A PRICE TO PAY

George Smullen

ISBN-13: 9781492145103
ISBN-10: 1492145106
Library of Congress Control Number: 2013915334
CreateSpace Independent Publishing Platform
North Charleston, South Carolina

This book is dedicated to:
My wife, Lori, whose patience is endless;
Myles Walter Marshall, ex-inmate who put his life on the line in order to save mine;
Maj. Randall "Hoot" Kahelski, riot field commander, deceased;
Capt. Jerome "Jerry" Elliott, riot emergency response unit leader, deceased;
Novelist Christine DeSmet, mentor.

•••

This is a work of fiction. Any similarity to persons living or dead is merely coincidental.

After Lucy Cox and the Ho Chunk guide, Evergreen Tree, finished conversing in his native tongue, the Indian turned north into the biting autumn wind and headed off. Lucy, her dark hair drawn in a bun under a flowery bonnet sewn from the remnants of a depleted flour sack, turned to her husband. "The lines of your forehead, James, look like the furrows of a drunkard's field."

"I have a good reason. Where is that heathen off to?"

"Evergreen Tree is no heathen. He's a devout Catholic. He is returning to Fort Green Bay and his loving family."

"But I paid him expressly to take us to our land."

A grin formed as Lucy pointed west beyond the wind-blown cattails. "See that stand of red oak on the far side of the marsh? That is where our land begins."

"Well, then, we no longer need Evergreen Tree as our guide."

Lucy patted her husband's shoulder. "No, we no longer need him."

"Why did Catholic parents name their child Evergreen Tree? I do not believe a Saint Evergreen Tree ever existed."

"They're Indians, James, and Indians name their children with Indian names."

Accepting the clarification, her husband called to Moses and Lucas, veering the horses west with a slight pull of the reins. The Belgians were a wedding present from his parents.

Lucy tended to the sky, darkened with countless V formations of Canada geese, while the wagon drooped and rose and wheezed and squawked, following a natural dike that cut through the twenty-six-mile-long Horicon Marsh in northwestern Indiana territory in what would be later become part of Wisconsin, the thirtieth state. The state's name comes from the Chippewa Indian word, Ouisconsin, which means "Grassy Place."

"The cattails," mused James, "sound their hellos to us as they scrape against one another."

"Your words, dear husband, so remind me of—"

Three white-tailed deer, two doe and a buck, shot in front of the horses, spooking the Belgians. The wagon leaped forward. Lucy held fast to the seat as each part of the wagon desperately attempted to separate itself from the whole.

James pulled hard on the reins, halting the horses, although they nervously whinnied and shuddered and stomped and snorted.

"Poetry," Lucy finished. "Your phrases are poetic."

"Nonsense," said her husband as he checked the wagon's load. "Nothing has fallen out, including you. This land, those deer, the geese—there is enough game here to keep us well fed, do you not agree?"

"You couldn't have known, but Evergreen Tree said our land is like Waubun, which means 'dawn of a new day.' It is truly the dawn of a new life for us."

"And from this very moment on, we shall call this place, our home, Waubun."

Lucy's smile was radiant. "Oh, James, that is so tender of you."

CHAPTER ONE

Ego was beside himself. *His post orders say he's gotta maintain vigilance throughout the shift. I should know. I wrote them words.* He stirred here, then there, and back to here again as a circus lion would pace its cage.

The sergeant's simple task was to recognize bona fide prison staff members and let them in by pressing a button that electronically disengaged the entry door's locking mechanism.

Naturally, Ego was irritated. Any other day, he would've already fired the turnkey for not looking in the proper direction, but Ego also recalled his wake-up pledge: "Nobody's gonna upset me on this day of all days, no matter what," and here it was the start of the shift, and he was within a clock's tick of violating his vow.

Look at 'im. He's snagging nose oysters and stabbing 'em to the bottom of the stool he's sitting on. That stool's state property. He's defacing state property. Any other day, he'd be outta here in five minutes flat and looking for a factory job.

Many Waupun citizens, most prison staff, and all correctional officers called him Ego—behind his back and out of earshot. His personnel folder officially listed him as Marion Richardson, Wisconsin State Prison's major of the guard.

Removing his gray Smokey Bear hat with gold state seal, Ego scrubbed at thinning salt-and-pepper hair while desperately wishing his steel-gray eyes could burn holes through the turnkey's head. *Nada, nada, not a thing I do is gonna wake 'im up.*

Turning to his reflection in the entry door's bulletproof glass and scowling at both the start of jowls and a gut that protruded over the

Sam Browne belt, he inspected everything attached to it: a handheld, portable two-way radio; handcuff pouch; mace spray can and another of CS tear gas; and the zap, or blackjack, which only Ego could curry and carry.

As to his name, it didn't take long for fellow guards to call him Ego because he insisted he knew all the answers to any question regarding prison security. "Someday I'm gonna be warden, and nothing's gonna stop me," he told them. The name stuck as a blob of seagull poop invariably sticks to a brand new car's paint job, ruining it.

His starched uniform shirt was blindingly white, thanks to his wife Joanie's care. It was the sole supervisory correctional officer shirt in Wisconsin that bore gold oak leaves at both collar tips. Naturally, in Ego's heart of hearts, he knew he, alone, deserved them.

Turning slightly and bowing his right shoulder a tad, he saw two of three vertical creases Joanie had pressed into the shirt's backside. Using a wet towel and hot iron, she also pressed the most obvious pleats in his dark blue trousers, as well. "They're so sharp," Ego often told her, "they can cut through a chicken fried steak." Joanie beamed. He knew she accepted his statement as a compliment of the highest order. He rarely uttered words of affection. Actions were more honest than mere words.

Eyeing the sergeant again, Ego sighed and dropped his gaze in order to inspect the black brogans, spit-shined Friday night while he watched Walter Cronkite on the boob tube. *They shine better than LBJ's limo.*

His head popped up just in case, but the turnkey continued his nose-to-pinky-to-stool defilements.

Today, Ego was not just overseeing one of his Inmate Prison Manners 101 classes. Today's class was special, being held for a special inmate, Brother-men jailhouse attorney Earl Davis.

Although Ego hadn't understood the meaning of the polysyllabic terms, he memorized, word for word, Davis's handwritten legal writ's final paragraph: "Wisconsin State Prison inmates view Maj. Marion Richardson as a monster possessing a human body. Even his subordinate staff fears his malice. This devil incarnate, with sadistic and evil temperament, seeks to increase his malevolent gratification by continually changing the rules under which we inmates must live, each modification more repressive than the rule it replaced. Although the major violates our constitutional rights, his venomous actions continue to meet state constitutional standards and state court approval. Thus, your petitioner is forced to seek redress in federal court for all Wisconsin State Prison inmates."

Lawbreakers got no damn rights.

Federal Judge Boyle of Wisconsin's eastern district obviously and publicly disagreed with Ego's opinion. "As far as I can ascertain from the records, all of Wisconsin's convicted felons are United States citizens," Boyle wrote in his decision. "True, they are citizens found guilty in Wisconsin Circuit Courts of feloniously violating state laws and sentenced by those courts to Waupun's maximum-security institution, but they are sent there *as* punishment, not *for* punishment. Thus, it is the order of this court that Waupun's inmate rulebook must be changed in order to reflect the constitutional guarantees to those incarcerated citizens having lost only one basic freedom, the freedom of movement."

Prompted by the head of Wisconsin's Department of Corrections to appeal Boyle's ruling, Governor Avery Todd promised in front of TV cameras to "look into the matter."

Three weeks later Warden Mitchell Palestine, wearing a god-awful blue herringbone leisure suit with white plastic belt and white plastic slip-on shoes, called Ego into the warden's office.

Palestine, in his snarky college graduate way said while grinning, "I know you're not going to like this, Marion, but Attorney General Robert Ward is giving me three weeks to submit to him for his review an inmate rulebook, reflecting Judge Boyle's decision."

If he had faithfully followed the state's administrative table of organization, Palestine should have been talking to his associate warden of security, but the man holding that position feared his own shadow. That's why Palestine chose Ego to be his hatchet man. Palestine was fully aware that Ego was afraid of only two things: a negative annual employee evaluation and a demotion.

"But boss, the governor said he was gonna look into the ma—"

"Tut, tut, Marion, you aren't listening."

Why does he keep calling me that? "But—"

"Which rulebook do you prefer, Marion, ours or the one that will be authored by Judge Boyle?"

That is the precise moment Ego planned Davis's kick-ass:

> An inmate-rat enters Davis's cell and places a shank under Davis's pillow. The cell hall sergeant discovers the shank and Davis is hauled off to the Greenhouse, the hole. The Inmate Disciplinary Committee's chief judge—guess who—finds Davis guilty and gives the inmate shyster a year in solitary, the first three days on bread and water. With a promise for a transfer to a federal joint, a pair of locked-down Latin King Cobras promise to kick Davis's ass while the three are in the Greenhouse's group dog run (chain-link fence recreational area, the size and shape of an actual outdoor dog run).

Unlike the warden, Ego unfailingly followed the state personnel board's administrative pecking order and handed down verbal or written orders exclusively to his three shift captains, utility captains, and administrative captain. The only exception was his implementation of his "manners classes." Regarding those, he dealt directly with Greenhouse supervisor Sgt. Jim Smith, willing to do Ego's bidding as long as Ego continued to look the other way regarding Smith's reporting to work somewhat wobbly and with booze-burdened breath.

And since Davis's manners lesson had possible exceptional legal problems, Ego thought it wise to wait for a Judge Boyle-certified reason to be in the hole on Davis's Day of Days. Somebody might think a relationship existed between Ego's being in the building on the same day that Davis got his ass kicked. Thus, Ego needed a legally legitimate cause for being there.

That cause landed in his in-basket on Friday afternoon. It was an inmate kite from the notorious Aryan Nation gang leader Theodore

"Wing Nuts" Kopfmueller, serving two consecutive life sentences for murdering in cold blood a pair of Milwaukee police officers. He was in the hole for continually violating institution rules.

In the kite, Kopfmueller wrote: "Major Richardson, sir, I need to meet with you ASAP. I'm going crazy in here with all these nut bags screaming twenty-four hours a day. I haven't had a good night's sleep in weeks. If you transfer me to general population, I'll obey all your rules—no ifs, ands, or buts." *Denying him a transfer to GP will be frosting on today's cake.*

Ka-flam. Finally, the sergeant, red-faced and avoiding Ego's glare, triggered the unlocking mechanism.

I didn't lose it, did I? It's a sign of good things to come.

As Lucy and James Cox's horse-drawn wagon made it to a clearing on their land, James halted the animals.

"Is this where we shall build our home, dear husband?"

"With your approval." James was already off the wagon and at her side.

Although she could have easily dismounted herself, she formed a plan as her husband helped her down. "James, let us celebrate our good fortune in a dance."

"Dance? There is no music. How can we dance without music?"

"I will sing."

James looked around, his head shaking. "I do not think—"

Lucy chortled. "Dearest husband, our audience is limited to God, his flora and fauna. No human shall make sport of our dance."

"I am not so certain, dear, if I can dance. I am not constituted as lively as you."

"Oh, James, at times you are so solemn." Taking his rough hands into hers, she hummed a pitch before she sang, "Rock of ages, cleft for me, let me hide myself in thee. Let the water and the blood from thy riven side which flowed, be of sin the double cure, save from wrath and make me pure."

Lucy moved James's hand, urging him to hold her closer. "Not the labor of my hands can fulfill thy law's demands. Could my zeal no respite know, could my tears forever flow. All for sin could not atone; thou must save, and thou alone."

Lucy brightly smiled; James appeared ill at ease.

"Nothing in my hand I bring. Simply to the cross I cling; naked, come to thee for dress. Helpless, look to thee for grace; foul, I to the fountain fly. Wash me, Savior, else I die."

Lucy stood on tiptoes and lovingly kissed her husband while his fingers outlined her breasts. He held to her as she swooned; he let her fall gently to the grassy spot. James followed his wife, his breathing profound, and the mission earnest.

CHAPTER TWO

The moment Ego pulled open the prison entrance door, three blocks west of the institution on Waupun's Brown Street, Dawn Griffin would not let go of her tall, well-built United States Marine son in dress blues.

With close-cropped auburn hair and Windex-blue eyes, Sgt. Zak Griffin was her little boy no more. Twenty-two years old, wounded and battle tested in Vietnam, he'd told Dawn the previous night that he was returning to the Nam on another tour. When she started crying, Zak said, "Ma, I'm as invincible as an M-forty-eight tank."

In one hour, he had to board the Hiawatha train in Columbus, eventually ending in San Diego by way of Chicago. In two months, he'd ship back to the Nam.

His mother's fingers reached to touch the ribbons on his uniform jacket.

"We gotta get going, Zak," yelled Earl Noble, Zak's cousin, while revving the Volkswagen Microbus's air-cooled engine, "or you're gonna miss the train."

"The train's leaving at two fifteen, Ma. The Union Pacific is leaving Chicago for San Diego at six tonight. If I miss either train, I'll be AWOL."

Holding on to the Purple Heart ribbon with oak leaf cluster, Dawn whispered, "You'll take care, won't you, son?"

"I promise."

"Your dad told me the same thing—promise me you won't do anything foolish, Zak."

"You don't have to worry. I'm no hero, Ma."

Her fingers picked a dandelion seedpod the wind had blown onto his jacket. "Like I believe that," she said, swiping at a tear.

Earl pushed the accelerator pedal to the floor.

"One more hug, Zak."

They embraced one another, and then Zak backed away, retaining eye contact. Finally, he turned and headed for the VW's passenger door, opened it, bent over, and stuffed himself in. Waving, he shouted, "See you, Ma."

Dawn swallowed hard. *Please, God,* she prayed, *please. He's all I have.*

Together, Lucy and James Cox constructed a log cabin, mixing up mortar of mostly mud and marsh grass. When winter arrived, James set traps. Whenever he checked them, half were filled with game.

In early spring, he began fencing the land and held fast the plow, Moses and Lucas earning their keep. The couple planted oats, corn, potatoes, and garden vegetables. James harvested alone since Lucy was with child.

Welcoming occasional strangers passing on foot or horseback on their way to Fort Winnebago, the Coxes were pleased to receive old newspapers. They devoured each and every word. Even the advertising was intriguing.

When firstborn Ethan arrived, James assisted with the delivery. Soon, other settlers arrived and endured hardships of pioneer life with the Cox family. A hamlet rose from the clearings.

After folks urged Lucy to make Waubun the community's official name, she sent for the proper forms from the territory's commissioner. When they arrived, Lucy filled them out dutifully.

Months passed. The document she awaited arrived. Lucy was fully shocked when she opened the official letter of congratulations from the commissioner. Her **b** *had been mistaken for a* **p**.

"Waupun—whosoever has heard of such a word?" cried Lucy. After that, she and the commissioner exchanged letters.

"A transfer back to Waubun can be worked out," she told James, "but it necessitates additional filings, affidavits, and five extra dollars."

James was well aware that promises made were promises to be kept, but the management of money had gained its foothold. "As for me," he told Lucy, "the word Waupun (Wau-PON) is even rarer than Waubun."

Lucy's eyes sparkled. "Why hadn't I thought of that? You are indeed a poet."

So, Waupun it remained.

CHAPTER THREE

Sgt. Mark Ericson sat on what could easily have been described as a barstool. His post, the Bubble, looked similar to a movie theater's ticket booth with three angled, four-foot-square, four-inch-thick pieces of bulletproof glass. A time ago, Ericson had been a fourth-grade teacher at Waupun's Jefferson Grade School but applied for a job at the prison in order to make enough money to support his growing family.

As Ego approached the first of three gates, Ericson punched a button, and the opposing gates rumbled as they parted.

The only lethally armed officer inside the walls, Ericson packed a Smith & Wesson .38 revolver. If that wasn't enough firepower, an Ithaca twelve-gauge slide action shotgun stood in a rack beside him. The Ithaca was loaded with four double-ought shells, each packing nine .33-caliber pellets, weighing 53.8 grains each. When discharged from the barrel, they would travel at about 1,200 feet per second, faster than the lead from his .38 pistol, but a tad smaller in size and weight. Ericson was certain his "target" wouldn't know the difference. He turned on the Bubble's microphone. "How are you doing, boss?"

Ego did not face Ericson, nor did he answer.

• • •

Next were the Overpass gates. Manning Overpass was Sgt. Jimmy Helm, Overpass sally port turnkey and union organizer. He pulled out two large, brass Folger Adam keys that manually controlled his pair of gates' manual locking mechanisms. Ericson, the Bubble sergeant, controlled their electronic locking mechanisms.

Because the two Overpass gates led directly to "the back," where inmates were housed, neither officer could override the other's decision making.

"Going to the back, boss?" Helm inserted Key Number One into Lock Number One, turned it, held, and nodded to Ericson. *Of course you're going to the back. Why the hell did I ask you that?*

Thwock went the electric lock. Helm pulled open the heavy gate.

Ego stepped through, passed by Helm, and approached the final wood and steel affair, fifteen feet away. Helm manually locked the first gate, stepped up to Gate Number Two, peered through the window to the circular security mirror on the opposing outer wall, saw no inmates on either the south- or north-side stairway, inserted Key Number Two, turned it, and held the turn. Lastly, Helm jerked to face Ericson and nodded.

Sock.

Helm swung open the door and watched Ego descend two stairs to the landing and make a sharp right before heading down the north-side stairway.

•••

Outdoors, between the Food Services Building and the North Cell Hall, bakery exhaust fans were blowing hard. Ego took in the rich and delectable aroma of baked bread. *I could go for a hot slice right now with plenty of butter. Maybe, I should...nah.*

He continued walking toward the Greenhouse. Inmates approached, their right hands holding on to paper passes, allowing them to move in the back without officer escort. When each nodded or bid Ego hello, his jaws clamped together. *We gotta respect the line. I'm on one side. They're on the other. It's always been that way and will always be that way. I'm the keeper. They're the kept. And that's that.*

The Greenhouse, its exterior walls painted lima bean green and frosted windows fortified with interior and exterior vertical and horizontal steel bars, looked like a millionaire's mausoleum in a big-city cemetery. Surrounding the building's grassy courtyard was an eighteen-foot-high chain-link fence, swirled concertina razor wire on its top.

Tower Six controlled the fence's entrance gate. As with most towers, except for the inner tower, it was built on top of the concrete-reinforced exterior wall that surrounded the prison. The wall measured twenty-two feet high, ten feet thick at the base, and six feet thick at the top.

Ego waved at Kevin "Pretty Boy" Blake, manning Tower Six. *Joanie swears he's the spitting image of Troy Donahue, and everyone knows Donahue's a fag.*

Blake exited the tower and stepped onto the steel grate catwalk, grabbed the top guardrail with one hand, and waved with the other. "You want in, boss?"

You think I'm here for my health? Ego rotated an index finger.

Blake reentered the tower and triggered the mechanism. *Thwack.*

Ego pulled the gate open, looked up, pushed the gate shut, and said, "See ya, ricky-tick."

"That's a ten-four, boss," returned the grinning sycophant.

•••

Greenhouse turnkey Steve Blankley, silent as the granite Recording Angel in Waupun's Rocky Run cemetery, keyed Ego into his ten-by-ten-foot sally port. Vertical bars rose from concrete floor to twenty-foot-high ceiling, crisscrossed by a number of equally spaced horizontal bars. On the other side of Blankley's sally port was No-Man's-Land, the fifteen-foot space between his and the Greenhouse sergeant's sally port. Access was virtually impenetrable. Two officers manned four locked gates twenty-four/seven.

Sgt. Jim Smith sat on a gray steel chair behind a gray steel desk, both bolted to the concrete floor. Nothing in the building was movable except for staff, inmates with wrists cuffed to belly chains and ankles cuffed to leg irons, and the singular, four-wheeled stainless steel food cart with well-oiled wheels. It made no noise whatsoever.

Smith wrote something in the logbook; Ego assumed it had to do with his entrance. Finally, closing the book and tidying up the desktop, Smith nodded.

Blankley keyed Ego into No-Man's-Land and then locked the gate. Smith rose, stifled a yawn, and keyed his gate to No-Man's-Land.

"I wanna see Kopfmueller," whispered Ego. "Put that in your book."

"That's a ten-four, boss. He's in Eleven."

"After I see him, we talk."

"Yazzuh, boss." Smith keyed the lock of the inner gate and yawned.

In the cellblock waited Officer Bret Westra, responsible for segregated inmates' needs and feeds. Ego passed by the young officer as if he wasn't there.

Cell One's inmate rushed to the rear of his cell and flushed the toilet. By the time Ego passed Three, toilets on both ranges were being constantly purged, which meant only one thing: he was in the block.

• • •

Ego stopped at Eleven. In it and on the floor, a hairless inmate with ears that looked like handles on a Grecian earthen jug executed one-arm push-ups while a big toe pushed the commode button. Suddenly, he stopped and growled, "Hey," and stood.

Wet with sweat, rippling arm and chest muscles, obviously in his prime, the Aryan latched on to vertical bars with sausage-size fingers. With Arctic ice eyes, he drilled holes through Ego. His salmon-colored skin bore multiple tattoos, the most prominent a swastika in the middle of his forehead. A pig on each triceps symbolized the police officers he murdered. "I see ya got my kite."

"I did—and I got good news. I'm gonna free you ricky-tick."

Wing Nuts's fingers relaxed their grip. His eyes softened. He even managed a grin. "When?"

Ego waited his Jack Benny moment. "When Werner Harmsen Funeral Home hauls your dead ass outta here. That's when."

Knuckles turning snow white, jaws dead-locking, eyes turning red hot, Wing Nuts growled, "My boys on the bricks said if you turn me down, they're gonna file a federal suit on your fag ass."

"Tell 'em to get the name right. It's R-i-c—"

The mucus-laced saliva gob held to Ego's right cheek. While it made its slow slide, he retrieved a handkerchief in his rear trousers pocket and blotted the scuzz. "That's a rule violation, Theodore."

"What are you gonna do, lock me up, Major Egomaniac?"

That's when the building went totally crazy, as most Greenhouse residents screamed, "Egomaniac, Egomaniac, Egomaniac."

Turning, the major headed for the sergeant's sally port, hoping Smith and Westra were the only ones in the block who could see his smirk.

In 1848, Waupun residents celebrated their being part of the thirtieth state of the union—Wisconsin. Among other news, the new state legislature let it be known it wished to locate and approve a state prison site, requesting state communities to volunteer.

James Cox, Waupun's village chairman, thought the institution could yield personal profits and garner the village additional jobs. Thus, he requested the proper papers in an official letter. Receiving the questionnaire, he filled it out and sent it off to Madison.

The legislature eventually announced five finalists, Waupun among them.

Legislators' on-site visitation dates were announced, which gave rise to a James Cox brainstorm.

His scheme, if worked properly, called for four volunteers to partake in a petty fraud—of sorts. Of the more than a dozen men who volunteered their services, James picked those individuals he felt were the most cunning.

When the time was right, each volunteer bade his family farewell and journeyed to a rival community, the buckboard's belly filled with gunnysacks, fully keeping in mind James Cox's written instructions:

First: make camp outside the community.

Second: locate the community's central water well.

Third: wait for the night before the legislative committee's inspection.

Fourth: without being seen or heard, dump into the well all the salt the gunnysacks hold.

Fifth: return and report to me regarding your successful mission.

Each volunteer swore to Cox he was successful in following the directives. No matter, Cox still fretted that the plan might not work. However, on July 8, 1851, he received an official envelope from Nelson Dewey, Wisconsin's governor. Inside was this brief letter:

Dear Mayor Cox. As to the location of this state's prison, Waupun, with its hardworking citizens, sweet water, and nearby stone quarries, is deemed by this state's legislature and my office to be the proper choice for such an undertaking.

State officials will soon advise you as to how funds will be disbursed.

Congratulations to you and your town's fine citizens.

God bless us all.

Sincerely,

Nelson Dewey
Governor
State of Wisconsin

CHAPTER FOUR

Outside the prison wall and on a sidewalk adjacent to the street on which Dawn Griffin lived, Ego looked up to Tower Six, overlooking the intersection of Brown and Drummond streets. He peered down both streets before barking, "Clear."

Blake inspected the same streets from his vantage point before bawling, "Clear," after which he lowered a rope with a clasp on its end holding a Folger Adam key. Snagging the key, Ego removed it and tugged the fastener. Blake hauled in the line and coiled it. Then, he performed another look-see. "Clear," he yelled.

"Clear," echoed Ego. He keyed and opened the hatch, took the key out of the lock, stepped inside, closed the hatch, and keyed the lock. The *ka-blam* sound echoed inside the hollow-concrete tower base. After locking the hatch, he ascended the winding steel staircase. He heard each step echo off the walls.

Finally, on the tower's floor and momentarily blinded by the bright light, he asked, "Smith let 'im out yet?" Ego shielded his eyes with a hand.

"Not yet, boss. I think Jim's waiting for you."

Together, they checked. Smith waited below, looking up. Ego performed a serious, extended nod. Smith keyed the gate. Down and out, stepped a tall, thin, and elegant black man with an Afro hairdo, his eyes green like a leopard's. He wore a khaki long-sleeve shirt, trousers, no belt, and brown work boots with no strings.

Two minutes later, Smith let the Cobras into the same group dog run, keyed the gate shut, and headed to his desk.

• • •

Young Westra stiffened as if bitten by a snake. "Sergeant Smith," he called, "there's a shank in group dog run." Jerking out his handheld and punching the on switch, Westra yelled into it, "Control, this is Bar Forty-Two."

"Go ahead, Forty-Two. This is Control."

"Control, there's a ten thirty-four, repeat, ten thirty-four in the Adjustment Center group dog run. Inmate with knife."

Smith was at the gate, screaming, saliva shooting in all directions. "Ruiz, drop that knife—an' I mean now, dammit."

"That's a ten-four, Forty-Two. Attention all bars, this is Control. There's a ten thirty-four in the Adjustment Center, inmate with knife. Repeat, inmate with knife in Adjustment Center group dog run."

Westra saw so much blood it looked like the kill floor in the meatpacking plant at which he had worked before becoming a correctional officer.

Tower Six's shotgun blast sounded as if a stick of dynamite had been detonated right next to Westra. Ears ringing, he grabbed the handheld. "Control, this is Bar Forty-Two. Noise, can't hear. Inmate stabbed and down."

Finally, in exultation, Ruiz plunged the knife into his victim's gut and left it there, Westra's eyes welded to the blood-smeared masking tape-covered handle.

The equally bloodied Cobras grinned as they pushed hands high above them.

Davis, sitting, legs straight out, hands holding on to the shank's handle, tried to say something, but blood, instead of sound, spewed out between his lips.

"Control, this is Bar Forty-Two. Aggressors have surrendered. Repeat. Aggressors are giving up."

•••

Emergency Response Unit (ERU) officers, dressed in black jumpsuits, black spit-shined boots, and black helmets with see-through plastic visors, holding on to glossy black nightsticks, tumbled through the opened group dog run gate like steaming potatoes being dumped from a huge, overturned cast-iron pot. Each rose and yelled, "Down, down, down," slashing batons so fast that Earl Davis could hear the air whistle. *Can't you see the blood? It's mine. Not theirs. Help me. Cold, I feel hot. Jesus Christ Almighty, can't you see I'm the one who needs help?*

Davis couldn't see the ninjas draw white plastic tie-offs around Cobra wrists and ankles faster than rodeo participants could rope and hogtie bawling calves. He heard what he thought was a gurney slam next to him. Most of all, he heard his teeth clattering like castanets. *Shirleen, you were right. I should've done my time and kept my mouth shut. What are they doing? Why the cuffs, the leg irons?* "Do you have to?" pleaded Davis, which were the last words spoken in a too-brief life.

Prison construction began as newly employed shotgun-toting guards, mostly farmers, living within riding distance of Waupun, supervised convicts who chopped, limbed, and debarked a forest of trees owned by James and Lucy Cox. Oxen hauled logs to the building site where a local carpenter, contracted with the state, acted as convict tutor in proper construction techniques.

Completed in 1851, the wood stockade had a guard tower at each corner and an eighteen-foot-high wood wall a foot thick that enclosed a total of 4½ acres. Within the compound were the Administration Building, carpentry shop, guard barracks, cellblocks, surgeon quarters, horse barn, kitchen, dining hall, and a small chapel.

The legislature pronounced Waupun State Prison as its official name and decreed the facility would adhere to the Quaker philosophy of penitence, accepting adults and children of both sexes, sentenced by circuit court judges to confinement at hard labor of at least one year. Lesser sentences were served in county jails.

County deputies dutifully transported newly convicted felons to Waupun in horse-drawn wagons called Black Marias, literally cells on wheels with prisoners in view of the public.

After it was made certain prisoners' legal papers were in order, Waupun's captain of the guard accepted the convict. After delousing the new convict, the registrar interviewed her or him—that is, if the prisoner could speak English.

After the interview, the registrar assigned the new prisoner an institution number. A guard or matron soon locked up the new individual in a one-person cell. Staff referred to each prisoner by number only, the silent system strictly enforced.

Using heavy wood canes with brass tips, male guards struck out beats on objects that resonated sound, the thumps announcing reveille, time to dump "honey buckets," work, count, meals, and bedtime. Canes were also used to calm down disputatious prisoners if that need arose.

Prisoners were allowed to talk only during the thirty-minute Sunday Bible study class, the discussion pertaining exclusively to salvation.

CHAPTER FIVE

If that jungle bunny dies and Smith tells anyone the kick-ass was my idea, that'll make me party to a crime, second degree murder. Jesus, I could get twenty-five years behind bars. What am I gonna do? What can I do? Jesus. The first thing you gotta do, Butch, is to calm down. Calm down. Ya gotta square away Blake. You gotta deal with Blake.

Ego inhaled all the air he could and then exhaled slowly. Finally, the words came. "All we was gonna watch was a kick-ass—right?"

Blake's eyes jerked and rose and dove and skidded this way and that.

Don't push. His balls are the size of June peas.

Blake's lips quivered.

Don't say nothing. Wait 'im out.

Blake stopped trembling. "Smith," he said, "couldn't have strip-searched that man or else he would've found that shank."

I got me a partner. "You're a hundred and ten percent correct," said Ego. "He couldn't."

• • •

Warden Mitchell Palestine expected the crashing knock on the door. Still, it took him by surprise. "Come in, Marion."

After carefully shutting the office door, Ego just stood there.

"Yes, Marion?"

"Boss, I was in Tower Six, checking Officer Blake's knowledge of his post orders and all of a sudden below us in the Greenhouse's group dog run, a beaner—there were two of them and one jungle bunny—well, this one beaner had a shank—and the other held the jungle bunny—the jungle bunny got shanked. He's hurt real bad, boss."

Palestine sighed. "Marion, the media would have a field day with you. It's not the Greenhouse; it is the Adjustment Center. Prisoners use the word *shank*. We are to use the term *prisoner-manufactured knife*."

"Yes, boss, bu—"

"Nor are the aggressors beaners. They're Chicanos, Latinos, or Hispanics. Jungle bunny, Marion? You'd be lucky if you retained your job for one second if you dared use that term with reporters. You'd be at Mercury Marine alongside many of the officers you let go."

"I understand, boss, but you're not a repor—"

"We identify them as colored or Negro."

"Yes, sir."

"Marion," pursued Palestine, "does the prison employ dogs?"

"No, boss, why?"

"Then, why do you use the term, dog runs? Those are Adjustment Center recreation pods."

"Yes, boss, pods."

Palestine arranged a pad of paper before him, withdrew a Mont Blanc fountain pen from his shirt pocket, separated the cap from body with a flourish, and thoughtfully laid the cap on the desktop. "Now, what are the aggressors' names and institution numbers?"

"As soon as I find out, boss, I'll let you know."

"And the victim's name?"

"Davis."

"Our writ writer?"

"Yes, boss."

Palestine winced and spoke and wrote at the same time. "A pair of segregated, unidentified inmates attacked another segregated inmate we are unable to identify until family members are informed. He was stabbed with a prisoner-manufactured knife in the Adjustment Center's group recreation pod."

Palestine placed the cap back on the pen's body, tightening it. Lifting his head, he scrutinized his hatchet man. "After we contact Davis's family, we'll release his name. How bad is he really?"

"Boss, if I was a betting man, I'd say he ain't gonna make it. You shoulda seen the blood."

Palestine grimaced. "Marion, your grammar."

"Boss?"

"It's atrocious, and since neither you nor I possess medical degrees, we really can't make a determination regarding his medical condition, now, can we?"

"I shoulda thought of that, boss."

"Should have, Marion. You shall in the future. By the way, which staff member, slash members, are we holding responsible for this unfortunate situation?"

"Smith, sir. Sgt. Jim Smith. From what I seen, he couldn't of strip-searched that be—"

Palestine smiled. "Are you looking for the word *Latino*, Marion?"

"Yeah, boss, Latino."

"The sergeant, you say, did not perform his responsibilities as required by his post orders?"

"That's right, boss."

"Then, when you leave this room, advise Mary to type Sergeant Smith's letter of dismissal. After that, get in touch with Detective Weems. We need to have Dodge County investigate this matter. You've given me enough information to temporarily satisfy Kyle Marston, the governor's aide."

"Yes, boss."

Palestine leaned back in his chair. "Resolve our problem, Marion, before Madison or the media attempt to resolve it for us."

• • •

Ego strode past Mary, the warden's secretary, without saying a word. After phoning Weems, he made his way to Jon Powers's office. Powers was the personnel director. After explaining the situation, Ego asked, "Can't we do something so Smitty don't lose his retirement?"

"That's it," said Powers, "we'll let him retire."

"Huh?"

"He's eligible for full benefits right now."

"I didn't know that." *Palestine could go for it if I lay it out right.* "Yeah, why don't we do that?"

•••

Behind Detective Joe Weems's thick eyeglasses were alert but comfortable brown eyes. In his early fifties, calm and smooth shaven, he wore a conservative gray suit, white shirt, and striped tie. He looked more like a successful salesman than a cop. Of medium height and build, he was in excellent shape—no beer gut for him, unlike most Dodge County deputies. Soft-spoken, he had one fascination: he loved to tell one-liners. "Major, you know what the definition of a gentleman is?" Weems waited and then said, "Aren't you going to guess?"

Ego shrugged. "I know I ain't one."

"A gentleman," said the smiling detective, "is a fellow who knows how to play the accordion—but doesn't."

Ego groaned.

Weems then got down to official business. "As to the assault, I need to interview staff and all inmates housed on the dog run side, both tiers." Joe waited. "There anything wrong, Major?"

"Yeah," said Ego. "Hospital Sergeant Dunlop got a hold of me after you and me finished talkin' on the phone. Davis, the victim, he's dead."

Weems, a daily communicant, made the sign of the cross. "May God have mercy on his soul."

•••

In the Greenhouse's basement hearing room, Weems and Ego sat on gray steel straight-backed chairs bolted to the concrete floor behind a long steel table, also bolted to the floor. Directly opposite them on the other side of the table sat Juan Ruiz, hands cuffed behind him, knees popping like a racecar's pistons.

Standing behind Ruiz were two NFL-size blueshirts, arms crossed against their chests, eyes glommed on to the inmate. At the far end of the table stood Officer Two, Frank Sanchez. The room's only door was closed. Its walls were mainly steel-framed windows. Outside the room, four blueshirts, arms crossed against their chests, looked in.

"Juan," said Weems, "I assume you understand English, but if you don't, we have Officer Sanchez who'll translate for you."

"I understand," said Ruiz.

Weems turned on the tape recorder. "Juan, I'm going to record our conversation, OK?"

Ruiz nodded. "I don't need no trans—what you say?"

"Translator," said Weems. "I'm still going to let Officer Sanchez remain here because if there's even one word you don't understand, he'll help you understand, OK?"

"OK."

"A moment ago," continued Weems, "you signed a paper that stated I, Joseph R. Weems, Dodge County corrections investigator, state of Wisconsin, read you your Miranda rights with Major Richardson and Officers Schmidt and Brown and Sanchez as witnesses. Is that correct?"

"Yace."

"Does *yace* mean yes, Juan?"

"Yace."

"Good, did you, Juan Ruiz, stab inmate Earl Davis while he was being held by inmate Pedro Gonzalez on June tenth, nineteen hundred sixty-eight, at or around one o'clock in the afternoon in the Waupun State Prison's Adjustment Center's Group Recreation Pod, commonly called group dog run?"

Ruiz examined the floor, trying to look bored, as he answered, "Yace."

"Did you repeatedly stab inmate Earl Davis, causing his death?"

Ruiz's head popped up. "I kill him?"

Both Weems and Ego nodded.

Ruiz grinned. "Hey, that's good."

Weems took off his glasses, a habit of his whenever he faced the totally unexpected. "Juan, did you just say it was good that you killed Davis?"

"Yace."

Weems lifted the plastic evidence bag that held the bloodied shank with masking tape handle. "Juan, I'm holding before you a clear, see-through plastic evidence bag, marked with two big black letters, D and C, for Dodge County, and a larger numeral one. Also, it has today's date, June tenth, nineteen hundred sixty eight. It has two signatures on it, written in black, Officer Bret Westra's, there, and mine, right here. Juan, do you see this bag I'm talking about?"

"I ain't blind."

"I didn't ask you if you were blind. I asked you if you could see the knife in this bag."

Ruiz's knees were doing triple time. "Yace, that's my shank."

"It's your shank, you say?"

"Yace."

"With which you repeatedly stabbed inmate Earl Davis, causing his death?"

Ruiz let out a long sigh. "Yace."

Weems reached for his cigarettes, knocked out two, and offered one to Ruiz. Ruiz accepted. Weems first lit Ruiz's and then his. Together, investigator and confessed murderer inhaled deeply and exhaled two cloudbanks that collided with one another.

Ruiz began laughing.

Weems removed his glasses. "Juan, why are you laughing?"

"I dunno."

"Where did the shank come from?"

"Up my ass."

Weems shook the large evidence bag. "You fit *this* up your rectum?"

Ruiz's eyebrows formed carets; Officer Sanchez interpreted the word in Spanish.

Ruiz nodded and then faced Joe. "Yace, up my, whatever you say."

"Rectum. Didn't some other inmate," pursued Weems, "give you this shank, perhaps the general population janitor—or what you guys in here call a tier tender—or could it have been an inmate barber who comes here once a week to cut hair?"

"No, I make it."

"You say you made the weapon. Where'd you make it?"

"In my house."

"Your house? You mean your cell?"

"Yace."

"The locked cell you live in twenty-three hours each and every day, a cell that's inspected by correctional officers at least once, sometimes two, three, or even more times a day?"

"Yace."

"Are you sure nobody gave you the shank, Juan?"

"Listen, I kill the muhfockuh, and I ain't saying no more."

"Juan," said Weems, "the recorder's still running. I want you to know we're not like law enforcement where you come from. We're not going to use a cattle prod or attach telephone wires to your bag or hit you or slap you around or anything like that. Do you understand?"

"Yace."

"Then, that's it, unless you want to say more."

"No," snapped Ruiz.

"I'll let you go in a minute, but first I must tell you that my questions and your answers are on this tape. Somebody's going to type them up and you'll be able to read them, and if you can't read them, a translator will read them to you. Then, we'll ask you to sign the paper, stating that what you and I said is typed on those papers and is the truth as far as you're concerned. Are you willing to sign that paper?"

"Yace."

"Good," said Weems, shutting off the recorder.

• • •

Weems told Milwaukee-born and bred Pedro Gonzalez that Davis had been killed. "Yeah, I held him."

"Why'd you hold him?"

"I lost."

Weems squinted. "You lost? What did you lose?"

"Rock-paper-scissors to see who'd get to shank the dude. I lost."

Weems's glasses came off. "Why'd you guys want to kill him?"

"Because he was there."

"And that's your explanation?"

"That's it," said Gonzalez with a shrug.

• • •

Before escorting Weems out of the institution, Ego told Smith to wait for him by the inmate chapel. Smith yawned and nodded.

• • •

Theodore "Wing Nuts" Kopfmueller lay on his bunk. *Ego and that tower screw was laughin' their asses off until that greaser shanked the nigger. That's when they look as if somebody started throwin' elephant-size turds down their throats.*

Theodore, don't blow this. It's a gift from God. Take time, think about it, plan with the boys on the bricks, tell 'em what happened, and listen to what they say. Don't be in a hurry.

Lifting a hand, Wing Nuts spat into it. "Tonight, Lady Five Fingers, you're gonna do me better than that West Allis high-dollar whore, Julie, with her corkscrew tongue."

As more and more settlers made Wisconsin their destination, the state grew its towns. Naturally, some unseemly citizens broke laws. Apprehended by constables, charged by county district attorneys, and found guilty by circuit-riding judges and hometown juries, the felons were sentenced to a minimum of one year at Waupun, where space was always at a premium. Although inmates were assigned to build new cells, the institution was consistently short of prisoner living space.

In addition, a fire set by a convict killed not only him but also eighteen other inmates. Legislators howled and the governor growled. The warden was discharged. One Wisconsin newspaper editor had the temerity to mention that a year earlier the dismissed warden had begged both governor and legislators to support construction of fire-resistant lockups.

"They refused," said the ousted warden, "because inmates can't vote."

Most other state editors rallied, demanding, "Give Waupun the resources, or else."

In 1861, convicts began construction of the stone, mortar, and steel 250-inmate-capacity South Cell Hall, completing it the day John Wilkes Booth shot Abraham Lincoln.

In 1890, female prisoners were separated from the men by a newly constructed wall, but three more men's cell halls were built and in full use by 1910. Equal in size to the South Cell Hall, they were simply named the Southwest, North, and Northwest cell halls. Because inmates filled every cage, each cell hall had to add fifty double bunks on the first floors for the glut.

Whenever prisoners rioted, the warden lost his job, but guards remained to lock down riot leaders and their followers. That act was termed a "screw-down," which is why guards are called "screws."

Daily diet on a screw-down was bread and water. Every fourth day, the rebels were given a full meal. Then, it was back to bread and water. If men in the hole wished to communicate with guards, they wrote their requests on slates, using chalk that had been provided. If the inmate was illiterate, tough nuts. No talking was allowed. Period. That's about the time an adage took hold: "In Waupun, payback's a motherfucker."

Security reigned until 1963, when the US Supreme Court ruled that Florida wrongly failed to provide counsel for inmate Clarence Gideon, too poor to pay for a defense lawyer. Soon, inmates in every state bypassed state courts and flooded federal benches with habeas corpus and cruel-and-inhumane-condition suits.

Judges warned states that their need to maintain prison order had less import than the protection of inmates' constitutional rights. "Either apply the least restrictive rules, or else the courts will run the prisons."

Waupun obeyed those judicial orders—unenthusiastically.

CHAPTER SIX

Two minutes past midnight, a phone in the state-owned warden's mansion jangled. Mitchell Palestine did not hear it; Nora Palestine did. "Dear," she whispered.

The phone continued ringing; Palestine continued snoring. "Mitchell," she said aloud. Nothing changed. The phone continued to ring. Nora elbowed her husband. "Mitchell."

He popped up like a jack-in-the-box. "Jesus Christ, Nora. That hurt, dammit."

"It's the red phone. You said I can't answer it. So—"

"The red phone? It can't be. It's most likely the white phone—and it's probably your daughter, who had another row with that drunken, no-good husband of hers."

"My daughter? Susan's our daughter." Nora turned on the night-light. "Now, look, you damn fool. It's the red phone."

"Incredible," said Palestine, lifting the phone. He had no time to say hello. "Yes, Kyle. Yes. At the mansion in Maple Bluff. Yes, I understand. In one and one-half hours? Yes, we'll be there."

Quietly laying the phone onto its cradle, Palestine slid off his pajama top without unbuttoning.

"What're you doing?" asked Nora.

"What does it look like? I'm getting dressed."

"Why?"

"My top staff and I must meet with the governor in an hour."

"Why can't the governor wait until morning, like decent, normal people?"

"Nora, as you well know, Avery Todd is neither decent nor normal."

Nora put her head back on the pillow. “Good night, Mitchell.”

“And good morning to you, Nora.”

• • •

What a bunch of assholes, thought Governor Avery Todd. In his midfifties, bald, champing at a stogie, dressed in a red silk smoking jacket with black lapels over black silk pajamas, he sat alone at the head of a long, shiny mahogany conference table, his aide standing by his side.

At the other end of the table sat five obviously uncomfortable suits and a uniformed correctional officer wearing gold major insignias on his shirt collar points. Todd turned to the young man standing beside him. “Did he have to bring a goddamned army? What time is it, anyway?”

Kyle Marston crooked his left arm, wrestled with a shirt cuff, and exposed an Omega with white face and gold Roman numerals. “Sir, as I told you earlier, I advised Mitch to bring his top staff with him. It's one thirty-five.” Sighing, he added, “A.m., sir.”

Todd fumed. “Do you think I'm some dipshit who doesn't know a.m. from fucking p.m.?”

Marston answered with a smile.

The governor turned and glared menacingly at the prison employees. *What a bunch of pricks.* He lifted a water glass and stared at it, relishing the anxiety his actions were causing them. *Four, three, two, one.* “Warden, gentlemen, and, uh, Major, it seems like the media is handling the murder at your institution to our liking—so far.”

Mitchell Palestine pumped his head and smiled. “I agree, Governor. My staff and I only mean to do our job efficiently, effectively, an—”

Todd jerked to face Marston. “Does he think I'm some tit-squeezing hayseed from North Podunk who paid his two bits so he can see cells and actual convicts at the prison?”

Eyes slightly above his eyeglass rims, Marston looked like a nineteenth-century English schoolmaster. “Mitch, the governor prefers you to save the window dressing for the public and the media. Let's stick to the facts, OK?"

Palestine patted his forehead with a folded white handkerchief. "Thank you, Kyle. I'll do just that. Governor, uh, Maj. Marion Richardson advised me that Sergeant uh—"

Palestine froze for an exceedingly long time, causing discomfort to his staff. "Uh, Marion, could you help me? I, uh—"

Ego's eyebrows looked like twin carets in a hastily written note. "Smith, sir," he said, "Sgt. Jim Smith."

He couldn't remember Smith? He's either dumber than a box of rocks or drunk or the old bastard's totally fucking lost it.

Palestine continued. "Sergeant Smith's written post orders clearly state he is responsible for making full-body cavity searches on each segregated inmate before said inmate is allowed to recreate. Obviously, Smith failed to follow those orders, and I thought it best we let him retire."

"Retire? Why didn't you fire the bastard?"

"Believe me, sir," said Palestine, "I was sorely tempted to do so, but according to Major Richardson and our personnel director, the media could have easily seen the dismissal as part of a conspiracy that started at the very top of state government—meaning all the way to you, sir. The inmate who was murdered was Earl Davis, the very inmate who had Federal Judge Boyle in the palm of his hand, so to speak."

Todd felt Marston's hand on his shoulder. The young aide whispered, "Mitch could be right, sir. Everything we do is put to task by Boyle, aided by our pinko UW law professors, their SDS followers, and the liberal media."

Sometimes, the snot-nosed kid makes sense. Todd harrumphed. "OK, Warden, I'll buy that—for now. Continue."

"Thank you, Governor. I have a friend who writes for the *Milwaukee Sentinel*. Sensitive to prison issues, he advised me in a phone conversation that this morning's paper will feature his article referring to Sergeant Smith's, uh, drinking problem."

Marston cleared his throat.

Now, what the hell does he want? Todd turned to his aide.

"Could work to our benefit," whispered the kid.

"If it doesn't," whispered back the governor, "your balls will be hanging in the capitol rotunda."

Todd turned to Palestine. "What about the murdered inmate's family?"

"That's my area of expertise, Governor," volunteered a suit sitting next to Palestine.

Exper-fucking-tise. My God, what's next? Viable fucking alternative?

"I'm Jack Deutch, associate warden of treatment. Later this morning, I'll telephone the deceased inmate's immediate family, and after I offer my condolences, I'll—"

As Todd yanked Marston's sleeve and whispered, Deutch looked like a deer caught in headlights.

"The governor wishes you all a safe trip back to Waupun," Marston announced to the Waupun crew. "Have a good evening."

Palestine and his staff stood as Todd harrumphed and bugled, "Good evening?"

"I meant morning, sir," said Marston.

Todd drilled fingers on the table until the nitwits were gone and then performed a jerk and glare. "That asshole better be right about the *Sentinel*. If not, you're looking for his replacement. Also, I want you to work out a plan with Bob Ward to get that place investigated. I don't trust those assholes."

Marston looked as if he had been forced to suck on a lemon. "You did say Bob Ward, the attorney general?"

"Do I have a fucking speech impediment?"

"No, sir. Number one, Ward's a loyal Democrat. Two, he's so anal-retentive it'll take years for him to move his people on this."

"Kyle, the voters elected Ward. I didn't. You and me hafta work with the prick 'cause he's the only AG we got. So, tell me, what're ya gonna do?"

"I'll call Bob first thing in the morning. Good night, Gov—"

"Good ni—? Why do I keep a knob who doesn't know morning from night?"

Kyle studied the brass locking mechanisms of his Louis Vuitton briefcase. "You retain me, sir, because I am your most devoted employee, not to mention that my dear grandfather has donated over eight hundred fucking thousand dollars to your campaigns."

Todd, already making his way up the curved staircase, raised both hands and burst out, "Oh, what a beautiful mornin', oh, what a beautiful day, I got a beautiful feelin' ev'rything's goin' my way." Finished, Todd watched Kyle salute, open the front door, and quietly exit, the door softly clicking shut.

In the nineteenth century, each inmate's movement was tracked and entered on the Daily Change Sheet the very next morning. Tracking inmates is still accorded high priority this very day. Carefully noted are any changes in his security status, job assignment, move to a different cell or prison hospital or hole, return to court, or mandatory release—and, lastly, in the event he died.

Deceased inmates were promptly laid out in plain pine coffins after a Waupun medical doctor pronounced their deaths official, the coffins constructed by Carpenter Shop inmates,

Buried on grounds the next sunrise, the remains were accorded brief Christian services conducted by either a minister from one of Waupun's many Protestant churches or a Catholic priest from St. Joseph's. Which one officiated depended upon the decedent's professed religion at the intake interview.

Inmates with no stated religious preferences, along with heathen American Indians or foreigners who spoke little or no English, were buried without rite. The warden or his designee, however, usually read from the Book of Common Prayer at the gravesites.

Inmates assigned to the yard gang dug the graves and also refilled the holes. Within the year, no longer able to hold back the load of earth piled on it, the casket imploded, the ground above making a "whoosh" sound, frightening nearby inmates or prison guards. The yard crew filled in the crater.

After each Christian burial rite, the priest or minister was escorted to the Officers Dining Room. There, he was given a breakfast of fried pork steak and as many fried eggs as he desired along with potatoes and onions smothered in gravy. Also included were buttered toast with jelly, milk, and plenty of piping-hot coffee with fresh cream and a bowl of sugar. Finishing off the fare, the prison chef offered the reverend a large piece of fresh berry pie in warm-weather months and pumpkin or mincemeat during the winter.

After the reverend consumed his breakfast, the warden or his representative heartily shook the reverend's hand before a guard escorted him to the front gate and out the institution.

CHAPTER SEVEN

In the kitchen and midway through Isaiah and a mouthful of toast, Auntie Louise Hammer was startled by the telephone's sudden but insistent jangling. She swallowed. "Shirleen, would you answer it, please?"

A female police officer, a beauty at that, poked her head out the bathroom door. She had foamy lips. "I can't," she said through the foam. "I'm brushing my teeth."

Auntie shook her head. "That child—she's always running late." Addressing the phone, she said, "Alexander Graham Bell, you can just wait." She nevertheless picked up. "Hello. Yes, Mr. Deutch, this is Louise Hammer."

Her smile vaporized. "Yes, he's at your place where, God knows, the boy needs to be. He got mixed up in all those drugs while serving in the army—but why do you—?"

Cup and saucer hit the floor and shattered. Auntie slumped into a chair.

Tugging on her Afro hairdo with a pick, Shirleen just stood there, burnished skin and brown eyes moist like a whitetail doe's. "Auntie?"

Louise waved off her niece.

"Auntie, plea—"

"Are you certain?" asked the aunt. "There's an Earl W. Davis there, too. My nephew is Earl R. Davis. They got their mail mixed up all the time. Maybe you have them—"

Louise Hammer's voice reflected passive acceptance. "Yes, Mr. Deutch, I shall take full financial responsibility for my nephew's funeral."

"Funeral?" screeched Shirleen. "Earl's dead?"

Auntie Louise's hand pushed out as she attempted to quiet her niece. "Funeral home?" she asked. "Is that what you said, you have to release him to a funeral home?" Louise nodded. "Yes, Mr. Deutch, I understand. O'Bee. I'll spell it for you. Capital O, apostrophe, capital B followed by two e's. It's on North Holton, H-o-l-t-o-n. Yes, that's a street. As soon as we hang up, I'll call them. Yes, Mr. Deutch, God has a reason for everything that takes place. We must accept that. Thank you and good-bye."

Auntie succeeded in returning the phone to its cradle. "Shirleen, child, look up O'Bee's phone number, will you, please? Oh, Poor Earl, you poor, dear boy."

Shirleen knelt before the older woman, dropped her head on her aunt's lap, wrapped her arms around her aunt's waist, and soon she and Auntie cried together, long and uncontrollably.

•••

Dodge County District Attorney Glen Matthews argued a point with Milwaukee County District Attorney E. Michael McCann at the Wisconsin District Attorneys Association annual convention. "Mike, you can't be serious. It's first degree—pure and simple."

McCann shook his head. "Nothing's pure and simple, Glen. You ought to know that. Chicago intelligence advised our office the Cobras are hiring Michael Brooking, the Harvard law professor. I assure you he doesn't lose—easily."

Matthews chuckled. "I have signed, written confessions from both men. They were given Miranda warnings with a translator present even though both claimed they had no need for one. We also have their confessions on tape. Mike, it's a slam dunk."

"Tell, me Glen, are the walleyes biting at Fox Lake? I took the kids there last fall, and we caught some pretty nice ones."

•••

Marine Sgt. Zak Griffin had stopped writing letters to his mother. Dawn Griffin wrote to the Marine Commandant in Washington, DC, asking if her son was wounded or missing in action.

Three weeks later, she received a letter from Zak. *Dear Ma, as to your contacting the Marine Commandant, don't ever do that again. Your son, Zak.*

On the first workday morning of January of each year in the nineteenth century, the warden's secretary dutifully penned inmate death announcements from the previous year. After the warden signed each letter, she addressed the envelopes and mailed the letters to next of kin, if next of kin was listed on inmate face sheets.

They were called face sheets because each sheet had an inmate's picture affixed to it ever since Frederick Scott Archer developed the photographic set plate, which resulted in a negative image that was infinitely reproducible, photography a criminal justice ally since its birth.

Because many inmates offered no next of kin's name because free citizens' treatment of inmates' spouses and children was less than kind, the warden's secretary addressed the letters to clerks of courts from the counties in which inmates were sentenced.

As to an inmate who lived long enough to serve the time the judge gave him, a month before he was released, he was measured for a new suit of clothes produced by fellow inmates in the Tailor Shop. New boots were fashioned by the Cobbler Shop. On the morning of his release, an inmate barber visited him after breakfast and gave him a decent haircut and shave. After that, he was allowed to bathe even if he had his weekly bath a day or two earlier.

Fully dressed in his new outfit, the man was escorted to the Business Office, where the business manager handed the man a new saddle and three gold coins, two double eagles and a half eagle, value, fifty dollars. This was the freed man's "gate fee." Once he signed a legal document, in triplicate, that he had received the saddle and the money, the business manager told him, "Out front, you will find a tethered horse in good health, I am told. The horse is yours to keep. Good luck to you."

The front gate turnkey gave his usual advice: "Get out of Waupun and don't let me ever see you again."

Most men accepted that suggestion before urging their horse to turn in whatever direction they wished to head.

Released women convicts were given the option to forgo horse and saddle and instead accept train fare. In front of the women's prison, a buggy waited, driven by a matron who took the freed woman to the Waupun train station, where she waited for her freedom ride.

CHAPTER EIGHT

Five years had passed. It was 1973. Sgt. Zak Griffin was home on leave. At least, that's what his mother assumed. When Dawn Griffin was awakened by the *thumpa, thumpa, thumpa, thumpa* sound of her son's Plymouth coupe's Ford Mustang engine, her fingers clawed for the night table and felt for the glasses. Awkwardly, she put them on. The right bow made it; the left was at the side of her chin. Nevertheless, she made out Big Ben's luminous hands: twenty past three in the morning. As far as she was concerned, it was night.

Out of bed, she pushed aside a curtain. The Plymouth's headlights pointed into the backyard instead of at the garage door. Finally, the engine was silenced. At least a full minute later, Zak turned off the lights. She heard the car door eventually open.

She also heard Zak curse as he entered the house, thump into a wall, curse some more, and make it to his bed. Its springs gasped. Soon, they squawked in protest as Zak rose from the bed and cursed. She knew he made it to the bathroom because she heard the commode lid hitting the porcelain back. Her son retched and cursed and flushed and retched and cursed and flushed some more.

Finally, it was over.

She heard him stumble and bumble and tumble his way back to his bed. Seconds later, he snored so loudly Dawn couldn't get to sleep, but sleep, thankfully and finally, did come.

• • •

The back door slammed so hard Dawn Griffin thought a bomb had detonated inside the house. *Ten past six.* Struggling with the terry cloth robe, she jerked to face the picture of Lance Cpl. Michael Griffin, who dove on a Chinese hand grenade tossed in the center of a group of fellow marines in Korea. "Mike, I need you," she pleaded. A moment later, she ordered, "Now."

Rushing downstairs and outdoors, the screen door making a *ka-flam* sound, she found Zak pouring gasoline out of a red can onto his military sea bag. "Zak, what are you doing?"

"Wazz it look like?" His grin unseemly, he threw the lighted Zippo onto the bag. *Whoooosh.*

As son and mother backed away, another female inquired, "Is something wrong?" It was Edna Mayfield, dressed in a diamond-tufted pink housecoat, her hair looking like a jumble of brambles. "What's burning?" she asked.

"None of your business," snapped Zak.

"Son," said Dawn, "we Griffins don't talk that way. Apologize to Mrs. Mayfield."

"The hell I will," he growled.

Dawn grabbed Zak's arm. "Then, I'll apologize for you. He's sorry he said that, Edna."

"The hell I am," retorted Zak, shaking loose from his mother's grasp and heading for the house as Edna scurried to hers. Dawn was certain her neighbor was preparing to dial the first of many phone calls.

In the kitchen, Dawn stood there as she watched Zak pop open a cupboard door, snatch an aspirin bottle, dump a number of pills into his hand, toss his head back, and swallow.

"Zak, why did you burn your uniforms?"

Zak shrugged. "Who needs them?"

"You do."

"Correction. I needed them—past tense," he said.

"What?"

"My commanding officer said I drank too much and that *we* had a problem. He offered me a solution, an honorable separation, which I accepted."

"It's about that picture, isn't it?"

It was obvious by his reaction that her son knew what she was talking about.

"What picture?" he lied.

Dawn sighed. "Son, it's plain to see you're not at peace. Your drinking, it's—"

Zak's eyes flamed. "My drinking is nobody's business but mine. I'm a big boy, Ma." He exited the kitchen. The Plymouth's engine roared to life. Its tires squealed. Zak didn't return home until the next morning, drunk again.

•••

Harvard law professor Michael Brooking left doubt in the jury's collective mind as to who was the victim, inmate Juan Ruiz or inmate Earl Davis. "My client did his best to protect himself by trying to grab Davis's knife in the process of their hand-to-hand struggle over who would have control of the weapon. Thank God, Mr. Ruiz saved himself." Jury members found both Ruiz and Gonzalez guilty of involuntary manslaughter.

The Department of Corrections sent the pair to the federal penal system, due to problems that would arise between the Cobras and the Negro gang, the Brother-men, according to Waupun's recently promoted security director, Marion Richardson, the institution's former major of the guard.

As soon as a new Waupun cell hall was completed, its more than 250 one-man cells were filled to capacity, many even housed with two men each.

"Will building even newer, more up-to-date institutions end this inmate housing problem?" a Madison Wisconsin State Journal reporter asked the Waupun warden.

"This shall never be the case," answered the warden, "unless we witness the demise of man himself or the abolishment of democratic principles that enable our citizens to choose wrong actions."

The warden's answer made front-page headlines not only in Wisconsin but also in newspapers throughout the nation and the world. Unfortunately, Wisconsin's governor, prompted by his political party's legislative howls, responsively dismissed Waupun prison's honest and thoughtful administrator.

Giving the ax to the warden for being truthful and insightful didn't stop that governor or those very same politicians who howled from authorizing the construction of a reformatory, or training school, for younger male felons. The new reformatory was built near Green Bay's shores, which is one of the state's largest water inlets. It was given the blessing of not only state but local politicians, in addition to a variety of newspaper editors, college professors, religious leaders, and social engineers because the lockup isolated younger men from the older Waupun "career criminals."

Politicians eventually authorized younger children's institutions to be built in order to avoid having kids locked up with older teenagers at the reformatory who, it was thought, could mislead the younger set, not to mention take sexual advantage of the nippers.

Adult women convicts continued to be housed at Waupun until one-third of the twentieth century had expired.

The continued construction of additional inmate housing units in existing institutions and of new state slammers has not abated in America's dairy land to this very day.

CHAPTER NINE

Wearing handcuffs and leg irons, seventeen-year-old Jeremy Clark sat behind the steel grated cage in the back of the Portage County squad while both deputies sympathetically spoke of the weather and the corn and soybean crops and the number of Canada geese overhead.

When they arrived in Waupun, the ride down Main Street was too brief. The driver turned the Ford Galaxie 500 onto Madison Street. After checking in their weapons in the Visitor's Check-In area, the deputies wordlessly handed the court papers to a white-shirted lieutenant. "Follow me," he told Jeremy.

Jeremy was led to a single cell off the corridor between the Overpass gates. After showering and before he could put on the prison jumpsuit, two officers with two stripes on their uniform shirts and one officer with three stripes searched every orifice of his body with the aid of a flashlight before escorting him to the Northwest Cell Hall.

Jeremy was amazed at the cell hall's large size as the sergeant in charge led him up to the fourth, most upper tier. "Here's your temporary home, Cell Eleven." Above the cell, in gloss black paint was the letter *L* followed by the numeral *11*.

Two weeks earlier, Circuit Court Judge Albert Fontaine had reluctantly sentenced Jeremy to serve a sentence of five to twenty-five years for second-degree murder for the killing of his stepfather, a drunken lout who physically abused Jeremy's mother once too often.

Alone, Jeremy looked between a pair of vertical bars to the tall exterior windows, dirtied by legions of pigeons. A few gray birds with raggedy feathers hunkered in the lower crevices, cooing to their hearts' delights.

L-11's walls, painted an uneasy yellow, must've seen a legion of colors because their splotches dotted the white porcelain sink's rim. The stainless steel mirror above the sink returned a vague, almost ghostlike image. The commode was absent a hinged cover. As he turned to the front, he was startled. "God damn," he said.

"God damn what?" asked the hunched-over gnome with corrugated facial skin. His cackle was next of kin to Oz's wicked witch. Holding on to a blue plastic bucket's metal handle with one hand and a green plastic cup with the other, the dwarf could not have weighed much over a hundred pounds. "Want ice?" he asked, his teeth looking like charred corn kernels.

"Yeah," said Jeremy, jumping off the bunk and approaching the bars.

The geezer grinned. "You got a cup?"

Jeremy looked around the cell and then turned to face the gnome. "No, I guess I don't."

"I'll get you one. I'm your tier tender. That's what the screws and cons call us here. In Ella-noise, the bulls called us porters." The gnome eyeballed Jeremy's chest pocket, which held a nearly full pack of Pall Malls. "Ya got an extra square?"

"No," said Jeremy.

The geezer's lips curled, his eyeballs riveted to the pocket. "Ya sure?"

"Yeah, I'm sure."

Putting down pail and cup, the gnome looked up and down the tier, unzipped his trousers, pulled out a flaccid, horribly maroon penis, and began stroking and grunting and sneering and chortling, his jaw dropping, spittle falling over the lower lip in a stretching column.

"What the hell are you doing?" asked Jeremy.

"Unh, unh, unh, unh," was the gnome's answer as he increased his tempo. "Unh-unh-unh-unh-unh." His eyelids drew shut as his body thrashed in seeming exultation. Opening his eyes and grinning, he winged gunk through the bars. "Ice is on the state. Milkshake's on me."

"You little bastard, when I get outta this cell, I'm going to grind your puny ass into the concrete."

The gnome returned salvo. "You and the fucking French Foreign Legion." Then, he was gone.

Jeremy unrolled toilet paper as quickly as he could, doused it in the sink, and attended to the gunk.

Soon, inmates passed by his cell, some belching and patting their guts, toothpicks between lips. A few looked in. Most didn't. One laughed when he did. Another shook his head and said, "It's a kid."

Obviously filled with inmates, the cell hall settled down.

A guard stood before Jeremy's cell. "Hands on the bars," he ordered Jeremy.

When Jeremy stood, he wrapped his fingers around two vertical bars. The guard announced, "Eleven," and was on his way.

"Twelve, thirteen, fourteen—"

Typewriters clackety-clacked. Men coughed and cleared their throats. Loud farts and falling piss preceded sudden whooshes of flushing toilets.

The cell hall sergeant, who had escorted Jeremy to his cell, appeared with a stainless steel dinner tray with meat, mashed potatoes, gravy, applesauce, a waxed half-pint container of milk, and two slices of buttered bread. He pushed it onto the cell's food slot. "Dinner," he announced. "If you *lose* any of the silverware, you go to the hole." Then, he was gone.

Jeremy rose and grabbed the tray, sat on the bunk, and inhaled the offerings. He was hungrier than he had thought.

One gong rang out, sounding like the start of a round of boxing. Cell doors below opened. Their *clackety-clack* sounds reminded Jeremy of Chicago's Riverview Park's Silver Streak roller coaster being pulled up the first hill. He and his biological father rode it when Jeremy was seven. *Ka-blang*. Steel pounded steel.

Setting aside his tray, he rose and approached the bars, stepped up onto a lower horizontal steel bar that kept the vertical bars spread apart and evenly spaced, and lifted high to see inmates on the cell hall's main floor line up.

Returning to the tray, he ate hurriedly. Two gongs. *Clackety-clack*. The sounds were closer. Jeremy figured they came from the second tier. He heard shuffling on the catwalk. Then, shoe bottoms scuffed against steel stairs as the line of prisoners descended to the main floor. The guard who made count stopped before Jeremy's cell. "Wanna go to rec?"

"Wreck?" asked Jeremy.

"Night recreation—ya don't have to go if you don't want to."

"I want to."

The guard jammed two separate brass keys into two separate keyholes on the cell's side, turned them, pulled them out, and was on his way.

Three gongs. *Clackety-clack, ka-bang.*

Jeremy knew he'd have to wait for four gongs. After they sounded, he heard cell doors on his left and right ratchet open. Grabbing hold of his cell door with more effort than he thought he'd need, Jeremy pushed the sliding door aside, *clackety-clack, clackety-clack,* and *clackety-ka-bang.* He stepped through the opening and onto the catwalk. Men on both sides held on to the top guardrail and looked down to the main floor. He followed suit.

"Hey."

Jeremy turned left, then right. Neither inmate on either side looked his way.

"Yeah, I'm talking to you, kid, you stupid motherfucker."

Jeremy's eyes dove to the sound and settled on pink eyes belonging to a creature no taller than a six-year-old kid. He was as fat as a roasting pig, hair as white as a flash of night lightning, stumps for arms and legs. He had a cleft palate. He looked more like a large rabbit than a tiny man. "Didn't ya hear me? I said move, motherfucker."

By 1910, state legislators had decided the Waupun prison's twenty-two-acre walled-in enclosure had run out of room for raising crops and animals. The lawmakers decided to purchase six hundred acres of farmland from Ethan Cox, firstborn of the Waupun pioneers, Lucy and James, in order to keep the institution self-sufficient. Inmates didn't cost the taxpayers a dime. In fact, Wisconsin realized about one hundred dollars of profit a year from each inmate's labor.

Trustees were chosen by the security director to build the first buildings on the newly acquired land. Most everybody in Waupun knew that trustees were the prison's security director's sycophants.

Supervised by a civil-service carpenter, trustees erected a huge barn that could hold enough animals to feed all maximum-security prisoners, women and men. Once the barn was completed, a bunkhouse, large enough to hold seventy-five men, was next.

It did not make sense to the prison administration to have inmates leave the prison and return to it each day because of inherent security problems, not limited to smuggling in booze or other contraband.

Not all trustees were trustworthy. They were, first and foremost, inmates who still needed supervision but not as strict as those inmates behind the walls. A whiteshirt position was posted, and a handful of blueshirts vied for the few "farm jobs" that were offered.

Escape was easy. The inmate simply walked away. However, many "chicks" that flew the coop didn't make it past the first tavern. Others headed home, where local law officers apprehended them and returned them to Waupun—for a fee.

Eventually, the term "trustee" was dropped. "Minimum-security inmate" took its place.

During the day, minimum security inmates tended to farm animals and machinery, milked and butchered animals, and grew crops and vegetables for their maximum-security brethren until 1969, when the governor stopped sustaining farm work because it was "demeaning" for inmates from metropolitan areas.

In 1968, the state realized a profit of nearly three hundred dollars per maximum-security prisoner per year. Each maximum-security inmate now costs taxpayers over twenty-five thousand dollars a year.

CHAPTER TEN

Like a waddling king penguin, second-shift captain Fred Zerlaski, a burly, white-haired, blue-eyed, fifty-four-year-old Polack with fingers the size of kielbasa breakfast sausages, grinned mightily as he led two columns of nearly five hundred maximum-security prisoners to the rec field.

On the side of each column were blueshirts, one among them a sergeant calling cadence as the rest scanned the columns, looking for any illicit behavior.

Twenty feet behind the captain, inmate column leaders knew they had to remain a certain distance behind Zerlaski. If they dared to enter the captain's comfort zone, he'd order both columns to halt, perform an about-face, and he and his men would march the whole shebang back to the cell halls.

Zerlaski reached the chain-link fence that kept both staff and inmates off the field during non-recreation periods. He turned to face the standing columns. Twenty feet meant twenty feet. Zerlaski nodded his approval.

Next, he turned to face the heavy chain and padlock. Zerlaski inserted a key into the lock. After slipping the padlock into his right trousers pocket, he pushed against the gate with a ham-size shoulder. The gate groaned open.

Inmates held their ground. They couldn't move until Zerlaski gave the whistled signal, their knees cocked like hammers of Colt single-action .45s. Zerlaski raised his right hand. Index finger and thumb revealed the glint of the chrome pea whistle. With ultimate fanfare, the Polack placed the whistle between upper and lower teeth, their color similar to the ivory keys of an antique piano. His lips parted. He inhaled mightily, chest ballooning like a rooster preparing to announce sunrise. Lips smothered the whistle's shaft. The whistle blustered.

An explosion of howling inmates bailed out of the columns and scattered to separate ball diamonds, handball courts, horseshoe pits, iron piles, basketball courts, spots on the grass, and a number of steel card tables with four attached swivel seats, the tables' legs embedded in concrete.

• • •

Around fifty inmates did not move, including the newest prisoner. The other forty-nine glared at Jeremy Clark.

Am I standing in a sacred spot? Although uncomfortable, he remained in place but turned his attention to the cinder track that ran alongside the bottom of the gray, foreboding wall where a number of convicts walked or jogged or ran all out.

Two guard towers looked over the rec. field. Each guard stood on steel-grated platforms jutting out from the towers like flying bridges on battleships. Each leaned against the top guardrail. One foot rested on the middle rail, the other planted on the grated platform. Each studied inmate movement below through mirrored sunglasses, as in a movie Jeremy had seen. "What's a kid like him in here for?" he heard a nearby con remark.

"Hell if I know," was the answer, "and damned if I care, the pussy motherfucker."

"Where's the punk from?"

"Bum Fuck, Egypt, for all I know."

Jeremy headed to the cinder track. An inmate running against the flow and backward at the same time was a red-haired Caucasian in his midtwenties. Although his eyelids were closed shut, he collided with nothing and no one.

"Hey, Radar, how they hangin'?" asked a con.

Radar, smiling and shaking his head, continued his backward run.

What happened next was no accident. *They* forced Jeremy to stop.

Hemming him in were the shims (she + him) he'd heard about in the Portage county jail. As each shim came ever closer, he-she grinned and eye-raped the boy, their rococo moves overly achieved, more feminine than any girl or woman he'd ever seen or known. Each primped, pouted, grinned, and gazed, eyelids flashing explicitly, sensually, and sexually. Their asses appeared hooked to high-lobed camshafts. Each must've thought he-she was a *Vogue* or *Mademoiselle* front-cover model, facing the ever-clicking Hasselblad held by a queer photographer, accompanied by his queer assistant.

Songstress Billie Holliday stood at an awkward angle, seemingly enjoying Jeremy's unease. "Don't know why there's no sun up in the skyyyyyyyyyyyyy—sloppy blowjob." Billie stopped and wiggled her ass. "Since my man and I ain't to-geth-ahhhhhhhhhhhhhh, keep raining all the ta-iiiiiime."

"Get outta here, bitch," said an audacious black shim, pushing Lady Day away as if she were a gnat.

"Nipper, you didn't have to do that," complained Billie.

The more aggressive Nipper announced, "I'm in *love* with this boy."

Jeremy couldn't have known that Nipper had ruined forever Milwaukee's elite pimp Elmwood Brewster's sex life along with his mind. Brewster first picked up Nipper in Brewster's '57 Cadillac Eldorado Brougham, an authentic George Barris-designed Del Caballero, customized by Detroit's Universal Coach Corporation. After Nipper performed her specialty on Brewster, the pimp wowed Nipper by announcing, "That's the best head I've evah had. You're gonna work for me."

Nipper did tricks for Brewster with a special white male clientele, including lawyers, judges, cops, doctors, priests, and ministers. No rabbis.

Nipper fell head over heels for her pimp. One night, after she gave him a round-the-world, she pleaded with him to pay for a sex-change operation.

"The only thing I'm paying you for," announced Brewster rather coldly, "is for your tongue lapping at my jones."

Nipper's day job was a metal fabricator at the AO Smith Company. After Brewster flat turned her down a second time, Nipper fabricated a special steel pincer while at work.

That night, the ambulance took Brewster, minus his testicles and penis, to a hospital. Nipper had tossed Brewster's manhood into Lake Michigan. After surgery was performed, Brewster was sent to Madison's Mendota State Mental Hospital where he lived out his life, talking to himself but no one else.

Nipper moved around Jeremy in sheer ecstasy, telling him, "I'll do whatever you want, chile—suck, fuck, play with your titties. I'll even give you a round-the-world that'll make you come for a whole gawdam year, ah-hummm."

Just then, Lena Horne approached a Ho-Chunk Indian who held hands with Susie-Q, the Alabaster Queen. Lena loudly proclaimed, "Pokeahotass, honey. You see that young boy over there? Ain't he just wonderful?"

The Indian, who looked as if he were pissed off at the world, grunted and flexed his muscles before growling in a deep bass, "Fuck 'im."

A half-pint Oriental pushed to the fore and was soon in Jeremy's face. "Me suckee; you fuckee, hey?"

Nipper shot out her tongue. "Betcha that boy tastes like banana cream paaaaaaaaaah."

Jeremy broke through the barrier and ran headlong into the iron pile crew. Muscle-bound bodybuilders and power lifters with shaved heads and bandanna-wrapped foreheads, grouped by race, scowled, grinned, giggled, roared, sulked, whistled, ogled, pumped, and posed, most grabbing for their crotches.

A Caucasian behemoth with no body hair whatsoever exited the pile and blocked Jeremy with his humongous size. "Hubba-hubba, I'm Mr. Clean, and you, my little bitch, shall be my queen."

A bevy of shims sang out, "Hey, Mister Clean, wha'cha gonna do to that boy?"

The giant grunted. His muscles demanded escape from skin. "I'll tell you cunts what I'm gonna do. This bitch needs a man, and I am *the* man, Rrrrrrrrrrrowwwwwwwwwwwl." His muscles quaked and squirmed and snaked.

One of the tower guards laughed aloud.

Radar approached again, running backward.

"Hey, MC, it's your lift," yelled Mr. Clean's spotter.

Before the big man returned to the pile, he told Jeremy, "When you drop a bar of soap in the bathhouse, my fireman's hose is gonna be up your ass just like that." He snapped his fingers and added, "Tickling your tonsils."

Making it past the iron pile, Jeremy faced yet another group, its members looking like irksome, smiling used car salesmen, ready to offload junk bombs onto naive sixteen-year-old boys with recently acquired driver's licenses and a hundred bucks in their wallets. "Trust in Jesus," said the first.

"The Savior is your friend," offered a second. "Did you read your Bible today?"

A Negro with black-framed eyeglasses approached. "Repent, brutha. Come to the chapel, be you Cat-lick or Protestant, we don't care."

Jeremy skirted around the group as fast as he could and ran into some serious bearded Negroes, all wearing white crocheted kufi over shaved heads. One especially light-skinned member rose and said, "*Allahu akbar*, brother. Allah be praised."

Jeremy continued on as a white inmate screamed and raged at the wall. A squat Latino passed him, stopped, genuflected, made the sign of the cross, and blurted, "El Senor is my savior." A lone Negro, his girth twenty inches at most, stared into the sun as saliva dribbled over his bottom lip.

Someone was at Jeremy's side, matching strides. Jeremy stole a look. It was a dipshit Negro wearing a full-time grin and sporting a gold upper tooth with what looked like a diamond in its center. "These muhfukuhs," said Dipshit, "are trying to scare you, just like that tier tender tried, but I see you ain't gonna lets 'em, uh-huh. I can see that."

Dipshit's head nodded a dozen times before he added, "You're one tough dude, uh-huh."

How'd he know about the tier tender? "The tier tender," said Jeremy. "How'd you know about him?"

Dipshit's grin grew even wider, looking as if he just cracked Fort Knox and was freely walking away with billions worth of gold. "Listen to the bro. You sound mighty white to me."

"How'd you know? Did you put him up to it?"

"Hell, no. Little muhfukuh told me. That's how. He stay in his cell, afraid you gonna kick his old-as-hell ass." Dipshit offered his hand again. "Muhfukuhs around here and elsewhere call me G-Money. Moms named me Milo, Milo Washington."

As they entered shim territory, G-Money said, "These bitches 'bout nothing, but they'll hump your bootie if you give 'em half a chance, uh-huh. Wass your name?"

As other inmates moved in to listen, G-Money scowled. "Move on, muhfukuhs."

"Jeremy."

G-Money drew in a deep breath. "Jeremy," he said. "That's a nice name. Where you from?"

"Stevens Point."

"Never heard of the muhfukuh."

"It's up north in Portage County."

G-Money howled. "You sounds like these country and western muhfukuhs here. I ain't used to no brutha who talk like that 'cept Zombie and some eastern Neeeeeegroes. What were black folk doing up north in—where you from again?"

"Stevens Point. My dad worked for the Green Bay and Western Railroad."

"And he be a porter, making beds, cleaning nasty-ass white men's toilets, carrying white folks' baggage, scratching his head for his two-bit tip, huh?"

"No, he was an engineer."

G-Money scratched his head and howled. "I don't believe you. I surely don't."

Two tall and expansively shouldered Negro inmates left the iron pile and approached Jeremy and G-Money. G-Money's grin went AWOL. "Sheeit, Curly and Moe is coming our way."

"I see you made it through our gauntlet," said the taller and more handsome of the pair to Jeremy. He had flashing dark eyes, brilliant white teeth, and a ready smile that instantly faded as he eyeballed G-Money. Then, he turned once again to Jeremy. "Or should I say, just about."

"He's mine," objected G-Money. "I have first dibs."

"I know. Unfortunately, it's the code," said the big man, once again addressing Jeremy. "Randy Smith's the name and strong-arming is my game. Everyone calls me Zombie. I'm leader of the Brother-men. This here is Jack 'Rude Boy' Worthington, my second in command."

Zombie's nudging Rude Boy caused his second in command to snarl a hello.

"I'm Jeremy, Jeremy Clark."

"Glad to meet you," said Zombie.

Rude Boy addressed Zombie. "He sounds just like you, a fay."

"Fay?" inquired Jeremy.

"It's Pig Latin," explained Zombie, "but with a wrench thrown in. In Pig Latin, the word for 'foe,' or 'enemy,' is 'o-fay.' However, modern style Brothers like us took away the *o* to further outflank Mr. Charlie so his po-leace couldn't understand. Thus, we arrive at 'fay.' Got it?"

"Got it," said Jeremy.

"Changing the subject, Rude Boy and I have this bet. I say you're that kid from Stevens Point, valedictorian of your senior class. He says no. Who wins?"

"Neither," said Jeremy. "Although I am from Stevens Point, I was in jail during graduation ceremonies and the student with the second-highest average was chosen as valedictorian."

"Killed your ol' man," said Rude Boy.

"Stepfather," corrected Jeremy.

"A lot of dudes here did worse," said Zombie, "including baby rapists, chicken fuckers, and"—Zombie eyeballed G-Money long and hard—"bootie bandits."

"And don't forget the horse fuckuh," a nervous G-Money said with a laugh.

Zombie paid G-Money no attention. "Jeremy, the reason I wanted to meet you is the Brother-men need a legal adviser."

"Ain' it enough you got Earl Davis killed?" demanded G-Money. "Besides, Zombie, you ain't got nothing coming because I got first dibs." ("First dibs" was a linchpin of the inmate code, giving G-Money primary rights over Jeremy).

A shrill whistle interrupted everyone in the vicinity. "Screw's coming," warned Zombie.

Zombie and Rude Boy headed back to the iron pile while G-Money jogged ahead on the cinder track. Jeremy walked alone, no longer hassled since he was now G-Money's property.

•••

As Zombie prepared to benchpress 365 pounds, Rude Boy, his spotter, said, "G-Money's gonna turn that boy out, and there ain't nothing you can do."

"That boy will not become anyone's bitch," declared Zombie. "Of that, I am certain."

"We need more elbow room," wrote the Waupun warden in his 1931 annual report to the state legislature. "Because a mere forty-two female inmates are separated from over one thousand male convicts by a walled-in space that takes up fully one-third of the available space, the fairer sex simply does not belong."

Two years later, Wisconsin legislators approved the purchase of a summer estate, lost by a millionaire stock speculator who went broke in the 1929 stock market crash. His estate was located in the unincorporated village of Taycheedah. Twenty miles from Waupun, it was first named Tee-Charrah by local Indians. In English, it means "lake camp." Nearby Lake Winnebago is the largest lake inside the state's boundaries.

Construction crews erected a six-foot-high chain-link fence and only twenty-five feet in length at the front of the property. Waupun inmates were not displeased over the double standards between the two prisons, but an Appleton Post Crescent editor chided lawmakers, "The fence at Taycheedah keeps free citizens out rather than holds convicts in." Although female prisoners could easily walk away from the Taycheedah institution, few ever did.

After Taycheedah opened, it didn't take long for Waupun's administration to order male convicts to dismantle the wall that kept them separated from the females. Neither did it take much time for both legislative houses to accept the plan that the buildings formerly used by female convicts be adapted as a hospital, segregation unit, and a place for inmates to meet with social workers.

CHAPTER ELEVEN

Although the telephone's rings came from another room, each one slammed into Zak's skull as if it were a ball-peen hammer. Head mashed between two pillows, he prayed his mother would soon answer the phone. When she did, it didn't take long for her to knock on the door. *Damn, that hurts.*

"Zak, it's for you. It's the prison."

Stomach churning like menacing black clouds preceding a tornado, Zak opened the door and lurched. Soon, he put the phone to his ear. "Hello. Yes, ma'am, this is Zak. Yes, ma'am, I was responsible for overseeing a number of prisoners in the Portsmouth brig. Number two, you say? No, ma'am. Yes, ma'am, Madison Street, visitor's entrance door. Yes, ma'am."

Zak put the phone down. "I have a job interview tomorrow morning," he announced.

Remaining home that night, he and Dawn watched Johnny Carson. Later, as Zak lay in bed, he was certain that a couple of boilermakers would have helped him get to sleep.

• • •

The next morning, Visitor's Entrance Officer Two Biggs studied a typed sheet attached to a clipboard while he hummed a stanza from "Tie a Yellow Ribbon Round the Ole Oak Tree." Biggs looked up and shook his head. "Nope, no Griffin here."

"How about Correctional Officer Applicant Number Two?"

"Yes, sir, there's Applicant Two. See it?" Biggs placed an X on the sheet and handed Zak a wooden box. "Put all your loose metal in here."

Zak placed a watch and Buck jackknife along with loose change into the box.

"You can have the watch and change but this," Biggs lifted the knife, "you can't. You can pick it up before you leave."

Next, Biggs waved Zak through the metal detector.

•••

A wisp of a woman sat behind a desk in the personnel office, clacking away at the typewriter. After she acknowledged Zak with a nod and a grin, she stopped typing, stood, and approached him. She smelled like Double Bubble chewing gum. "And you're Zak, Applicant Number Two."

"Yes, ma'am."

She took Zak's hand as if he were a boy and led him to the hallway, where four wooden chairs were backed against the wall. "I'm Laura," she said. "You can have Number Two chair."

"The one closer to the door, or us?"

"The door." She returned to her desk.

Applicant Three and Four checked in. Laura directed each to his assigned chair. Number Three had unruly long hair and jutting side-burns. His attempt at a walrus mustache, thought Zak, was almost too funny for words.

Number Four's shoes were spit shined, his hair cropped closely. He reached over Number Three in order to shake hands. "Army?" he asked.

"Marines," said Zak, grabbing the applicant's hand and shaking it.

"Army here, name's Judder, Judder Brown. Before I was born, Mom and Dad hauled out a *Webster's*. Dad came up with *jerk*, Mom, *shudder*. Judder's a combination of the two."

The door to their left popped open. Out came a man about Zak's age. He took over Number One chair. The man accompanying him wore a suit that was probably fashionable in the forties. "Correctional Officer Applicant Number Two," he announced.

Zak rose and accepted the man's hand. "I'm Jon Powers, personnel director."

"Zak, Zak Griffin."

"Your mother sings in our church choir. She has such a sweet voice." Powers nodded Zak toward the door.

Zak stepped into a room with off-white walls. Two narrow barred windows provided natural light. Eight-foot fluorescent tubes attached to the ceiling flickered, since one appeared to be on its last gasp. A long brown Formica conference table overwhelmed the room. One man stood; the other who didn't said, "I'm Richardson, security director."

"Good morning, sir." Zak reached out to shake Richardson's hand; he declined. Zak had heard plenty at Otto's Bar and Grill about the security director. Guards called him Ego. The standing man offered his hand and said, "I'm John Deutch, associate warden of treatment."

"Glad to meet you, sir," said Zak.

"You may sit, Zak," said Powers before he and the others silently studied copies of Zak's job application.

Finally, Powers lifted his head. "Since you're a Waupun native, the prison shouldn't seem unusual to you."

"That's right, sir," said Zak, "it's not.

More silent study.

"I remember seeing you at football games some years back," offered Deutch. "And you were a sergeant in the marines, awarded three Bronze Stars, the Silver Star, and two Purple Hearts. Gentlemen, we have a hero before us."

"I was no hero," objected Zak.

Deutch chuckled. "That's exactly what I'd expect a hero to say."

"Semper fi," said Ego. "I was in the corps a long time ago, and I ain't no hero, neither."

"But you're security director," said Zak.

Ego leaned forward, gazed at Zak, and then looked to Deutch and Powers. "He's got a point, don't he? Haw, haw, haw."

Deutch lit his pipe with a farmer match, drew in, and exhaled a cloud. "I was in the navy and served in the Pacific. Zak, could you tell the committee why you applied for the job?"

"Yes, sir, I need the money."

"Amen to that, and a second reason?"

"My military experience at the Portsmouth navy brig will help me be a better prison guard."

Ego erupted like Mount Vesuvius. "What did he just say?"

"Zak," warned Deutch, "the word *guard* is perceived as a negative term here. We use *correctional officer* or *blueshirt*."

"At Portsmouth, we—"

"As you said," Ego bellowed, "you ain't in the corps." Then, most surprisingly, Ego turned to the others and added, "He's got the makings of a first-rate correctional officer."

"Will you accept the job?" asked Powers.

"I will," said Zak, still amazed at Ego's sudden outburst.

Powers rose. "I'll go over salary, hours, insurance, vacation, holidays, etc., after we interview the other two candidates. You can wait outside." Powers opened the door.

As Zak stepped out, Powers called, "Correctional Officer Applicant Number Three."

Number Three and Zak bumped into each other. "Sorry," said Zak.

"That's OK," said Long Hair. A moment later, he turned in the opposite direction and sped down the hallway. "I didn't want the fucking job anyway," he called out.

Zak shrugged.

Marvin Miller, Wisconsin corrections chief in the late sixties, rumored to be a boozing buddy of Edward "Ted" Kennedy, told cheering UW students, "Farm work is demeaning to urban convicts." Those remarks were so tantalizing they made front-page headlines the next morning.

"Demeaning?" thundered Wisconsin Farm Bureau Chief John Manley at the capitol building entrance as he passed out numerous copies of the local papers to legislators. "If you guys think farm labor is demeaning, I want you to tell our dairy farmers that. I'll guarantee they'll come to this building and kick all your asses with boots loaded with cow shit."

"Take it easy," said State Senator Albert Stone. "Marvin's statement was taken out of context."

"Out of context, my freaking ass," screamed Manley. "My people won't even wait to vote you out of office; they'll call for special elections. The only state jobs available to you and yours, Senator, will be cleaning wayside shithouses at the Illinois, Iowa, and Minnesota borders. Demeaning, indeed."

"You should be speaking to the governor. He's the fella who appointed Miller to the corrections job. Todd shoulda never appointed that drunken East Coast son of a bitch to head up an important Wisconsin bureaucracy."

Most other legislators assured Manley they agreed with his viewpoint—as usual—even if they didn't.

More than a few citizens penned letters to various editors concerning Miller's statement, among them Jane Gately, a farm wife near

Waunakee, the town with the slogan "The only Waunakee in the world," (thank goodness).

Jane's letter was brief. "Dear Editor: Corrections Chief Marvin Miller declared farm work demeaning for urban inmates. Maybe next week, His Royal Corrections Majesty could get up at four in the morning and venture to the countryside and visit law-abiding folks who milk cows, plow fields, and tend to honest farm work, which yields taxes to pay for His Royal Corrections Majesty's salary."

Obviously, Miller had a tin ear for the public forum because a story in the Capital Times stated he had pleaded with Madison's University of Wisconsin president to send professors to Waupun in order to teach on-site university courses to inmates.

So infuriated was Jane that she announced to husband, children, and grandkids after Sunday services and before serving lunch, "Dad raises corn. Marvin Miller raises my blood pressure. Now, I'm going to raise hell."

"Give it to 'em," roared Michael, her sun-burnished husband. With a hand on Jane's shoulder, he faced his family. "I am so proud of my wife." He brought his gray-haired beauty to him, kissed her fully on the lips, and when they parted, he roundly blushed.

"Enough of that," said the family's matriarch. "Let's pray and eat. I'm hungry."

CHAPTER TWELVE

With a smudge of black soil on her cheek, Dawn Griffin obviously enjoyed tending her flower garden, even as Edna Mayfield said she admired the flowers while attempting to uncover anything unseemly concerning their neighbors. As expected, Dawn did not oblige. Edna, however, never gave up trying.

At that moment, Zak dressed in his correctional officer blue uniform, exited the home, and chatted pleasantly with both women. A short time later, he checked his watch. "Oops, gotta go," he said.

"Be safe," said Dawn.

Smiling, Zak opened the 1935 Plymouth coupe's driver's side door and stuffed himself in what his mother called a teakettle-size interior. Waving, he and his roaring car disappeared around the corner.

"My," offered Edna, "that son of yours certainly looks good in blue."

Grinning and swiping at perspiration on her forehead with a forearm, adding another smear of dirt, Dawn agreed. "Like my flowers, Edna, he looks good in any color."

"Besides," added the gossipmonger, "he doesn't stay out all hours every night like he used to—if you know what I mean." Edna sighed and added, "It's the nights before his days off that he—"

"He's a grown man, Edna," reminded Dawn.

"That he is, and what young lady wouldn't be interested in catching him as a prize?"

"What Zak does with his time is his business. Just like what you do is yours, don't you agree?"

Edna's cheeks were now the color of a harvest moon. "That's just what I was going to say."

It was obvious Dawn was no longer consumed by her son's drinking.

•••

Erected in 1910, the red brick building that housed the Alano Club was originally Beaver Dam's English Lutheran Church before its membership dissolved and sold the building to a community theater group. After purchasing another idle and larger church, the theater group sold the smaller building to Gene and Big Larry, a pair of recovering alcoholics whose fellow AA members were getting heat from a pastor who didn't like the odor of cigarette smoke in his church's basement, where AA meetings had been held for many years.

Apprehensive, Dawn opened the entrance door and entered the building, which smelled of stale cigarette smoke. A white cardboard sign with a black arrow and freehand lettering pointed right to "Alanon room." A second arrow pointed downstairs to "AA meetings."

Trying desperately to be quiet, she discovered that with every step she made the floor creaked. The Alanon room's door was open. Close to a dozen women of varying ages and a balding man in his forties looked directly at her. They sat on older chairs one would find in a home, set up in a large circle so their occupants could look at each other.

Wearing blue jeans, a white blouse, and tennis shoes, the obviously oldest lady with the whitest hair and most wrinkly face stood. "Hi, honey. I'm Alice. You looking for an Alanon meeting?"

"I am," said Dawn, more than a little nervous, "and my name is Dawn."

Grabbing Dawn's hand, Alice turned to the others and squawked, "Hey, guys, this here is Dawn."

"Hi, Dawn," the others called out.

They seem, Dawn thought, *to be almost—can I think it—happy?*

"Have a seat," said Alice. "You want coffee?"

"That would be nice," said Dawn, taking her place in a straight-back chair. She reached into her purse.

"Never mind," said Alice, "it's on the house. How do ya like it?"

"How do I like what?" asked Dawn.

"Your coffee?"

"Oh, black."

"Black it is." Alice's chuckle seemed somewhat deeper than her speaking voice.

The meeting began. Alice, obviously the leader, called on three ladies to read from different books. Then, she announced they'd say the Serenity Prayer after a moment of silence. Everyone bowed heads. "God, grant me the serenity to accept the things I cannot change, courage to change the things I can, and wisdom to know the difference."

Alice turned to Dawn. "Honey, would you care to start? You might want to tell us about your drinkin' problem?"

"The name's Dawn. I don't have a drinking problem. It's my son. I need to know what I can do in order for him to quit—for his own good. If he doesn't stop drinking and driving, he's going to kill himself, or he might kill someone else, a child, God forbid, because he drives drunk." Dawn told the group how Zak was tossed out of the Marine Corps due to his excessive drinking.

Alice started to laugh.

Shocked, Dawn glared. "I don't think what I've just said is one least bit funny."

"I agree," said Alice. "Every one of us in here—we were just like you. We thought we could fix our drinkers, by Hannah, and that's exactly what we had to stop thinking. We had to admit defeat. We can't fix them. No way, honey, although we can begin to fix our overreacting to our loved one's drinking behaviors."

"I just can't believe what you've said," said Dawn.

"Well, I'll tell you this, Dawn. You'd have a better chance of putting out the sun's light with water from a watering can than to stop your son's drinking."

"I must have hope."

"Hope all you want," shot back a girl who couldn't have been older than eighteen. "I'm Neva, and I'm a grateful member of Alanon."

"Hi, Neva," the others chimed in.

"Your son," Neva continued, "isn't going to stop drinking until he makes up his mind to do so. He can't stop drinking for you. He has to stop drinking for himself. Besides, drinking isn't his biggest problem. I know. Ronnie, my brother, won't quit for anyone. He still drinks every night, but you know what? It doesn't bother me like it used to—and I have to thank Alanon for that. With that, I'll pass."

"Hi, everyone, I'm Doug and a grateful member of Alanon," said the lone man.

"Hi, Doug," the others called out.

"It's your son's thinking," he continued. "We call it stinking thinking, and it'll be with him for the rest of his life, whether he's sober or drinking from a jug in a brown paper sack. That was my Amy. That's the way I found her after she left me and I hadn't heard from her in months. I—I thought she was dead—" Doug's eyes watered. He made a manly swipe at them and continued. "Neighbors who went on a weekend holiday to Chicago came back and told me they were certain they saw her, panhandling for drinks on Diversy. Well, I went there the very next morning, and sure enough, I spotted her. She looked terrible. She lost a lot of weight. Her face was filthy, and she was wearing rags. I mean r-a-g-s. When I parked the car and stood next to her, she smelled like the inside of a barn needing cleaning." Doug stopped. This time, he let the tears fall. "Amy—she started crying. To make a long story short, I talked her into coming home. The next day, on her own, she went to a meeting downstairs. A couple of months later, I joined these fine women of Alannon."

"And we're glad to have you," said Alice.

Doug reached for a handkerchief and unfolded it carefully. "Amy's been sober for seven months now, and whenever she starts acting cockamamie, I'll ask, 'Hon, might you need a meeting?' Usually, she'll answer, 'Yeah,' but sometimes she doesn't answer, and that's when I gotta really detach from her."

After the meeting, Dawn knew she'd return and eventually accept that Zak's drinking was his problem, not hers.

Jane Gately gave up any hope for sleep. So, the good woman counted words instead of sheep and produced her next letter to various newspaper editors.

Dear Editor: My loving and hardworking husband, Michael, and I toiled many years in order to make our farm one of the area's top milk producers. We've not taken any vacation for more years than I care to admit. I bore and reared three fine sons and two wonderful daughters who not only helped with chores but also helped to plow and harvest neighbors' crops, tended to their animals, and even bicycled into town in order to pump gas at the Standard station. My kids also delivered newspapers, babysat, and waited tables at Waunakee's two restaurants. They banked seventy-five percent of their earnings for college. The rest they used to buy Cherry Cokes at the drugstore and any clothes they needed.

Michael worked part time at Montgomery Ward on weeknights while I waited at Woolworth's food counter in order to enable us to have the necessary finances for our kids to attend and graduate from the University of Wisconsin in Madison.

Now, Wisconsin's prison administrator, Marvin Miller, not only claims farm work is demeaning to convicts but also intends to offer UW on-site courses to them at the Waupun prison.

I say Marvin Miller is wrong on two counts. Count number one: If farm work is demeaning, my husband and I and thousands of other Wisconsin farm families should be hanging our heads in humiliation, but that is not the case, nor shall it ever be.

Michael and I and all other farm husbands, wives, and their children shall continue to hold our heads high. We are proud of our ability to work the land and raise animals for milk and meat in order to feed our neighbors, and in return, we are able to afford the necessities of life.

Count two: Farm families are law-abiding families. Many of us work our fingers to the bone and save what we can from our earnings in order for our kids to obtain college educations, if that is their desire.

Marvin Miller thinks convicted thugs, murderers, rapists, and burglars should get their college education free—using our tax dollars—just because they are convicted thugs, murderers, rapists, and burglars.

I said to Michael, "Maybe we should've gone on welfare and our kids should've been raising hell instead of listening to us and behaving like the good citizens they are."

Shocked, my husband said, "Jane, whatever happened to your sense of values?"

"Whatever happened to our governor's?" I shot back.

"Don't ask me," complained Michael, "ask Governor Todd."

So, here's my question, Governor: Just what has happened to your good old Wisconsin values? Are they going to hell in a hand basket, as some folks think, me included?

CHAPTER THIRTEEN

Officer Two Zak Griffin, Sgt. Judder Brown, and Capt. Mark Ericson stood before the grinning Ego, sitting behind his desk. The inmate swamper must've used plenty of pine oil that morning. The odor was almost sickening. On the desktop was a family portrait of Ego, his wife, Joanie, their two grown sons and one daughter with a gaggle of smiling grandkids, some with missing teeth. Next to the portrait was a plaque with chrome handcuffs, its inscription:

Marion "Butch" Richardson
Completed
FBI Tactical Training Course
Quantico, Virginia
June 18, 1976

"At ease, men," said Ego. "What I'm holding are letters from Madison. You fellas are now Major Ericson, Lieutenant Brown, and Sergeant Griffin. Congratulations, men. Major," he told the former bubble sergeant, "you're now responsible for the prison's security of all three shifts."

"Thank you, sir."

"Judder," said Ego, "you're gonna be my investigating lieutenant. Since it's a new position, I'll talk to you later about your duties."

Ego turned to Zak. "Sergeant Griffin, you'll be second-shift Adjustment Center supervisor. I'll make all your promotional announcements tomorrow at the shift meetings. Major and Sergeant, if you don't have anything more to say or questions concerning your new positions, you can go. Lieutenant, you stay."

•••

After Judder closed the door, he sat nervously.

"I thought you'd be pleased with your promotion," observed Ego. "What's the big problem, Lieutenant?"

"Sir, I think you should know that Zak has a—how do I say it—uh, a drinking prob—"

"Butch," said Ego. "Now that you're on the management team, you can call me Butch—as long as cons or blueshirts ain't in earshot, got it?"

"Yes, sir," said Judder.

Ego sighed, his eyes searching the ceiling.

Judder's face reddened. "I mean, yes, Butch."

"Just so you're aware, Lieutenant, I know just about everything about everyone who works here, but not every *little* thing. That's where you come in. I already know about Zak's drinking, and I also know his union-organizing buddy, Walters, is gonna apply for that second-shift officer two vacancy in the Greenhouse, or my name ain't Butch Richardson. So, whatever I don't know is what you're gonna find out for me, understand?"

Judder squirmed in his chair. "But how will I know what you don't know?"

Ego sighed. "You won't. Your job is to tell me everything you heard or seen. You wanna be security director someday, doan' cha?"

"Sir, I wouldn't ever think of taking your job."

Ego mimicked the lieutenant but with a voice two octaves higher, "I wouldn't ever think of taking your job. Well, you'd better start thinking. Who do ya think's gonna be warden after Palestine retires?"

"You, sir?"

"Stop," warned Ego, "before you say another frigging word. Go up to the staff lounge and get me a cup of java. After that we'll—as the warden likes to say—explore your duties in more detail." Ego leaned back. "Didn't that sound purty?"

Judder grinned. "How do you like your coffee, Butch?"

"Hot, white, and sweet, like I like my women," said Ego, laughing, although his lieutenant wore an obvious question mark on his face. "Cream and sugar," added Ego. "Extra sugar and extra cream."

Flashbulbs exploded and klieg lights beamed like the sun as TV cameras documented the moment Governor Avery Todd formally and publicly appointed University of Wisconsin-Madison law school professor Delmar Winston as corrections chief a week after Todd fired Marvin Miller—due, it was rumored, to a citizen's letters to Wisconsin's newspapers.

The media started to ask Todd the same questions.

The coup de grâce was evident as the letter writer herself, Mrs. Jane Gately, was feted at the new corrections chief's induction ceremony.

It was aide Kyle Marston's idea for Todd's appointing Jane to the state Corrections Board. She eventually enabled Todd to go on a prison-building binge.

It did not take Marvin Miller very long to get out of "This goddamned hayseed state," he said to a Milwaukee Journal reporter. Days later, Miller was living near Hyannis, Massachusetts. Rumors had it that the Miller was on the team that helped whitewash Teddy's "Chappaquiddick misfortune."

Teddy drunkenly drove a car, took a wrong turn, and headed the car over a bridge and into the water after attending a party. Teddy's wife was not present at the get-together but single women were, including twenty-nine-year-old Washington, DC, Mary Jo Kopechne, a campaign worker for Teddy's brother, Robert. Mary Jo, a good-looker, according to friends, was the only passenger in Teddy's car.

Teddy swam to shore but didn't report the mishap until eight hours later. Mary Jo was found inside the car the next day. Her death, according to a coroner's report, was due to drowning. A number of US citizens, including many loyal Democrats, felt the senator was either too drunk or a coward, or both.

Many citizens concluded the senator had not tried hard enough or long enough to save Mary Jo. They also believed the Kennedy clan paid Mary Jo's parents a good sum of money for their silence.

Silent, the Kopechne parents have remained.

CHAPTER FOURTEEN

Jeremy Clark jogged on the cinder track alone because G-Money was on a visit. Although encouraged by social workers to maintain family ties, inmates could refuse visits. Jeremy wrote almost daily to friends and his mother, Alicea, but warned them he would not meet with them while he was an inmate.

In his last letter, Jeremy described how Canada geese flew over the institution and how minimum-security farm inmates unloaded a year's worth of liquefied cow and pig manure onto state-owned fields surrounding the city, causing not only discomfort to Waupun's free citizens but to its incarcerated men, as well.

Zombie and Rude Boy stepped out from the iron pile. Rude Boy signaled Jeremy to stop. "Congratulations," said Zombie.

"For what?"

"For getting the law librarian's job. You can help Brother-men with their legal appeals."

"If they put in a request to Officer Mortenson, he'll send them a pass," said Jeremy, "just like he does for everyone else."

Rude Boy stiffened. "You're so smart, ain't cha? Wait'll G-Money gets into your hocks. Then, we'll see who's—"

A shrill whistle meant a screw was making rounds on the rec field. "Hey," said Zombie, "it's only Griffin. He probably wants to take me on again."

The sergeant stopped, grinned, and crossed his arms. "How's the mighty weightlifter doing today?"

"Not bad, Sergeant," said Zombie. "That is, if you aren't going to try to show me up on the bench press again? By the way, what are you doing here? I thought you worked in the—"

"Greenhouse. I do. I was called in because Sergeant Haskins is ill. What do you mean—try?"

The sergeant turned to Jeremy. "And you are?"

"Clark, 207406."

"Better watch out," warned the sergeant with a smile. "Before you know it, these guys will have you pumping iron and weighing two hundred and fifty pounds."

"Not likely," said the young inmate, who must've spied somebody he'd been looking for. "Nice meeting you, Sergeant. I gotta go."

When the sergeant saw whom Clark met up with, he frowned. "G-Money's his friend?"

"He is for now, Sergeant," said Zombie, "if you know what I mean."

"I hope for his sake you're right. Well, the boss man said I can't lift weights with inmates anymore."

"Aw, that's too bad," said Zombie, kidding, "I was hoping we could go at it again."

"Later," said the sergeant.

"Later," answered Zombie.

•••

"What did Curly and Mo want?" asked G-Money.

"If I'd help the Brother-men with legal work."

"And?"

"I said I'd help them same as I'd help anyone else. What's the big deal?"

"No big deal, Jeremy. I just wanna know what them bastards is up to, that's all."

•••

Kyle Marston held to his chest a manila file folder with a red stamp warning "For eyes only" plainly in sight. He knocked on Avery Todd's open office door. The boss man stood by a window, peering out of it almost wistfully.

"May I come in, sir?"

"Course you can."

As Kyle crossed the thick blue carpeting, he held out the folder. "You won't believe this."

"Believe what?"

"This," Marston said with a big grin. "Bob Ward came through—finally."

"What're you talking about?"

"Remember when Palestine and his staff met with us the night that inmate was murdered—and you told me to get the AG to investigate Waupun?"

"Yeah, I remember. It was morning, not night, you boob."

Kyle used the file folder as a fan as he backed away from a fog bank of cigar smoke. "As usual, sir, you are one hundred percent correct, but I bet you can't guess whom Ward's sending to investigate?"

"I don't have to guess," shot back Todd. "It's your responsibility to keep me informed."

"Get this—he's sending the sister of the murdered inmate to be his undercover investigator."

"You're bullshitting me," said Todd.

"I'm not."

"You're telling me Bob Ward has a sense of humor?" Todd shook his head as he made his way to the black executive chair.

"Perish the thought," said Kyle.

Sitting, leaning back, and grinning, Todd said, "So Ward has a sense of humor, does he?"

"That's hardly likely, sir. He's so anal."

"Siddown, Kyle, and let's talk about more important matters."

Dutifully, the aide sat.

After Todd blew a cloud of cigar smoke at his loyal lackey, he asked, “Kyle, have I told you lately that you’re a dumb fuck?”

Fanning the smoke away with the file folder, Kyle said, “A thousand times, sir.”

“You keeping count?”

After both men laughed, they discussed more important matters, such as which clerk in the legislative typing pool had the nicest hooters *and* most stunning ass.

Selling photographic "penny postcards" of Waupun's "Crow Bar" hotel's exterior, interior, officers, and inmates was one way Alfred Stanley Johnson Jr., who preferred to be called Stanley, supplemented his photo studio's bottom line in the early 1900s.

As a child, Stanley lived in a house on Madison Street, directly across from the prison's South Cell Hall. His father, Alfred Sr., ran a portrait studio, called Picture Rooms, located up the street, a half block north of Main Street.

Stanley headed up the studio in 1891. Nine years later, he and his wife, Myrtle, worked together to produce a number of photographic images of the prison, selling them to locals and tourists as "picture postcards." Interestingly, their first postcards referred to the prison as the "State Penitentiary."

One photographic card featured a rather large pig, wallowing in mud. Above the pig's image was a handwritten inscription, "I am at Waupun but not in the pen." Another card featured female prisoners clothed in neck-cinching floor-length dresses, standing in what looked like a large vegetable garden with the twenty-two-foot-high wall and a single guard tower utilized as background. The card was entitled, "Female Convicts at State Penitentiary, Waupun, Wis."

Some of Stanley and Myrtle's postcards were offered for sale in either color or black and white. The Johnsons sent a number of their postcards to Germany, where they were "colorized," returned to Waupun, and sold for a higher price.

One colorized card didn't list Stanley as photographer but was definitely his photograph. On its backside, it stated, "Published by Dr.

J. Turner, Waupun, Wis. Made in Germany." It also bore the trademark "Litho-Chrome."

The photographic postcards of inmates didn't normally show their faces. One such card was entitled "Prison Dining Room, Waupun, Wis." Evident were the faces of four somber guards, dressed in dark uniforms with white Roman collars, worn by contemporary ministers and Catholic priests. They stood silent watch over inmates sitting at attention at long tables, some wearing striped uniforms while others wore solid color clothes.

In another card entitled "Convicts Baking Bread at State Penitentiary, Waupun, Wis.," pictured on the rear wall in the prison bakery was a pair of coal-fired baking ovens. One inmate, seen from the side, was tending to an oven's fire. The doors were open, displaying thirty loaves of freshly baked bread. One could almost smell their aroma. Another inmate to the right of both stoves stooped over a large wooden bin, most likely filled with flour.

Johnson's most famous card's foreground was ominous with black vertical bars. On the other side of the bars, pictured were inmates marching in two columns. The postcard's title? "Grand March for Dinner, State Prison, Waupun, Wis."

CHAPTER FIFTEEN

"We have other women, nurses and clerks, who work in the back," Personnel Director Jon Powers advised the new hire, "but you'll be our first female mid-manager. And you're our first colored female mid-manager."

Shirleen squirmed in her chair, recalling Auntie's warning to always be gracious. "Mr. Powers, I prefer the term *black*."

Powers's cheeks turned the color of fresh beets. "Black it is," he said, adding, "How times have changed. When I was a child, mother almost killed me when we visited Chicago and I called a Negro *black*. Back then, *black* was offensive."

"Yes," said Shirleen, smiling, "times have changed."

Promptly leaving the sensitive subject to rest, Powers said, "As you know, Miss Hammer, under normal circumstances, you'd report to our associate warden of security, but Judge Boyle made it perfectly clear your position shall be as independent as possible. As with our chaplains, you're answerable only to our warden."

Which is what the AG demanded. "Yes, that's my understanding as well," agreed Shirleen.

Powers fidgeted. "Speaking of our security director, he informed me yesterday he'd give you a tour of the back." Powers checked his watch. "He should be here. If you don't mind, I'm going to find out what the holdup is."

"No problem," said Shirleen.

Powers rose and exited the room while his clerk in the adjoining office stopped typing, stood, left her desk, and appeared at the doorway. "Miss Hammer?"

"Yes?"

"I just want you to know how good it is that we finally have a lady in the prison's administration."

"Why thank you, uh—"

"Call me Laura."

"And you can call me Shirleen."

The sprite laughed. "I should warn you, Shirleen, as a subordinate staff member, I am expected to address all members of the administration as *Mister* or *Sir.*"

Shirleen rearranged the pleats in her skirt. "As you can see, Laura, I'd have a problem with being called *both.*"

Powers returned. Accompanying him were three men, one in a blue suit and two guards, wearing white shirts. The suit had on a white dress shirt, striped tie, miniature chrome handcuff tie tack, and spit-shined shoes. His trousers were cinched above the waist in an effort to conceal the paunch. The officers were totally military.

"Gentlemen," said Powers, "this is Miss Shirleen Hammer, our inmate complaint investigator."

The suit stepped forward, took Shirleen's hands into his, and said, "Pleased to meet cha. I'm Butch Richardson, security director."

"I'm pleased to meet you, Butch," said Shirleen. "Madison personnel said so much about you." *More than you'd ever know. You were in a tower while my brother was being attacked.*

"All good, I hope," said Ego, turning to his whiteshirts. "Let me introduce you to Major Ericson."

Shirleen nodded warmly. *Nothing negative about him.*

The major stepped forward. "Ma'am," he said.

"And," continued Ego, "this is Investigating Lieutenant Brown."

Judder stepped forward and clicked his heels. "Glad to meet you, ma'am."

Richardson's snitch and hatchet man. "Likewise," said Shirleen.

Ego cleared his throat. "Shirleen, I'm busier than a hive of bees on a hot, humid day. That's why I brought the major and lieutenant along. But, young lady, if you smile at inmates like you're smiling right now, I'll hafta lock down the whole damn institution."

"My smile would cause such a drastic measure?"

Shirleen was certain she and everyone else in the room were aware that the antique regulator clock's ticks and tocks had become much louder. The red climbed all the way from Ego's neck to his cheeks to his forehead.

That's the moment the major came to his aid. "Ma'am, what Mr. Richardson meant is we have men in here who don't respond appropriately to normal social cues."

Ego's eyes lit up. "That's what I meant," he said. "Thanks, Mark."

Shirleen squeezed Ego's hands. "Butch, I prefer your directness to a gentleman's hypocrisy any day."

Ego was obviously pleased. "Why, thank you, Shirleen," he said, turning to his subordinates. "Men?"

"Yes, sir," the pair answered as one.

"Take our ICI on a full-scale tour—wherever she wants to go."

The major addressed Shirleen. "Ma'am, please allow us."

Milwaukee's WTMJ-TV News Four reporter Betty Bower envisioned toppling Walter Cronkite as she and her cameraman waited in an inmate attorney interview room in the Administration Building at the Waupun Correctional Institution, there to interview an inmate endorsed by a Milwaukee Mafia capo whom Betty had known intimately.

As soon as Frankie "The Italian Bull" Colacicco made his entrance, squired by two blueshirts, Betty took in the inmate's body aroma. Its main ingredient she was certain had to have been oil of cloves. She couldn't have known that Frankie had paid two packs of Camels to a kitchen worker for the "cologne."

Secretly, Betty adored his wavy ebony hair after he removed a blue knit cap. Frankie wore dark sunglasses, starched khakis, and spit-shined boots.

Love was in the air. Betty touched Frankie in all the right places while setting him up for the camera. Each time, she said, "Excuse me."

The Bull grinned. He knew what time it was.

"Lights, camera, action," Betty advised her cameraman before facing the lens head-on. "We have before us this morning Francis Colacicco, an inmate at the Waupun Correctional Institution." She turned to Frankie. "What's your take, Francis? What is the inmate take on the present situation in Waupun?"

She noticed that the klieg lights could not penetrate his sunglasses. "Frankie," he said. "Call me Frankie. Da way me and my fellow political prisoners see tings is dese agricultural staff members, correctional officers to you, are hopin' we'll overreack. Dat way, dey get to lock down our asses."

Both officers moved uneasily as Betty sniffed, "Lock you down, you say?"

"But we can take what dey dish out. We're men. Dey're just a bunch of fags."

Betty signaled the cameraman to zero in on her caring, empathic lips and eyes. "Francis, explain to our TV viewers what a lockdown is."

"Dey lock us up in our cells and don't let us out. Dese dogs can fuck with us 'cause dere ain't no witnesses, if you know what I mean."

Betty knew those words would never do. "Say mess with us, officers, beat," she whispered.

"Mess with us, officers, beat, whatever," Frankie said aloud.

Betty looked to the cameraman, who was checking the recorder's dials.

He grinned, and nodded.

"Then, it's a wrap," said Betty, who hugged Frankie, her fingers caressing his crotch. At once, she grasped the significance of Frankie's mob name.

"Interview's over," said one blueshirt.

"See what I mean?" said Frankie. "Dey're nothin' but dogs."

After the officers submitted written reports, the security director ordered Frankie to be placed in Temporary Lockup, pending investigation.

CHAPTER SIXTEEN

School Officer Alex Mortenson grinned. "It's not often I'm asked to escort a movie star."

"I'm no movie star," said the appreciative Shirleen, chuckling.

"Well, you certainly look like one."

"Why, thank you, Officer Mortenson."

Mortenson escorted Shirleen into the first classroom. Most inmates were working diligently at their assigned work. Mortenson introduced Shirleen to the teacher.

Tranquility disappeared when an inmate blared out, "Who you?"

"May I answer?" Shirleen asked Mortenson.

Mortenson nodded.

Shirleen turned to the entire class. "I'm Miss Hammer, the new ICI, inmate complaint investigator."

Additional hands pierced the air.

"One more question," announced Mortenson, "and that's it."

"Hey, sistah," said a brash young man as he rubbed his crotch and sneered, "you and me, we be tight. Am I right?"

Shirleen struck a defensive pose. "I don't believe we ever met, Mistah. So how can I possibly be your sistah?"

The other inmates laughed.

Shirleen added in a normal tone, "However, your apology is accepted."

Back in the hallway, Mortenson said, "You did good."

"I did, didn't I?" Shirleen said with a chuckle.

After visiting the dining hall followed by the chapel, the three entered the Social Services Building, where Shirleen met the supervisor.

Upstairs, she met psychiatric social workers, psychologists, and a psychiatrist who ran inmate therapy groups.

"Last, but not least, is the Greenhouse," said Ericson, pointing to the fenced-off jail within a prison, which is the moment a king-size boulder fell into the pit of Shirleen's stomach.

"Officially," added the lieutenant, "it's the Adjustment—"

"Center," completed Shirleen.

"That's right," said Judder. "How'd you know?"

"I was told by Madison personnel, since it's the building where I'll be performing most of my work."

"Oh," said Judder, "I see."

Did you? I'd better be on my toes with this guy.

Officer Steve Blankley, Greenhouse turnkey, would've been the perfect greeter at a deaf-mute convention as he keyed the three into his sally port.

Ericson pointed to Zak and whispered, "The sergeant is writing in his logbook. When anyone comes into the building or leaves, he must note who specifically and the precise time in his logbook."

A stud muffin—and he's not wearing a wedding ring.

Blankley keyed the three into No-Man's-Land.

The sergeant finished writing, rose, and keyed the three into his sally port.

The major made the whispered introduction. "Ms. Hammer, this is Sergeant Griffin. Zak, this is Ms. Hammer, our inmate complaint investigator."

"Pleased to meet you, ma'am," whispered Zak.

"Shirleen," she said. "Call me Shirleen." *Oh, please do.*

"Shut the fuck up," an inmate inside the block yelled. "I'm trying to cop me some Z's."

Shirleen looked down the bottom tier. Fingers of differing sizes and colors wrapped themselves around steel bars. She looked up to the second tier. The same.

"There's a bitch in here," yelled one. "She's on the rag. I can smell it."

"Pipe down, asshole. Didn't you hear me? I'm trying to get some Z's."

A blueshirt inside the cellblock burst around the corner of the other side of the tier and put on the brakes when he saw the visitors.

The sergeant whispered, "And that's Officer Walters." Next, he spoke in a conversational tone. "Mr. Samuels?"

"What do you want, Sergeant Zak?"

"We were whispering. Please do likewise."

In charge, but he shows respect.

"I wasn't talking to you, Sergeant. I was yelling at them other faggots."

"Watch your language, Mr. Samuels. Anyway, that's not your job to keep order. It's mine."

Firm but fair. "Will I be allowed to tour the block?" whispered Shirleen.

"The men are riled up," said Zak. "Perhaps another day."

"Do new male employees tour the block their first day?"

"Yes, ma'am, but they wouldn't now. I think we better let things cool off a bit."

Shirleen turned to the major. "Didn't Butch say to take me wherever I wanted?"

"Zak," said Ericson, "we're going in."

"I will note my objection in the logbook," said Zak.

"That's your prerogative," said the major.

Frankie "The Italian Bull" Colacicco's being locked up in segregation made headlines. "The correctional officers who escorted inmate Francis Collacicco to the attorney interview room for an approved television interview between the inmate and Betty Bower, Channel Four reporter, are willing to take lie detector tests. The two officers stayed with the inmate, Bower, and a cameraman throughout the interview. These officers will swear under oath that they personally witnessed Bower fondle inmate Colacicco and kiss him passionately," said Officer II Reggie Walters, correctional officer union organizer.

"No comment," replied the warden's secretary to all press phone calls regarding the Bower-Colacicco incident. "You may contact our central office in Madison for information regarding this matter."

"What da fuck happened to da Bull?" asked Joey "Big Lips" Fortunato, Milwaukee's Mafioso don of Roy "Rat Face" Pasquale, Big Lips's number one hit man.

"Fuggim," said Rat Face. "I wouldn't pay no attention to that cocksucker because he don't know his ass from a hole in the ground—and never will."

"Here I was trying to help the bastard," said Big Lips, his head shaking "maybe get him out on time served for good behavior. When he fucks up, he fucks up royally, don't he?"

"Fuggim," said Rat Face.

They stopped talking in order to listen to Betty Bower on the tube. The camera focused on a solitary tear as it descended her cheek as slowly as a slug in search of love in all the wrong places. "I report the news; I do not invent it," she said.

Reggie Walters fired off letters to editors of state newspapers. "The correctional officer's job is tough enough as it is. However, when media members fabricate stories as to how we supervise inmates, the task becomes not only thankless but also potentially dangerous because inmates think they no longer have to obey our orders. Betty Bower, as far as I'm concerned, is a prevaricator of the worst sort."

Inmate letter writers fired back. "As to Officer Walters's letter, he and other bluesuits are intent on committing genocide. Don't believe a word they write or speak."

Thomas Dray, University of Wisconsin-Madison Students for a Democratic Society chieftain, joined the fray. "Instead of behaving like the civil servants they are, gangs of hobnailed, tax-supported hooligans, who call themselves correctional officers, are more than ready and willing to shoot and kill any political prisoner who might not grovel at their feet. We must stop these Gestapo members now. End genocide now. Wake up, Amerika, now."

CHAPTER SEVENTEEN

Reggie Walters cautiously scanned both tiers as Shirleen, Ericson, and Judder made it to Cell One, its occupant, a huge, grinning black man, erupted like Old Faithful. "Sister, sister, sister, my queen of the Nile, come over here and let us talk of blackness."

Shaking her head and grinning, Shirleen made it to Cell Two and discovered its occupant, a Caucasian, was not only nude but his eyes were glazed. "Nigger whore big-lipped Brillo-pad cunt," he screamed.

Cell One yelled, "You hunky muhfuh, don't speak that way to my queen or—"

"Or what, you fucking faggot?" snapped Two.

"Ah'll faggot your ass, you sissy muhfuh, with my black snake."

The flash of a light green object that flew out of Cell Three turned out to be an airborne plastic coffee cup, its contents spilling and splattering on bars, walls, floor, and Officer Walters's shirt. "That's a conduct report, Michaels," said Walters.

"Fuck you, fuck that report, and fuck that bitch you're trying to impress," shrieked Michaels, who exposed himself. "What do you think of this? Now, you knows what a maaaaaaaaaaan looks like."

Earl was in here? I can't believe it. These men are—animals.

"Add disrespect," said Reggie.

"And fuck your disrespect, you punk-assed hunky."

As she looked back but still kept walking, getting nearer and nearer to the cell's bars without noticing it, the next inmate latched on to Shirleen and reeled her in.

Obscenities, their decibel level beyond belief, muffled her call for help.

Officer Walters's scream was not at all encouraging. "Hogan," she heard, "let her go."

The entire cellblock went crazy.

"Hogan's got her," roared inmates.

"Let her go, Hogan," shouted Walters.

"Son-a-bitch got her. Fuck her up, Hogan. Fuck her up good."

"Hogan, let her go."

Hogan's voice surged through her bones. "Shuddup, shuddup, shuddup."

"Control, this is Bar Forty-Two. Inmate holding staff member in Adjustment Center."

Auntie Louise. What are you doing here—and in your Sunday best, your navy blue suit, white blouse, and frilly silk tie?

"This is Control, Bar Forty-Two. That's a ten-four, inmate in adjustment center holding staff member. Emergency radio traffic only. Attention all bars. Ten thirty-three. Emergency radio traffic only."

Wearing a wide-brimmed, navy-and-white hat with long and luxurious peacock feathers, Auntie stood before Shirleen, holding her Bible close to her chest. "Trust in God's power, not in your abilities, my child."

Shirleen slacked up, ending her struggle.

"Attention all stations, this is Control. Emergency in Adjustment Center. Escort all inmates back to their cells. Repeat, escort all inmates back to their cells."

Shirleen could hear Zak's voice. "Listen to me, Hogan."

"Don't I always, Sergeant Zak? Don't I always?"

"Don't let that bitch go, Hogan," screamed an inmate from the second tier.

"You usually listen," said the sergeant.

"Did ya hear me? Don't let her go."

•••

Blankley keyed Ego into the sally port. The usually reticent turnkey said, "Hogan's got the colored lady."

"How's she doing?"

Blankley shrugged. "I only hear. I can't see."

Just then, a whiteshirt and a group of tense, black-suited ERU ninjas appeared outside Blankley's entrance sally port.

"Let 'em in," ordered Ego.

Blankley nodded. The captain and the others packed the sally port.

"Hogan's got the new ICI. Her name's Shirleen," Ego announced to the ERU crew.

Sgt. Morris Dunlop, standing behind the captain, moaned, "Hogan? Not *that* asshole? He's so stupid he doesn't know if he's on foot or horseback."

• • •

Shirleen slumped to the floor. "She ain't dead, is she, Sergeant Zak? That's not my fault, is it?"

"No, it's not your fault," said Zak.

"That cocksucker, Hogan, let her go."

"Hogan, you chump sissy," yelled an inmate housed down the tier.

"Are we tight, Sergeant Zak?"

"Can you believe this?" yelled a nearby inmate. "That big, dumb Hogan let her go."

"We're tight," said Zak.

Reggie Walters grabbed Shirleen and pulled her to safety against the wall. Zak went to her, knelt, and carefully rearranged her skirt. "Are you OK?" he asked.

"I am, thanks to God, you, and Auntie Louise."

Reggie was next. "You all right?"

Shirleen nodded. Tears breached.

Zak and Reggie gently helped her up.

•••

Inside Blankley's filled sally port, ninjas softly touched Shirleen's shoulders. "Good girl, that's a good girl." Surrounding her, protecting her, directing her, urging her, they exited the sally port and were outside.

Tower six electronically unlocked the fence gate.

On the road that led to the Administration Building and overpass, inmates being led from their work sites to their cells wisely got out of their way—and fast.

Jimmy Helm opened one overpass gate at a time, and the group made it up to the squad room, lit cigarettes, borrowed money, dropped coins in machines that dispensed cold sandwiches, apples, oranges, coffee, hot chocolate, popcorn, candy, and soda.

Shirleen needed to use the bathroom. A nurse led her to the ladies' room. Its aroma was a mix of pine oil and cologne. After the nurse closed the door, she looked into the mirror, caught Shirleen's eyes, and said, "I'm Katie Hendricks."

Shirleen snorted as she fought tears. "I'm—"

Katie brought Shirleen to her, patting her back. "Cry, honey, it always helps."

•••

Later, after Shirleen splashed cold water onto her face and patted it with paper towels, she and Katie giggled over Shirleen not liking her bloodshot eyes.

"Want to go out and face the world?" asked Katie, attempting a smile.

Shirleen nodded. Katie opened the door. "Here she is," she announced, "all better now."

Laura, the personnel director's clerk, was first to greet and hug Shirleen. "Good girl," said Laura, "good girl."

Laura backed off to let others come forward. Shirleen thanked each and every one of them.

She noted a distinguished-looking older gentleman who took his place beside Butch Richardson. Smiling, the gentleman approached, his hand pushing forward. "I'm Warden Palestine," he said.

"Everybody," said Shirleen, looking to the others and then to Palestine, "has been so kind."

Loud applause, followed by "Good girl, that's a good girl."

"Let's go to my office," offered Palestine.

• • •

The warden lifted the red phone. "Palestine here. Yes, Kyle. Ms. Hammer has met adversity with poise and courage."

The warden turned to Shirleen and smiled. "Yes," he said, "we always like to give you good news, Kyle, and you have a good day, as well."

Palestine put the phone down. "That was Governor Todd's aide, Kyle Marston. I was hoping to speak with Avery personally. First, let's discuss dinner. I intend to take you to the Wild Goose Inn for dinner. It's on the other side of the Horicon Marsh. Marion, you come too. I'm buying."

Marion? Shirleen watched the security director's cheeks turn red.

• • •

After the three finished with dinner and drinks, the warden advised his inmate driver to let Shirleen off by Stoffel's drugstore, very near her apartment. He didn't want the minimum-security inmate to know precisely where Shirleen lived.

After she exited and closed the car door and watched it take off, Shirleen noticed the bright red but old coupe across the street. A tall man stood by it; his cigarette glowed orange. An oncoming car's headlights lit him up.

Grinning, Shirleen crossed the street. "Sergeant Griffin, I'm so happy to see you. I wanted to thank you personally."

"Forget the sergeant stuff," said Zak. "I'm Zak, Joe Citizen, and as to your thanking me, I don't deserve anything special. I was just doing my job."

He looks just as wonderful out of uniform. In fact, better. "Zak," she said. "That's a unique name."

"So is Shirleen. You don't mind if I call you Shir?"

Shirleen smiled. "Go ahead," she said. "Shir sounds special, coming from you." She offered Zak her brightest of smiles.

"Uh, Reggie and I were wondering if you'd like to join us at Otto's Bar and Grill. It's a blueshirt hangout."

"Reggie?"

"Officer Walters," said Zak, "that is, if a member of Waupun's management team doesn't mind fraternizing with a few lowly blueshirts."

Shirleen laughed. "That would not be a cause for turning you down. The thing is, I need eight hours of sleep, or I'll turn into a hag." *Zak, you don't realize it, but you're certainly complicating matters.*

"I can hardly believe that," he said.

He opened the rider's side door. Shirleen got in. Then, he went around the other side of the car and literally squeezed himself into what little space was available. "It's a thirty-five Plymouth," he told her. "I named it Shoofly Ply a long time ago after the song 'Shoofly Pie,' my mom's favorite."

"That's one of Auntie Louise's favorite old-time songs," said Shirleen. "Didn't the Andrews Sisters sing it?"

"I think so," he said, turning the key.

The engine roared to life.

"She's souped-up," Zak announced with pride. "Did it myself, with the help of friends. I drag raced it at the KK drag strip in Kaukauna, and a few times at Union Grove near Kenosha." He turned from her to look through the windshield. "Hold on." He hit the gas pedal and tires squealed. Shirleen yipped as she held on to the sissy bar for dear life. *He's so cute and so strong, the silent type, too. Ummmmmmmmm.*

The Southwest cell hall sergeant rose from his chair. It was time to make rounds of all four tiers. After he managed to make it by both sides of the top tier, he was as tense as a stretched-to-the-max rubber band. Inmates were plainly hostile. What he couldn't have known was that most had watched the Betty Bower interview with Frankie "The Italian Bull" Colacicco, and they were pissed.

Escorted to the hole that day, Frankie continued with his foul language, which got him additional tickets. To the Greenhouse staff, he was a virtual pain in the ass. To the general population, the heretofore-unsympathetic braggart had magically turned into a hero.

One man started catcalling. Then another. Then a hundred. As the sergeant passed men standing at the bars growling epithets in obvious anger, soon the entire cell hall was howling, "Free the Bull. Free the Bull. Free the Bull."

A sheet of paper on fire was tossed over a guardrail. Within a minute, flaming debris lay on the main floor of the cell hall.

Blueshirt reinforcements were called in. First, they donned Scott Air-Paks that let them breathe as they stomped out smoking newspapers, magazines, inmate clothing. Eventually, inmates stopped. They had difficulty with their breathing.

The cell hall sergeant requested exhaust fans.

"Hell, no," was the line captain's response. "Let them eat smoke, the bastards."

In a tersely worded memo to all inmates the next morning, approved by Kyle Marston, Warden Palestine declared a slowdown. The only inmates allowed out of their cells were members of the kitchen crew, garbage haulers, and laundry workers.

Channel Six interviewed Charlie Wonker, an Ego snitch, who claimed, "The Milwaukee Mafia's responsible for the inmate unrest."

Charlie was a known punk. Those men in his cell hall raged through the night, "Charlie, you're dead. Charlie, you're dead. Charlie, you're dead."

Requesting protective custody (PC), Charlie was duly cuffed and leg-ironed. As he walked the catwalk with two officers in front, two behind, in order to protect his backside, inmates spat and heaved "milk-shakes"—blends of body excreta in foam cups—at the child molester. Most of the shit had landed on the blueshirts, instead.

On the main floor, Charlie bawled like a baby as the escort officers puked and cursed and tore off their clothes and showered.

Years after, he was freed from PC directly to the streets. Naturally, Charlie preyed on kids again and told cops, "Children entice me. It's not the other way around."

He was arrested, charged, found guilty, and was given a ton of time to be served at Waupun. Inmates gangbanged him in the shower room of the Big Top, the indoor rec hall. After every man who wanted a chance at him got one, they hanged him. The Dodge County Coroner ruled Charlie's death a suicide. Make no doubt about it: payback in Waupun is invariably a motherfucker.

CHAPTER EIGHTEEN

In September, Zak's high school football coach gave him a pair of Green Bay Packers tickets. Zak asked Shirleen if she'd like to go along.

"I've never been to a Packers game," she said. Waiting a moment, she smiled and added, "Yes, I'll go. It sounds like a lot of fun."

They were pointed to a special spot at Lambeau Field's parking lot because of the car's uniqueness, most likely, and Shirleen's extraordinarily good looks.

The Packers and Detroit Lions tied at thirteen.

That night, when Shirleen telephoned Auntie Louise, her aunt said, "Zak, Zak, Zak, that's all I've been hearing. Maybe it's about time your Auntie meets this Zak."

Shirleen considered the problems that might rise from the visit, but said, "Remember, Auntie, you can't tell him about my *real* job, and don't dare mention Earl."

"Why not, girl?"

"Because, Auntie, you know why. I'm an undercover agent. That means we can tell no one, not even Zak."

"If you're getting serious about that boy, and it sounds like you are, you'd better reconsider your lying ways."

"I can't."

Long pause. "Do you still read the Bible, girl?"

"Yes, Auntie, I do, but that doesn't change the fact of my job."

"Your dishonesty could jeopardize your happiness—and his."

"I have to take that chance."

•••

Zak and Auntie Louise got along famously. He devoured two large pieces of sweet potato pie along with inhaling three cups of her famously strong coffee. "This pie tastes better than Mom's pumpkin pie, and she's the best pie maker in Waupun."

"Oh," said Auntie Louise, taken aback with the tall, well-built, and handsome white man, "that's nice."

When Zak excused himself to go outdoors for a cigarette, Shirleen remained indoors. "What do you think?" Shirleen asked.

"That boy's a true gentleman."

"Yes? Go on Auntie, I know you want to say more."

Auntie crossed her arms and stomped a foot. "Where are your manners? Will you give me time to answer, girl? Anyway, I've always imagined that you'd marry a churchgoing colored man."

Shirleen stood, arms akimbo. "Auntie—that's so old-fashioned."

"Exactly," said the resolute aunt, not giving in one inch. "Besides, if you're so serious about this boy, why can't you tell him the truth?"

"When the time's right, Auntie, when the time's right."

"James, four-seventeen," said Louise. "So whoever knows the right thing to do and failed to do it, for him it is sin—and I'll add for her, as well."

On the ride back to Waupun, not a word was uttered until Zak turned the car off US 41 and onto Wisconsin 49, a few miles outside Brownsville.

"Zak, I have a question."

"Shoot."

"Could you turn down the radio?"

Zak turned it off.

"Does...?" asked Shirleen.

"Does what?"

"Does my being colored bother you?"

"What color you talking about?"

Shirleen laughed so hard she nearly cried. "What color you talking about?" she repeated.

When they arrived in Waupun and Zak saw her up the stairs to her apartment, he said, "Look, there's something—"

Shirleen could wait no longer. "Yes?" They laughed nervously. She waited but hated the silence. "Damn it, Zak, what were you going to say?"

"Shir," he said, "I—" Zak turned and faced the stairs.

Certain he was going to leave, Shirleen gasped as the big guy twirled to face her once again. "Shir," he whispered, "I know this sounds crazy but I think I love you."

•••

They lay next to each other on her bed. "Anything wrong?" asked Zak.

"I hope you don't think less of me," said Shirleen.

"Why would I?"

She pouted. "Because," she said in a voice that might have belonged to a little girl, "that's why." A fingertip outlined a star-shaped scar under his ribcage. "What did this?"

"A fastball."

"Fastball?"

"Sniper's bullet."

"Zak, why are you giggling?"

"It's what you're doing to it," he said. "I'll give you a half hour to quit."

Kissing the scar, Shirleen turned to study his left hip, which bore a number of jagged scars.

"Shrapnel scars," he explained, "from a Claymore mine. The way you touch, I'm almost pleased they're there."

"They must've hurt, Zak. Did they hurt?" Tears came.

Zak kissed them. Their lips touched, at first softly. Certain she was in love, and not in lust, with this virile, reticent man, she placed her head on his chest. She closed her eyes. *He is so absolutely beautiful.*

•••

Five nights later, Zak put the key—that Shirleen gave to him just this day—into the lock and turned it. When he opened the door, he just stood there, gazing.

"What's wrong?" Shirleen asked, wrinkling her nose.

"You're wearing an apron," he said.

"How observant of you, kind sir. I didn't bother to ask you if you liked spaghetti and meatballs with marinara sauce and Parmesan cheese."

"Is the pope Catholic?"

As Shirleen mulled over the question with some seriousness, Zak laughed. "I love spaghetti and meatballs and Parmesan cheese," he said, adding, "and I love you."

They came together and when they parted, Shirleen said, "Just two minutes ago, I finished talking with Auntie Louise. 'Girl,' she said, 'why can't you find a nice college-educated, churchgoing colored man?'"

"I'm not college educated," said Zak, "and—he carefully inspected an arm— "I'm sort of pink in color."

It was around midnight when they ate the spaghetti and meatballs with Parmesan cheese.

•••

Since Greenhouse officers weren't allowed to smoke in front of inmates, Reggie waited to be relieved by a utility officer.

In the basement where the staff john and inmate hearing room were located, he listened to Zak making his way down the stairs. Their eyes met.

"Haven't seen you at Otto's," said Reggie. "Where've you been?"

"Where've I been?" echoed Zak.

"That's what the man asked. How come you stopped coming to Otto's?"

"Why," asked Zak, "do I get the feeling you're upset?"

"Upset?" questioned Reggie. "I can't blame you for trying to change your luck, but don't you think you're carrying this a little too far?"

A haymaker flew out.

After Reggie realized he was lying on the floor, he rubbed his aching jaw.

Zak bent over and tried to help Reggie get up.

Reggie shook his head. "I don't need your help. Furthermore, I don't want it."

Zak turned away and ascended the stairs to the cellblock.

• • •

Reggie remained on the floor for some time before he got up. Heading to a sink adjacent to the bathroom, he applied cold water to the hurt. After drying off with a terry cloth towel, he looked into the mirror and saw that his cheek was already turning purple.

• • •

The next morning, Dorothy put Reggie's transfer request on top of Ego's in-basket.

The klieg lights blinded him as the warden stood behind the wooden podium slowly adjusting his reading glasses before announcing to the media, "Good morning, ladies and gentlemen. I want each of you to know that third-shift cell hall sergeants delivered to the inmate population copies of my letter, which each of you have also received. Copies of my letter were also handed to all staff who reported to work this morning."

Clearing his throat, Palestine continued, "I will now read the letter I wrote and was given to all inmates. Copies of it were handed out to my staff as they reported to work this morning." He held off momentarily, and then began to read.

"To all Waupun inmates: As you well know, the prison has experienced a good deal of tension in the past two weeks. It was my conclusion the institution was in need of a cooling-off period. I requested my Madison superiors to approve a lockdown of all inmates, including those in general, segregated, and hospitalized population. That request has been approved.

"Accordingly, all inmates shall remain in their cells. Staff will deliver food trays to you. Visits will be canceled temporarily. If inmates are in need of legal material, staff will locate it for you, but please have patience.

"Correctional officer staff shall report to the squad room, where they will be assigned emergency lockdown tasks. Civilian staff will be assigned housekeeping duties that were formerly accomplished by inmates, including kitchen, garbage pickup, laundry pickup, cleaning, and sorting, and cell hall tier tender work.

"Highly trained search dogs plus state-of-the-art metal detectors shall aid officers in their institution-wide search for weapons and drugs. Correctional officers shall search inmate living quarters, including dormitories and individual cells. Inmates shall be body searched." The warden looked up to study the response. "Any questions?"

Betty Bower jumped up. "Warden, might not those dogs bite defenseless inmates?"

Warden Palestine shook his head. "I assure you these are well-trained dogs."

On Channel Four's news report that night, after showing the warden giving Betty his answer, the TV screen then revealed for six seconds Betty's silent, concerned look.

CHAPTER NINETEEN

G-Money had known from the moment he opened his eyes that this was the Promised Day. He quietly sang, "Raindrops keep falling on my haid."

As a guarantee that it must, in fact, be the Promised Day, he stuck the shank neatly between his buttocks with the aid of masking tape.

Later, in the school, G-Money checked out the janitor's storeroom, officially called the swamper locker, located in the rear of the school. The swamper locker was one of only three rooms in the entire building that did not have windowpanes in their midsections. The other rooms were the staff and inmate toilets.

After finishing with cleanup, which took about fifteen minutes, G-Money and the other swampers sat on overturned buckets, played cards, smoked, and boasted about driving Cadillac Del Caballeros on Milwaukee's Wisconsin Avenue or Madison's State Street. While he had been an authentic pimp, his fellow swampers were pimp-wannabes.

"But that don't mean my eyes will be turnin' red," G-Money sang as he pushed packs of Salems or Pall Malls, their choice, at each man, motioning to the locker. "That room," he pointed to the swamper locker, "be all mine at nine thirty. That's when you skedaddle, right?"

The pimp wannabees nodded their assent.

"Raindrops keep falling on my haid."

•••

At precisely nine thirty that morning, Jeremy Clark placed the Back in Fifteen Minutes sign on the lower portion of the law library's Dutch door before he headed to the swamper locker for his morning break.

With a flourish, G-Money bowed and pointed to two overturned buckets inside the swamper locker. Without hesitation, although it was usual for them to sit outside the storeroom, Jeremy entered and sat.

"Raindrops keep falling on my haid, but that don't mean my eyes will soon be turning red."

G-Money turned on the deep sink's hot water spigot and let it run, soon filling both cups before placing them on the back of the deep sink. "Crying's not for me. Nothing's worrying me, da-dee-dum-dum-da-dee." Dumping spoon after spoon of instant coffee into each cup, he stirred with poise and handed a cup to Jeremy along with a cigarette. "Raindrops keep falling on my haid."

"You're sure into that song, aren't you?" said Jeremy as he leaned back, lit his cigarette, blew out the match, closed his eyes, and inhaled.

That's the moment the door banged shut and Jeremy's eyes jerked open. They beheld a grinning G-Money holding on to his erect penis.

Jeremy shot up and flung everything into the deep sink, the cup bouncing and making resounding sounds.

"Just stroke it," urged G-Money.

Jeremy looked to the door. "Let me out."

"That ain't happening."

"Let me out, or else." Jeremy was now standing.

"Else what the hell you gonna do, punk?"

Jeremy searched the room.

G-Money knew what time it was. "I took care of everything. There's only one man in this room that's gonna do the hurting."

"You're going to have to kill me," said Jeremy, "because I'm not going to do it."

"Stroke yourself, then," urged G-Money, "and I'll watch, and that'll be that."

"No. Let me out of here."

G-Money grabbed the young man where no other male ever had, other than a doctor. G-Money unzipped Jeremy's trousers, reached in, and pulled out his penis at the same time the shank rose like a red-tailed hawk before making its swoop. Down came the blade. Jeremy fell to the floor and lay there in a fetal position, feeling both fire and ice in his crotch.

"You're a bitch now," declared G-Money, his gold tooth gleaming, flushing the flesh down the deep sink's drain.

"Why don't you kill me?" pleaded Jeremy.

"If you don't give me no sugar, you're gonna wish you be dead."

G-Money rubbed the knife's handle with a towel before sticking the shank into Jeremy's hand.

G-money turned the knob, lurched out of the room, and took off in a run, his pounding footsteps drawing attention from teachers and students, as he knew they would. At the school office, he caught one end of the doorway before coming to a full halt. He wore his best frightened look. "Officer Mortenson."

Mortenson, who was busily talking to the female civilian school clerk, jerked. "What's wrong, G-Money?"

"Something bad. Something real bad happened, Officer Mortenson."

•••

Maj. Mark Ericson, already in the school, greeted Ego. "It's all sound, no fury."

"What happened?"

"Inmate law librarian says he cut off the head of his dick in the swamper locker. Says he hopes to die. I don't think he will—die, that is. I contacted health services. Inmate nurses are up here, attending to him. I halted all classes and library passes for the rest of the day."

"Why'd you do that?"

"It's possible somebody else might've done it to the kid."

"Why do you say that?"

"His main man is G-Money."

Ego grinned as he looked down the hall toward the swamper locker. "I see."

"I also stopped all inmates from communicating with each other," added the major, "so they couldn't get their stories lined up. I also ordered blueshirts to set up a modesty shield in order to strip-search all the men before questioning them individually and then escorting them back to their cells."

"Good job, Major, as good a job as I would've done when I was wearing those oak leaves. Since things up here are running like a Swiss watch, I'll let you get back to taking care of the rest of the institution."

Ericson smartly saluted the security director and exited the school a moment before Judder, in full investigative mode, approached Ego, saluting. "Sir."

"What do ya have so far?" asked Ego.

Judder took out his little notebook. "Jeremy Clark, law librarian, says he cut off his schwanz because he wanted to be a gir—"

Sudden, loud movement came from down the hallway. Utility officers performing shakedowns halted their body cavity inspections as the gang of four inmate nurses rushed up the hallway carrying an inmate on a gurney. The wounded inmate moaned, "Let me die, please let me die."

Ego's palm came up like a traffic cop's.

The nurses halted.

Marty Pulaski, a former Chicago cop who murdered his wife and dumped her body in Lake Geneva, spoke up. "We have a medical emergency here, Mr. Richardson. We got to get him to the doc—fast."

"Well, you're just gonna hafta wait 'cause I said so, understand?"

Marty nodded. "Understood. He's lost plenty of blood, five-hundred cc's, or more, maybe a lot more."

"Well, then, you better get going," said Ego.

He and Judder followed the nurses onto the landing and watched them descend the stairs, run down the truck alley, and then turn at the corner of the far end of the Food Services Building.

That's when Ego turned to Judder. "How many shims we got in here?"

"Who knows? Maybe fifty, maybe more," said Judder, adding, "I don't know exactly."

"How many don't have dicks?"

"Susie-Q, the Alabaster Queen, is the only one I know of, except now there's Clark."

"Did you notice his neck wound?"

"I did."

Ego drew in a ton of air, looked down at his gut, tugged at his belt, and said, "I gotta lay off the potatoes and gravy. By the way, did you know that inmate that doesn't have a pecker anymore is G-Money's girlfriend?"

Judder turned white. "G-Money?"

"How many times I gotta tell you that you gotta learn these guys' street names?"

Judder nodded.

"How many, damn it?"

"More than a few."

"More than a few, he says. The investigating lieutenant should know that G-Money, aka Milo Washington, the chief swamper up here, is a frigging bootie bandit. He targets new inmates, the younger the better, gets their trust, and then, wham, he screws them silly before he pimps them off to the general population for cigarettes or dope or what have you. You getting the picture?"

"I am," said Judder.

"OK," replied Ego, "here's what you do. Question staff, Mortenson first. After you finish, come to my office and you and me will go to the Left Guard in Fond du Lac and order those big Black Angus steaks, rare. After we finish 'em off, we'll come back, shoot the bull until midnight, and then we'll wake up G-Money and have a heart-to-heart. I'll be bad cop. You be good."

Judder grinned. "Sounds like a winner to me, boss."

• • •

Two hefty blueshirts escorted the sleepy and obviously nervous G-Money to the security office at five minutes past midnight.

Twelve minutes and six seconds past midnight, after being bombarded by Ego and Judder, the bootie bandit's eyes lit up and the gold tooth sparkled almost blindingly so.

Ego knew. He knew that G-Money knew exactly what time it was.

"Say," G-Money said to Judder, "you be the good cop, huh?"

Judder did not have a ready answer. Then, the grinning bootie bandit turned to Ego and said, "And you? You be the bad cop."

"Listen here, Washington," started a red-faced and obviously irate Judder, "I, uh—"

Ego grinned. "It's no use, Lieutenant, he's onto us. G-money's been under more sweat lights and questioned by the best police officers in the state more times than you or me could ever add up. Isn't that right, G-money?"

G-Money laughed out loud. "I understand you hunky poh-leace—completely."

With a jagged index finger pointing, his eyes aflame, Ego warned, "And I'm telling you right now, fella, if any of my snitches tell me that you had anything—anything, you understand—to do with cutting that boy in the school, I'll toss your ass in the hole so fast you won't even know what hit you—and I also guarantee you that you'll do the rest of your time there. And if I could, I'd have you on bread and water the entire time. Do you understand where I'm coming from?"

G-Money saluted Ego. "Yazzuh, boss."

Ego turned to the blueshirts. "Get him the hell outta here, will ya?"

The night that Milwaukee Mafioso members pushed the drunken Betty Bower and her car over a ravine of an abandoned stone quarry will long be recalled by an emergency medical technician (EMT) and a Racine County cop.

Her friends and fellow workers felt she'd screw a snake if somebody held it long enough. That night, she looked for a place where she and her two Mafia "sweethearts" could manage some troika sex without interference. Although the gangsters had orders to do her in, the olive-skin boys had to do something about those erections that could drill holes in concrete.

A late-arriving sheriff's deputy stuck his head through the rider's side window as the EMT studied a humming device he had extracted from the dead news reporter's crotch. "Know what this is?" asked the attendant.

"Sure, it's a dildo."

"Do you know who that is—I mean, was?"

"No," said the deputy, "should I?"

"This woman," announced the EMT, "was the famous, or infamous, depending upon what side of the fence you sit on, Betty Bower of Milwaukee's Channel Four."

"Now, I know," said the cop. "She got that Mafia inmate in Waupun into a helluva lot of hot water."

"Right-o," said the EMT as he turned off the dildo. Now wearing a straight face, he added, "I can hear it on tomorrow's newscasts: TV news reporter Betty Bower comes moments before she goes."

Both cop and the EMT doubled over and shed tears of laughter.

A couple of years after Betty met her demise, a doctor at the Madison University Hospitals detected malignant growths in an inmate's testes that belonged to Frankie, the Italian Bull. Frankie was so upset he ordered two Chicago thugs to get rid of the MD. Days later, a hair blower fell into the doctor's tub while he was taking a bath.

The Dane County coroner ruled the death accidental. Why he had not questioned the need for a bald bachelor to own a hair dryer was not probed. The coroner's secretary wondered how her boss had suddenly become the owner of a year-round cottage on Bear Lake when she knew he didn't have a pot to urinate in or a window to throw it out.

In order to soothe ruffled Waupun blueshirts over the Bower-Colacicco matter, Governor Todd arm-wrestled legislators so they'd boost correctional officer wages. When the lawmakers approved of the pay hike, Todd told Kyle Marston, "That'll keep the pricks quiet." Todd torched a stogie, inhaled, lifted a cheek, tooted, and deftly added, "For a while, anyway."

CHAPTER TWENTY

Otto's Bar and Grill smelled like a morning-after ashtray of mashed-out butts onto which someone had poured stale beer. The jukebox blasted and thumped as if a large crowd of boisterous customers were there. Zak was Otto's singular customer. Seven minutes from closing time, he ordered another drink.

While Al Preston, first-shift sergeant at the prison and part-time bartender on nights and weekends, poured Zak a double Jack Daniels along with an eight-ounce beer chaser, Zak stared at the picture he held in his hand of the Oriental girl who solemnly sat next to her father, a smiling, pith-helmeted North Vietnamese Army (NVA) major.

NVA officers didn't wear collar-tab insignias in the field for fear of becoming special targets or being ferreted out for intelligence gathering if captured. However, the major kept on his person the photo that showed his insignia of one star over two parallel bars.

The NVA major and Zak were in Quang Tri province near Dong Ha on the same day. Zak and Delta Company, along with other marine companies, were assigned to kill or capture retreating NVA regulars who'd be fleeing US Army Cavalry. Anyway, that was US joint force headquarters' plan.

At the time, Delta found itself about two clicks north of the Ben Ha River, which flowed close to Route N9 and the DMZ.

Pvt. Earl "Shotgun" Washington from Roanoke, Virginia, said above a whisper, "You get a whiff of the lieutenant? He stinks like a three-story shithouse."

Other Delta members chuckled. A few whistled. Not Cpl. Alvin "Chipmunk" Fuller of Neskowin, Oregon. "It's the smell of fear," he said with all seriousness.

Pvt. Matt Johnson, Delta's newest member, in country a mere nine days, asked, "You really think so?"

"No," said Shotgun, "he don't know how to wipe his ass. That's what this is all about." Laughter.

Something's not right, thought Zak, certain Shotgun wouldn't misconstrue his glare. A second later, Shotgun warned the others, "Keep it down, bros."

After several minutes, which seemed like hours, they had advanced a couple of hundred yards. Zak stopped. Halting his forward movement was a ten-foot-high jungle plant with huge leaves. After pushing his M-16A1's barrel against one of those leaves, he froze. *Jesus Christ.* His suddenly raised, closed fist stopped Delta's forward movement.

A squatting gook, answering nature's call, was a mere thirty feet away, while beyond him Zak heard gooks involved in a gabfest, obviously unaware they were supposed to be running from army cav.

Zak turned, his men as silent as morning fog hovering above the Horicon Marsh back home. When he turned, the gook he had spotted was now diving for his out-of-reach AK, trouser bottoms still tied around his ankles, his bare ass in the air. Zak aimed and shot once, twice.

All hell broke loose.

Much later, med evac copters picked up the Delta wounded. Another copter picked up four KIA, among them Shotgun Washington.

"Where's Doc?" Zak asked Lance Cpl. Max Schulman. Since marines were killers and not corpsmen, Doc was US Navy Hospital Corpsman Second Class Scott "Doc" Chandler from Winter Haven, Florida.

"Last seen him working on a gook," said Schulman, pointing the direction.

Zak found Doc kneeling beside the very gook Zak had shot. "We got us a big one here, Zak, a gook major. I figure HQ can get beaucoup intel from a major."

"How do you know he's a major?" asked Zak, sighting in on the gook's right arm, its hand under its lower back, its eyes drilling holes through Zak.

"This," said Doc, handing Zak the photograph. "He gave it to me, said I should write to the girl, his daughter. That is, if he dies." Chandler shoved the print at Zak, who didn't look but stuffed it into a pocket.

"Can you believe?" continued the medic, "he speaks English better 'n you an—"

The major's hidden hand was out. Zak heard the shot before he saw the pistol, its report no louder than a car door being shut. It was now pointing at him. Zak shot first. He'd later compare the resulting sound to that made by a muskmelon he and fellow students on a senior class trip dropped from the ninth floor of a Chicago hotel onto the sidewalk below.

The wound was red; the skin surrounding it, black. The gook's eyes remained open, although it was obvious they could no longer see.

Tearfully, Zak knelt beside Doc, holding him up. Doc swayed like a huge tree responding to an ax's final bite. Too fast, much too quickly, the corpsman turned from a human being into a distorted heap on the jungle floor.

• • •

At Portsmouth's sickbay waiting area, Zak sat almost at attention on a stiff steel chair for nearly three-quarters of an hour before a corpsman dressed in whites called out, "Sgt. Zak Griffin?"

Zak rose.

The corpsman pointed down the hallway. "You're to see Dr. Nobles in Room one-oh-fiver."

"Why?"

"It's at Colonel Hayrick's request," the sailor said, reading from a form. Hayrick was Portsmouth's commandant.

Zak stopped at 105 and rapped on the closed door.

"Come in," he heard.

Zak turned the knob and opened the door. A green-shaded desk lamp with at most a forty-watt bulb was the room's single light source. Although the room had windows, their Venetian blinds were shut tight. As with all naval and marine floors, the office's floor was waxed and buffed to a luster.

"Sergeant Griffin?" asked the bespectacled, tall, thin Negro dressed in navy khakis, over it an open white doctor's jacket holding a gold-and-black nameplate. He stood behind a battleship gray desk. Nobles's hair bore flecks of white.

"Reporting as ordered, sir," said Zak.

"Come on in and shut the door, Sergeant, and have a seat. I'm Lieutenant Commander Nobles." The doctor smiled.

Zak sat and waited as Nobles thumbed through a file with Zak's name and serial number inscribed on them.

After what seemed like an inordinate amount of time, Nobles lifted his head, removed his eyeglasses, and said, "By the way, Sergeant, I'm a psychiatrist, and—"

Shrink, why am I seeing a shrink?

"—Commandant Hayrick, himself, recommended you see me. He reports you're a top-notch and gung ho marine with a number of medals for bravery—a born leader. Does that sound like a fair assessment?"

Zak rearranged himself in order to feel more comfortable. "If that's what he reported, sir."

"Also," Nobles added, "he states he's concerned that you drink too much, that you drink to excess. Does that also sound fair?" Putting his glasses back on, Nobles stared straight into Zak's eyes.

Feeling uncomfortable once again, Zak swallowed hard. "Most marines I know drink, sir. I feel as if I'm being singled out."

"Singled out, huh?" Nobles's eyes remained zeroed in on Zak. "The colonel further describes your drinking as a nightly occurrence unless you're pulling duty.

"Sir," Zak almost snapped back, "during my entire Marine Corps career, I've never been in violation of general orders. I've been present for each and every muster, and I've always carried out my superiors' orders to the best of my ability. I've never been disciplined for doing anything wrong."

"Sergeant, are you experiencing any pain from your wounds?"

How could I have known that gooks were real people and got married and had daughters? Gooks were monkeys, the enemy. That's all. I'm not going to tell you the major's daughter chases after me in my dreams, calling me, "Killer. American Pig Killer," but when I drink enough she doesn't appear—until the next time I don't drink myself to sleep.

"Zak, it's closing time and you gotta go so I can lock up," warned Sgt. Al Preston, part-time bartender.

"It could be," said Dr. Nobles, "that your drinking is a simple matter of self-medicating."

Zak gazed at the glossy floor. "No, sir, I don't feel any pain. My wounds healed a long time ago. Can't I drink without receiving Colonel Hayrick's permission?"

Nobles sighed. "Colonel Hayrick is only interested in getting you help. Can you understand that?"

"No, sir, I can't."

"Are you able then, Sergeant, to tell me what your problem is?"

"Sir, I'm not aware the marine sergeant has a problem, sir."

"Did ya hear me, Zak? It's closing time."

Nobles shook his head. "If you have no problem, Sergeant, then we have nothing to discuss, do we?"

"You are one hundred percent correct, sir."

Nobles opened a desk drawer, took out a *Playboy* magazine, and thumbed through it.

Zak shrugged. "Sir, since we don't have anything to discuss, may I be excused?"

At this point, Nobles held the magazine sideways. It was obvious he was scrutinizing the magazine's centerfold. "No, Sergeant, you may not be excused."

"Zak," pleaded Al, "I gotta lock up or Kathy's gonna think I'm fooling around." Zak watched Al turn off the jukebox lights and exterior neon lights.

Sighing, Zak rose. "All right, I know when I'm not wanted," he said, tossing a crumpled dollar bill on the bar and making his way to the rear exit. He pushed open the door and was gone.

During second shift, Ed Black's assignment was Tower Eight in the center of the prison's front wall on Madison Street. After dark, literally nothing happened inside the prison front yard. Thus, Ed became notorious for providing the action by calling Control whenever he saw anyone make her or his way on the sidewalk below. "There's somebody beneath my tower, probably a communist," he told Control Officer Thomas Hayes.

"It's Ed," Hayes warned Control Sgt. Brad Sheen. "Says there's a comrade under his tower. Wanna talk?"

Sheen glared, removed the S&W police air-weight .38 from the holster, and aimed it at Hayes.

"Ed," said Hayes, "I'll alert Waupun PD."

A Waupun City police dispatcher responded to Hayes's call. "Somebody told me Ed was gonna transfer outta eight. That right?"

"Tomorrow ain't soon enough," said Hayes.

Following SOP, Sykes radioed a prowler report to Officers Don and Ron Schmidt. "Ed saw another communist," said Ron. "Let's go to Tony's Pizza and take us some beaver shots."

A car's headlights on Madison Street exposed a longhair carrying a briefcase, which he placed on the sidewalk and then bent over and tied his shoes. A moment later, he rose and walked away, the briefcase still lying there.

The Waupun dispatcher radioed a 10-89 to the Schmidts.

"Hmm," said Ron, checking the 10-code explanation chart. "What's a ten-eighty-nine? Here it is. Jesus H. Christ."

"What's the deal?" asked Don.

"Bomb."

It didn't take long for them plus Dodge County deputies and Waupun's volunteer fire department to arrive below Tower Eight. The fire department chief, as usual, drunk, wanted to test his new federally funded bomb cage. Soon, he and the county deputies and Waupun cops argued who should place the briefcase in the cage.

"Goddammit, I'll do it," said the tipsy fire chief. He picked up the satchel and inspected its contents while everyone else had already started eating dirt, concrete dust, grass, and asphalt chunks.

When Ed went home that night, he gave Noreen the usual peck-on-the-cheek routine before dropping into the La-Z-Boy. Noreen, as usual, went to the kitchen to make Ed a sandwich.

Meanwhile, Ed's stepson, Larry Black, a high school senior who headed up the local chapter of Students for a Democratic Society, stormed into the house. "Did you phone the cops about a briefcase holding a fucking bomb?" Larry's beard, all forty-seven hairs, bristled with animosity.

Ed pushed the La-Z-Boy into upright. "And where did you learn that foul language, young man?"

Larry stomped to the kitchen. A heartbeat later, the boy and his mom returned. "You paranoid prick," yelled Larry, "that quote, bomber, unquote, was me, you asshole. I forgot to pick up my briefcase after I tied my shoes. Is that such a crime—to forget?"

Ed didn't get his sandwich nor did he toast his toes on Noreen's ass that night. Instead, he foundered on the La-Z-Boy until dawn, when he awakened from fifteen minutes of uneasy sleep, feeling as if he were frostbitten.

CHAPTER TWENTY-ONE

Ego's ranch-style home on a one-acre lot with two-stall attached garage was just beyond Waupun's northwest city limits. The side door opened to three stairs that led up to the kitchen. Joanie greeted him with her usual warm smile. "A package for you, dear." She handed him a manila Bubble Wrap envelope.

After he gave Joanie a peck on the cheek, he checked the return address. It was from a Milwaukee lawyer. Inside the envelope, he discovered a microcassette tape labeled Exhibit One. *Why would a Milwaukee shyster send this here—and not to the prison?*

Ego felt as if he'd been dropped on an iceberg, icy waves rocking it. He nearly slid into the frigid waters. Nevertheless, he stuffed the cassette into his shirt pocket as if it held no significance.

After supper, Joanie washed the dishes while Ego dried with a towel. "I'm going down to the workshop," he said. He'd play the tape there.

"Me, I'm going to watch TV," said Joanie.

• • •

Ego's basement workshop had a microcassette player, which usually played Johnny Cash or Lefty Frizzell tapes. Inserting the law office tape and closing the cover, he pushed the play button.

"Hello, Mr. Richardson, this is attorney at law Malcolm Vergenz, spelled V-e-r-g-e-n-z. By way of introduction, I represent an organization whose goal is to protect the American way of life. One of its leaders, Theodore Kopfmueller, is an inmate at the institution where you are associate warden of security.

"Soon, you will hear the sworn affidavits of two citizens who desire to set the record straight involving a murder at the prison."

Ego hit the stop button. His teeth chattered, head shook, eyes ached. He needed to urinate. Still, he needed to listen to the rest of the tape. Vergenz stated the date and time and asked somebody if that was correct.

"Yeah," a woman answered.

"Yeah," repeated the attorney. "Does *yeah* mean yes?"

"Yes," she said.

"What is your name?"

"My name is Ann Secamore," said the woman.

"Could you speak a little louder, please, and spell your last name?"

She coughed and cleared her throat. "Excuse me, I thought I was speaking loud enough. It's Secamore, S-e-c-a-m-o-r-e."

"And Miss Secamore, where do you reside?"

"I live at three-oh-nine West Main Street in Waupun."

"You said three-oh-nine West Main Street in Waupun?"

"I did. I'm moving to another place real soon."

Ego wrote the name and address on a notepad advertising Stam Auto Body.

"And why are you here—in my law office?"

"It's like this. My boyfriend told me about an inmate in Waupun being murdered. According to my boyfriend, the murder was ordered by a prison staff member, a higher-upper, if you know what I mean."

"Your boyfriend told you about a murder at the prison, you say. And who is this boyfriend?"

"Smith, Jim Smith, uh, I mean James Smith. He's a retired guard, lives in Waupun above the R&R Bar. He used to work in the prison's hole, the place they call the Greenhouse."

That son of a—he gets boozed up and gets a piece of ass, and tells this woman, whoever she is—she ain't from around he—

"You say an inmate was murdered. Do you recall the murdered inmate's name?"

Ego's teeth clattered like loose ball bearings knocking against one another. *Davis.*

"I do. It was Earl Davis."

"How does your boyfriend—James Smith—fit into this?"

"He was a sergeant. A major, Major Richardson, but now the prison's associate warden of security, set up the murder, according to Jim. The way Jim, I mean James, told me, it was like reading one of those novels that keep you on edge until the last page. Well, I'll tell you this: I was shocked beyond belief. That's why I came here."

"Thank you, Ms. Secamore. This ends the first interview."

Ego turned off the machine, picked up the extension phone, and dialed the prison. The Bubble shot him through the security office. "Security Office, Sergeant Williams speaking."

"This is Richardson. Check and see if we have an Ann Secamore, S-e-c-a-m-o-r-e, on the authorized visitor list."

"OK, boss, I'll check."

Ego's fingers drilled the workbench top until Williams said, "Mr. Richardson?"

"Yeah."

"An Ann Secamore's on Theodore Kopfmueller's visiting list."

"Thanks."

"Anything else?"

"Nah." Ego hung up, looked to the ceiling, and called, "Joanie." She didn't answer. Ego pushed *Play.*

"For the record, could you please give me your name and address?"

"Yeah, it's James Smith. I live at two sixteen West Main Street in Waupun, Wisconsin."

"Anything the matter, dear?" Joanie called from the top of the stairs.

Ego punched the off button. "No, the tape I got in the mail; it's work-related stuff—as I thought."

"That's good," his wife sang back.

He listened to Joanie close the door and return to the La-Z-boy as he relieved himself in a Roets Dairy milk bottle.

Returning home the next night after the shift, Ed Black hoped Noreen would, at the very least, speak to him. After he loosened his uniform tie and undid the top shirt button, he scurried to the refrigerator, retrieved a cool one, stepped into the parlor, turned on the tube, took off his shoes and socks, and settled into the La-Z-Boy. "Noreen must still be pissed off," he said to no one as he brought the cold one to his lips.

Upstairs, a door slammed. Floorboards banged. Ed, like a coil spring meeting dry ice, rose in a dozen different directions. He looked down to a beer-soaked shirt and recliner. Ed pictured a pack of wolves stalking a herd of yaks. However, it was stepson Larry who zipped down the stairs and roared, "You're history, asshole."

After the kid gave Ed the bird, the boy lunged out the door, Ed giving chase until a foot plunged into a pile of fresh dog shit, causing the entirety of Ed to slip and fall, the dog's emission sticking to him like super glue.

Ed returned home but couldn't change clothes because the bedroom door was locked. After whispering "Noreen" a couple of times, he placed an ear to the door and listened to silence's deathly chill.

At two o'clock in the afternoon three days later, while Ed was in Tower Eight, Madison Van & Storage transferred anything that wasn't nailed down from his home to an undisclosed location.

At about the same time, Deputy Joe Weems found a parking spot near Ed's tower. He got out of the detective's squad, holding onto papers that Noreen's lawyer had filled and Dodge County's Circuit Court Judge Schlitz had signed.

Ed appeared on his catwalk. "How ya doing, Joe?"

Weems waved the documents and said, "These are for you."

"Wha'cha got?" asked Ed as he lowered the clip on a rope.

Shrugging, Joe jammed the documents into the clip. As Ed pulled on the rope, Weems turned, unwrapped the cellophane, and exposed a rum-soaked Crooks cigar. Then, he headed for his car. "Disgusting work if you ask me, but no one asked."

At ten fifteen that night, Ed was home. He traced on one wall the darkened outline where a family portrait had hung. He couldn't even find his twelve-gauge shotgun in order to end his misery. Movers had taken everything except the dust bunnies.

Ed checked his wallet. In it were a five, two singles, a Sears credit card, and a three-pack of rubbers he didn't get to use. He shuffled off to Otto's, where fellow second-shifters heard his mournful story in fits and spurts amid tears of anguish and angry expletives.

His fellow second-shifters bought Ed many more drinks than he could handle.

CHAPTER TWENTY-TWO

Waupun's Brooks Ambulance returned Jeremy Clark to the prison after a Madison University Hospitals' surgeon made Clark as whole as possible, according to Ego's investigating lieutenant, Judder Brown.

A barrage of questions followed. "How come every school swamper had at least three packs of tailor-mades in his cell? Clark cut hisself you say—huh? Where's the proof? How long are you gonna let his bullshit ride?"

"What do you mean, sir?"

"Butch, the name's Butch. What do you mean what do I mean? I mean this. We're gonna put Clark's ass back into GP—if he doesn't come clean. That's what I mean."

"I hadn't thought of that, Butch."

"Well, start thinking."

"Yes, sir. By the way, Butch, I have something else to report."

"Yeah?"

"Yes, one of my snitches, Avener Smith, told me our inmate advocate, Shirleen, asked him what he knew about the murder of an inmate that took place in the Greenhouse before I started working here."

Ego stiffened. He couldn't breathe. *Jesus, am I having a heart attack?*

"Anything wrong, Butch?"

Finally, Ego started sucking air. “Nah, but did Smith say anything else?”

“No, just that Shirleen asked him, that’s all.”

Judder stood and opened the door.

“Where you going?”

“Health Services,” Judder stridently announced. “Either Clark talks or it’s GP for his ass.”

Ego watched Dorothy at her desk, twirling an index finger in mock horror. She had never been impressed with Ego’s loyal foot soldier.

Ego grinned. “Go get ‘im, Lieutenant.” *Why did Shirleen ask about Davis? Aw, it’s probably about nothing. At least, I hope so. Get ahold of yourself, Butch. It’s about nothing.*

•••

Jeremy opened his eyes.

Judder stood at his bedside. “Remember me?”

Jeremy nodded.

“Think you can walk to a nurse’s office so we can talk in privacy?”

Jeremy eyeballed the other sickbay inmates. Four paid rapt attention. “Nah, I don’t think so.”

“OK, I’ll ask you right here. Do you stick by the story you told me in the school?”

“Story?” asked Jeremy.

“Story. That’s what I said.”

What’d you think I was going to say, Sherlock?

“What’d you cut it with?”

Jeremy started counting ceiling tiles.

“You don’t know or you won’t say?”

“Lieutenant, there’s one thing worse in here than being called a punk, and that’s being tagged a snitch.” Jeremy put his head back on the pillow and closed his eyes.

"I'm not asking you to be a snitch. I talked to Dr. Murphy. He thought you were real smart. Said when he and his students checked up on you, you were reading a medical book. What was its title?" Jeremy heard pages flipping. "Yeah, *Gray's Anatomy*."

Jeremy opened his eyes. The lieutenant looked like a cat playing with a cornered mouse.

"Why'd you do it? Were you the catcher and G-Money the pitcher? Did you tell him the price went up?"

Jeremy started counting tiles once more.

"I talked with our doctor and he says you can be released to GP. Is that what you want?"

"Lieutenant, you and I live in two different worlds."

"Are you G-Money's whore?"

Jeremy lost count. So, he began anew.

Within the hour, inmate Clark was released from the Health Services Unit and sent back to his cell hall with the same job assignment.

• • •

Jeremy stood in the chow line.

Protected by the inmate code, G-Money plainly laughed in contempt while at least a hundred more inmates made kissing sounds.

After he returned to the cell hall, Jeremy lay on his bunk rereading Eldridge Cleaver's *Soul on Ice*, fully expecting what was coming.

G-Money stopped in front of Jeremy's cell. "You gonna be my bitch, or you gonna dead. It's your choice."

Jeremy returned to Cleaver. He heard G-Money snicker before he entered his cell.

Although Jeremy wasn't crazy and didn't look forward to the jeers, grins, and catcalls he'd have to face during night rec, he knew he had to go. He needed to meet with Zombie.

• • •

The next day, as Jeremy stood in the lunch line, he blinked three times toward Rude Boy. Rude Boy turned to Zombie and said a few words. Zombie turned to eyeball Elmer Johnston, welding teacher aide, sitting at the far end of the dining hall. Elmer nodded while Zombie scratched his nose. Elmer took out his handkerchief and blew. Zombie and Rude Boy began chatting. Elmer made eye contact with Jeremy and nodded. Jeremy tugged at an earlobe. Elmer turned to his tablemates and laughed along with them.

Jeremy, with empty food tray, headed to the scullery but stopped behind G-Money, who jabbered excitedly to fellow swampers who stared.

G-Money turned. Jeremy and he made eye contact. Jeremy smiled and then made his way to the scullery, handing in his tray.

Outside the dining hall, he stopped, taking in the fragrance of the next meal. It reminded him of home, his mother a superb cook. What he expected happened. Elmer slammed into him. "Watch where yo going, bitch."

Jeremy pushed at Elmer and said, "I'm no bitch."

Elmer reeled backward and slammed into the Southwest cell hall, its old and longtime sergeant banging on the window, shaking his head, and waggling an index finger.

Jeremy and Elmer went their separate ways.

Sergeant Barnes, arms crossed against his chest, watched as Jeremy climbed the stairs. The bridge officer—*Bridge* was his working title—was perched on a chair on the catwalk that connected G-tier to the outer wall. Bridge was talking to an officer on F-tier about some party. He should've been watching Jeremy. Jeremy stopped at his cell and ratcheted its door shut before slipping into G-Money's cell.

Inserting under G-Money's mattress the shank that Elmer Johnston had passed to him, Jeremy turned in the opposite direction and whipped back to face the bunk, hand plunging under the mattress, fingers grasping the masking tape-covered handle. He did that again and again.

Satisfied, he undressed and rolled his clothes around his shoes and stuck them under the bunk's pillow before going to the rear wall.

Surprised, G-Money pulled the toothpick from his mouth as he ratcheted shut the cell door, whispering his pleasure.

Obediently, Jeremy went to his knees, looked up, and smiled.

G-Money, breathing heavily, was likely fighting off premature ejaculation. His eyelids dropped; his facial muscles contorted.

Jeremy, quicker than lightning, was up, his hand under the mattress. He slammed the sharpened steel into G-Money's chest before G-Money could exit his reverie.

A moment later, Jeremy watched G-Money's eyes scream as he writhed in pain while Jeremy worked to get the shank out.

G-Money fell to the floor, sounding like a dropped baseball bat bag.

Jeremy screamed and pulled harder. Finally, the bloodied steel was out but in a split second it was plunged into the gut. With a sawing motion, Jeremy moved it upward, G-Money's innards disgorging his latest meal and a tarry, stinky blackish-red substance.

Blood pelted the walls, soaked the floor, struck the ceiling, hit the mirror, fell onto the commode and into the water, lashed the chair and bunk and bars. Blood everywhere, pools, smears, splotches, streaks, spots.

Bridge was outside the cell. He screamed, "What are you doing?"

Inmates shouted.

Sergeant Barnes screamed to Bridge, "Get your ass down here right now."

Jeremy saw that Bridge had pissed his pants. Jeremy dressed. It took longer than he expected. He heard sounds of ERU. Finally, a ninja appeared. He looked at Jeremy and then down at G-Money. "Jesus H. Kuh-rist."

"You want this?" asked Jeremy, offering him the shank.

"Leave it where it is."

"In my hand?"

Ninja's eyes couldn't or wouldn't leave the body on the floor. "No, put it on the floor and back up to the food slot and show your hands."

Jeremy placed the shank on top of G-Money and turned his back to the bars, fingers finding the food slot. His hands and wrists were through. A moment later, he felt the cuffs.

"They too tight?"

"No."

"Step to the rear of the cell."

Jeremy stepped over G-Money to the rear of the cell as he heard the door go clickety-clack.

"Come out on the catwalk." Jeremy had to step over G-Money again.

"Stop." A ninja ratcheted the leg irons.

As they marched down the catwalk, Jeremy in the middle, two ninjas in front, two behind, inmates screamed, banged bars, and started fires. An inmate with bass voice called out, "He bad."

"Bad," other inmates took up.

As Jeremy and ninjas made it outside the cell hall and on their way to the Greenhouse, he heard the chant, "Bad, bad, he bad. Bad, bad, he bad. Bad, bad, he bad."

Ed Black was in a state of shock. The judge not only ordered him to pay alimony to Noreen but support payments for Larry, as well. Ed screamed, "But he's not my kid and I'm not his dad!"

"I'm aware of that," bellowed Judge Schlitz, slamming the gavel, "but you're paying for his support."

Hitchhiking to Madison, where he checked into the Hotel Washington, Ed followed the deskman, whose breath smelled like boiled cabbage. He led Ed to a sleazy room the size of a prison cell. "Welcome to our bridal suite," said Bad Breath.

"For which couple, the Count and Countess Dracula?"

"Sixty a week, no hair off my ass if you wanna take it or not."

"I'll take it," said Ed. "I always wanted to live in a frigging palace."

"Funny, funny, funny. Under what name do you wish to register?"

"John Smith. By the way, has anyone told you your mouthwash ain't hacking it?"

"Better men than you. You're the fourth John Smith to register this week."

"It's John M. Smith. Ever try Listerine?"

Bad Breath snatched the cash. "Tried it once but gagged on the shit."

It did not take long for John M. to run out of money and take up residence in a cardboard box in the rear of the Yellow Jersey bicycle store, where he guzzled muscatel.

Andy, chief bike mechanic, woke Ed each morning, sending the bum on his way.

Lingering in a public toilet before a smudged mirror, John M., that is Ed Black, watched gnats crawl between knotty beard hairs and filthy cheeks. Blackheads looked like freckles, and the whites of his eyes were egg yolk yellow with numerous red zigzag lines that had no particular beginning or end in mind. The hair on top of his head looked like a mop that was dragged through drain oil. His once pearly whites looked like yellowed stalactites and stalagmites that led to the entrance of hell.

Shaking, he sought out a University Avenue street vendor who daily offered him hot dogs that had blanched in the kettle. "Juan, tell me the truth. How do I look?"

"Like you always do," said the peddler, laughing and lifting an insipid wiener from the pot. "You hungry?"

CHAPTER TWENTY-THREE

Shirleen jerked as if electrically shocked. Startled, she sat up in bed. Feeling the lamp, she found the switch. Studying the clock's numerals, she finally understood it was three minutes after three o'clock. "Zak, is that you?" *I thought I heard something, but maybe I was dreaming.* "Zak?"

Her fingers found the living room wall switch. There he was, eyes sad-sack and glossy. "Why?" Shirleen cried out. "Why?"

"I don't know," he said. "All I know is I love you."

Shirleen shook her head. "In order to love someone else, you first have to love yourself."

"You don't think I love me?"

"No, Zak, I don't."

•••

Besides having his all-time worst hangover ever, Zak nonetheless abided by Shirleen's order. He telephoned Milwaukee's AA hotline. "Yes," he said. "That's why I'm calling. Shir, she's my girlfriend, she thinks you guys can help me."

Shirleen squeezed Zak's shoulder.

"No, I can't," said Zak. "I work second shift. Yes, two until ten." Zak shook his head. "No, that won't do either. That church is only a block away from the prison. That's where I work. What about Fond du Lac or Beaver Dam? Yeah, Beaver Dam's closer. Got it. One fifteen

Lincoln Street. Yeah, I think I can find that. Cellar Dwellers? OK." Zak wrote down the words. "They meet at nine this morning, and I should ask for George? OK. Thanks. I'll do that, and you have a good day, too." He put down the phone and sighed.

Shirleen kissed Zak on the forehead. "I knew you could do it," she whispered.

She seemed so pleased.

•••

After Zak entered the side entrance, he heard them, downstairs. He had wished he was normal size because the stairs' squeaked under his weight and loudly announced his entrance.

They sat around a conference table, a coffee cup before each. *They don't look like drunks.*

A man wearing a black T-shirt with a Harley-Davidson logo rose and approached, extending his hand. "You Zak?"

Zak nodded.

"Great, Sam from Milwaukee called and said I should be on the lookout for you. I'm George." George turned back to the group. "Say, you guys, this big fellow is Zak."

"Hi, Zak," they called out in unison.

"Have a seat at the table," said George, "and I'll get you a cuppa, if you want one."

"I want one."

"Decaf or high-test?"

"High-test." Zak's head pounded and his stomach churned. He sat next to a woman around his age. Cute, she wore tie-dyed jeans and a loose-fitting blouse. She reached out with a hand. "Hi, I'm Judy."

"Zak," he said.

"Yeah," she said, "I know. Your first meeting, huh?"

"Yeah."

"Good for you."

George brought Zak coffee before sitting at the head of the table. "It's about that time, folks. Hi, everyone, I'm George and I'm an alcoholic."

"Hi, George," the others yelled back.

Zak felt his head was just about to split into two.

"Welcome," said George, "to the Cellar Dwellers closed AA meeting. Those who have a desire to stop drinking are welcome to attend." George paused to look at Zak. "Zak, I'm going to accept your presence as conformance to our single requirement. Will somebody please read from the book, *How It Works*."

"Hi," said an older gentleman with white hair and trimmed mustache. "I'm Don, alcoholic."

"Hi, Don," the others yelled almost gleefully.

Inside Zak's head was this ball-peen hammer.

"This is from chapter five of the Big Book," said Don, who began reading, "Rarely have we seen a person fail who has thoroughly followed our path."

When Don finished, a blonde, identifying herself as "Neva, alcoholic-addict" read the meditation of the day, which included the lines, "Some things I do not miss since becoming dry: that overall awful, sick feeling, including the shakes, a splitting headache, pains in my arms and legs, and bleary eyes."

She's talking about me.

A straw basket was sent down the line after George said, "We are self-supporting; we accept no outside contributions."

Most everyone put in a buck, as did Zak.

"It's time for introductions and affirmations," said George.

The man to George's right introduced himself. "Hi, I'm Arkansas Charlie, and I'm an alcoholic."

"Hi, Charlie," the others called out, much too loudly for Zak.

Marcie was next. "Hi, Marcie," they happily shouted.

When it came time for Zak, he said, "I'm Zak, and I don't know what I am."

"Hi, Zak," they shouted as happily as ever.

"We're going to have a first-step meeting," said George, looking at Zak.

Am I supposed to say something?

George continued. "The first step is, 'We admitted we were powerless over alcohol—that our lives had become unmanageable.' Who wants to start?"

Marcie started. She told how she got blitzed just about each and every night and many mornings would wake up in strange beds with even stranger men she'd never have anything to do with when sober.

Others talked about their *bottoms*, when they felt totally whipped and had a moment of clarity about the reality of their situation.

Eva, an octogenarian, said, "Zak, just so you know, denial's not a river in Egypt."

After the meeting, Dick M., a navy Vietnam vet, shook Zak's hand and said, "Welcome home, bro. You can admit a basic, unpleasant truth about yourself today. You can choose this day as your bottom like right now, or your bottom can choose you, which could be prison, a nuthouse, or a cemetery plot. It's up to you."

"Thanks," said Zak, not really meaning it.

George collared Zak and handed him a card. "It has my school and home phone numbers. Call anytime, night, day, it doesn't matter, but call before you take that first drink. If you already had that drink, don't bother. By the way, I teach English at Wayland Academy." George then spent the next few minutes talking about his Harley.

On the drive back to Waupun, Zak passed a Ford Fairlane with dual mufflers. The Ford's driver gave Zak a thumbs-up.

Zak thought about the possibility of his being an alcoholic. Shaking his head, he said aloud, "I don't know. I just don't know."

On a frostbitten morning, ice chinks hanging from beard and mustache, John M. Smith, ex-prison guard Ed Black, who chose to become a bum rather than pay monthly support payments for a kid he did not father, shook so hard he could hardly grasp the doorknob of Madison's Mifflin Street Cooperative.

Opening the door for him was Winnie, the Wine Head, whose lips looked like whitewalls, induced by his inhaling day-old sugar doughnuts. "How, John M.," greeted Winnie, who swore he was full-blooded Lakota. He wore a frayed kid's Indian chief's headdress with the message Visit Wisconsin Dells on its headband. The frazzled chicken feathers were faded green, yellow, and red.

At once, John M. dropped to the floor and vibrated like a John Deere tractor hitting on one cylinder.

Winnie whooped and war-danced. A customer, the Reverend Donald, a 137-pound, six-foot-five recovering drug addict, knelt beside the downed bum and recalled while on a bad LSD trip, he staggered onto the plowed fields of an Iowa Trappist monastery. The monks, as was their wont, silently nursed him to health while Donald babbled from dawn until dark as to how he would devote his life to spiritual matters. The monks breathed not-so-silent sighs of joy the day Donald left them.

Donald got a job as a dishwasher at Ella's Deli and was led by God through the restaurant's rear exit to a Dumpster with an American Handgunner magazine on top. Turning to the personal ads, he spotted Bishop Tommy "Tell it like it is" Smithfield's display ad. Smithfield's ad stated he was the leader of What a Friend We Have in Jesus Christ

Almighty—What a Pal—Pentecostal Church, its headquarters a post office box in Dallas, Texas.

Donald became a minister of Smithfield's church, his proof a thirty-five-dollar Doctor of Divinity sheepskin signed by Smithfield.

John M. Smith didn't give a damn about the reverend because Smith was surrounded by foot-long, iridescent, hairy-legged spiders with green eyes and clicking pincers. Right behind the arachnids slithered red-and-blue Gila monsters on steroids, their yellow pitchfork tongues darting out menacingly. "Help me, for chrissake," yelled the wino.

Donald turned aside and gagged, certain Smith had gargled that morning with the dregs of an outhouse.

At the same time, Winnie, the Wine Head, noisily executed his version of the Lakota Rain Dance, vaguely similar to the Lakota War Dance.

CHAPTER TWENTY-FOUR

Wearing a T-shirt, faded jeans, and black cowboy boots, Kevin Blake made his way downstairs to Ego's workshop. Ego stood beside an old refrigerator, its door half-open. Holding on to two Miller High Life beer bottles, Ego stretched one out to Blake. Blake accepted and took a long swig before he wiped the beer from his lips with the back of a hand. "Man, that hit the spot, and how."

"You park your car out front like I told you?" inquired Ego.

"Yeah, boss. What's up?"

With index finger pointing to the first floor, Ego approached the stairs and called, "Joanie."

Joanie was at the entryway. "Hi, Kevin. Yes, dear?"

"We have this gang problem Kevin and me need to talk about." He looked at his watch. "It'll probably take the better part of an hour."

"I was counting on you coming with me. Reverend Mike was anxious that you had volunteered for—"

"I know," said Ego, "I know, but this is high-priority work stuff."

"Reverend Mike is expecting both of us," reminded Joanie.

"Later, when you come back, you can tell me what was said and done, and it will be as if I was there with you."

Joanie shook her head. "It's always the institution, isn't it?"

Ego blew her a kiss. "Love ya."

She giggled and wiggled her behind and was gone.

As Ann Secamore and Jim Smith answered attorney Vergenz's questions, Ego watched Blake strain and twitch.

Finally, Blake mumbled something, which Ego didn't make out. He hit the stop button. "You say something?"

"Yeah, I asked what you're planning to do."

"I'll tell you what *you're* gonna do," said Ego. "You're gonna take care of Jim. I'll take care of Secamore."

"What do you mean, 'take care'?"

"Well, something like this: you're gonna take Jim fishing, and he'll have an accident, or something like that. Use your head. Come up with your own idea. Know what I mean?"

"Christ, are you serious?"

"As cancer," replied Ego.

No longer answering to John Smith, Ed Black took back his real name after the Reverend Donald baptized him. Ed not only quit drinking, but he also rented a clean apartment, bathed, shaved, got regular haircuts, wore clean clothes, and got a job.

A dishwasher at Chi-Chi's, Ed made amends to Noreen and eventually paid her all the alimony and child support he owed her.

Noreen told him stepson Larry, a loyal member of Students for a Democratic Society, was now a staff attorney with the ACLU.

When not working, Ed volunteered at Reverend Donald's State Street storefront chapel. One day, certain God had talked to him, Ed asked, "Are you sure, Lord?"

"Watt yo mean, yo crazy-ass hunky?" questioned Howard "Toofless" Washington, who had tossed away at least a dozen pair of choppers fitted and provided to him by various governmental and charitable organizations. "Yo one crazy-ass watt bo'."

It didn't matter what Toofless said. Ed sent a one-hundred-dollar money order to Bishop Smithfield, who was netting a yearly six-figure profit from selling mail-order divinity degrees to mostly prison inmates.

In time, Ed purchased a used eighteen-wheeler. On its cab door was heralded Jesus Highway Crusade. On the trailer's sides and rear was the same message, "Honk if you want to go to Heaven."

Ed visited just about every interstate truck stop in the country, where he stuffed Bible verses behind toilet paper and prophylactic dispensers in the men's rooms and held religious services in the parking area.

Attending were short-order cooks and red-eyed waitresses with dangling Pall Mall cigarettes; black men and women with Afros; white men with sideburns and scraggly beards holding on to their bra-less women with granny glasses, dressed in bib overalls and tie-dyed T-shirts; out-and-out bums, wearing paisley double-knit shirts stuffed into double-knit trousers; oil-stained mechanics; and lastly, Ed's fellow truckers, smelling of cigarettes, pie a la modes, french fries, Jim Beam, coffee, and Double Bubble bubblegum.

After opening the trailer's rear doors, Ed turned on the lights that exposed a chapel with stained glass windows, Hammond organ, and altar. Climbing aloft, Ed sat at the organ and sang his original, "Meet Me at the Toll Booth, Jesus, on the Highway of Life," while strobe lights flashed and ersatz blood flowed through see-through veins on the plastic Jesus hanging on the simulated-wood plastic cross.

Jane Rutherford, wayward daughter of coffee bean scion Earl Stanley Rutherford, watched and clapped and fell in love with the highway preacher man. Swearing off all mind-altering drugs, she joined the Highway Crusader in bed. The next morning, she said, "Before we fuck each other to death, maybe we oughta make this a long-term affair."

Daddy Rutherford purchased the newlyweds a Montana ranch as a wedding gift. Ed hired real cowboys to raise beef he and Jane eventually sold to an exclusive Christian clientele. The chief financial officer, Ed's stepson, Larry, forsook the ACLU for the John Birch Society.

CHAPTER TWENTY-FIVE

After Jeremy pleaded guilty in Dodge County Circuit Court to the plea agreed charge of second-degree murder for killing Milo "G-Money" Washington, Waupun's Program Review Committee placed Jeremy in administrative segregation status.

The first step toward rejoining general population was to receive written approval from the security director before committee members would even consider such a move.

When Ego toured the Greenhouse, Clark asked him, "What are my chances of getting out of here in a year?"

"Nada," said Ego. "Nada frigging chance as long as I have anything to say about it."

Jeremy's neighbor to his right was John "Injun" Doxtator, a Ho-Chunk from Keshena.

In time, staff and inmates referred to Jeremy and Injun as the Bobbsey Twins. One night, as Jeremy sweated out numerous push-ups, Injun whispered, "Say, you shouldn't work so hard. You need to take a vacation."

Jeremy looked to the ceiling as if he were inspecting some strange object. "How do I do take a vacation from this place?"

Injun snorted a laugh. "How. That's what us Injuns say. Keep staring at a lit light bulb until you think you can't."

"Like self-hypnosis?"

"Don't hurt your brain."

Jeremy lay on the bunk and stared at a bulb that was beneath the second tier's catwalk. His eyes watered, his gut rumbled, and night became day as tarantulas performed the boogaloo on his skin. Day became night. Muscles, sinew, bone howled with pain. His eyes shut, he rose. *I'm floating.*

Astoundingly, he saw himself on the bunk, his eyes closed, as if it were a body in a casket.

A tiny light beckoned and half mocked him by drifting toward him, and when he reached out to touch it, it floated away.

Suddenly, he was outdoors and above the Greenhouse—how did that occur?—as the tower officer in Six scratched himself and yawned.

"Hey," Jeremy yelled as loud as he could. The guard paid him no attention.

In a flash, Jeremy flew ever higher, above Waupun. Under the full moon, he watched Canada geese fly toward the Horicon Marsh. To the west he saw a patchwork of corn, alfalfa, and soybean fields.

He looked north, the direction his body took. In a flash, he flew above Waupaca's Chain O' Lakes, their dancing waves reflecting moonlight. An instant later, he hovered above Stevens Point. Below was his mother's home, his home.

Inside, he heard a WSPT radio announcer read the local news while his mother sat at the kitchen table. "Mom," he called to her.

She rose, turned off the radio, and put the jar of Hellman mayonnaise on the top shelf of the fridge and then closed the door.

A heartbeat later, Jeremy lay on the bunk. As he rose, his leg muscles ached. He stood, grappled with the bars, and whispered, "Injun, it worked."

"Better be careful," warned Injun.

"Why?"

"The next time you might not return."

•••

Jeremy took a number of vacations. Each one lasted longer than the previous one, but he never worried. He always returned as he did this time, although he did not have the strength to rise and stand. Nevertheless, he whispered, "I'm back."

"So?" asked someone in a strange-sounding whisper.

"Injun?"

"Nah, he's gone. I'm Ted Kopfmueller."

"Where's Injun?"

"On the bricks. Judge Boyle cut him loose."

"When?"

"Two, maybe two and a half years ago."

In the fall of 1948, Wood County Sheriff Al "Big Al" Westhuis (pronounced West House) led accused killer William Anderson in shackles, a pair of deputies holding on to each of Anderson's arms, from the county jail across Baker Street to the courthouse for the eighth day of Anderson's trial.

Anderson, attired in a rumpled, double-breasted, light brown suit with blue pinstripes, crinkled white shirt, and paisley tie with multiple gaudy colors, voluntarily took the witness stand, an action that his attorney strongly advised against, which is why he declined to ask Anderson any questions.

Judge Ronald Bilkins arranged his pince-nez glasses before announcing, "District Attorney Adkins, you may question the witness."

"Thank you, Your Honor," said the balding, overweight Adkins. He wore a navy blue suit—its coat unbuttoned—a matching vest with gold pocket watch chain dipping from vest button to vest pocket, white shirt, and somber tie.

Adkins faced the jury of twelve men, seven of whom wore rumpled suit coats over bib overalls. He nodded.

Then smiling, Adkins turned to face the gallery of news reporters and array of citizens. Finally, he made an about-face in order to confront Anderson. He inhaled profoundly. His vest buttons strained as he exhaled in deepest chant, "William Anderson, you have heard over the course of the past seven days, long days I might add, numerous witnesses declaring the circumstances surrounding the murders of your wife, Miriam Anderson, your best friend, Paul Jennings, and Wood County Deputy Sheriff Dale Bennett. Did you, sir, commit those crimes?"

"You betcha," said Anderson, "and that's the God's honest truth."

While Anderson's lawyer protested, the gallery whooped and hollered as Judge Bilkins pounded the bench as if he were nailing shingles on a roof in a hailstorm. Finally, the racket succumbed to silence.

With his next election in the bag, DA Adkins melodiously intoned, "Mr. Anderson, would you care to elucidate your response?"

The defendant turned to the judge. "I don't know what he means. Do you?"

"Mr. Adkins?" queried the judge.

Adkins covered his mouth as he cleared his throat. "Yes, Your Honor. Mr. Anderson, please state what happened next."

"I stuck Jennings and Miriam and blasted Bennett with my thirty-thirty."

Adkins's eyebrows rose to their absolute pinnacles. "You stuck them? You shot him? What you mean, Mr. Anderson, is that with a hunting knife, you stabbed Paul Jennings's anus, severing internal organs before thrusting it repeatedly into your wife's chest." Silent only momentarily with his head down, fingers touching a brow, Adkins asked in deepest bass, "After stabbing Jennings and your wife, what did you do next?"

"I went to the phone and cranked it."

"Then, what happened."

"The operator said, 'Number plee-uz.'"

Just about everyone in the courtroom laughed out loud.

CHAPTER TWENTY-SIX

Joanie Richardson looked out the kitchen window while she washed a head of lettuce under a gush of cool tap water. A pork loin and German potato salad were baking in the oven.

Ego took in the aroma with a long inhale, getting hungrier by the second, half listening to Walter Cronkite on the boob tube. The phone rang.

"Would you get that, hon? I'm expecting a call from Mike." Mike was their firstborn.

Ego stretched, yawned, and pushed the recliner's handle forward. Rising, he muted the news before lifting the phone. "Hi, Mike."

"Good evening, sir. This is attorney at law Malcolm Vergenz. Am I speaking to Marion Richardson?"

Ego felt as if some supernatural creature had just ripped out his heart, encased it in ice, and then reinserted it into his chest in one hideously swift move. "Yeah, this is him."

"How are you this fine evening, sir?"

"Who'd you say this was?"

"I suspect you know why I'm calling, sir."

Why now? Why? "No," lied Ego, "why?" He needed to urinate badly.

"I assume you received the cassette tape. Is our connection OK, Mr. Richardson?"

"Yeah, I received that gang-activities tape a long time ago."

"You must be mistaken, sir." A moment later, Vergenz came out of the ether. "Oh, I get it, somebody's listening, right? Your wife perhaps?"

"On the money," said Ego. "Hold on, will ya? I'm going to go to the extension phone in the basement." Ego covered the mouthpiece and whispered, "It's Madison, hush-hush gang stuff."

Joanie wiped her hands on a kitchen towel, accepted the phone, and covered the mouthpiece.

"OK, Joanie," Ego called out when he reached the downstairs' phone, and after hearing the click, Ego growled, "Why'd you call me here?"

"If you prefer, Mr. Richardson, I'll contact you at the prison tomorrow. However, if I recall how things are run there, you have no such thing as phone privacy—for reasons of institutional security—am I correct?"

Ego felt a blast of cold air hit him although it was eighty and the humidity was higher yet. "Yeah."

"Mr. Richardson, I called to let you know that you must meet with Theodore Kopfmueller within a week."

"Tell me, Mr.—"

"Vergenz," helped the attorney.

"Vergenz," repeated Ego. "Tell me what kind of man represents animals like Aryan Nation thugs?"

"They are giving you six days for the meeting to take place. One week from today, I shall phone you."

"If my wife answers," quickly warned Ego, "tell her you're the gangs' liaison officer in Madison."

"Gangs liaison officer, Madison," repeated Vergenz, "I understand, Mr. Richardson. I'll say good-bye for now. Please enjoy the rest of the evening."

Ego dumped the phone on the cradle, hefted a Phillips screwdriver, and nervously tossed it from one hand to the other.

"Hon," sang out Joanie at the top of the stairs, "supper's on the table."

"Be right up." Ego rose and placed the screwdriver on the tool shadow board.

• • •

Shirleen waited for Warden Palestine to finish reading the day's daily change sheet. *I was wrong to fall in love. Then, to believe Zak would stop drinking. Girl, you can't control him, and you can't live the way you've been living.*

"Yes, Shirleen?"

Last night, he fell flat on his face and grinned all the while as if nothing was wrong. You shouldn't have been surprised, Shirleen. Afterward, he's so absolutely filled with remor—

"Shirleen," repeated the warden.

"Oh, excuse me, sir. I was daydreaming. I'd like to have the rest of the day off, if that's OK."

"Are you—all right?"

Why'd he ask? "Why'd you ask, sir?"

"Well," said the warden, "it appears by the looks of your eyes that you might have been crying."

Shirleen rushed out of the office and past Mary, and minutes later she parked her car in front of Piggly Wiggly. Soon, she filled the trunk and rear seat with empty cardboard boxes.

On the way home, doubt visited her. "Maybe," she said, "he'll change." Head shaking fiercely, she pounded the steering wheel hard with the heels of both hands. "No, damn it, I have to change."

• • •

Zak finally noticed the cardboard boxes after he tried to turn the key in the lock the third time. *Those boxes. They're filled with my personal stuff. She's changed the lock.* Grabbing the doorknob, he shook it. "Shir, it's Zak." He put an ear to the door and heard music. This time, he whispered, "Shir, it's me, Zak. I'm sorry."

Still, there was no response.

Kicking the door, he descended the stairs, making a helluva lot of noise. Then, he slammed the outside door shut, which could have been mistaken for a rifle shot.

• • •

After Al Preston returned with the change, Reggie wiped beer foam from his lips. "You serious? You're gonna live with your mother again?"

Zak shrugged.

"Tell you what," offered Reggie. "My place has an extra bedroom and a bed. We could halve all the costs and share cooking and cleaning duties and live happily ever after. How's that sound?"

"Like a plan," said Zak, hitting the bar with the empty shot glass.

At his trial, William Anderson continued his story. "After I told the telephone operator what I done, the next thing I know is Deputy Smolinski's on the line."

Even members of the jury couldn't maintain straight faces at his murder trial.

"And, sir, what did you tell Deputy Smolinski?"

"I stood in our bedroom and watched Miriam and Paul, naked as jaybirds, on my bed, licking each other's you know what's. All of a sudden, Miriam starts screaming, 'I'm coming.' That's when I figured I was going to let them both go from that bed and straight to hell."

Judge Bilkins pounded the gavel time and time again—all to no avail.

• • •

Click. "Car two, what's your location?" asked Richard "Dick" Smolinski, Wood County sheriff's dispatcher. Click.

Why do you care, you nosy bastard? Deputy Dale Bennett was in Car Two, parked in the parking lot at the Baker Street A&W root beer stand. He'd just finished his second chilidog, washed it down with root beer, grabbed the mike, and pushed the button. Click. "This is Car Two. I'm near Sixteenth and Baker, why?" Click.

Click. "Car Two, report to the William Anderson residence, next door to Smoky Joe's tavern." Click.

Click. "Why?" Click.

Click. "'Cause he told me he murdered his wife and her boyfriend." Click.

Bennett snickered. I can see why Big Al assigned that Polack to radio operator and janitor duties. Click. "Killed 'em, you say?" Click.

Click. "That's what I said. Proceed with caution." Click.

Yeah, he likely killed him a squirrel or a deer or something like that. Bennett remained at the root beer stand, ogling Janie Meyers, the carhop with boobs the size and shape of muskmelons.

When he started the engine, Janie came running, her dumbbells a' jumping. "Hubba, hubba," intoned Bennett before he headed the Ford toward highways 13 and 73 north.

Although the flathead V-8 sported an Offenhauser intake with twin Stromberg 97 carburetors, Bennett drove to Smoky Joe's tavern as if he were on a Sunday ride.

Arriving at the Anderson place, he eased the squad onto the gravel driveway and sighted Anderson standing behind a screened door on the back porch.

"Proceed with caution, my ass," Bennett said with a laugh and then killed the engine, exited the vehicle, and arranged the family jewels before dusting off his brogans on opposing pant legs. That's the moment Anderson leveled the lever-action .30-30 and shot three times.

"Jesus Christ," whispered Bennett as he collapsed onto the gravel.

Anderson stood over the deputy as Bennett moaned, "You fucking killed me, you bastard."

Wood County Deputy Sheriff Dale Bennett did not hear the fourth shot.

CHAPTER TWENTY-SEVEN

Judder Brown and four blueshirts escorted Wing Nuts from the Greenhouse to Ego's office in the Administration Building. The lieutenant pointed to the hot seat in front of Ego's desk. "Up there and sit down."

Listen to King Kong. He's lucky we ain't on the streets. I'd bitch slap him so hard he'd feel the sting for a month. Sneering at the lieutenant, whose right eyelid shuddered, Wing Nuts made it up the stairs and performed the ankle chain shuffle to the chair. He sat and grinned at the five screws, whose eyes followed his each and every move.

Jerking from their stares, Wing Nuts checked out Ego-fuckin'-maniac's workspace like a pawnbroker inspecting with a loupe a diamond ring brought in by a foul-breathed wino. The office was twice the size of his cell. It stunk like a confusion of pine oil, paste wax, and stale cigar smoke.

Fluorescent ceiling tubes produced a greenish haze on the off-white walls. On the wall to his left hung a framed airbrushed portrait of a grizzled cowboy with a week's worth of salt-and-pepper stubble, his black ten-gallon hat sweat-stained and dusty, and a faded red-and-white bandanna tied around the neck of his sun-bleached chambray shirt. The brass plaque on the frame's base stated, "They didn't promise me much when I took this job."

Opposite the ramrod was a framed, glass-covered, cross-stitched admonition, "The more you sweat in peace, the less you bleed in war."

On its lower right were the initials JR. *JR, huh? Secamore said his ho's name was Joanie, Joanie Richardson. Yeah, JR.*

The lieutenant and blueshirts separated like the Red Sea when Ego barged through their midst and climbed the stairs. Standing before Wing Nuts, Lord Almighty gazed downward, nostrils flaring like a Doberman's whiffing a trembling Chihuahua's ass. "Why, if it ain't Theodore Kopfmueller hisself."

The lieutenant and four screws scrambled up the stairs and formed a phalanx around the notorious inmate.

"I wanna be alone with Theodore," said His Majesty.

"Sir, do you think you should?" objected the lieutenant.

"You don't have to worry," said His Majesty. "Theodore's a pussy–cat. Go ahead, Theodore, and show the lieutenant you're a pussy cat."

"Meeoooooooow," went Wing Nuts.

His Majesty waited for the four blueshirts and Judder to descend the stairs before he clicked the door shut and returned to his Doberman persona. "What the fuck do you want?"

Wing Nuts had been practicing the lines for a long time. "Remember, Mr. Security Director, the day that that nigger was offed by those spics in the group dog run? I remember it as if it happened yesterday. There I was, mindin' my own business as I'm bein' strip-shook by Sergeant Smith. Remember him? Yeah, you do. You and him were buddies, weren't cha? Smitty finished strip-shakin' me and was takin' me to a dog run when Westra yells at him. Maybe it was God warnin' me to look, but who do I see in that tower, grinnin' like a pair of shit-eatin' dogs?"

As Wing Nuts rose, he reveled in the bulge that pushed against his khakis. "It's all about the law, Your Majesty. The same law that put me in here is gonna lock your ass up in a cell next to mine. At least, you'd better hope so because most of these bad motherfuckers in here will want a piece of your action, but I'll protect your ass—that is, if you give me some of it."

Wing Nuts couldn't help it. He loved every second it took for Ego's face to turn the color of body remnants in a seventy-mile-per-hour head-on crash.

"If that's what you and your Aryans on the streets wanted," said Ego, "Vergenz would've sent that tape to a TV or radio station or, better yet, to the state's attorney general—and not to me. So, stop the bullshit."

Wing Nuts tapped his index fingers together, giving His Majesty his due. "Give the man a kewpie doll." Wing Nuts was past the point of sheer delight. "You're a hundred percent correct, Your Majesty. Everyone's got a price to pay, includin' you."

"What's the charge, Theodore? I'll hafta see if I'm willing to pay."

"Ya got two weeks to transfer me and my next-door rappie, Clark, to GP. Then, you get me outta this shithole within six months—and I ain't talkin' about a transfer neither."

"Look, my hands are tied. DOC directives won't let me get you outta the hole unless you get a recommendation from the inmate advocate."

Feeling as if he just topped off the best sex of his life, Wing Nuts wanted, needed, no, demanded time to bathe in this, his moment of moments. "So, are you willing to pay the price?"

"I am," said His Majesty. "Once I get the advocate's blessing, then we can plan to get you outta here, but not until then."

"OK by me," said the Aryan.

Ego rose and jerked open the door. "Lieutenant?"

"Boss?"

"Take 'im away. Get him outta my sight."

"Right away, boss. OK, Kopfmueller, let's go."

"Meeeeeeowwww."

•••

Ego closed the door and sat for a considerable length of time. With reluctance, he rose from the chair and approached the cowboy on the wall. "I got a story for you. Care to listen? It's a good 'un. Well, there's this guy named Pierre. Him and his men build a suspension bridge longer than the Golden Gate. Yeah, that's what I said—longer than—but get this—after he and his men build it, nobody calls him Pierre, the bridge builder, which kinda pisses him off. Well, after that's finished, Pierre and his men go off to Jap Land and put up a tower higher than the Eiffel. And get this, not a soul calls him Pierre, the tower builder. But—and this is a big but, Pierre sucks one lousy cock. Guess what? Yeah, everyone calls him Pierre, the cocksucker, even his mother."

Ego pulled out a handkerchief and honked. "All these years I been loyal to the state, to this institution, Joanie, the kids." Tears fell like water from a downspout during a mega-storm. "But you know that, don't cha?" Ego sat. "I'm so alone," he told the portrait. "So frigging alone."

After Deputy Dale Bennett breathed his last mournful breath, his killer, William Anderson, got into Bennett's squad, lifted the mike, and pressed the knob. Click. "This is Bill Anderson. I'm heading your way to turn myself in." Click.

Click. "Wha-what happened to Deputy Bennett?" asked the startled Smolinski. Click.

Click. "Right about now I guess him and Saint Pete are having a heart-to-heart." Click.

Click. "Deputy Bennett's dead?" Click.

Click. "Yeah, I killed him." Click

Click. "You killed him?" Click.

Click. "I did." Click.

•••

Anderson drove to the Wood County Jail and said to Sheriff Albert "Big Al" Westhuis, (west house), "You need to lock me up."

Chugging on a stinky stogie, Big Al crushed the killer's nose against his lips with a ham-sized fist. Anderson sank to the floor, exhaling pig-like oinks. "Shaddup, you murdering bastard, or I'll give you something to squeal about."

At the trial, Wood County Coroner Dr. James J. Mullins, poet at heart, described Anderson's knife as "next of kin to Ahab's harpoon." As to Deputy Bennett's cause of death, he said, "Three rifle slugs, like sharpened lava rocks hurled from Mount Vesuvius, tore through the deputy's midsection, lacerating and rupturing multiple organs. The fourth embarked its journey under his chin and exited the skull's crest."

Bennett's widow, sitting in the front row, fainted. Behind her and rising noisily was a red-faced, sun-burnt man wearing bib overhauls and blue chambray work shirt that had seen better days. With salt-and-pepper nostril hairs looking like porcupine quills, he wore the bouquet of a cow barn in addition to a Give 'em hell, Harry reelection button. "Lynch the bastard," he bellowed. Deputies hauled him out of the courtroom.

At the sentencing hearing, Judge Bilkins told Anderson, "The acts of savagery you committed against your unfaithful wife and her lover might be understood, perhaps, but reprehensible, in fact." Pausing, taking off his glasses, and glaring, the judge continued, "But why, sir—why did you kill the deputy? He arrived at your home—at your request."

"He took too much time," said Anderson, "and I don't like waiting."

The magistrate kneaded the bridge of his nose for some time. With spectacles back on, he declared in straining tone, "William Lewis Anderson, you will get used to waiting. You have been found guilty of three premeditated murders. The law leaves me no choice but to sentence you to three life terms at the Waupun State Prison, to be served consecutively."

Anderson looked almost pleased as he told his attorney, "I got only one life to give and he gave me three."

Anderson couldn't have known then he was destined to become Waupun's longest-serving prisoner in the institution's history.

CHAPTER TWENTY-EIGHT

Shirleen had remained in her office the previous week in order to avoid Zak. Her Department of Justice supervisor and handler, Walt Kensinger, had warned her to avoid a relationship.

On Friday, Walt telephoned and told her, "Either carry out your duties as inmate advocate or return to the DOJ for a different assignment."

Monday morning was picture-perfect, with a cloud here and there marbling the azure sky. Locals seemed to be in a good mood as they greeted her.

In the joint, men assigned to the yard gang attending to flower beds or lawns waved. She waved back.

Somehow, she made it to the chain-link gate that would get her into the Greenhouse compound.

Tower Officer Jay Wilkins punched the button that electronically unlocked the gate. She sighed and pushed the gate open, closed it, halfheartedly waving and trudging on. When she opened the door, the reticent Steve Blankley had the Folger Adam key ready.

"Hi, Steve, and how are we today?"

Unbelievably, he answered, and not with one word. "We are doing well, Shirleen, very well, as a matter of fact. How are you? I haven't seen you in—by golly, I haven't seen you in—I don't know how long it's been. How long has it been?"

"It hasn't been that long."

Luckily, Officers Maureen Kelly and Glen Sommers were downing cookies and coffee in the cellblock.

Sommers put down his cup and made his ascent to the second tier. Hesitating momentarily, he looked to Zak's sally port and then back to Shirleen, shaking his head. A moment later, he made his way down the tier and was out of sight.

"We just finished with showers," said Maureen. "I assume you're coming in."

"Yup," said Shirleen, giving Zak a sidelong glance. Thankfully, he was writing in the logbook.

After Blankley keyed her into No-Man's-Land, Zak looked up, smiled pleasantly, and rose to let her in. Shirleen pictured herself falling to the floor and going up in smoke like Oz's wicked witch. "Whom do you want to see?" he whispered.

Don't faint. "Kopfmueller, one zero four four six seven eight."

"Cell Eleven," said Zak, locking the gate and following Shirleen to the cellblock's gate.

Shirleen dared not look into his eyes, fearing she would act the fool. *We're like a pair of opposite pole magnets. Get too close, and—*

"Keep a close watch on our inmate advocate," Zak warned Kelly.

What does he—?

"Will do," said Kelly.

I don't need him to babysit me.

When she reached Eleven, its occupant grabbed the bars, contracting his muscles, inflating his chest. *If you're trying to impress, you've failed.* "Mr. Kopfmueller?" she asked.

"Yeah."

"I'm Miss Hammer."

"Niiiiiice," was his response, his tongue darting in a way that could be interpreted only in a sexual manner.

With amazing speed, Shirleen turned and began her return to the sergeant's sally port.

"Ms. Davis, I apologize."

Shirleen stopped.

"I apologize," the Aryan said again. "I shouldn't have disrespected you."

Shirleen returned. "I accept your apology, but I shouldn't," said Shirleen. "What is it you want, Mr. Kopfmueller?"

"Me and my main man next door—we been locked down so long we don't know what the sun looks like."

Shirleen looked to the cell in order to determine its occupant's name. His fingers were wrapped around the cell's bars. They belonged to a black man. *That an Aryan Nation leader would consider a black man his best friend is bizarre—but for a black man to accept Kopfmueller and what he stands for—that's unthinkable.*

"As to Mr. Clark, he'll have to put in a pass request." Turning to address Wing Nuts, she said, "The fact is, Mr. Kopfmueller, I have read your file, and it's replete with conduct reports. It seems you've had difficulty abiding by institutional rules not only in general population but here in segregation, as well. You've received twenty-three conduct reports since you've been here. As far as I'm concerned, the administration has every right to maintain you in segregated status until you change your negative behaviors."

"Haven't you heard of someone changin' his ways?"

"There's nothing in your files, absolutely nothing," declared Shirleen, "that would prompt me to think that any change has taken place."

Kopfmueller shoved a folded piece of paper through the bars. "Maybe this will change your mind."

After opening and reading the note, Shirleen couldn't remember how she made it to Zak's sally port.

"Anything the matter?" he whispered.

"Yes," said Shirleen, obviously distressed. "Could you come over to my place tonight?"

"Why?"

"I can't tell you here."

"OK."

"That is, before you go to Otto's."

"You know how to hurt a guy." Zak keyed her into his sally port and then keyed open the gate that led to No-Man's-Land.

When Shirleen exited the building, she didn't look back.

Some circuit court judges, wishing to hone tough images for future elections, throw a ton of concurrent sentences at multiple-offense lawbreakers, knowing full well that Joe and Jane Six-Pack don't realize that ten concurrent sentences of ten years each equal one ten-year sentence. Run consecutively, that sentence would be one hundred years. That's why career criminals avoid judges who hand out consecutive, or "wild" sentences.

Judge Bilkins ran William Anderson's three life sentences wild. Thirty-three years and nine months had to pass before Anderson was eligible to meet with the parole board for the first time. In 1973, having served twenty-five years, the gray-haired Anderson was the master of ceremonies at the new inmates' orientation, held monthly on the rec field during warm-weather months and in the Big Top during cold or inclement weather. "Listen up," he started out. "Us inmates have this code. If any one of you violate our code, we'll—" Halting midsentence, he waited for the usual idiot to ask the question.

"You'll what?" queried the month's nitwit.

That was the signal for murderer Willie "Big Man" Hampton to join Anderson. Weighing three hundred and fifty-seven pounds, the six-foot-five Big Man could easily rip apart prison-issue shirtsleeves by a simple contraction of his biceps.

As he scowled at the fish, his eyeballs nearly leaped out of their sockets, his teeth reminiscent of Arlington National Cemetery markers. Finally, a gorilla-size paw defiantly latched on to the prominence that bulged in the center of his crotch, his eyes studying the questioner. "If' you break the code, muhfukuh, the second thing I'm gonna do is to force you to suck a bucket of my love juice."

With that said, Big Man turned one incorrigible degree at a time, eyeballing each new man. No idiot among them dared inquire of Big Man's first act as their collective Adam's apples bobbed like apples floating in a water barrel during a hurricane.

Big Man didn't keep them guessing. "Because the first thing I'm gonna do is bust all your teeth outta your heads—one tooth at a time."

CHAPTER TWENTY-NINE

Smelling like a mixture of talcum powder and English Leather cologne, Zak was dressed in T-shirt and Levi's as he drove to Shirleen's, parked Shoo-fly, zipped up the stairs, and knocked once on the door.

As she opened the door, he noticed she also wore jeans but with a salmon-colored sweater that enhanced her bronze skin. *If she touches me,* he thought, *I'll do anything, say any—*

"Thank you for coming," said Shirleen, pointing to a dark blue love seat with white throw pillows on each corner. "Have a seat. Coffee's on the stove, or perhaps you prefer a Coke?"

"No, thank you. What did you want to see me about—that is, before I go to Otto's?"

Shirleen's nostrils flared. "You of all people should know I didn't want you coming here soused to the gills."

"I'm sorry, Shir. I really didn't mean to start off on the wrong foot."

"But you did." Shirleen handed Zak the note. "This is what Kopfmueller handed to me after I turned down his request for a GP recommendation."

Zak unfolded the note and read: Don't try to conceal secrets. Aryans are everywhere. If you don't do what I want, my boys and I will tell everyone in this shithouse of a prison who you really work for and who your brother was.

After Zak reread the note four times, he lifted and looked at Shirleen. "What's this about?"

"I'm trying to tell you, Zak."

"You're trying?"

"Yes." Taking a seat opposite him, she finally made eye contact. "Zak, I work for the Wisconsin Department of Justice, not the Department of Corrections. I'm a DOJ agent, an undercover agent. My real boss is Attorney General Robert Ward, not Warden Palestine. The warden nor anyone else here is aware of my real job, and that is to investigate Inmate Earl Davis's murder at Governor Todd's request. Years later, it's a helluva time to start an investigation, I tell you."

Zak stiffened, aware if he said anything else, it would be in anger. He counted to ten, but the swirling volcanic gases he felt became ever hotter, ever more explosive. He started counting again.

Shirleen added, "And there's more."

"More? There's more?"

"Yes, Earl Davis was my brother."

Zak drew in a deep breath and let out a whistle.

Shirleen continued. "I was born with the last name of Davis, but after my parents were killed in a car accident, Auntie Louise cared for me and Earl. She's always been like a mother to me. That's why when I became old enough, I legally changed my last name to Auntie's last name, Hammer. I did it to honor all of what she had done for me."

"Why didn't you tell me?"

"Zak, I couldn't. I wanted to. Oh, how I wanted to. Zak, those Cobras who killed my brother almost got away with murder and then were transferred to a federal prison, due to the efforts of Marion "Ego" Richardson. To this very moment, I believe he had something to do with Earl's death. I know he was in the tower while my brother was killed. He was watching the Cobras murder my brother. And get this: the tower officer he was with at the time is now Captain Blake. I have a strong hunch Ego had something to do with Earl's death, but I don't have enough evidence to bring yet. I realize this all sounds like some cheap novel, brother and sister on opposite sides of the law and—"

"This is too much," said Zak.

"What do you mean, too much?"

"Why should I believe you now?"

Shirleen's eyes were ablaze. "You don't believe me?"

"I don't know if I can. Can't you understand?"

"I want you to leave, Zak. Now."

Zak stood. "Aren't you afraid I'll blow your cover?"

"I have no control over what you do. I never have had control over you and never will."

When Zak stepped into the hallway and before he could turn back to face her, Shirleen had already slammed the door shut and at once locked it.

Bounding down the stairs, Zak knew one thing for certain: he needed a drink.

• • •

The next day, Betty's Corner Café locals gawked at Walter Kensinger as he entered the restaurant. Wearing a camel sport coat over an impeccably white dress shirt, vertically halved by a striped brown, gold, white, and red tie, his attire was complemented with dark brown trousers, dark socks, and satiny not glossy cordovan wingtip shoes. His well-combed white hair, intense blue eyes, and deeply tanned skin prompted him to look more like a successful CEO of a Fortune 500 company than a bureaucrat. Smiling, he said "Hi" to Shirleen as he sat opposite her in the booth.

Jeanne Marie was there instantly. "Hi," she said. Turning to Shirleen, Jeanne remarked, "If this is what you traded Zak in for, take my word for it, honey, you made a wise choice." The waitress turned back to Walter. "Care for something to eat or drink, honey?"

Walter grinned. His teeth were as white as his shirt. "How about a large Tab?"

"One large Tab coming up. Care for anything to eat?"

"No," said Walter, "I have to watch my waistline."

"You don't have to worry a bit about your waist, honey. You're in excellent shape."

"Thank you," said Walter. "I'll accept that as a compliment for an old man."

"Old sha-mold," said the waitress. "You're just the right age." She headed for the fountain, wiggling her attributes.

Walter looked out the window and spotted a Waupun squad car, its driver a former DOJ agent. Walt turned to Shirleen and then twice jerked his chin toward the squad. "That's Max Steenbergen. He used to work for us. I'm pretty sure he just made me."

Walter harrumphed before he changed the subject matter. "Didn't I warn you to not mix your professional life with your personal?"

"Walter, I'm a grown woman. I—"

Jeanne Marie returned with the Tab, a straw already in the glass. She leaned toward Walter, displaying her cleavage.

"Thank you," said Walter. "You're the most beautiful waitress I've seen today."

"Aw, I betcha you tell every waitress that." Jeanne Marie eyeballed Shirleen. "Is he married?"

"I'm afraid so."

"They're always the best ones," said the waitress.

"If I weren't," said Walter, "married, that is, I'd come courting you."

"Isn't he sweet?" Jeanne Marie grinned and left, wiggling her behind even more than normal.

"She's quite the gal, isn't she?"

"Yes," said Shirleen, "but don't you want to see the note?"

"Naturally," said Walter, accepting it and quickly reading before asking, "And all this Kopfmueller wants is—?"

"A recommendation that he and a Brother-men gang member be released to general population. A formal recommendation from the inmate advocate is SOP."

"Who's the other inmate?"

"Clark, Jeremy Clark."

"Clark? Hmm, name's not familiar."

"He killed his stepfather and while in prison murdered another inmate who I'm told cut Clark in a very bad place after he tried to rape him."

"OK," said Kensinger, "give Wing Nuts what he wants. By the way, we have a hunch who our mole is, but we can't prove it. It's only a matter of time. In the meantime, if Zak—drunk or sober—says anything about your being with us or you hear anything, and I mean *anything* about your being with us, we close up shop at once—you hear?"

Shirleen nodded. "I hear."

"Everything's going to be fine," said Walter before he lifted the glass of Tab and drank.

Jeanne Marie slid a quarter down the jukebox's coin chute. A few moments later, Carly Simon sang, "Everybody have you heard/He's gonna buy me a mockingbird/And if that mockingbird don't sing/He's gonna buy me a diamond ring/And if that diamond ring won't shine/He's gonna surely break this heart of mine."

Howard Carter, a thirty-one-year-old ne'er-do-well, on a sun-dappled day barged into a Madison, Wisconsin, draft board office. The clerical staff were so astonished that they watched in awe as Howard seized an armload of file folders and scooted outdoors, where he held them aloft in front of a gathering of mostly youthful protesters and a few scribes plus TV reporters and their camera operators.

Sporting whatever facial hair could be finagled, the male revolutionaries were outfitted by Goodwill Industries in deliberately ripped blue jeans and long-sleeved plaid flannel shirts. Most of the young revolutionary ladies had long, straightened, and ironed hair framing innocent faces. Wearing a mixed bag of granny glasses, tie-dyed T-shirts, bib overalls, fatigue pants, cutoff jeans, GI raincoats, and combat boots, leather sandals, or earth shoes, they did not shave legs or armpits.

"What do we want?" Howard screamed to the band of wannabe subversives.

"Peace," they howled with vehemence and protracted anger.

Howard seemed to be foaming at the mouth. "When do we want it?"

"Now," answered the crowd.

Howard stooped before he rose, lifting a red gasoline can and dramatically baptizing the files with the flammable mixture. (Having a modicum of sense, media folks backed away, camera operators exchanging wide-angle lenses for telephotos). Poised betwixt Howard's thumb and forefinger was a wooden match. Zapping the Lucifer head down the legs of his blue jeans, Howard watched as a puff of smoke preceded the flame.

Meanwhile, the crowd chanted, "Burn! Burn! Burn!" In that very moment, Howard earned his moniker, penned first by a Capital Times reporter—Howard "Burn" Carter.

Raising the match high, Burn released it with Hollywood flamboyance. Whoosh. Pandemonium. Helmeted cops came out of nowhere and were upon the group, flailing away with shiny batons, all of which made good TV film footage.

Burn made his getaway in a VW Microbus, driven by a dude who shared his Thai-weed stash. The pair headed to Canada. (On the same day, William Jefferson Clinton of Hope, Arkansas, met with communist officials in Moscow, where Clinton reportedly accepted a Russian-style doobie, its contents grown in Cuba. He did not inhale.)

The FBI discovered Burn in Canada. Mounties arrested him. After much haggling, Canuck jurists extradited him to the United States, where a Madison jury found him guilty of state charges of burglary and destroying government property. Solemnly, the judge handed Burn two concurrent ten-year sentences.

In response, Burn turned to his followers and held high the V for Victory sign. "Peace," he yelled. With an abject loathing of authority, he faced his honor, lifted a leg, and farted like a horse. Young folks followed suit in addition to mooning press members, their flashbulbs popping, reminiscent of a Chinese New Year celebration.

CHAPTER THIRTY

Joanie's snoring hadn't kept Ego awake; a busy brain had. He lay there, recalling a conversation he had with one-armed Tommy "The Greek" Stephanapolous. Like many Italian-connected mobsters doing time, Tommy bragged about his associations with the Milwaukee Balistrieri family. "They got this contract killer who's so goddamn good, there ain't a coroner in the world who can tell his victims died from anything but natural causes. And nobody knows who the killer is. He's that anonymous."

"So, how do your guys get in touch with him—in the Yellow Pages under Murder Incorporated, and how do you pay him, by Western Union?"

"Nah," said Tommy the Greek, "the boys place a personal ad in the *Journal*—not the *Sentinel*—and it's gotta say, 'Jessie or Kitty or Tom or Mike,' or whatever, 'all is forgiven. Call home.' We leave a pay phone number. It protects us—and him."

"Yeah?" said Ego, playing along.

"Yeah, the way he gets his moolah is he tells the boys to send a young gangbanger with his money to a public establishment like a tavern."

"So, why doesn't the gangbanger tell your boys what this guy looks like?"

"When they return, they don't know nothing, won't say nothing, and get pissed off if anybody questions them."

More than a few men were doing time at Waupun for having attempted to contract the murder of an estranged spouse or business partner. Most contract killers actually turned out to be wired undercover DOJ operatives. "How do ya know if he's not some undercover cop?"

"Cause this dude's gonna call you the day after the ad runs, and it's gonna be one minute after noon exactly. Not one second earlier. Not one second later. It's gonna be one fucking minute exactly, sixty seconds, not sixty-one, not fifty-nine, after noon."

What more can I lose than the money it costs to run the ad?

Joanie had stopped snoring. As quiet as a cat on the prowl, Ego got out of bed, descended the stairs to his shop, and pulled out the next-to-bottom drawer of the black Sears Craftsman six-drawer toolbox. It rolled out silently on ball bearings.

Yawning, he lifted the three-eighths-inch drive socket set tray. Under it was the plan. Picking up the sheaf of papers, he sat on the stool and swiped at his eyes before he put on his reading glasses. Although the plan was not totally fleshed out, it was close.

He'd have a riot to cover Wing Nuts's attempted escape. Inmates did not normally riot if they were having a bad day or the institution's chef screwed up the menu. They needed a cause. Eventually, he'd have to make a cause happen.

Watching his head movie starring Theodore Kopfmueller, the Aryan hides in the Industries Building basement while the riot gets underway. Theodore is armed with a zip gun Ego has made in this very workshop, along with enough .22 long rifle cartridges to get the other jobs done.

Kevin Blake arrives, prepared to bash in Wing Nuts's skull with a baseball bat Ego has hidden inside the building. Theodore surprises Blake and shoots him dead. Theodore goes upstairs to the third floor, sees the Tower Four officer below him, and takes him out. *Too bad,* Ego thought, *if Ben doesn't have the day off. He's a good man.* Ego shrugged. *But better Ben than me.*

Theodore tosses a grappling hook supplied by Ego to the tower's guardrail. The hook catches. He ties his end to the handrail of the Industries Building stairwell, exits the window, and takes one, maybe two arm swings.

Sharpshooter Jack Blaine exhales, inhales, and holds, trigger finger squeezing ever so slightly. *Ka-snap. Splat.* Theodore drops to the concrete, looking like road kill.

Jesus, that hurts. Ego grabbed his chest, thinking he might be having a heart attack again. *Nah, it's a sour stomach. Must've been the garlic.* Checking his watch, he made his way up the stairs and headed for the fridge. *Warm milk's what I need.*

"Honey, is that you?" Joanie called out.

He drew near the bedroom door. "Yeah," he whispered. "I can't sleep. I'm warming up some milk."

"Oh," she said.

"Armpit Annie approaching," Tower Eight officer yelped into his handheld as below him strode Ms. Ann Knepler—the K was not silent, nor was she. Ann was the ACLU attorney in charge of state prisoner issues. A liberated woman, she had forsworn shaving even one strand of body hair. Furthermore, she enhanced her nearly unseen mustache hairs with an eyebrow pencil.

Behind those thick spectacles, her irises looked like jumbo black olives floating in a martini glass. Her scuffed earth shoes offset the matronly paisley granny dress, its loose cut sheltering bantam-size breasts. Toting an attaché case almost half her size in one hand, she carried a long-stick black umbrella with the other, no matter the weather.

She had this peculiar habit, which earned her the Waupun moniker "Armpit Annie." While in a conversation with anyone, she scratched opposing shoulder blades, exposing underarm jungles from which Sgt. Morris Dunlop claimed he saw a pair of bats escape and fly in formation like a couple of fighter jets. She also gained Queen "Dip Wad" status with her salty greeting to blueshirts, "How the fuck ya doin'?"

Sgt. Greg Moen, bubble sergeant, responded, "Not so fucking bad. How about you?"

Up came her bad finger.

Annie asked for and received permission to meet with inmates perceived as leaders, including Howard "Burn" Carter, who did not know that a certain female law student was among the peaceniks who exhorted him to burn draft board files. "How the fuck ya doin'?" she said, clamping on to Burn's paw.

Thinking she could be his ticket out of Waupun, Burn wrote Ann a letter so steamy the envelope nearly sealed itself. Since attorney mail was privileged and could be inspected for contraband only from its exterior, the letter was sent on its way.

After she received his letter, Annie and Burn began writing daily and passionately via their official legal mail. In time, she requested to be placed on Burn's official visitor's list. The warden approved her application since he feared legal action if he failed to do so. On their one permissible kiss, Burn all but checked out what Ann ate for breakfast with his tongue. "I bet your pussy tastes like a cherry Popsicle," he whispered, Annie nearly overcome by Burn's poetic phrasings.

Soon, Ann decided to make a political statement by marrying Burn. She arrived, wearing earth shoes under a wedding dress that bore a Christian Dior label.

Klieg lights on, TV cameramen juxtaposed bars and smiling bride with mustachio. Dodge County Circuit Court Judge Monty Hackworth was opposed to prison marriages but officiated anyway in the ceremony held in the prison's Visiting Room.

While Ann intently listened to His Honor, she scratched and reporters, cameramen, the Visiting Room officer, inmates, visitors, even His Honor, swore they witnessed a couple of bats emerge from those hairy armpits and fly in precise airborne maneuvers.

CHAPTER THIRTY-ONE

While sitting across Ego in Ego's office, Kevin Blake refashioned the tower scene that occurred years ago. "No, major," he objected, "we did not set up that fight, you did, and I'm not going to lie for you. You'll have to suffer the consequences of your actions."

Reality, however, kicked in. Blake's right eyelid shuddered, which upset him. He pushed a fingertip to the offending fold.

Ego looked up. "What's wrong?"

Blake's jaws clenched. His knees pumped as if he were running in place.

"I asked, what's wrong?"

"Two things."

Ego waited. "Well?"

"You really want to know?"

"Would I be asking if I didn't?"

"OK, I got a tape in the mail from Vergenz."

Ego's face turned blotchy.

"It's the same as yours." Valiantly, Blake fought tears. "Kathy, she wanted to know what it was."

"What'd you tell her?"

"Like you, I said it was a tape from the lawyer who works with us on gangs."

"OK, and the second."

"Shirleen. I don't know why it slipped my mind but a couple of months ago, she asked me if you and I were in the tower the day Davis was killed."

Ego waited. "And?"

"And I said yeah, that I had to shoot a warning shot in order to stop those guys from killing Davis, but he died anyway."

"Did she say why she was interested in something that happened so long ago?"

"Yeah, she said she knew Davis's aunt in Milwaukee."

•••

Juan Medina was found guilty of second-degree murder in a Waupaca County circuit court. He was to be transported by deputies to Waupun on Monday. Thus, on Sunday, his family members attended Mass at five thirty in the morning before they headed the '48 Ford F1 pickup truck with its straight-six flathead engine and patina of surface rust to the county jail. Everyone, including Juan's wife, was dressed in her or his Sunday best. The men wore cowboy hats and cowboy boots.

Not allowed to speak Spanish, they did their best in American English. When the nice deputy rose and whispered that visiting hours were over, Juan's eldest brother, Pablo, warned his younger brother, "Juan, do not trust nobody at that place, no Chicano, no gringo, no nigger, nobody. Those bastards will turn you into *marciones*." Pablo halted and looked to the nice deputy before adding, "Girl."

Nodding, the deputy offered his two cents' worth. "Pay heed to what your brother says, Juan."

Juan inflated his chest as far as his torso permitted. "I swear to everyone here and to the virgin"—he made a sign of the cross—"that I will remain a man."

Rising first from their chairs were Mama and Papa with etched facial lines from years of working in the fields under a scorching sun. Papa used a cane. They made it to their youngest, touched him, and nodded.

Pablo, his wife, Anita, and their two daughters were next. Two other brothers and two sisters and their husbands waited for their turn.

Felicita, Juan's eighteen-year-old wife, was last. Hanging on to Juan, she wailed as the nice deputy, with Pablo's help, finally broke her grasp.

• • •

Juan Medina jumped up from the dining room table and backed off, his fork's tines pointed at a pair of Anglo inmates with whom he had been sitting. "I kill you," he howled.

The dining room became as silent as the falling snow inmates could see through the barred windows.

Sergeant Griffin, ordered in on his day off and performing dining room duties, made his way to the table. When Zak was within a few feet of the table, the more nervous of the two sitting men shouted, "He started it, Sarge. I swear he don't understand a fucking word of English."

"He's crazy, Sarge," agreed the other.

Zak pushed open palms at them. "Calm down," he ordered.

"I am calm," screeched the flighty one.

"You speak English, amigo?" asked Zak.

Juan nodded and said, "Yes."

"What's your name and number?"

"Juan. I am Juan Medina, number eight nine eight six six four eight."

"OK, Juan, I want you to give me that fork."

"I will kill them before they make me a girl."

"Honest, Sarge, we said nothing to him," said the edgy inmate.

"Me," said the other, "and my rappie, we said or done nothing wrong. Here we was, eating our meal, minding our own business, and that little fella jumps up and says he's going to kill us."

Zak's eyes were riveted to the fork. "Juan, give me the fork."

Medina's head shook. "I done nothing wrong. They did."

"We was just talkin' and all a sudden he goes ape shit, says he's goin' to kill us. Honest, Sarge, that's the way it went down."

"You can explain yourselves later," said Zak, holding out his hand. "Juan, give me that fork."

Sighing, Juan handed the fork to Zak before Major Ericson and six utility officers zipped into the dining hall. "OK, Sergeant, what seems to be the problem here?"

"I witnessed this inmate"—Zak pointed to Medina—"threatening those two inmates with a weapon, this fork." Zak pointed at the seated men. "He told me he was defending himself because those two were trying to coerce him into having sex."

"We done nothing of the kind, Major," said the anxious inmate.

"Fuck it, I'm coming clean," said the other inmate. "I done nothing wrong, but him"—he pointed to the nervous man—"he was trying to put a hit on the beaner."

A number of nearby inmates looked to each other and nodded and grinned.

"We'll take care of this, Sergeant," Ericson told Zak. "Gentlemen, I want you to rise for a pat-down." He turned to Juan and said, "We're going to pat you down too, Pablo."

"My name is Juan."

"Sorry about that, Juan," said Ericson. "Empty your pockets and put whatever you have in them onto that table."

Zak returned to the cafeteria line alongside a pair of blueshirts, arms crossed against their chests. They watched officers escort each cuffed inmate out of the room, one at a time. The dining hall resumed its normal hectic pace. "It's noisy as hell," observed Zak with a smile.

Although Howard "Burn" Carter married Armpit Annie mainly to get out of prison, that didn't happen. So, he decided that if he had to do the time, he wanted to do it in style by making a "close association" with Ego. Burn, one day made up an extra juicy story, involving multiple inmates and conspiring blueshirts, a social worker on drugs, a pair of lesbian nurses, and Miss Victoria Prim, the school clerk, who, he alleged, blew inmates in the principal's office when the principal was absent.

Ego placed the cons in the hole while the warden suspended alleged wrongdoing staff members with pay, pending investigations.

That evening, down to bra and panties in a shady game of strip poker with three blueshirts, Miss Prim leaped onto the bar at Otto's Bar & Grill and did a slow grind to the strains of Charlie Rich's "Behind Closed Doors."

"It's time I spread some wild oats," she shrieked, unhitching the bra and tossing it to a mob who stretched for the grab as if it were a Green Bay Packer football.

The next morning, loud, rattling sounds awakened her. Lying next to her was Jack Blaine in all his nakedness, holding his penis as if it were King Arthur's sword. Instantly, Miss Prim got down on her knees and prayed for a crop failure.

The lifers put out a contract on Burn for his most outlandish prevarication. His wife, Armpit Annie, met with Warden Palestine, who contacted Kyle Marston, Governor Avery Todd's aide. The next day, Annie visited Todd in his office. "If you help my husband, I'll do anything," she pleaded, Todd's fingers exploring her thigh.

"Anything?" he asked.

The next morning, Warden Palestine ordered an emergency summit of the Reclassification Committee, whose members pissed and moaned but nevertheless approved Burn's immediate transfer to a minimum-security prison camp near Superior.

Awaiting Burn were Sgt. Robert Smeltz and inmate Richard "Wretched" Riley with shaved head, pig nose, squinty eyes, no neck, and biceps the size of Desoto Hemi pistons. Wretched was known for granting lifetime disabilities to inmates who refused to meet his sexual demands. "If you don't hum on this, you commie draft-card-burning motherfucker, you'll be tied in a wheelchair for the rest of your brief life."

"Sergeant?" begged Burn to the three-striper, who turned his focus elsewhere as Wretched attempted to detach Burn's head from the rest of him.

"Ever hear of Officer Dan Spaulding?" asked Sergeant Smeltz.

"Yes," gasped Burn, writhing on the floor, "he works at Waupun."

"You shoulda said 'worked.' Dan's my nephew, but a certain lying son of a bitch got him suspended on bullshit charges."

Smeltz disappeared a moment before Wretched waggled what should have been attached to the underside of a steamy Clydesdale stallion. "How about Moon River? Even a commie-pinko snitch-ass punk oughta be able to hum Moon River."

CHAPTER THIRTY-TWO

Ego drove to the *Milwaukee Journal*'s offices on West State Street, where a clerk, a pretty young thing standing behind a counter, asked, "May I help you, sir?"

"Yeah, I want to put this in Personals." Ego handed her a folded sheet of paper, which she opened and placed on the counter, smoothing it out. After counting each word, she asked, "And when do you wish this to run?"

"As soon as you can."

She attempted a smile. "Sunday would be best. More people read the Sun—"

"That's fine."

She punched buttons on an adding machine, pulled the handle, punched in some more numbers, and pulled the handle twice. She ripped the paper from the machine and handed it to Ego. "That'll be eighteen dollars and ninety-five cents."

Ego handed her a twenty.

Smiling, she gave Ego the change and said with a pout, "I hope Jessie calls."

Ego momentarily blanked out. Then, he finally recovered. Jessie was the name he used in the ad. "Oh," he said, "me and her mother hope so, too." Then, he added to the drama of the moment, "Maybe, we were too hard on her. We were strict for her own good, you know."

Nodding, the clerk looked as if she might cry.

When Ego arrived back in Waupun, James Biggs, visitor's entrance officer, was his usual self. "Didja hear, boss, about Jim Smith? Used to work in the Greenhouse?"

"What about 'im?"

"He's dead, boss. Folks say he drowned in his own vomit."

• • •

Wearing his usual casual and uncoordinated outfit, Mayor Fred Johnson, Ego's best buddy since grade-school days, entered Chief of Police Maurice "Maury" Rogan's office. Johnson seemed a bit edgy, which was rather unusual. "Anything I can do you out of, Mayor?" Rogan pleasantly asked.

Johnson went to the window behind Rogan's chair and lifted a blind. "Sorry, Maury," said the city leader. Grinning, he added, "I'm a poet and don't know it, but I sure as hell ain't Longfellow. Maury, I need your help. We gotta help Butch Richardson. He's got a problem we can handle—that is—I think we can. His problem is this gal, Ann Secamore. She hasn't been living in town long. Butch says this Secamore gal is the Aryan Nation's main source of intelligence between inside and outside members. Butch—he'd like to get rid of her, make it a lot easier for him to run that prison, if you know what I mean."

The chief swallowed what must've been kin to a cat's hairball. Next, he rearranged some papers on his desk. Then, he answered cautiously, slowly. "Fred, I don't think I need to remind you that these aren't the frontier days. I can't run off citizens just like that. My men and I represent the law and uphold it. We would never think of dishonoring it."

"I'm not asking you to break the law, Chief. Butch is a lifelong friend, and this gang stuff is tearing him apart."

"So, he thinks this Secamore's the communication source between the outside Aryans and the insiders, eh?"

"No, Maury, he's certain she is."

Rogan's head bobbed. "Let me put on my thinking cap," he said, leaning back in his chair, picking up a stogie he'd left in the ashtray, knocking off the ash, and relighting it. He exhaled more than a few clouds while carefully examining his fingernails. Finally, his eyes jumped up and made contact with the mayor. "Say, I got this nephew, Joey Miller, a Rock Hudson look-alike. My sister Joanne keeps pestering me to hire him, but you know the city's policy about nepotism. If you let me hire him, I'll assign him to court Secamore, if you get my drift, and see if we can't interest her in leaving town."

The mayor let out a long sigh. "Chief, you have my blessings to hire this movie-star nephew of yours—on a temporary basis, that is—and if she leaves town, I'll grease the skids so he can get a permanent job here."

"I couldn't ask for a fairer deal than that," said the obviously pleased chief.

•••

Lt. Judder Brown couldn't figure out where he'd gone wrong. Butch had canceled their office meetings and had been treating the lieutenant like a red-haired stepchild.

Judder had difficulty getting any sleep. So, he made an appointment with Dr. Damon, who prescribed Valium.

One yellow pill followed by a few shots of Old Forester did the trick. Better yet, Judder increased the dosage along with a few extra shots and slept like a baby.

•••

Almost noon. Ego pretended he was interested in a pair of boots in Brooks's shoe store window. An outdoor pay phone, its number he used in the *Milwaukee Journal* ad, was a mere ten feet away.

Turning away from the window, he looked across the street at the National Bank, but a Greyhound bus, being put through its gears, came between him and the bank and fouled the air with diesel exhaust. It smelled like an old kerosene stove his father had in the machine shed when Ego was a kid.

He checked his watch; it was taking its good-natured time today. The prison whistle began its noontime wail. One minute later—sixty seconds exactly—not fifty-nine, or sixty-one, the payphone rang. Shaking, he lifted the receiver. "Hello," he said.

"To whom am I speaking?" asked a male voice.

"Bob Roberts," said Ego, "Mr. Bob Roberts."

The man on the other end chuckled. "Sounds OK to me, Mr. Roberts. Most of my customers pick John Smith. I assume you have work for me."

"I do."

"How many?"

"How many?" Ego's bladder announced its need to be evacuated. "How many what?"

"How many students do you want dismissed?"

Students. Dismissed? "Oh, I understand. One. I want one dismissed."

"That'll be ten thousand dollars in small bills, no consecutive numbers."

"I don't make much more than that in a year," complained Ego.

"You have two days. On the third day, we will converse at the same time, same phone number. Please bring with you a pen or pencil and some paper to write on."

"That's not much time," was all Ego got out before the dial tone blared in his ear.

The next day, he cashed a Vanguard Prime money market check for ten thousand five hundred dollars at the National Bank. The money was for his and Joanie's retirement buffer. He spent the rest of the day traveling north on Highway 41, getting off at different exits, buying a candy bar or a cup of coffee and getting change for hundred-dollar bills. Two days later, exactly one minute after noon, he lifted the ringing pay phone. "Mr. Roberts?"

"Yeah," said Ego.

"I assume you have the cash in the proper denominations?"

"I do," answered Ego.

"Good. You'll need to write down my instructions."

Ego fumbled for a piece of paper in his wallet, placed it on the booth's shelf and next fumbled for his pen in his shirt pocket. Finally, it came out.

"Is that a Mont Blanc?"

Ego froze. No doubt about it, he had to urinate. Now.

"If you continue to look for me, Mr. Roberts, I might be forced to dismiss you."

Ego's eyes glommed onto the shelf. "I'll be no problem," he whispered.

"Good. Have a male courier meet me at the La Cage in Milwaukee at five thirty tomorrow afternoon."

"Courier at La-what? How do you spell that?"

"Capital L, small a. Then, add the word cage like in a zoo—or prison. It's at eight zero one South Second Street."

"Eight zero one South—"

"Second," repeated the killer. "Your courier is to be athletic, a good-looker, and a good deal younger than you."

"Athletic, good-looking, younger than me." *Blake. Women go gaga over him. He looks like Troy Donahue.*

The driver of a blue-and-white '66 Ford Galaxie 500 two-door hardtop slammed on the brakes because he followed too closely a '70 maroon Olds Ninety-Eight whose driver had stopped in order for an adult cat to cross Main Street.

Tires squealed, chrome crunched, metal brayed, glass broke, and soon both drivers were out of their cars, shouting at one another, but the contract killer continued talking and Ego continued writing. "He'll bring the money in a dark blue gym bag. Inside, with the money will be the student's name, picture or pictures if you have them, home, work addresses, and any other pertinent information. When your man arrives at the La Cage, he should tell the bartender his name—which is?"

"Hold it," said Ego, who turned away from the fender bender. "Did you say blue gym bag?"

“Yes, also the student’s name you want dismissed, home and work address, pictures, info—I also need the name of your courier.”

“Ballad, Jim Ballad.”

“Ballad,” repeated the contract killer. “Like a song, right?”

“On the money,” said Ego, writing down Blake’s fictitious name in case he forgot. The dial tone blared. Ego placed the phone on the hook. He knew better than to look down the street at Waupun’s only other downtown pay phone.

•••

The jukebox was playing nonstop at Otto’s. Temporary cop Joey Miller sat on a stool next to Ann Secamore and politely asked her if she cared to be his pool table partner in a doubles match.

“Sure, why not?”

After winning two games in a row and downing a second beer, Ann said, “You know, you look just like—”

“Rock Hudson,” completed Joey. “Everybody says that. Speaking of movie stars, you wanna go to a movie in Fondy on Friday night?”

“Fondy?”

“Fond du Lac. Let’s say I pick you up at six thirty.”

“Sure, why not?”

“If ya tell me where I should pick ya up, that is.”

“At the upstairs apartment at three-oh-nine West Brown.”

Joey arrived in a turquoise ’69 Mustang convertible with white top and an eight-track tape player. “Which movie are we going to see?” asked Ann.

“Steve McQueen’s in it along with that fag, Dustin Hoffman. It’s called *Papillon*,” said Joey.

“Why do you say Dustin Hoffman’s a fag?”

Joey shrugged. “A man knows those things.”

“Well, you’re wrong. He’s married and got kids.”

While McQueen was making it with a native island girl, Joe dropped five and copped a feel. Ann turned to him, smiled, and pressed his hand harder. In no time at all, he was playing with a nipple. Their tongues engaged; Joey's free hand rubbed her crotch.

They did it all night long and into the morning, taking yet another turn after brunch. Without any prompting from Joey, Ann confided to him why she was in Waupun.

Naturally, Joey reported everything to Uncle Maury.

The next evening, Joey and Max Steenbergen arrived at 309 West Brown. Max did the knocking.

Opening the door, dressed in a nearly see-through negligee, Ann didn't seem surprised but instead appeared disappointed. She exhaled smoke directly at Joey. "Is Joey your name?"

Joey nodded.

Ann turned to Max. "What is it you fellows want?"

"We know you work for the Aryan Nation and are a go-between between the cons and their members on the street. That's not a good thing, not good at all," said Max, shaking his head.

Tossing eye daggers at Joey, Ann then turned to eyeball Max. "Like I asked, what is it you want?"

Max shrugged. "Get lost and never be found."

Ann took a long drag and exhaled another cloud. "Tomorrow soon enough? Greyhound comes at noon."

"Tomorrow it'll have to be."

Placing thumb and forefinger less than an inch apart, Ann placed those digits a foot from Max's eyes.

"What's that?" he asked.

Ms. Secamore laughed derisively. "It's Joey's wee-wee size. His thumb's longer than his dick." And with that said, she slammed the door shut.

Max glanced at Joey's thumb. "Now, don't even think for a second I believed her."

"She's a lying bitch," growled Joey.

Max couldn't wait to tell the rest of the shift about what the Secamore gal had said about the department's Rock Hudson look-alike.

•••

Kevin Blake headed the blue-and-black-striped '69 Mustang Mach I on Highway 41 South to Milwaukee. He gazed in the side mirror. His hair billowed as fingertips stroked it. The sunglasses were damned expensive. He could've been in an Ipana toothpaste commercial. He'd chosen a simple, elegant, light blue sport shirt, the gold chain birthday present from Kathy, its glitter highlighting the chest hair.

When he first saw the present she had purchased for him, he was not happy. "Jesus, Kath, women wear necklaces, not men."

She and their two teenage daughters snickered and laughed. "Plenty of with-it men wear gold chains," declared Jenna, his older daughter, "including just about every big-name Hollywood star."

"That's because most of 'em are fags," retorted Blake.

His negativity caused Kathy to cry. Feeling like an all-time heel, he let Jenna put the chain around his neck as Jill and Kathy applauded and complimented him.

So pleased was his wife that she gave the birthday boy another surprise—this time in bed.

"Why are you putting Vaseline up there?" he demanded.

"So I can push these up there."

He stiffened. "What the hell are they?"

"They're beads."

"They got a crucifix on the end of them?"

"No, silly," she laughed, "they're special beads. When you are just about to come, you have to let me know somehow."

He was not sure what she was up to.

A moment later, she licked at his chest, ever going downward. Blake tried to think of anything but what Kath was doing. Ultimately, as he knew it was impossible to hold out forever, he felt himself losing. He yawped, "I'm coming."

Kathy raised and karate-chopped the erect penis.

Moaning and rolling and writhing, Blake pulled himself into a fetal position. "For golly sakes, that hurt."

"Shhhhhhh," she warned and then squealed in laughter.

"What's so funny?"

"Hush," she said. "You're gonna wake the girls."

"Those beads. What're they about?"

"You'll find out."

With deliberation, her own needs to be met, Kathy knelt, hands cupping her fine breasts as she leaned ever forward and urged her husband to suckle. After his tongue darted out and visited the aureoles, he bit.

It was obvious that was exactly what she had wanted, demanded, and needed because after she exhaled in utter joy, Kathy caressed him once again to a place of intensity.

Head bucking from side to side, he ushered forth, "I'm com—"

She yanked the string of beads.

Instantly, Blake was launched to another world beyond a hundred galaxies to a black hole where physical joy was intensified a hundredfold.

Much later when he came to, he managed to whisper, "Where'd you learn that?"

Kathy smiled and whispered with pouting lips, "In one of my magazines."

"Times," said Blake, chuckling, "they are a'changing."

•••

He found the La Cage, its exterior made up of Milwaukee cream brick, its architecture reminiscent of Europe's Middle Ages. The roof's copper towers had turned green. Its interior was pink and blue neon, the music loud. He approached an empty bar stool, placed the gym bag on the floor, and sat. Brass Buddhas, lit incense sticks in their crotches, looking like huge erections, astonished him, Blake certain the incense meant to hide the odor of marijuana smoke.

An effeminate, portly red-haired bartender approached, extending the wrong hand for a shake. "Sir, would you like me to put that bag behind the bar?"

"No, I want it where I can keep my eyes on it."

Red grinned politely. "I'm Michael, sir. I'm just trying to be helpful. And what are we drinking?"

"We're drinking a brandy Manhattan on the rocks—Korbel if you have it."

"Brandy Manhattan. Korbel, it is, sir."

As to the jukebox, Andy Williams now crooned "Moon River," slowing down the tempo. Blake thought it a wretched tune. Kathy liked it. Stunned, he watched men dance with men, women dancing with women.

Just then, the entry door flung open and in stepped a well-built, over six-foot-tall swarthy stud with stunning blue eyes. Blake figured he was in his midthirties. A well-scuffed black leather motorcycle jacket was draped casually over a shoulder. His combed Wildroot Cream Oil hairstyle was fifties all the way.

Mr. Hollywood, thought Blake. Hollywood's choice of a Hawaiian sport shirt, Levi's jeans, and scuffed black engineer boots placed him in *I'm an individual* category.

"And how are we this fine evening?" asked Michael.

"Thank you, Michael, I'm just fine. The usual, please."

Hollywood hung his jacket on the back of the stool next to Blake and sat. Michael delivered the drinks. "Don't you think he looks like James Dean?" asked Michael, referring to Blake.

Hollywood studied Blake. "More like Troy Donahue, I'd say." Turning to Blake, he said, "To your health and happiness, Mr. Smith."

"Ballad. Jim Ballad," corrected Blake.

After Michael left, Blake whispered, "I assume you're the one I'm—"

"I am."

Hollywood displayed a pack of Camels, knocked it against the side of his palm, exposed two cigarettes, and offered one to Blake.

"No, thanks."

"The name's Smooth," said Hollywood.

Blake didn't know what to say. So, he offered a hand. Smooth sneered, lit up, took a drag, and exhaled three distinct trails through mouth and nostrils. "You pout like James Dean, but you still look like Donahue." Smooth began a pat-down that no one would have suspected. It was just two male friends, enjoying each other's company.

"I'm not wired or strapped, if that's what you're worried about," said Blake. "I came only to deliver—"

"If you would've been strapped or wired, it would've made my life all the more interesting, Jack."

"Jim." Blake felt instant pain; Smooth was crushing his testicles.

"Don't fuck with me, Bill, because there's only one other act that is more attractive to me than getting it on with you." He inhaled. The cigarette glowed. "You believe in life after death, don't you?"

The pain was too much; Blake couldn't answer.

Smooth loosened his grip, grabbed Blake's right hand, and placed the hand where Blake didn't want it, on Smooth's obviously erect organ. "No matter which option you choose, Jimbo, this gun goes off."

Blake swallowed what he thought was a tennis ball with long hairs attached to it. "I thought I was supposed to deliver the bag and that was that."

"Tell me, Angelo, do you believe in the tooth fairy?"

• • •

Judder Brown's relationship with fellow correctional officers was not good at all because he was blind not only to his shortcomings but to Ego's character, as well. Judder couldn't have foreseen that the star to which he had secured his lasso would forsake him for such a shallow individual as Kevin Blake, who relied on his good looks and a ready smile.

Obsessed by wrong choices and his loneliness, Judder dived deeper into a depressed state and talked Dr. Damon into increasing his Valium intake from five-milligram pills to ten. Damon couldn't have known that his patient was visiting other physicians in the area and talking them into similar advances.

At night, Judder crushed an ever-increasing number of blue pills into a powder on a piece of paper, folded it, tapped the pulverization into a water glass of Old Forester, and promptly downed the booze mixed with the potent powder with pleasure.

After inmate Wretched Riley shut his eyes, preparing for heaven on earth, the kneeling Howard "Burn" Carter rose, shot out of the cottage, and bounded into the prison camp's Administration Building, his heart pumping at mach speed. "I demand to speak to the superintendent," he yelled at the inmate night clerk.

"Fuck you, you punk-assed snitch," said the clerk.

Burn nevertheless remained in the building until Superintendent Donald Schultz, a gruff barrel of a man, arrived at seven forty-five in the morning. "Are you the camp superintendent?" asked Burn.

"I am," said Schultz.

"May I see you alone, sir?"

Schultz looked as if he had just stepped on a fresh cowpie with his new brogans. "No," he said, entering his office and slamming shut the door.

At noon, Sergeant Smeltz entered the building and knocked on Schultz's door. The door opened. Schultz greeted Smeltz as if they were brothers. Schultz told the day clerk, "Smeltz and me are going out to lunch." An hour later, Schultz returned and yelled at Burn to get into his office.

"Do you know who I am?" asked Burn.

Schultz's face turned beet red. "You bet your sweet ass I know who you are. You're the hippie asshole who burned draft card records in Madison, took off for Canada, and got your ass hauled back here where you and your Commie friends made a mockery of our court system. You married that ACLU broad who looks like Groucho Marx. And then to top it off, you made up a bunch of lies for extra favors.

"Now, either return to your housing unit, or I'll transfer your ass back to Waupun at once for disobeying a direct order. I'm sure you know what'll happen in Waupun. You'll be on the breakfast menu. I'm leaving the choice up to you."

"What you're saying," said Burn, "is it's either the fire or the frying pan."

"You turned up the heat, mister. Now let's see you turn it the hell off. Besides, there's an old saying in Waupun—"

Burn knew full well the rest of the maxim.

Schulz responded anyway. "Payback's a motherfucker, kid."

CHAPTER THIRTY-THREE

As Ego lay in the La-Z-Boy recliner, resting his eyes and taking in the pleasant aromas of pot roast, mashed potatoes, and gravy, he felt life was good.

The doorbell jangled. Ego lifted and went to the front door.

Waupun's chief of police, Maury Rogan, grinned as he waited for Ego to let him in. "Hey, Maury, what brings you here?"

"Hi ya, Butch. What I got to tell you I didn't think we oughta talk about over the phone."

"Well, come on in."

Ego turned to Joanie. "Me and Maury will go down to the workshop so we won't bother you."

Joanie smiled. "That's OK, you two are no bother."

"Sure smells good," said Rogan. "What's cooking?"

"You should know my Joanie's the best cook in town," bragged Ego.

"Now, don't say that, dear," warned Joanie. "I'll bet anything Maury thinks Jill's cooking rates the blue ribbon, but anyway, it's pot roast with the fixings."

"If she was here, you'd better believe I'd say that or I'd lose my happy home," said Rogan, adding, "How ya doing, Joanie?"

"Just fine, Maury, and you?"

"Hunky-dory."

What's he got to say that he can't say over the phone? "Let's go, Maury. I got some brewskis in the fridge."

"Guess I could have one," said the chief. "I'm a tad thirsty."

Downstairs, the men exchanged pleasantries before Ego popped the question.

"Well," said Rogan, "I thought you might be interested in what Max Steenburgen saw the other day as he passed by the Corner Café."

Jesus, it's gonna be another one of his novels. "What'd he see, Maury?"

"Well, ya know, Max used to work for the attorney general."

"You forget, Maury, I'm senior member of the Waupun Fire and Police Commission. I know just about everything concerning our boys in blue."

"And I'll always be grateful for your support," said Rogan. "Well, Max told me he saw a former supervisor of his from the DOJ, a Walter Kensinger, K-e-n-s-i-n-g-e-r, sitting in Betty's the other day."

Spit it out, will ya?

"So, Kensigner's in Betty's and he's talking to one of your employees as if they know each other real good."

"I understand, Maury. Continue."

"Well, he was talking to that colored, good-looking gal of yours, Shirleen Hammer."

Jesus, Shirleen again?

"And she's talking to this Kensinger like they know each other really good."

"Look, Maury, any moment now and Joanie's gonna be putting supper on the table."

"Wow, you're a tad antsy, aren't you, Butch? You better have another beer."

Ego shook his head.

"Well, after Max reports that to me, I decide to do a little police work of my own."

"That's why we hired you," said Ego. *Would you puh-leaze make your point?*

"That's kind of you to say so, Butch."

Please, dammit, get to the point.

"Shirleen's from Milwaukee," said Rogan.

So are fifty thousand other people. "That right?" said Ego.

"So, I telephoned Chief Breier. Jim and me—we go a long way back—well, I call him in order to get whatever lowdown I can about one of his city's former citizens."

I betcha he don't call Brier Jim, that's for certain, and I don't need a blow-by-blow description of Brier and his family? "Jim, huh?"

"That's right," said Rogan. "Well, he was happier than a queer in a pickle barrel when he realized it was Maury Rogan on the other end of the line. He was only too pleased to let me know that Shirleen had been one of his first female officers—and a good 'un, at that. Now, coming from Jim, who didn't want no women working for him as beat cops, that's really something."

A cop? She never said nothing about that? "Well, I didn't know she was a police officer. In fact, I don't know the background of most of the prison's employees because Madison Personnel has been doing all the background checks and hiring."

The chief's eyebrows rose. "You don't hire new employees?"

"That's right," said Ego.

"Well, I don't know much about that stuff, but I don't think Jim would tell me she was one of his if she wasn't, no, sir, he wouldn't."

"I didn't mean to tell you that Brier would tell you a—"

"I didn't think you were, Butch. You got another beer handy?"

Ego went to the fridge and uncapped two bottles, quickly handing one to Rogan.

I guess I can't hurry him up, no matter what.

"Where was I?" asked the chief.

"You were talking about Chief Breier and Shirleen."

"Was I? Well, OK. The chief told me Shirleen worked for him for only three years because Bob Ward hired her away from him."

"Ward? You mean Attorney General Ward?"

"The one and only."

Rogan stopped to catch his breath. "Hold on. It gets juicier. This Shirleen—she had a brother at your place, and he wasn't a guard, neither, if you catch the drift. Top that if you can: sister's a cop, brother's a robber. Doesn't that beat all?"

Hammer, I don't remember no inmate with that name. "I don't recall ever having an inmate named Hammer, and by God, Maury, I think I can remember all the cons that done time ever since I been there."

"You got a good memory. I'll hand that to you," said Rogan. "His name wasn't Hammer."

Well, what in hell was his name? "Well what was his name?"

"Davis. Earl R. Davis," said the chief. "That's what his name was."

Ego felt as if a vise were constricting his chest.

"He was murdered by a couple of Cobra gangsters some time ago. Now, do you remember? Butch, is something the matter?"

"I had something stuck in my throat."

"Well, that's about it." The chief finished the rest of his beer. "And that's about it for this bottle, too. I gotta go. Jill and I are going out to eat at the Wild Goose Inn tonight."

Ego followed Rogan up the stairs. "Joanie and me—we're stay-at-home types."

"Yeah," said Rogan, speaking louder for Joanie's benefit. "That's the main reason you should take more time away from the job and take that wonderful woman of yours out a time or two."

"Hear, hear," called out Joanie.

"Yeah, yeah," said Ego, grinning as best he could.

"And the state doesn't pay him a nickel extra for his dedication," she continued.

"You're right," said Rogan.

Ego patted the chief on the back, saw him out, and closed the door softly before returning to the La-Z-Boy, which wasn't at all comfortable. The kitchen aroma sickened him. Everything inside him either churned or burned.

When does it ever end? Now I know why she was asking about Davis all the time, and I gotta add Griffin to the list. They gotta be in this thing together. When does it ever end? Or does it?

A year passed since Ann "Armpit Annie" Knepler-Carter had met with Governor Avery Todd in order to plead with him to save her husband, Howard "Burn" Carter, from being maimed or killed by other inmates for his double-cross tendencies.

Todd ordered the Department of Corrections chief to transfer Burn to a northern camp after Todd received the only thing he asked for, which surprised Ann Knepler-Carter to no end.

Todd made mad, passionate love to her on top of the governor's conference table. Next, the Oriental carpet. Then, the guv lifted her onto the sink in the executive bathroom, Ann never feeling more like a woman.

With Todd's blessing and secretive financing, she saw a dermatologist who removed her mustache. Next, she commenced to shaving leg and armpit hairs. The aerial-performing bats would have to find another place from which to hang.

Exchanging Coke bottle eyeglasses for contact lenses, she tossed the umbrella she always carried into a garbage can.

A plastic surgeon implanted the largest set of Dow Corning's the company manufactured. After the surgery, she looked into a full-length mirror, and with a smile said aloud, "My, that is one fine rack."

Before tossing granny dresses and earth shoes into a Goodwill Dumpster, she visited State Street boutiques and purchased T-shirts that showcased her zoomies along with designer jeans one size too tight. She wrestled them on, filled the bathtub with water, and sat fully clothed. When the jeans dried, she stood before the full-length mirror and said aloud, "That, girl, is one incredible ass."

Delighting in Todd's never-ending sexual experimentations (Ann adored his numbering them), she sought a divorce, the reason, "My husband is a convicted felon." Subsequently, she handed her resignation in to her ACLU supervisor, joined an upscale law firm, the Republican Party, and a few of Madison's finest private clubs. Whenever she visited those nightspots, she was surrounded by scores of panting studs. Ann reveled in the attention.

As to ex-hubby, Howard "Burn" Carter, his ass pivoted more than Ann's. Even his voice tilted falsetto since he became Wretched Riley's Main Bitch.

When released from custody, Burn headed to San Francisco, where, years later, he became a spokesperson for government-subsidized AIDS research.

CHAPTER THIRTY-FOUR

Five fifty a.m., and it was as quiet as a cloistered convent at the governor's mansion. Kyle Marston keyed open the front door and headed to his first-floor office, the size of a closet, and not a walk-in one, either.

Marston sat and stared at the phone and drummed his fingers on the desktop, knowing full well he had to take the plunge. Lifting the phone, he dialed.

He heard the upstairs phone ring. It continued to ring. And ring. And ring. *I'm in deep shit,* he thought.

"Yeah," answered Avery Todd.

Sounds as if he partied all night at the Republican Ball. Kyle winced. "Kyle here, sir."

"Kyle, where?"

"Downstairs, sir. Hate to wake you, but we've had another unfortunate incident at Waupun." *He'll overreact as usual.* Toying with his desk calendar, Kyle looked out the window to see if he could spot any clouds. *Nothing—and nothing from the boss.* "A Latino inmate, nineteen-year-old Juan Medina, committed suicide while housed in the Adjustment Center."

"That's the hole, you boob," screamed Todd.

Kyle straightened his black horn-rim glasses with index finger and thumb. "Sir?"

"A spic killed himself, you say?"

Kyle grinned while he listened to Ann Todd lecture her husband to be more sensitive to people of other races.

"Jesus Christ," Todd complained without cupping the receiver, "there's nobody here but us and Kyle downstairs, who's talking to me this very second on this very phone." Then, to Kyle, Todd said, "We got plenty of spics in Milwaukee—don't we?"

"And most voted for you, sir."

"Give me five," growled the boss man.

Kyle slowly exhaled. "I'll be waiting, sir."

The chief aide was just about to hang up.

"Kyle?"

Marston pulled the phone back to his ear, eyebrows rising. "Sir?"

"Don't you ever fucking sleep?"

"I am not paid to sleep, sir."

"Attaboy," said his nibs.

•••

Wisconsin's most popular governor of the twentieth century descended the showy staircase, looking extremely hung over. Still he managed to strut and preen, dressed in a gaudy black silk smoking jacket with offsetting white collar. He was already biting into a stogie.

That smoking jacket looks as if it was stolen from a Tijuana whorehouse. "Nice jacket, sir," said Kyle.

"And fuck you, too," rumbled Todd. "I wouldn't wear this son of a bitch to a dogfight, but the Frau bought it as a present. If I didn't wear it, she'd probably de-nut me."

Kyle's lower lip made a downturn. "I thought—"

"What'd you think?" snapped Todd.

Kyle searched the ceiling as he whispered, "That Ann bought it."

"Didn't I tell you the Frau's hearing is at its peak when someone whispers? I swear if a gnat was trying to conceal a fart, she'd think it was an A-bomb going off."

Kyle's forehead ridged before he handed the folder to Todd. "Sorry, sir, I won't whisper." *Why is he weighing the folders?*

"Jesus, Kyle, what is this, a fucking novel?"

Kyle shook his head. "Uh, no, sir. It's a compendium of—"

"My head weighs a hundred and fifteen fucking pounds and my stomach feels like I been force-fed a bucket of snot and you say compendee-what?"

"It's a collection of reports, sir. As you are wont to say, bureaucrats cover their asses with reports."

Todd cleared his throat. "And you read everything?"

"I did."

"And you still want me to read?" Once again, the guv hefted the load of papers.

"Sir, I simply don't want you to have any surprises at your next press conference."

"OK, OK." Todd read and commented at the same time, "This kid didn't want some con's dick shoved up his ass. Good for him. So, he uses a fork to make his point. Makes sense to me." Todd eyeballed Kyle. "Why the hell does that prison allow inmates to have forks, anyway? Check that out, will ya? And, get this—he gets put in the hole for protecting his virgin ass. Palestine should've given him a goddamn medal. That's what he should've done."

"Yes, sir," said Kyle.

Todd resumed his scanning and vocal annotating. "Then, after a shrink *observes* the kid in the hole, the kid honks an oyster at the shrink and gets a bull's-eye. You know what *observe* means to a shrink, Kyle?"

Kyle offered his top toady smile.

"It means he stands there and asks the poor bastard if he enjoyed fucking Grandma while tugging on Mama's titties at the same time he's licking Sister's pussy before blowing Brother while packing fudge up Grandpa's ass."

Kyle laughed. "I don't think it's that bad, sir."

"You don't think it's that bad? So the shrink puts the kid into Control, which means the kid's bare-assed, lying on a mattress-less stainless steel bunk to which his wrists and ankles are shackled. Later, the shrink gets A: the guilts, or B: fucking falls in love with the bare-assed little shit—your choice—and lets him out of Control.

"Meanwhile, the spic thinks the world's gone ape shit, says 'fuck it' in Spanish, tears his skivvies into strips, makes a noose, and hangs himself under his bunk. That about it?"

"You're close, sir, very close," said Kyle.

"This shouldn't cause me any problems, should it?"

"As long as we have harmonious answers, sir."

"We? Why'd I hire you?"

Kyle shrugged. "I want to make certain you give them the best and most favorable politically correct response, sir."

"OK, OK, but don't forget we gotta be touchy-feely with the guards' union or they'll picket my ass. We don't want to give those fuckers a media field day. Say something like, 'Our loyal correctional officers work hard to avoid this kind of shit.'"

"*Loyal* might be a bit over the top, sir."

The governor glared.

"Got it," said Kyle, "guards are loyal."

"You can also say my staff is studying the matter in order to avoid any future problems, that kind of shit, OK?"

"OK."

"And Kyle?"

Kyle was busily lining up a blank sheet of paper in his typewriter, trying not to appear annoyed. "Sir?"

"Say something nice about spics, too, will ya?"

"Gotcha, sir."

Todd, obviously pleased with himself, waddled off. "Go get 'em, tiger. Meanwhile"—the politician stopped, lifted a leg, and blew one bodacious fart— "I'm gonna get myself some shut-eye. And Kyle?"

Kyle looked up from the typewriter in all the seriousness he could muster. "Yes, sir?"

"Quit breathing so goddamned hard."

This time Kyle laughed loud and long with the governor. "I can assure you I'm not even breathing. I loathe the aroma of Limburger cheese, sir."

Avery Todd ascended the stairs with gusto.

•••

At the same time the governor found just the right spot to nestle his head on the goose-down pillow, Ego withdrew the daily change sheet from his in-basket. He had been at the institution all night after receiving the call about Medina. He read, did a double take, and read again. *Somebody forgot to put in Medina's transfer from Control back to TLU. Everybody knows a con in Control can't wipe his own ass by hisself.*

And get this. Cell hall sergeants have already thumbtacked their copies of the change sheet to their bulletin boards so cons don't bother asking them where their buddies are. And when cons take a gander at this, they're gonna think we did something to that inmate, such as killing him—giving them reason to—yeah—riot.

Ego rose, closed the door, sat down, grabbed the phone, and lifted.

"Sir," said the Control sergeant, who handled weekend telephone operator duties.

"Outside line."

"Yes, sir."

Who would've thought the answer to all my problems would be handed to me in a change sheet?

Staff had nicknamed the piece The Cannon. Its official designation was 37mm MM1 Multi-Projectile Rocket Launcher. It sported dual pistol grips and a twelve-round rotary cylinder of nearly foot-long tubes. It looked like a portable Gatling gun on steroids.

The Cannon was mainly used as a welcomed diversion during annual Weapons Qualifications Week, when blueshirts exhausted soon-to-be outdated ordnance, turning the gunnery range into a Fourth of July-like rock-and-roar display. After expending individually assigned allotments, they strode to a wooden bench and sat, looking like fat farm cats lying near a corncrib plagued with mice.

The Cannon's projectiles were never used against inmates, but the weapon earned its mythology on a Sunday afternoon when ninety inmates declared an impromptu sit-down strike on the rec field, supposedly protesting prison conditions. Truth be known, most were plainly bored.

In response, Tower Six officer came out on his catwalk, cradling The Cannon as Treatment Director Jon Deutch, with weekend on-call duty, followed.

The strikers' leader, Jason Michaels, a convicted child molester, yelled to the other protestors, "As long as we're peaceful, he can't shoot."

"Do you men see this?" yelled Deutch, pointing to The Cannon.

All sitting inmates, except Michaels, nodded.

"It's called the MM1," continued Deutch. "I'm going to read you its handbook, detailing the weapon's capabilities." While Deutch read, blueshirts quietly escorted nonparticipating inmates to their cells at the same time ERU ninjas surrounded the strikers.

Finished with the manual, Deutch addressed the strikers. "I advise you to quit this felonious act and to rise and march silently in single file to the Adjustment Center. If you do not—" Deutch stopped, looked to the cannon, and shook his head, the threat left unsaid.

Strikers looked to each other as Michaels yelled, "They can't use lethal power as long as we're peaceful. Power to the people. It's the law."

Jack Bulbitz, a convicted bank robber, stood. "Fuck you, you baby-raping motherfucker, fuck the people, and double fuck the motherfucking law." He then pointed to the tower officer. "He can shoot and he knows it."

All the strikers except Michaels followed Bulbitz's lead. Glumly, they stood and formed a line, embarking on a hushed tramp to the Greenhouse as Michaels yelled, "Even though we're inmates, we have rights."

A moment later, six ninjas grabbed Michaels, lifted him above their shoulders, and on a dead run rushed him to the Greenhouse as a tower officer yelled, "There he goes, along with his rights."

This was indeed a moment for laughter.

CHAPTER THIRTY-FIVE

It was pitch-black as Madison Street turned into County Highway M. Zak let up on the hot rod's accelerator, switched off headlights, turned the ignition key to the off position, and turned onto the Catholic cemetery's crushed granite roadway, pebbles popping under tires, sounding like NVA Russian-made AK-47s.

Halting the coupe under a large maple, Zak tapped a cigarette from the pack and spun the Zippo's wheel. Although the wick flamed, it kept moving away from the cigarette's tip. "What's that?"

"You should've asked, 'Who's that?'" said Lanh Ngoc Than, the NVA major Zak had killed.

At first Zak was startled, but he caught himself. "Hell, you're nothing but a figment of my imagination."

"Then, you wouldn't mind if an idea originating in your brain smoked one of your cigarettes, would you?"

"Be my guest."

Accepting a Camel, Lanh leaned forward and grabbed Zak's shaking hand and held it. With fanfare, the major inhaled long and hard, grinned ever so widely, and exhaled. He spoke to the cigarette. "It's been a long, long time."

"You're dead," said Zak, "and it's all over for you but the shouting."

"Shouting—isn't that what my daughter does in your dreams?"

"How'd—?"

"Chasing after you with a knife. You'll discover how I know eventually, but this is neither the time nor place for that breakthrough.

My daughter, Thu, is not that child any longer. And she knows nothing about you. She's a medical school student, living in Ho Chi Minh City with my thoroughly self-centered sister, Ly, named after the lion. I am now my daughter's hero. If I had lived, she and I'd be fighting like cats and dogs. She's headstrong like her aunt. Besides, it was I who forced you to kill me. I took a chance with losing my life when I shot that med—"

"Sir?" A woman's voice.

Zak turned to the sound, the light nearly blinding him. Quickly, he shaded his eyes with the back of his hand.

"Please roll down your window, sir."

Zak turned to face the major. *Gone—?*

"You're Zak Griffin, aren't you?"

"Yeah," Zak managed as he rolled down the window and tried to hide the shotgun, "I'm Zak."

"I'm Officer Darmstadter, Waupun Police Department. I used to be Linda Weintraub. Remember? I was two years behind you in school. You probably didn't know, but I had the biggest crush on you. I'm married to Wayne Darmstadter, the mechanic at Bentz Shell."

"Oh yeah," Zak said, "I remember you."

His hand slipped. The shotgun's barrel smacked against the car's dash.

Her voice became tense. "Zak, is that what I think that is? Listen to me, Zak. Are you listening?"

Where the hell did he go?

"Zak."

"Yeah?"

"Did you hear me? Are you listening?"

"Yeah, I'm listening."

"Is that shotgun loaded?"

Zak must've taken too much time to answer.

"I said, is it loaded, Zak?"

"As a matter of fact, it is," he said.

"Zak, listen to me. Are you listening to me?"

"Yeah, I'm listening."

"I want you to place the palms of your hands against the windshield. Now, Zak. Do what I say."

"You got this all wrong."

"Zak, are you listening?"

"Yeah, didn't I tell you I was listening?"

"Then, do as I say."

All I need is a second. She'll turn off that light and it'll be over. "Linda?"

"Yes, Zak, do you have a problem following my orders?"

"Yeah, it's your light. It's too bright. Can you douse it for a minute?"

The light remained. Zak looked to the rider's side. "Where the hell did ya go?" he asked aloud.

"Zak, are you listening?"

Zak turned to the light. "Yeah, I'm listening."

"Zak, I'm going to open your door, but I don't want you to move. If you move, I might have to shoot you, and you don't want me to shoot you, do you?"

Zak figured she was serious. "As a matter of fact, I don't. OK, I won't move."

The door opened.

"Zak, I want you to clasp your hands behind your head."

Zak obeyed. "Am I under 'rest?"

"Now, exit the car," she said. As Zak's feet hit the gravel, he spun around and almost fell. "Oops." Righting himself, he twirled in the opposite direction and almost went down again. "Whoops."

She gave Zak a quick but thorough pat-down. "You don't have any weapons on your person, do you, Zak?"

"No," he answered.

"I don't think so, either. Zak, are you listening? I want you to lie down on your stomach on the grass over there." She pointed to a spot just off the roadway.

Zak made it there and got down on his knees. Groaning, he lay down.

"Now, put your hands behind your back."

"You want me to eat dirt?"

"I've been told we eat a bushel before we die," she said. "You shouldn't get any more than a teaspoonful." She cuffed Zak's wrists. "Zak, I'm placing you under arrest."

"For what?"

"DUI."

"Didja hear my car's engine?"

"Zak—"

"You didn't 'cause I was parked here but I didn't drive here. Somebody else drove me here."

"Who drove you here, Zak?"

"Somebody else. I'm not going to tell you who. I'm no snitch."

"If somebody else drove you here, as you say, then where is she or he?"

Zak looked around. "I don't know. He must've taken off."

"Zak, listen to me. Are you listening?"

"Yeah."

"I followed you all the way from Main and Madison. So, I know you were driving."

Major Than, sitting on a branch of a nearby hard maple tree, pointed at Zak and laughed heartily.

"You bastard," screamed Zak.

"Are you calling me a bastard?" asked the cop.

"No, him," said Zak, pointing with his chin.

"Who?"

"Major Lanh Ngoc Than—up there in that tree. I killed him."

"We'd better get you to the station so you can sleep off whatever you're on."

•••

Zak's head ached. His cell smelled like a mixture of Pine Sol and vomit. He tried to sleep. He tried sitting. Hours seemed like days. A month later, or so it seemed, he heard the cell door jiggle. In no mood for noise, he asked, "Do you have to?"

"You don't look so good," said Chief Maury Rogan.

"I don't feel so good."

"After Linda told me what happened, I phoned Butch Richardson."

There goes the job.

"And he said you were one of his best, that I should give you a break. Linda told me you were yelling at some major of the North Vietnamese Army, that he was in some tree, and that you had killed him. Are you still fighting that war?"

An electric motor buzzed. A faucet dripped. Zak's head hurt.

"I know all about your war record, but when a fella drinks like you do, he's got problems—big-time. Linda said you used to be quite an athlete, and she said you built a good-looking nineteen thirties car into a hot rod and even raced it. Why don't you help the coach at the high school or work on cars with teenagers at risk?"

"I don't have the time."

"You got time to spend in taverns, don't you?"

Zak hung his head.

"Well," said the chief, "I'm going let you go with a warning. Next time, I'll throw the book at you."

The chief disappeared.

Zak waited for a long, long time. *Which year did he say he was going to let me go?*

Finally, Officer Steenbergen appeared with a key, shaking his head.

"Do I look that bad?" asked Zak.

"Worse than that, like you've been drinking dog piss." The cop keyed open the door while holding on to Zak's car keys.

• • •

The Beaver Dam Alano Club's basement meeting room smelled like a mixture of stale cigarette smoke and Glade air freshener. Zak's stomach churned. His head ached.

Behind the counter was a well-built middle-aged woman with strikingly shiny eyes. Her brown hair had a hint of highlight. She dumped coffee grounds into the large percolator's basket, smiled warmly, and said, "You're Zak, aren't you?"

"Yeah."

"I'm Neva. You don't remember me, do you?"

"No."

"I know your mother. I'm in Alanon, too. You and I met down here—at your first and, I assume, last meeting. I'm this morning's leader, which means I'm responsible for making coffee and cleaning up after the meeting."

"Where's George?"

"Wayland's on break. So, he and Jan took off on their Harleys to their cabin near Rhinelander."

"Damn," said Zak.

Neva frowned. "So am I chopped liver?"

"No." Zak grabbed the back of a folding chair in order to prop himself up, the chair's legs galling against the floor. "Jesus," he cringed, "that noise. It's killing me. I have this splitting head—" Zak changed his mind and growled, "Hangover."

"You think grown men shouldn't cry. Don't you?"

"I'm not into the touchy-feely scene."

"I know where you're at," said Neva, "because I've been there myself. This could be your last chance, Zak. Please don't go."

He stopped.

"Zak," she pleaded, "we have the same disease. We also have the same solution."

She grabbed his arm.

"It's not good to cry," he said.

"Oh yeah?" said Neva. "You're wrong and probably wrong about a lot of other things, as well. Damn it, big guy, even if you don't need a hug, I do." She grabbed him and held fast.

"OK, Farney, I read you your rights," said the solemn detective wearing an empty pistol holster attached to his belt, "and you told me you understood them and signed a waiver to have a lawyer present. Is what I said correct?"

"That's correct, Inspector Huberty," said Farney Johnston, outfitted in a county jail oversized orange jumpsuit. Farney adjusted his glasses.

"See that light? Means the machine's recording. It's three seventeen p.m., July fourteenth, nineteen hundred and sixty-nine. You ready?"

"Yes, Inspector, I'm ready."

"Good, this is Sheboygan County Chief Detective Inspector Robert Huberty. Present with me is Detective Thomas Wright and Farney Johnston, a suspect in a multiple murder that took place on July twelfth, nineteen hundred and sixty-nine in Sheboygan, Wisconsin. How old are you, Farney?"

"Matter of fact, I turned twenty on the twelfth. Mom was chopping veggies with her sabatier. I took it from her and stabbed her with it."

"Can you spell the name of that knife for me, Farney?"

"S-a-b-a-t-i-e-r. Sounds like it should end in a-y. Doesn't it? Or e-y?"

"Doesn't look like it sounds. What'd you do next, Farney?"

"After I killed her?"

"Yes."

"I cleaned, changed clothes, and hid the knife in a paper sack, which I took to Susan's."

"You mean you took the sabatier in the bag to the James Watkins residence at five fourteen south Twenty-Seventh Street in Sheboygan?"

"Yes, sir, that's the place. Susan's mother answered the door and didn't want to let me in. I pushed hard, knocked her over, gutted her just like the whitetail buck when I went hunting the first time and shot it. It was a six-pointer."

"What'd you do next, Farney?"

"Climbed the stairs to where the bedrooms are. I found Gary in bed, asleep. I woke him up and told him he had to die. He pleaded I not use the blade on him. So, I straddled him, knelt on his arms, pinched his nose, and covered his mouth. Man, did I ride that bucking bronco."

"You're laughing, Farney. You think killing Gary Watkins was funny?"

"No, Inspector, but nobody in that house heard us. Can you believe that?"

"I believe that, Farney. Who did—excuse me—I mean what did you do next?"

"Well, the door was closed. After I put my ear on it, I could hear Tom Watkins inside, panting, you know what I mean. And the exact moment I kicked open that door, he was hunched over a bit and guh-roaning in sheeeeeeeeeeer exultation as he came."

CHAPTER THIRTY-SIX

With twenty-two years as a by-the-book blueshirt, Jack Peabody was sweating bullets. He fully expected a world of shit coming his way. *The cons. They're as quiet as meditative monks—and in the dining hall on a Saturday, to top it off.*

Trouble was, he hated to approach Captain Bragg, a first-class SOB who received his every promotion by not only bringing apples to his superiors, but shining them as well.

Duty was calling. Still, Jack, a former marine who never stopped being a jarhead, told himself, *I'd sooner face Nikita Khrushchev than Bragg.*

Finally, he couldn't live with himself if he didn't face up to Bragg, standing next to Officer Barney Johnston, whose post was by the stainless steel drinking fountain.

Barney winked at Peabody while Bragg looked in the opposite direction, busily picking a winner in his schnozzle. *I guess he hopes I'll go away, disappear.* "Captain, uh, we need to talk," whispered Jack.

Bragg turned to face Jack. His upper lip curled. "Then, why don't you fucking talk, Peabody?" Bragg almost yelled, causing inmates to glare at them.

You might want to switch to Lavoris. Your breath smells like pig shit. "Did you notice," Jack continued whispering, "that the inmates aren't yelling or talking or telling jokes?"

"Meaning?" posed Bragg with his usual display of arrogance.

"Meaning, sir, we could have a big problem on our hands."

Bragg snorted.

"What I'm trying to say, Captain, is they're like rattlesnakes—coiled, you know, ready to strike."

"Peabody, I want you to be the first to know that if those assholes ain't talking is a problem, I'll live with it."

What a knucklehead. "Captain, they ain't generally this quiet at mealtime. Something, by golly, is wrong."

Bragg's eyebrows nearly touched one another. "You got a yellow streak running down your back, Peabody?"

If my family didn't need to eat, I'd cold cock you. "No, sir, I was just trying to make a point." Peabody surveyed the inmates again. They were throwing eye-knives at Bragg, Barney, and him. "Something's wrong is what I'm telling you." *You knob.*

Bragg turned to Barney. "What do you think, Johnston?"

Barney shrugged. "About what?"

"What Peabody was talking about."

"I wasn't listening."

Barney, you lowlife coward. So, that's how much guts former sailors have.

Bragg snickered as he drew closer to Peabody and whispered, "You think I give a rat's ass these fuckers ain't talking? Well, I fucking don't give a flying fuck. You fucking got that?"

"Loud and clear, Captain." *If they raise hell and I'm still alive and he's still alive, I'm going to kill him.*

Thankfully, nothing happened. The inmates did not raise hell. Jack Peabody felt he got a free one that day. Still, the inmates remained as silent as a group of hummingbird babies that lay in their nest, awaiting the next meal.

•••

Minutes after all inmates were ensconced in their cells after lunch, Sgt. Nick Barnes ascended to D-tier. There, he made a complete round, and not one inmate gave him the time of day or made eye contact. That happened on C-tier, as well.

When he approached C-14, occupied by Jack Willing, a friendly, likable man, Barnes tried his best to make light of the situation. "How's it going, Jack? Did they serve spicy beef burritos again?"

"Who killed Medina?"

Jesus, so that's what this is about. "You talking about that inmate that hung himself?"

"How could anyone hang himself in Control, cuffed and leg-ironed to the chains?"

"Yeah, how?" sounded out a number of inmate voices throughout the cell hall.

Barnes didn't bother making rounds of A or B tiers but went straight to his desk, snatched the change sheet, scanned the entries, hauled in the phone, and dialed Control. After he explained matters to Control Sgt. Greg Moen, Moen contacted Major Ericson and read off the entries.

"Jesus," said Ericson, "I better give the boss a head's-up."

"I would if I was you," said Moen.

• • •

Ego was on the John Deere mower on the "back forty," cutting the lawn. He saw Joanie open the rear door. She wore the look of deep concern. He made believe he hadn't seen her and continued mowing, looking straight ahead.

Ten to one I know what that's about. As she approached, he grinned and waved. Joanie yelled something. He put a palm to his ear while shaking his head as Joanie put a closed fist between ear and mouth, pretending to be talking on a telephone.

Ego killed the engine.

"Major Ericson's on the phone and says it's urgent."

"What's up? Did he say?"

"No, but he said he needed to talk to you—now."

Nobody's gonna screw up my riot. Ego dismounted the mower and grabbed Joanie's hand. They walked to the back entryway like a couple of teenagers. "I like the aroma of a freshly cut lawn," said Joanie.

"I like the way you smell," said Ego.

"Oh, go on," she said, pushing him up the stairs.

Ego listened carefully to Ericson. *I'll put on a Hollywood.* "This ain't good, Major, not good at all. Inmates have—you-know-what—over less than that." *They'd better raise hell—if I have anything to say about it.* "Right. A modified change sheet is a darned good idea."

Joanie fidgeted.

"Give me a call after it's out. I wanna know how the cons react to it. Thanks, Mark, you done good." Ego ever so slowly hung up.

"Trouble?" asked Joanie.

I got me an Oscar. "Plenty," said Ego, certain he must've looked like the next of kin to a bloodhound. "It was the inmate change sheet."

"What about it?"

"It was about the guy who committed suicide last night, the reason I spent most of the night at the joint. This morning's change sheet showed that he was in control status, and if that was true—which it wasn't—he couldn't have killed hisself because his wrists and ankles would've been chained to his bunk. It's a royal screw-up because whoever typed up that change sheet forgot to put that he was moved out of Control and back into Temporary Lockup.

"So?" asked his wife.

"You see, these change sheets are posted to the cell hall bulletin boards so cons don't bother the cell hall sergeants and they can see what happened to their missing buddies. So, they'd rather believe blueshirts murdered the guy." *Which is what I'm counting on.* "Anyway," he continued, "I'm gonna finish cutting the lawn. When the major calls back, let me know, will ya?"

"You know I will," said Joanie. "I hope this doesn't mean you're going to be spending all weekend over there."

Ego shrugged. "Could happen." *Better keep looking like I'm worried.*

• • •

Major Ericson hit the button on his walkie-talkie. "Bar Four, this is Bar Three."

A squelch preceded Captain Bragg's answer. "This is Bar Four. Go ahead, Three."

"Your twenty?"

"Yard office," lied Bragg, whose feet were resting on top of a social worker's desk in the Social Services Department. He was staring at Big Daddy Garlits's Hemi-powered Swamp Rat dragster in the latest *Hot Rod* magazine.

"That's a ten-four. I want you to go to all cell halls. Tell the sergeants to advise inmates that inmate Medina, the guy who committed suicide last night, was in TLU, not Control status, when he committed suicide."

"Ten-four, major. It's as good as done." *And you can shove that up your ass.* Holstering his handheld, Bragg returned to the magazine.

In the Sheboygan County Jail's Prisoner Interview Room, Chief Detective Inspector Robert Huberty and Detective Inspector Thomas Wright listened as Farney Johnston detailed how he had brutally murdered five Sheboygan County residents, including his own mother.

Farney had put an ear to an upstairs bathroom door and listened to eighteen-year-old Thomas Watkins masturbate. "After I kicked that door in, I saw Tom's big ol' hard-on. I mean, he was built like a donkey. Well—let me tell you—after I stuck the sabatier into him, blood gushed like oil out of a Texas gusher."

"What happened next?"

"Next?" asked Farney, glowing from the thrill of recounting his final murder. "After Tom, I found young Glen hiding in a closet under a bunch of boxes and blankets. When I lifted them off him one at a time and very slowly, he whimpered like a baby. He continued to do so while I stabbed him repeatedly until I could no longer detect breathing or a heartbeat."

"You killed him, you say?"

Farney's eyebrows looked like one long one.

"Then what did you do?"

"Then I undressed, showered, and went to Tom's room, where I discovered he wore my size pants and shirt. I put on his clothes and waited for Susan. After she saw her mother and I told her what I did, Susan screamed like she did last summer when we rode on one of those bullet-shaped carnival rides. Then, she telephoned the police. Patrolman Huff was the first to arrive. He read me my Miranda rights and I told him I understood those rights, including the right to remain silent and that

anything I said could be used against me in a court of law. I also had a right to have an attorney present and if I couldn't afford an attorney, one would be appointed for me before any questioning could take place. At any time, I could decide to stop answering until I could talk to an attorney."

"And you fully understood them?"

"Yes," said Farney, "I fully understood them and relinquished those rights."

"Farney, why'd you kill your mother and Mrs. Watkins and her three sons?"

"I wanted them to be with Jesus in heaven."

"Jesus, you say?"

"Yes."

"Is there anything else you'd like to add, Farney, because that's all I need to know at this time. Detective Wright, do you have any questions?"

"No," said Wright, "I don't."

"I do have a question," said Farney.

"And that is?" pursued Huberty.

"Does Waupun have a chaplain like I've seen in those old black-and-white movies? I'd like to be a chaplain's assistant."

"I don't know much about Waupun, Farney, except it's the name of the prison."

"It's also the name of the city," added Wright.

"If they have one, I'd still like to work in the chapel," said Farney.

"I will make note of that," answered Huberty.

CHAPTER THIRTY-SEVEN

"Morning, boss," said Bubble Sergeant Moen as he punched the green button.

Ego offered a cursory nod. The gates' opening mustn't have sounded right. "Call maintenance," said Ego. "That worm gear needs attention."

"You got it, boss."

The gate made a *ka-thunk* sound. Quickly stepping between its partially opened steel jaws, Ego made his way to the security office, which smelled like a mix of Johnson's paste wax and Grampa's Pine Tar soap.

Sgt. Glen Waxing sat at Dorothy's desk. His eyes were attached to the Playmate of the Month.

Ego purposely harrumphed.

Waxing jerked, shot up, and stood at attention. He was red-faced and piss-in-the-pants nervous. "Can I help you, boss?"

"No," said Ego.

Waxing heaved a sigh of relief, sat, pulled out the bottom drawer, and let the magazine fall in.

Ego approached the wall where clipboards with inmate pass lists hung. He took down the Catholic and Protestant services clipboards and studied them. *Just as I thought—Theodore and his Aryans are at Mass, and Rodriguez and his Cobras are going to Protestant services. Can't blame 'em. I'd do the same so I could get outta my cage.*

Ego hooked the clipboards back in place, stepped up to his office, took off his suit jacket, and placed it neatly on the back of his chair. He grabbed the Sam Browne and trussed it, much like a sheriff of yore preparing his gun belt for a meeting with some bad hombres. He punched the handheld's on button. "Control, this is Bar Two."

"This is Control," answered Moen. "Go ahead, Two."

"I'm going out back and will be ten-seven in the chapel."

"That's a ten-four, Two."

•••

Under a focused morning sun, Ego eyeballed the guard towers as he made his way to the chapel. The chapel's organ and accompanying inmate choir reminded him of a movie he and Joanie attended while he was courting her. Bing Crosby was the priest and Ingrid what's-her-name was a nun. *Damn, they don't make movies like that nowadays. Everything's changed—for the worst.*

After he opened the large wooden chapel entrance door, more than half the inmates turned back to look. It took five seconds for the rest of the cons to know of Ego's presence.

Sgt. Tom Bella and Officer Two John Benet, arms crossed against their chests, turned to Ego and nodded. "Good work, men," he whispered.

Father Jerome offered his final blessing in Latin as he made a sign of the cross. Inmates, in turn, made their signs of the cross and began filing out of the pews. Eventually, Wing Nuts came near.

"Theodore, I saw the man next to you pass you something. I want it."

"I didn't get passed nothin', Mr. Security Director, honest."

"Downstairs," ordered Ego, "for a body search."

Theodore eyeballed his followers. "As usual, white guys get picked on."

•••

Sgt. Morris Dunlop tried his best to get Officer Two Mike Shanahan's attention. Shanahan eventually came to, but it was too late. He looked up the stairs, obviously spied Ego, glaring at him, and got rid of the girlie magazine as if it were a pin-pulled grenade.

"Since Officer Shanahan is so busy, Sergeant," Ego said as he and Wing Nuts made it to the basement floor, "I'll shake down Kopfmueller, myself."

"Mike or me can do it," objected Dunlop.

"Nah," said Ego, "remain at your post. Mike? He probably has some other place he needs to be." Ego pointed to Father Jerome's office. "I'll conduct the search in there."

Shanahan skedaddled up the stairs, three steps at a time, and was out of the building.

Wing Nuts preceded the grinning Ego into the priest's office. Ego put a vertical index finger to his lips, closed the door, and pulled the drapes, much as Father Jerome did whenever hearing an inmate's confession. "How are the cons reacting to this Medina thing?"

Wing Nuts shrugged. "Some of my guys said somethin' about not bein' able to kill himself because he was in Control. But Cobras, they ain't sayin' shit."

"Then, you gotta push 'em."

"Me?"

"You. I need a—"

"Yeah, what do you need?"

"R-i-o-t," spelled out Ego. "It's gonna cover your escape."

As hard as he tried, Wing Nuts couldn't erase his mile-wide grin.

Ego continued. "Rico and his boys are coming to Protestant services. I'm gonna be waiting in Social Services while you meet with Rico. Tell 'im to start the 'you-know-what' at eight fifteen Tuesday morning. If he buys in, turn to me and nod three times."

"Why Tuesday? Why not tomorrow?"

"'Cause they need time to make weapons. It's gonna take place at three locations." Grabbing a thumb, Ego said, "School." He moved to the index finger. "The old rec hall." Middle finger. "Kitchen."

"School, old rec hall, kitchen," repeated Wing Nuts.

"Ten Aryans—who don't need to know why you ain't gonna be with them—are gonna be in each of those areas. That means thirty altogether, got it?"

"Got it. But where am I going to be?"

"I'll get to that when I get to that."

"OK."

"So, thirty of your best. I'll pick up the list of their names tomorrow morning under your pillow. If Rico or his Cobras chicken out, your boys make sure everything happens as it's gonna, OK?"

"OK."

"Now, for you: When you report to work Tuesday morning, you're gonna find a pistol I made in my shop—it's twenty-two caliber—along with extra ammo and civilian clothes in your clothes locker. So, don't go opening the door so wide that everyone can see in. Get into your work duds and go to work. You're gonna get an eight o'clock pass to Social Services. So, when you return to your locker, get what's there, and without being seen, go to the basement and hide inside the middle of all those boxes. Eventually, it'll be discovered you ain't in your cell or in Social Services. Blake, Captain Blake, he's gonna enter the building and call out for you."

"He what?"

"I couldn't do this thing alone. I needed him, but he's shaky and he could snitch me out." Ego's Adam's apple rose and dove twice as hard. "With that pistol, you're gonna take 'im out and then go up the inside stairwell to the third floor."

"OK, I kill Blake. What if he's wise to me?"

"He won't be. Up on the third-floor landing, a window's on your left. Tower Four's below it. So, don't let 'im see you, 'cause under that window's sash there'll be a key to the Sign Department. Go in there. You'll find a rope and grappling hook in the middle drawer of a steel table closest to the stack of stop signs. Then, return to that window. Take out the tower officer. Nobody's gonna be the wiser 'cause all tower officers will be eyeballing the school, the kitchen, and the old rec hall. Toss the hook to Four's guardrail, tie your end to the stairs' handrail, and down the rope you go. Get Four's key and your get-out-of-jail-free ticket."

"How do I know I can trust you?"

"What do ya want—we should cut our hands and become blood brothers? I hafta trust you and you hafta trust me. That's it. Remember, I'll be waiting and you're gonna nod three times." Ego opened the door and told Sergeant Dunlop, "He didn't have no contraband."

"Which happens when I go fishing," said the sergeant.

"What do ya mean?"

"I don't catch 'em all."

Ego was halfway up the stairs when Dunlop told Wing Nuts, "I'll phone your cell hall sergeant and let him know you're gonna be late."

"Be careful with that coffin," Sgt. Al Preston, part-time bartender at Otto's Bar and Grill, warned the minimum-security inmates. "It's made out of heavy cardboard—and I've seen 'em bust apart when they're manhandled."

Mindfully, the inmates placed their shovels on both sides of the lavender casket in the back of the Ford delivery van.

"Cardboard?" said inmate Timothy Boyle. "You gotta be shitting me."

"You expected bronze?" Preston uncapped a small blue jar with white cap, reaching in with an index finger, and slathering the goop beneath his nostrils.

"No, but Mother of Mercy, cardboard?" said Boyle.

"What are you doing?" asked inmate Nick Kahelski.

"Vick's bouquet beats decay." Preston tossed the little jar to Kahelski, who followed the sergeant's lead, as did the other members of the inmate burial crew.

Everybody in, the van eventually turned off Highway 49 and onto what looked like a horse-and-buggy trail on Prison Farm One. Preston broke the silence. "I assume the dude in the box didn't finish his sentence."

"So?" said inmate Jimmy Joe Washington.

"So, we bury him standing up," said Preston. "Then, after his sentence is finished, we'll dig 'im back up and bury 'im lying down."

"You gotta be shitting me," Washington said, noticeably shivering.

The sergeant grinned. "Yup."

The inmate driver halted the van and killed the engine, and all hands looked out. In neat rows were white stone markers with numbers etched on each. Also, one open pit with a large pile of dirt and rocks next to it awaited the man in the box whose family members, if located, declined to bury him.

"Everybody out," said Preston,

Inmate Sylvester Hastings pointed to the box. "Him too?"

"Nah" said Preston. "First, you guys take a smoke break. Then, we'll plant 'im."

In spite of the strong wind, the inmates managed to light up as they formed a circle and someone cupped his hands around a burning match.

After taking a couple of drags, Hastings started for the open pit.

The others followed.

Due to an abundant rainfall that year, the water table was higher than normal, and actual waves with whitecaps lapped at the base walls of the rectangular pit.

"He probably weren't in the navy," said Washington, "but he gonna be buried at sea."

"Which is another perk I forgot to mention," said the straight-faced Sergeant Preston.

CHAPTER THIRTY-EIGHT

Ego heard something. *It could be the yard officer. He checks all buildings once an hour on weekends.* Ego stepped out of the social worker's office. The offender turned out to be a fan in the next office. It must've been left on since Friday, its blade hitting the safety cage every once in a while. Turning off the fan, Ego tweaked the offending blade and then turned the appliance back on. The whirring propeller pushed air inoffensively. Mission accomplished.

Returning, he pushed a Venetian blind's valance ever so slightly. He saw Wing Nuts leaning against the chapel's exterior stone wall, smoking. *Damn it, smoking's allowed only on the rec field. If a blueshirt sees him—*

And there he appeared: Rico Rodriguez front and center, bodyguards at his side, a half dozen Cobras taking up the rear. At Rico's left side was Hector Soto, a former contract murderer for a Chicago dago gangster before hooking up with Rico and Milwaukee's drug scene. Hector was handed a life bit—plus thirty running wild—by Judge Seraphim Christ for executing Rico's drug rival in front of an undercover cop.

On Rico's other side was Cobra enforcer Johnny Sanchez, an iron pile devotee who preferred large-muscled prison punks over soft, rounded women on the bricks. Waupun was his home of choice.

All Cobras dressed, walked, and resembled one another, their straight, oiled black hair combed back to form ducks' asses. Shirt buttons, including collar, were fastened. Pant legs, given extra starch by

Latinos in the laundry, were stiff as steel and begged for hinges at the knees. While one pant bottom stiffly lifted, the other stiffly fell, all high steppers, feet shod in black patent leather Johnson & Murphy wingtips.

• • •

"Look at that Aryan bitch," Rico said in Spanish, concerning Wing Nuts. "She's looking straight at me, the pussy. How does that Anglo, floppy-eared bitch get away with not being in her home?"

Hector Soto suggested, also in Spanish, "Maybe she wants to suck your fire hose, man."

The other Cobras chortled, clicked fingers, and wiggled their asses.

Rico, palm to the side of his mouth, called out to Wing Nuts, "Hey, dog, my boys say da po-leace are gonna lock your ass up."

"Nobody's goin' to do shit," replied Wing Nuts. "I got strip-shook after Mass because the Man thought somebody passed me somethin'."

"What did the dog find?"

Wing Nuts grinned. "Nothin' but dingle berries."

Rico and his men laughed and jived in Spanish about the incredible size of Wing Nuts's Dumbo-sized ears.

That was the moment the Aryan set the trap. "Say, what you and your boys gonna do about Medina?"

As mute as their grandparents' graves, the Cobras shucked and shrugged.

"What can we do, dog?" asked Rico. "He's not a Cobra."

Like nodding toys, Rico's men bobbled their accord.

"You tellin' me Greenhouse screws killed him, and you and yours aren't going to do shit? I can't believe my ears."

That's the way it is, you floppy-eared Anglo. You don't see no lettuce truck behind me. "I'm talking straight—that's just the way it is, dog."

"And I suppose you're going to tell me you didn't order your boys to off that Brother-men legal beagle, what was his name—oh yeah, Davis."

Rico's grin disappeared as fast as a pigeon inside a magician's silk top hat.

"Besides," added Wing Nuts, "how's it gonna look when white boys stick up for a wetback—but wetbacks—they don't do jack?"

"Go ahead," Rico told his men in Spanish, "I'll catch up."

•••

Ego witnessed Rico speaking maybe one or two words, at most, before he headed to the chapel while Wing Nuts turned and ambled down the roadway, heading into the turn. *Dammit, give me the signal.*

Wing Nuts stopped, turned slowly to face the Social Services Building, and shrugged, Ego certain the Aryan enjoyed detaching fly wings during his summer days off from grade school.

Finally, nodding three times and flicking away his butt, Wing Nuts took off for his cell hall.

•••

With Sunday off, Maj. Mark Ericson attended Mass at Saint Joe's with his wife and kids. Then, they went boating and water skiing on Big Green Lake.

Captain Bragg hadn't alerted Captain Gunderson, Ericson's fill-in, about Saturday's change sheet screw-up.

Naturally, Gunderson didn't mention the change sheet blunder at Sunday's preshift meeting.

By noon, inmates felt Medina's murder by Greenhouse guards was now indisputable. Why else had blueshirts acted dumb as hell when asked about Medina's death at breakfast and lunch? Not even the cell hall sergeants knew about it. They acted as if they hadn't even been aware of his death. Naturally, the officers' lack of knowledge had to be totally bogus.

In the afternoon, the heat was so stifling that one inmate suggested the warden had rigged a giant magnifying glass over the rec field—just to piss off everyone even more so.

• • •

With no compunction whatsoever while on the streets, Rico Rodriguez had ordered multiple contracts on perceived enemies and disloyal gang members. His foot soldiers took care of the details. Law enforcement was helpless, since nobody dared finger Rico. If the leader had even an inclination that something was afoot, the individual/individuals' time left above the ground was definitely limited to days, if not hours.

Thus, when one of his girlfriends with her face looking like ground beef met with DA Mike McCann, he and Chief Breier promised her a new life elsewhere, and on Milwaukee's dime, if she would tell a judge and jury what Rico had done to her.

She agreed.

Rico got ten years for assault and battery with great bodily harm, his absolute first run-in with the law as an adult. Anybody other than Rico would've have been placed on probation. In Waupun, he endeavored to be low-key. He wanted another run on the bricks. And he wanted that bitch dead. Most inmates underestimated him and his followers as being dope heads.

"When the sun goes down, Aryans are runnin' the show or the Cobras are," Wing Nuts warned Rico. "It's your call."

Rico was between a rock and a very hard place. He missed his wife although he'd never been loyal to her. He missed his kids although he never showed them a father's love and concern. When Wing Nuts questioned his manhood, Rico was going to show everyone that Cobras, unlike Anglos and niggers, don't bark like scared dogs. They attack.

Although it was more than possible he'd get additional time if he didn't lead this show, everyone in the joint would treat him and his Cobras like common, everyday punks. Rico and his boys were neither common nor were they punks.

As he stood in the middle of the rec field that Sunday afternoon, he defiantly spoke loudly and clearly—in English. "One of ours was killed by screws, and no blueshirt is gonna kill one of ours and get away with it."

Most inmates, other than Cobras, thought Rico's oratory was right on. Cobras found it troubling their leader spoke in English.

A member of the Mexican Mafia, Jose Fedora, protested loudly and clearly in Spanish, "One of ours?"

Looked up to by the Cobras, Fedora had committed separate armed robberies twelve years ago in Milwaukee and days later, held up a drugstore in Austin, Texas.

Nabbed first by Texas rangers, Fedora had to first complete a ten-year stretch in Huntsville before Texan authorities sent him to Wisconsin's Waupun. "As far as I know, the dog was no Cobra."

"He's Latino, isn't he?" shot back Rico, also in Spanish.

"Yeah," served Fedora. "A wetback like me."

Some Cobras broke grins.

"No matter," returned Rico, "Cobras are gonna stand tall. Besides, our bros, the Aryans, are gonna help."

Fedora slapped his forehead. "Aryans are our bros? You're talking heavy-duty shit there, dog."

Most Cobras remained silent. They knew the real Rico. If the exchange had taken place on the streets, Fedora would have been ground into hot dogs, bratwursts, or Polish sausages.

• • •

Meeting with Zombie, Rude Boy, and Jeremy Clark, Gregory Leacok, a Brother-men released from the Greenhouse, told them, "Screws didn't kill that Mexican. I was two cells down fum him and I swear on my mama's grave that sergeant, he didn't go into no cell until after the man hung his goddamn self."

Zombie turned to Jeremy. "I want matters to be on your level. Go tell Troll. Tell him what Leacock said and saw."

"How about I tell Wing Nuts?" asked Jeremy. "Troll gives me the chills."

Zombie glared.

Jeremy headed across the rec field. Zombie and Rude Boy shielded their eyes, watching both Jeremy and Troll.

Soon, Jeremy returned. "Wing Nuts bought into it. Troll isn't pleased. He warned Wing Nuts it could end up a disaster."

Zombie crossed his arms. "Did you say *could*?"

"Wing Nuts wants us to join them."

"He isn't going to get what he wants."

Rude Boy's chin jutted out as he said, "Brothers don't take orders from no hunkies." Holding off momentarily, he added, "'especially that hunky."

"Let's get one thing straight," said Jeremy. "I'm the messenger, not the message."

"OK," said Zombie, "you tell him that we won't join them but we'll do nothing to stop them either."

• • •

Sgts. Al Preston, Mark Spelling, and Leonard Stam, pulling rec that afternoon, approached Captain Bragg, "Something's up," said Preston.

"And it isn't good," added Stam.

With his usual show of hubris, Bragg drew in a deep breath before blurting out, "Maybe you boys oughta apply for a job at Mercury Marine in Fond du Lac. You won't get scared there."

As the three watched Bragg sashay away, Stam said, "Him and the horse he's riding on."

Preston and Spelling agreed with head nods.

• • •

Ego wished he was sprawled on the La-Z-boy, watching Matt, Kitty, and Chester instead of listening to Pretty Boy Blake snivel and whine. Adding to Ego's discomfort was Blake's overpowering halitosis.

"You want me to call the contract killer? Is that what you want?" asked Ego.

"Yes, I can't take it anymore," blubbered Blake.

"And you know his phone number?" pursued Ego.

Blake stared in obvious disbelief. "You're the one who talked to him on the phone."

"And you think he gave me his private number? Get a hold of yourself."

Ego grabbed two beers from the refrigerator and offered one to Blake. Blake shook his head. Ego returned that bottle to the fridge and popped his with a church key, gulped down half the bottle's contents, swiped at his lips with a shirtsleeve, and said, "Let me tell you how it is. We either pay the piper my way or we spend the next ten to thirty years in a federal joint, not as employees but as inmates—your way. I'm too old, plus I like my freedom, my job, everything I worked for."

Shaking his head, Blake made his way up the stairs, opened the door, stepped out, and quietly shut the door. Ego heard a car door open and shut, an engine start, and a car exit his driveway. He was no longer interested in watching what was on the boob tube. What was Blake going to do—snitch him out? That was a distinct possibility, and Ego wouldn't stand for that.

Avery Todd started his long tenure as governor after William "Bill" Daly, a commercial Realtor, preceded him in a one-term fiasco. Daly and his wife owned mostly dilapidated Victorian houses he bought for pennies and rented to University of Wisconsin students at premium prices.

One night, while attending an ad hoc meeting of Madison Democrats at Carlo's Restaurant, owned by the alleged Mafia Don, Carlos Caputo, Daly was drunk on his ass, as usual, when Donald Crumwell, that night's master of ceremonies, asked the group at the meeting's conclusion, "Anybody got any new ideas?"

Daly stood—well, almost. "I think we oughta close our state prisons."

"That's a great idea," said Crumwell in awe that such an idiotic statement could be made, and in public.

"Yeah," continued Daly, "the money we spend on keeping those poor bastards locked up could be used to bankroll community treatment centers."

"That's the dumbest idea I ever heard," spoke up the sensible Mitch Myers, who had much experience in law enforcement.

"Oh yeah?" said Daly. "Think of it. Psychiatrists, psychologists, and social workers could help lawbreakers overcome their childhood traumas that caused them to become thieves, rapists, and murderers."

UW law professor Delmar Winston stood. "I am truly impressed," he said. "What a novel and truly sensitive ideal, a Democratic ideal." Many in attendance agreed with head nods.

"Hear, hear," some said.

Myers glared at Winston. "You don't know what you're talking about."

Jonathan Sagehart, a practicing psychiatrist with a huge following of patients, the richest shrink in the city, stood. "It's plain to see Mr. Daly understands the criminal mind."

Actually, Daly understood one thing. He was on a roll. Attempting to stand once more but somewhat unsuccessful, he held on to the table and said, "Just think, our state will be the first in the nation to enjoy freedom from crime."

The majority stood, moved their chairs noisily, and headed for the bar.

With Robert's Rules of Order handbook held firmly aloft, Sagehart faced the few men left and resolved that Daly be the Democratic standard-bearer.

After the resolution passed, Myers returned and declared, "Are you guys out of your mind? Who's going to make sure Daly stays on the wagon?"

"I object," said Dr. Sagehart. "Mr. Daly's an adult and–

"Somebody's gotta make sure he stays sober," said Myers, "and I nominate Doc Sagehart."

As the others applauded, the psychiatrist knew he was had.

Eight months later, Sagehart's wife sought for and received a divorce. Since he'd lost most of his medical practice because he was too busy with his job trying to keep Daly sober. In addition, Sagehart lost his kids, cars, boat, and cottage, "up north," as folks in Wisconsin are prone to say.

CHAPTER THIRTY-NINE

Two scenes played in Ego's head theater all night long. They were on a continuous loop.

Scene One: Blake's sitting in the warden's office, crying like a starving week-old baby, spilling his guts, blowing his nose, relating each and every detail leading up to Earl Davis's death.

With Palestine's hand on the red phone, he kept asking, "Are you certain? Are you certain it was Marion?"

Scene Two: Two Dodge County uniformed deputies at his side, Joe Weems steps up to Ego's office.

Ego grins. "Hey, Joe, how they hangin', two in a bunch, I hope?"

Weems appears as if he's looking down on his mother's open coffin. "I'm sorry about this, Butch, but it comes with the territory."

"What're you talking about, Joe?"

"Marion Richardson," says one deputy, "we're placing you under arrest for being party to the crime of murder. Please stand and place your hands behind you."

Ego stands and the deputy cuffs Ego's wrists, clicks them shut, and keys them. "Are they too tight?" he asks.

"No."

"Good," says the deputy. "I'm gonna read you your rights."

Ego protests, "Joe, he don't hafta—I know my ri—"

Weems looks away and studies the portrait of the grizzled cowboy on the wall.

"You have the right to remain silent," says the deputy. "Anything you say may be used against you in a court of law. You have the right to have an attorney present before speaking to me or any other law officer. If you can't afford an attorney, one will be appointed for you."

"Joe," screams Ego, "you guys don't hafta do this. I'll walk out, I don't want to be cuffed, and I promise I won't give you guys no trouble."

"If you decide to answer questions now without an attorney present, you will still have the right to stop answering at any time until you talk to an attorney. Knowing and understanding your rights as I have explained them to you, are you willing to answer my questions without an attorney present?"

With Joe Weems leading the way, Ego walks between the uniformed deputies. They pass by slack-jawed blueshirts. In a second, a horde of blue scatters like a group of teenagers at a raided beer party.

Ego hears them yell, "You won't believe this. You won't believe what we just saw—Dodge County cops—they're marching Ego's ass outta here. He's cuffed. No, we aren't lying."

•••

In the morning, more tired than he could imagine, Ego took his place in the breakfast nook, picked up the *Milwaukee Sentinel*, and made the usual front-page go-around.

On the top right was a picture of a suit, wearing wire-rimmed eyeglasses. It was an obituary. Ego figured the suit must've been somebody important. After he read the cutline, Ego's heart thumped like frenzied drums accompanying a jungle voodoo rite as sweating, singing natives leaped in swirling hysteria around a blazing fire.

So that's what Vergenz looked like. Says he was in a drug treatment program a few months ago. Drug overdose. Smooth's a pro. No doubt about it.

Then, reality hit. *Jesus, what if Kopfmueller sees this? Easy, big guy, he ain't gonna see diddly, 'cause today's paper don't go out back until tomorrow. I'll take care of his TV when I pick up the list. The only thing he'll be reading is the Bible, and the only things he'll be watching are three blank walls and the cell hall's windows through steel bars.*

Bill Daly, oblivious to both Jimmy "Ace" Smedley and Jack "Click" Cassidy, who were surreptitiously shadowing Daly, enjoyed being treated as if he were a king.

Ace and Click worked for the Madison Capital Times.

The paper's managing editor telephoned Daly and asked His Royal Highness if he minded that the editor read to him Ace's first story, word for word, before requesting comment.

"No comment," said his nibs.

"Do you have a drinking problem, Governor?"

"Did you hear me? No comment." The hung-over governor answered with a hang up.

The next day, the Cap Times' front-page headline screamed in three-inch-high letters, "Bill Daly No Friend of Friends of Bill."

It was the first story of a promised series focusing on Daly's troubling lifestyle.

Accompanying the first story were Click's photographs showing Daly after a night on the town, booting the front door of the governor's mansion, his trooper-bodyguard-driver, Scott Ellison, looking on.

According to the cutline, Daly and his wife had spent that evening at Porta Bella Restaurant's basement dining area, boozing and brawling all night.

"Clarice Daly preceded hubby into the mansion before slamming and locking the door," wrote Ace. "Behind her was her husband, holding desperately on to the trooper, and not for moral support, either."

Another photo, entitled "After the Kick," showed Daly lying flat on his back with Trooper Ellison attempting to rouse the boss man.

The second story led with, "Governor Bill Daly nightly—no pun intended—prowls Madison's bar scene with wife Clarice in tow, an unfortunate situation for state citizens who voted for sober leadership."

Donald Crumwell, Daly's chief of staff, attempting to apply a Band-Aid to a mortal wound, told an impromptu press conference, "The governor's personal life is personal. I wish to remind you this ship of state is not rudderless but is in the hands of a competent, hardworking, and dedicated captain."

The next morning, Daly and his flack, Crumwell, made a surprise visit to the Waupun prison, followed by a bevy of media sycophants.

He didn't realize Ace and Click with bogus facial hair were also present.

The next day, Ace's article, in part, stated, "Daly treated inmates as if they were long-lost friends but backed away from prison staff members as if they had a highly contagious disease."

The Cap Times was forced to order additional paper stock in order to meet the ever-growing readership.

CHAPTER FORTY

As Ego rearranged the plaques and photos on his desk Monday morning, Dorothy called out, "Lieutenant Brown's on the line."

Ego snatched his phone. "Yeah."

"It's Judder, sir. You wanted me to call you?"

"Yeah, I been hearing all kinds of things since I came in this morning. I want you to check out the back and then report to me personally in my office."

"Now, boss?"

"You think I want it done tomorrow?"

"I'll check it out—pronto."

"Go get 'em, Lieutenant." Ego put down the phone. *Kick that boy's ass, and like a puppy, he comes back and licks the boot that did it.* "Dorothy."

She looked up. "I'm still here, boss."

"I don't wanna be disturbed by anyone except for Lieutenant Brown. Him I wanna see right away."

"Gotcha," she said.

Ego shut the door, sat, sighed, and grabbed the morning paper. He leaned back and sighed again.

• • •

Judder didn't know if he should be pleased or suspicious. What was Ego's real reason for his sudden change of heart? *Why didn't he ask Blake to check out the back?*

Inmate library workers were, as usual, too enthusiastic in their greetings. Most inmates treated the investigating lieutenant in such manner.

As he passed by the law library, Jeremy Clark sullenly turned away. *Well, one thing's normal.* Judder stopped at the double steel fire doors, one opened to the school hallway, which revealed School Officer Mortenson at his desk, swapping stories with his chief swamper.

The swamper is trying to warn him.

Finally, Mortenson did get the message and jerked to face Judder. The school officer's lower jaw, if it could have, would have struck his chest.

He can't even make believe he knew I was standing here.

Mortenson turned back to his swamper. "What you doing, sitting there? Me and the lieutenant—we got official business to tend to."

"Yowzah," offered the swamper, righting the empty trash basket on which he had sat. He took off for the swamper locker, most likely to get the word out that Judder was in the school.

As the lieutenant and school officer strode the hallway, peering into classrooms but not at each other, Judder whispered, "Have you been hearing anything?"

"You talkin' about Medina?"

"Medina?"

"Well, me and my swamper feel the same way."

"You feel what?"

"He couldn't have done himself in."

Judder tried to say something.

"You know, suicide," continued Mortenson. "Anyway, that's all I been hearing—Medina, Medina, Medina—ever since I picked up my workers. The way I sees it, Lieutenant, no way could Medina have hung himself—but Saturday's first change sheet showed he did—and get this—while he's in Control status. How can a guy kill himself if his ankles and wrists got iron on 'em and they're locked to the bunk's chains?"

Judder was having difficulty sucking air. "First change sheet, I understand."

"Yeah, but when the major puts out the second that says Medina was in TLU and not in Control, the shit hit the fan...but I'm telling you what you already know."

"That's OK," said Judder, trying with all his might to retain his seeming aloofness while the chest pains started to diminish. "It doesn't matter what I think or know or don't know. What I need to hear is your point of view, not mine." *I should've been called in. Ego—he should've called me in to invest—*

"Now, tell me, Lieutenant, if you was an inmate—but of course, you ain't—but just for a moment put yourself in their place—wouldn't you think we're trying to blow smoke?"

"Covering up the fact that staff had something to do with Medina's death?"

"You got it," declared the school officer. "Nobody warned us this morning at the shift meeting. We could've been warned. We could've talked to the inmates that other inmates respect. You know what I mean, get out the word and receive feedback?"

"Yes, I know what you mean."

"My chief swamper says him and most cons figure that at least one blueshirt in the Greenhouse, or a group of them, killed Medina, maybe by mistake—that's the way I got it figured. My swamper was just telling me Brother-men don't want no part of a—"

"Yes? Part of what?"

"You know," whispered Mortenson, "a riot."

Judder reached into a pocket, scored two Valium, and tried not to be obvious as he turned away from Mortenson in order to slip them into his mouth. He swallowed and felt them drop.

"So," continued Mortenson, "if you're really asking me where I stand, you can tell Ego—I mean, Mr. Richardson—that we oughta lock her down and keep her locked down until everything cools off, or else there's gonna be blood—maybe plenty of it."

Returning to the Administration Building and up to the squad room's bathroom, Judder splashed cool water on his face for a full five minutes. Patting his face with a succession of paper towels, he looked into the mirror, hoping he'd appear with normal facial color when he reported to Ego.

•••

Dorothy did her level best to be civil to Judder. "You don't have to knock, Lieutenant. He's expecting you."

Judder nevertheless tapped the door hesitantly.

Ego's voice was loud, clear, commanding, and decisive.

Judder turned the knob and cracked open the door.

Ego was grinning. "Come on in, Judder, and close the door."

Judder stepped up, entered, turned around, shut the door with a soft click, and stirred the chair facing Ego's desk. The chair squawked, Judder obviously not pleased with the noise. As he sat, he was fully aware he was shaking. *Those pills should've already started working.* "Sir, you must be aware of the—"

"How many times have I told you to call me Butch when we're alone, huh?"

"Butch, you, uh, must be aware of the inmate suicide, correct?"

"Yeah, what about it?"

Judder felt as if a semi truck had just slammed into him. "Why wasn't I called in? I'm the investiga—"

"Judder, let me make it plain and simple. I didn't want to bother you. You got enough problems as it is. That's why I—" Reaching into his out-basket, Ego grabbed a stack of file folders. "If you wanna read the reports, here they are."

"I have enough *problems,* sir?"

Ego puffed like a blowfish. "For chrissake, Judder, you know what I'm talking about."

"No, I don't know what you're talking about, Butch."

Leaning forward, eyes moving left and then right, Ego said, "It's no secret you been chewing tranquilizers like they was M&M's."

"Sir, I disagree with you, but I, uh, never mind, because I've got something more important to talk to you about."

"Then, by God, do so," commanded Ego.

"After interviewing a number of blueshirts and inmates throughout the institution," lied Judder, "I believe an inmate riot is imminent."

Ego's cheeks turned dark red. "What? Say that again."

"They could riot today."

"Are you willing to stake your reputation on what you just said?"

Judder felt as if somebody had just shoveled a cup of concrete dust into his mouth. "Yes, I am."

Ego grinned. Picking up his phone and punching the numbers, he said, "You and me, son, we're gonna see the boss—right frigging now."

A voice on the other end caused the grin to disappear.

"Uh, hello, Mary, this is Richardson. I need to speak to the warden." He frowned. "No, it can't wait. It's an emergency."

He winked as he cupped the phone's transmitter. "Good work, son. Good work."

Aware no staff member would ever dare use the word *emergency* unless there was an actual crisis, Judder felt vindicated. *He's treating me as if I am somebody.*

Ego's fingers did a number on the desktop until, "Uh, oh, good morning, boss. Yes, sir, me and my investigating lieutenant need to meet with you—now. Yes, sir, I—" Ego pushed the phone from his ear and eyeballed the ceiling in mock horror before he brought the phone back to the ear. "Yes, sir, I meant my investigating lieutenant and I will meet with you. Yes, sir, we'll be right down."

After Ego placed the phone on its cradle, he practically yelled, "What am I—a frigging English teacher or the security director?"

After highlighting state prisoners' lack of rights, Governor Bill Daly did what every good politician does. He formed a committee. With the lack of any kind of Midwestern common sense, members of the Committee on Offender Rehabilitation insisted they be shown the site where a nineteenth-century harlot prisoner and her bastard baby were buried.

"Nobody knows the location of that cemetery," Palestine told committee members. "Besides, what does an old prison cemetery have to do with present-day offender rehabilitation?"

That quote made the front page of the Milwaukee Journal. After reading it, inmate Wyoming Brewer had a hell of an idea. The wino and ne'er-do-well from Marshfield had passed out in a furniture store he burgled. Cops spent five minutes trying to roust him from a couch in order to tell him he was under arrest.

Wrinkled ears, crumpled face, salt-and-pepper stringy, greasy long hair, basset hound eyes, and a bugle nose with a blue wart on its tip, Brewer was a sight. Whenever he opened his yap, he exposed a black hole guarded by eyeteeth, the color of the Yangtze River. Only Frederico Fellini could have appreciated Wyoming's gander.

Naturally, Wyoming had no idea of the cemetery's location, but that didn't stop him from writing to Don Crumwell, Governor Daly's aide. "Dear Sir, I know where the whore and baby are buried. Signed Wyoming Brewer, Inmate."

Crumwell wrote an appointment letter for Governor Daly's signature and secreted it into the governor's in-basket. Daly hardly ever scanned letters he signed.

Hearing of Brewer's appointment, prison shims tried to help him improve his raggedy-ass looks. Lena Horne shampooed and styled his hair. Saucy starched and ironed his clothes as stiff as overdone pancakes at a VFW breakfast, while Susie-Q loaned him her red patent leather platforms.

Looking like an exhumed Dorothy of Oz, Brewer led the committee to the fence that enclosed the Greenhouse, open palm to his ear. "Hear that? Do ya hear them babies crying?"

"I hear," said Betty, a committee member who leaped excitedly, jiggling like Jell-O on a vibrator. Unbeknownst to Brewer, Betty was School Sisters of Notre Dame Sister Mary Elizabeth, who had recently switched her penguin-like habit for blouse and miniskirt.

"They're whores' babies," said Brewer, "buried under that building, mostly nuns' kids sired by priests. If the truth got out, the pope would lose his gold phone."

Betty was speechless; Mother Superior was not. She tongue-lashed Governor Daly, who in turn screamed at Crumwell, "The letter you'll write to Brewer shall say, 'We no longer need your services, thank you.' And—it's for your signature. Once that's finished, I'll accept your resignation."

After he was kicked off the committee, Wyoming Brewer sued the state and the Notre Dame nuns, seeking millions and demanding the pope's gold phone.

Months later, Marty Showalter of Waupun swore he saw Crumwell at Chicago's O'Hare airport. His head shaved, Crumwell was saffron-robed and, along with fellow Hare Krishna's, circled annoyed airline passengers, chanting, "Wanna buy a flower?"

CHAPTER FORTY-ONE

After Judder recounted his made-up investigation to Warden Palestine, Judder couldn't believe the warden's reaction: it was a huge, juicy, cat yawn. Palestine's swivel chair squeaked as he turned to Ego. "Would you care for a cup of coffee, Marion?"

"Thank you, boss," said Ego, "my usual."

Palestine next turned to Judder. "And you, Lieutenant, how do you like yours?"

I tell you this place is ready to blow up any minute, and you ask how I want my coffee. What is with you? "Two sugars, please, and extra cream."

Palestine lifted from his chair, padded across the carpet, and opened the door. "Mary, Marion and I want our usual coffees. Lieutenant Brown wants his with—" Palestine turned to Judder.

"Two sugars and extra cream, sir," said Judder.

"Did you hear the lieutenant?"

"I sure did," said Mary.

The warden shut the door and padded back to his chair. He sat. As to Judder, the minute seemed like an hour.

Palestine finally broke the silence. "Tell me, Marion, do you agree with the lieutenant's call for an institution-wide lockdown?"

Judder fully expected the security director's forceful, affirmative answer.

Amazingly, the room remained silent.

Ego finally shook his head. "Sir, I wouldn't go as far as recommending an institution-wide lockdown."

What did you say? Did I hear right? Judder stiffened; his chair made a protesting sound.

Palestine jerked. "Did you say something, Lieutenant?"

"No, sir, I didn't. It was my chair." He forced a smile. "It squeaked."

Quickly, Palestine turned to Ego. "Well, just how far would you go, Marion?"

I am being sucked into in a whirlpool of deceit.

As Judder entertained black thoughts, he emerged from them temporarily and heard Ego say, "Zak Griffin and five of my best officers from the second shift will support first-shift program blueshirts. If you assign Shirleen to the school, I'm sure she'll be a big help with the large number of inmates there."

"Your plan sounds economically feasible, Marion, something that we in management must always be concerned about. Your implementation plan is approved. It is as good as done." Palestine removed his Mont Blanc and wrote on a pad before him. "Well done, well done, Marion." Palestine put the cap back on the fountain pen. "Lieutenant?"

"Sir?"

"If I had requested a lockdown as you—"

I've hit the river's bottom. They hope turtles and assorted fish will tear away my flesh until my bones sink below the muddy bottom.

"Lieutenant, are you OK?"

I give my all, and this is what I get in return? "Sorry, sir, I was thinking about something else."

"Lieutenant, you should know that legislators would have called my request for an institution-wide lockdown 'fiscally irresponsible.' It's likely the governor would have ordered Madison Central Office to prepare my retirement papers. So, you can understand why Marion's plan is—"

"Sir," said Judder, "may I say something?"

It took much time but eventually the warden, wearing a stunned look, said, "Lieutenant, I'm shocked. You should know you can say anything at any time in my office—without question."

"Sir, do you recall what happened at Attica in New York?"

"I certainly do, young man. Commissioner Oswald blundered by bargaining with those inmate riot leaders. By the way, as an aside, did you know Oswald worked here in Wisconsin corrections?"

"No, sir, I didn't."

"Russ Oswald could have spent time in Waupun as my understudy, learning the ropes—the way you are learning them right now. He most naturally would have handled matters much differently at Attica if he had been trained in Waupun." The warden looked to Ego, "Marion, you remember Russ, don't you?"

"Yes, sir," said Ego.

"There you go, Lieutenant," said Palestine.

There you go, Lieutenant. How dare you question me? That's what you really meant.

"One thing for certain, Waupun will never become Attica because we—Marion and I—have plenty of experience with these matters. We now have a plan in which to thwart any untoward inmates."

A knock on the door. Everyone in the room turned to it. "Come in, Mary," called out Palestine.

Opening the door with one hand, carrying a platter of coffee cups that tinkled like bells, Mary first served the warden, then Ego, and finally Judder.

I've got to get out of here. Judder placed the cup on Palestine's desk. "Sir," said Judder, eyeballing Ego, "may I be excused?"

Ego's forehead became ridged like an old zinc washboard. "Aren't you gonna drink your coffee, Lieutenant?"

"Sir, since I didn't foresee any other response other than a lockdown, I'll continue to investigate the back, and if I hear anything above and beyond what I've already heard, I'll report back to you."

Ego turned to Palestine. "Warden, is it all right with you if the lieutenant leaves?"

Palestine shrugged, his lower lip sticking out. "That certainly presents no problem to me, Marion."

"Then, go ahead," Ego said to Judder.

As Judder shut the warden's door, he was certain he had heard giggling after Palestine said, "Indeed, Marion."

That is the precise moment Investigating Lieutenant Judder Brown performed a swan dive into the inky waters of mental breakdown.

It was an ordinary night in the Northwest Cell Hall, or so everyone thought—that is, except for Ben Dixon in K-11. He was planning to escape that very night, realizing that if he had confided in one inmate about his intention, the entire institution would have been talking about it. It was his secret, his alone.

Although edgy, he managed to zero in on Jack Malone, K-tier's tier tender, treading the catwalk, coming ever closer, handing out ice.

It was Sgt. Wilbur Jenkins who drove Ben to distraction. "How's it going, Ben?"

When Ben shrugged his answer, the sergeant stopped. "Don't tell me you had a shitty day."

Ben shrugged again.

"Too bad," said the sergeant. "Well, I gotta go because it's close to that time that my relief will report here and take over."

Just then, Ben heard Susie-Q, the alabaster queen, yip for her sweetheart, J-41's Pokeahotass, a huge Ho-Chunk queer. Pokeahotass despised the new terms "Native American" and "gay" and just about everything and everyone else except for Susie-Q, with turquoise eyes, strawberry lips, and not one body hair. She was housed below in I-14. Susie was the former John Devlon, Milwaukee's middleweight Golden Gloves contender in 1965. A moment after the wolf yip, she called out in her finest fem faux, "I love you, babe."

It took years of incarceration for Devlon to finally understand that the woman inside him was desperate to get out. That's why he hacked away his male plumbing with an X-Acto knife and flushed the works down the shitter before calling the cell hall sergeant. The shitter's security screen caught the chunk of meat, but it wasn't until a week later the civilian plumber was called to fish it out.

Brooks Ambulance Service took Devlon to Waupun Memorial Hospital, where an Oriental doctor who spoke Pidgin English stopped the bleeding and sent the inmate on his way to Madison University Hospitals.

Returning to Waupun a week later, Devlon announced to Sergeant Barnes and his tier tenders, "From now on, you and your tier tenders will please call me Susie-Q. I'll answer to no other name." Disrobing, she made like Marilyn Monroe as tier tenders whistled, raised hands over their heads, cried tears, and howled.

"She be lak a department store dummy," croaked tier tender Oscar Washington.

"Mannequin," corrected Barnes, who wrote in the cell hall logbook, "Hobby tools are not allowed in Devlon's cell. Inmate self-destructive."

CHAPTER FORTY-TWO

After taking a long, soothing shower, Shirleen rubbed her body with baby oil, patting dry with an extra-thick terry cloth towel. She applied just the right amount of lipstick. She shook her head and wiped off the bathroom mirror and countertop. She stepped into her bedroom, put on bra and panties, and slipped into jeans and a soft white cotton sweater.

Finished, she traipsed into the kitchen, grabbed a Tombstone pizza from the freezer, and put it in the hot oven. Returning to the fridge, she poured a glass of Chablis, sipping it as she left the kitchen, turned on the TV, and sat on the loveseat.

As she took in the delightful aroma of Italian herbs, Walter Cronkite bid his, "And that's the way it is." She rose, switched off the TV, and chose an Ahmad Jamal LP, recorded at Chicago's Palmer House. It was a present from Zak.

Delicately, she blew away a few dust flecks on the platter. Jamal's "Medicine" came pouring through the JVC floor speakers as she thought of what Katie Hendricks had said: "You and Zak ought to get together again."

"Why would I want to do that?" asked the incredulous Shirleen.

"Because he's a changed man, and you two make such a nice couple."

A couple of days earlier, Dorothy, Ego's loyal secretary, told Shirleen, "If I was twenty years younger, I'd grab Zak and haul him off to my cave."

"Zak's always talking about you," Reggie said to Shirleen at the Business Office on payday.

"He hasn't said anything to me," declared Shirleen.

"Maybe he's bashful."

"And I'm Mary, Queen of Scots."

She made a time check. Six minutes to go. Reaching for the latest *Motion Picture,* she read aloud its front cover message: "You wouldn't treat me this way if my father were alive. She shook her head. "If that wasn't so damned pathetic, I'd—"

She heard a knock on the door. *It could be a Fuller Brush salesman or, worse, Jehovah's Witnesses. I'm not ready for either.* She cleared her throat. "Who is it?"

"Zak."

If you know what's good for you, girl, go back and sit and "let things be," as Auntie would say.

She unlocked the door but let the safety chain remain and peeked through the crack. *Why? Please tell me, somebody tell me why did I open up this goddamn door?*

Zak was dressed in T-shirt and jeans. *He's so damned hand—*

"I've been working on my car's engine. Smells like pizza in there."

His eyes. They're clear. He's not slurring his words. He doesn't look or act drunk. "It was a toss-up," replied Shirleen, "between a pizza or a Swanson's frozen chicken dinner. Pizza won out. What do you want, Zak?" *If you stand here, gawking like a teenager, he's going to think all is forgiven and that you—calm down, Shirleen.*

"That's sounds like the Ahmad Jamal record I bought you," said Zak.

"What do you want, Zak?" *Heart, stop beating so hard. He'll hear and know.* "Have you been drinking?" *His forehead's wrinkling. He's turning red. Good.*

Zak shrugged. "I suppose I deserve that, considering my track record, but no, in answer to your question, I've quit drinking."

"Those are words, Zak, just words."

"Right now," he explained, "words are all I have."

Shirleen's upstairs neighbor, Tom Delaney, descended the stairs to her level. "Hi, Shirleen, Zak." Tom continued down the stairs and was out the door, Zak looking after him. He turned to Shirleen. "I know my past record isn't much to brag about. I said I loved you, I treated you like—"

"Chopped liver," Shirleen finished for him. "Go ahead and say it, Zak."

"You're right. I am my main problem. It wasn't the corps or what happened in Nam. It was me and my self-centeredness—all the way. I've been behaving like a spoiled brat."

Shirleen swiped angrily at the tears that dared fall. "You've made so many promises before, Zak. Why should I believe you now?"

Zak reached to touch her.

Shirleen backed away. "Uh-uh, no you don't."

Normally, Zak would have made an abrupt about-face, thundered down the stairs, slammed the door, and headed to Otto's. "I can understand," he said, "why you can't forgive me."

"Zak Griffin, here you are—apologizing to me so you'll feel better. What about me? Oh, yes? I forget. I should forgive you and take you back because you've gone to a few meetings and haven't had a drink in a short while. What do you expect from me, a medal, applause, pat on the ba—"

"I—"

"No, Zak, let me finish. How you treated—no, I should have said mistreated me, was...Damn you, Zak Griffin, why should I forgive you? You hurt me to the core, you hear? I gave you everything, my heart, my body, my soul."

Slamming the door, she ran to the couch, stopped, stood there, and yelled, "Damn you, Zak Griffin." Crazily, she flew back to the door, unhooked the chain, and opened the door.

Zak wasn't there. She looked down. He was slowly descending the stairs. Shirleen whispered, "Zak."

He stopped.

"Please come back."

He did not move.

"Please."

He bounded up the stairs, lifted her clear off the floor, and brought her to him.

"I must be insane," she said. "Added to that, the pizza's burning."

They laughed and cried together as Zak put her down.

•••

Joanie Richardson picked up the phone. "Hello. Yes, he's here." Smiling, she handed the phone to her hero.

Sighing, Ego reluctantly accepted it. "Yeah?"

"Blake here."

"Yeah?"

"I want you to know—"

"What? I'm busy. I—" He looked to Joanie. She was shaking her head, her way of warning him to cool his heels.

"Nah." Ego changed course. "I shouldn't have said that. I, uh, I got mucho things on my mind." *And if anyone pressures you at all, you're gonna break like cheap china.* "What? You saw his car in front of Shirleen's place? Interesting. Thanks for the information."

Ego put down the phone as gently as possible before he snatched the phone book. It opened to the H's. *Maybe it's an omen. Hammer, Shirleen. There it is, three two four, one nine seven two.* "Honey, I'm gonna use the workshop phone so I don't bother you."

"Such a gentleman," joked Joanie.

•••

The bedside phone demanded attention with its incessant ringing. "Don't answer," warned Zak.

Reluctantly, Shirleen reached for it. "Hello. Why, yes, Mr. Richardson, this is she. Yes, he's here. Just a moment, please." Palm covering the mouthpiece, she whispered, "How did he know you'd be here?"

Shrugging, Zak accepted the phone. "Hello," he said and then listened for a full minute before saying, "Tomorrow's my day off, but I'll be there. I understand. No problem, boss. OK, good-bye."

After Zak handed the phone back to Shirleen, she placed it on the cradle. "How did he know you were here, and what did he want?"

"Reggie must've told him I was coming over here, but he didn't know I'd stay. Well, anyway, the boss man says inmates are uptight. He wants me to help Mortenson in the school tomorrow."

"Guess who else is going to be at the school tomorrow?"

In one hour, Ben Dixon in Cell K-11 would escape.

He listened to Sergeant Jenkins lift the phone and report that all Northwest Cell Hall cells were deadlocked and each assigned inmate was counted by Barnes personally. Missing were men in the hospital, hole, outside court, or on a funeral visit.

Freddie Johnson, the jailhouse Muslim imam, announced Isha in his heavy cornpone, "Eeeee-shaw."

Ben shook his head. The day Freddie would hit the bricks he'd be right back to shooting smack, getting higher than cirrus clouds. A dozen Muslim converts, however, took the dope head seriously and grunted their "Allahu Akbars" as they most likely laid down their prayer rugs on cell floors.

A throng of typewriters takkety-tak-takked as inmate scribes churned out catalog orders, love and hate mail, and lawsuits, along with great American novels minus the slightest hint of following grammar or spelling rules. Belching, coughing, pissing, and plenty of farting rounded out the dissonance. The supper meal had been chili with red beans.

Pissing was loudest. Ben visualized multiple yellow arcs vaulting high as inmates stood with their backs against the bars, pissing an impressive seven feet to the commode. He did the same thing when bored out of his skull. If the flow missed the bowl, the sound was second cousin to a Holstein cow pissing on a flat rock. Arcs hitting their mark sounded like Italian fountains, the subsequent flushes changing any idyllic mental pictures Ben could conjure.

Just then, H-8's Michael "Big Mike" Langston inhaled deeply and made an "Ngggggggggh" sound before honking what must've been an especially adhesive gob, hacked hopefully between his cell bars.

On cue, tier tender Jackie E. Ellingsworth screamed, "You're gonna clean up that mess, motherfucker. I ain't gonna."

Big Mike yelled back, "Suck my love muscle, you punk-assed, motherfucking chump."

Laughter and giggles sprang from cells, since Jackie E. held Waupun's record of sucking a man from dead-assed limp to a pulsating ejaculation in thirteen seconds flat.

As expected, Henry Olson detonated his mighty blast before laughing like hell. In Waupun for thieving five packs of Camels from Habeck's Standard gas station on the corner of Eighth and Baker in Wisconsin Rapids, Henry was viewed as a total dildo.

"Jeeeeezus, that boy has gotta sheeee-it in his pants," squealed Johnny Rutherford in J-23. Armed robber Rutherford was the man with the ax in the prison's R&B band. On the streets, he bonked bandleaders' wives, mamas, girlfriends, daughters, cousins, aunties, and on one occasion, a great-grandmama, which got his black ass fired. Out of work, he held up folks with his Roscoe in order to buy drugs.

CHAPTER FORTY-THREE

Zak tiptoed from bathroom to bedroom, put on socks but not shoes. He didn't want to wake her but still approached her side of the bed, bent over, and kissed her on the forehead.

Purring like a tabby cat, she opened her eyes. "I'll give you a half hour to quit that." Stretching, she added, "I had a dream, Zak. I dreamt we were in love."

"We are, but right now I've got to go."

"Too bad. I was thinking of something else. Guess we don't have time for that, do we?"

"I love you," he said with a smile.

She stood and kissed Zak tenderly. "I'll see you soon," she said.

•••

Outdoors, Zak stopped and lit a cigarette as a robin on a nearby tree branch chirruped.

Zak saluted. "And the rest of the day to you, sir."

•••

Ego sat there, thinking about so many years ago when he held on to the bottom of his father's corduroy mackinaw while "Big Ole" Richardson held on to the tractor's steering wheel while the John Deere's engine sang out its *thackety-wock-wock, thackety wock-wock exhaust pulsations*. Calling out in his deep bass, "Six more passes and then we're done."

"I wished it was a hundred," said young Marion.

Ole laughed as only Ole could. He enjoyed the simple pleasures of life: sipping a beer with Marcella, his wife, and young Marion in tow at Four Corners Tavern, a country inn, on a Friday night's fish fry; arm draped over Marion's shoulder as both sat on a couch, listening to *The Shadow* on the Philco on Sunday night; having Marion sit between him and Marcella in the Chevy with its Stove bolt six sounding similar to Marcella's Singer sewing machine; or like today, with Marion standing beside him on the John Deere.

Marion spotted a field mouse running on a ridge of freshly turned loam, its tiny legs skittering so fast it looked as if it had sixteen rather than four.

Suddenly and without warning, out of nowhere, or so it seemed, a red-tailed hawk stabbed the mouse with talons and flapped its wings until it steadied itself. The bird then lifted one yellow leg, assuring it had gaffed the prey. Its scalpel-sharp beak ended the squirming.

Then, looking straight at the boy, the bird jumped and flapped its wings, lifting ever so slowly, carrying its prey with dancing tail to a gnarly branch of a dead elm along County Highway M, which is where the raptor stabbed and stripped fur before horsing down fragments of flesh. After each swallow, it turned and inspected the boy.

Marion tapped Big Ole's shoulder.

Ole looked.

The boy pointed to the bird.

Nodding and grinning, Big Ole exclaimed, "Big 'un, ain't it?"

• • •

"No talking in line," warned School Officer Mortenson, trying to be Mr. Security Conscious. At least, that's what Zak figured, because Zak was working with Mortenson this morning. It didn't take long for the group to reach the school stairs.

Mortenson led the way up, keyed the lock, and opened the door. Inmates followed him in. Zak and Mortenson made the second count of the morning. "Twenty-two," they called out as one.

"OK, guys," bellowed Mortenson.

The inmates scattered like bees in an upended nest in order to retrieve cups along with jars of instant coffee before heading for the deep sink and the hot water.

•••

On her way to work, Shirleen paused to feed a squirrel that seemed to wait for her five mornings a week. Shirleen laughed. "You're such a pest." She tossed the wood rat a peanut.

•••

Mortenson collected passes from both inmate students and those seeking to use either the library or law library. "Morning, Stumpy, how's your mom doing?"

"Lot better," said the burly inmate, a member of the Outlaws. Stumpy had lost a leg in a motorcycle accident. With intense eyes, shaved head, walrus-like mustache, and a Maltese cross tattooed on each earlobe, Stumpy sounded as if he gargled with gravel. "I had rec last night and talked to her on the phone. She said the doc might release her from the hospital as soon as today."

"That's good news," said Mortenson.

"Sure is," said Stumpy as he moved on.

"Me and my men," Mortenson told Zak while locking index fingers, "we're like this, not like you and your yahoos that toss piss and shit bombs at you any chance they get. My guys aren't like that."

Zak smiled.

Next was the leader of the Brother-men. "Hi, Zombie," Mortenson greeted.

"How're you doing, Mr. Mortenson?"

"Fine, how about you?"

"Good. I'm getting my high school diploma this morning. Moms said she was going to frame it and hang it on her living room wall. How about that?"

Zak and Mortenson offered their congratulations.

Zombie took off for the first classroom on the left, Mrs. Broker's room.

Zak heard a commotion in the library. He turned to the sound.

Shirleen had just stepped inside the library. She was stunningly beautiful. *I don't deserve her.*

Wearing a navy blue suit, white blouse, and navy blue-and-white low-heeled shoes, Shirleen glowed as she headed straight for Zak, extending a hand. "Sergeant Griffin, it's so good to see you. What are you doing in the school?"

•••

Just about every inmate in the Metal Furniture factory wore leather work gloves. Huge machines slammed and clanged and clattered as shear operators sliced large sheet metal pieces into smaller pieces, handing them off to assistants.

The assistants, in turn, handed the smaller pieces to brakemen assistants who handed them off to the brakemen. Pushing foot pedals, the brakemen bent flanges into pieces that were destined to become desk drawers, bookshelves, and desktops. Once the piece was bent, they handed them to number two assistants who pushed them off to welders, flipping their masks from half-mast to full down as they turned on their wire-fed welding guns, the wire crackling and flashing blue-white, melting and fusing one steel piece to another.

An ah-oogah horn blared, a signal for everyone to stop whatever he was doing and turn to Robert Tank, shop officer, holding high an inmate pass. "Kopfmueller," he shouted.

The Aryan removed his helmet and fixed his gaze on the officer.

"Social Services," yelled Tank.

"Yo." Handing the helmet to his assistant, Wing Nuts waited for another inmate to take the assistant's place before he headed to his locker in order to change into his khakis.

The factory floor once again began its earsplitting work.

Opening the locker, Wing Nuts saw one of his Aryans busy Tank with a personal matter while another follower engaged factory manager Jack Stephenson in a shear machine problem.

Holding everything, including the zip gun, bundled up inside his khakis, he closed the locker door and quickly slipped down the stairway, unnoticed by staff and most inmates.

• • •

Shirleen shared small talk with Mortenson while Zak felt "the chill," the very first time since he was last in the Nam. A number of Cobras in the law library was "observing" him.

• • •

Marine Gunnery Sgt. Braxton had shared with Zak that his great-grandparents had been slaves on Tybee Island, Georgia, while a Salem cigarette dangled from Braxton's lips. "At oh-nine-thirty," he told Pvt. Griffin, "we're gonna backtrack through bush we covered yesterday. So, I don't expect no problems." Braxton nodded as some men greeted him. "But don't think that don't mean there won't be none," he warned.

While Zak listened carefully to the sergeant, he nevertheless surveyed other marines in the company. Most were close to his age. Most calculated him in disregard as they dropped laundry and drained the lizard, sweated profusely from both heat and humidity, and slapped at stinging gnats.

It didn't take long for a few of the old-timers to give the new guy a hard time. "Where you from?"

"Wisconsin," said Zak.

"Where in the hell is what-you-say?"

"Wisconsin," chimed in Pvt. Ron Ceridono of Los Angeles, "is north of Alaska, am I right?"

"No, Whistle Dick," said Lance Cpl. John Bullock, "there ain't no such place. It's a figment of Rand McNally's imagination they put between California and New York."

The only exception was Pvt. Mark Hellestad, taller than Zak and much heavier. The blue-eyed blond wore a perpetual grin. "That makes us neighbors. I'm from Ida Grove, Iowa, where right about now—if I wasn't here—I'd be in my thirty-seven Tudor Ford, slant back, with my gal, Mary Beth Jennings, holding on to me."

"Thirty-seven, huh?"

"Yeah, with a fifty Olds rocket eighty-eight under its hood. It goes like a bat outta hell. Took it to the drag strip in Cordova, Ella-noise, and Union Grove in your state, where it ran in the high fifteens."

"I've a thirty-five Plymouth coupe," said Zak. "It has a Ford three-oh-two I took out of a rolled-over Mustang. I took it to Bill Gerrits, who ported and polished it, balanced the crank, dropped in a Crower racing cam, oversized pistons, larger valves, and dual carbs. I saw Big Daddy Garlits at the Grove race, his Swamp Ra—"

"OK, girls," broke in Sergeant Braxton, a lit Salem dangling from his lips, "let's lock and load."

His men moaned and groaned.

"Does he ever inhale?" asked Zak.

"I don't think so," said Hellestad. "He even sleeps with a lit one, hanging between his lips."

Ben Dixon stood before the commode and prayed for patience. He couldn't begin the actual escape until lights-out and after Charlie Tuna made his round of the tiers.

Ben listened to Willie Sommers in L-37, pounding off and singing in falsetto, an every-night occurrence, "You are my everything."

"It is better to cast your seed in the belly of a whore than to spill it on the ground," preached F-8's Charlie Ames, a born-again Christian who spent just about every day in the chapel, hitting on young inmates.

"That ain't in my Bible," countered Willie as Ben checked his watch. It was time to start tearing strips. He lifted the footlocker's lid and retrieved the extra fart sack for which he paid a box of Pall Malls to Jake Malone, K's tier-tender. There'd be no screw on K until Charlie made his round. After that, Ben would perform his Houdini act.

Ben never dealt well with authority, including parents, teachers, and cops. His parents forced him to see a counselor who gave Ben his first blowjob.

He received a GED in Walla Walla, Washington, because the Parole Commission told him he'd either have that diploma in hand or languish in prison until his time was up. He passed the tests without a hitch. As promised, the commission cut him slack.

He didn't like emotional tangles. Once, he hooked up with a brown-eyed brunette waitress. Sarah was soft, silent, thoughtful, and downright beautiful. One night in a motel room, she asked, "Why do you keep doing things that get you locked up?"

Ben filled up a water glass with Old Overholt, kicked back, took a swig, and grinned.

"You could be in prison most of your life," she continued, "and that would be such a waste."

The fluid lit up his mind where smart-ass answers dwelt. "What about you? You wait tables eight hours a day, six days a week, and what does that get you?" Taking a deep breath and singing with a voice that attempted at sounding like Tennessee Ernie Ford, "Another day older and deeper in debt. Me? I steal what I want and get plenty of dough and live like a rich man until, that is, I get caught."

Sarah shook her head. The next morning when he awoke, Sarah was gone. He found out a couple days later that she even quit her job.

Although he never saw her again, Ben thought of her from time to time.

If he only had paid her heed...

Finished with the first strip, Ben felt tears coming, but tears were for sissies. He was no punk.

CHAPTER FORTY-FOUR

Foxtrot Company moved out at a cautious pace. Most of the eighteen- to twenty-year-old men were combat-proven vets. Zak was not. As the others searched for anything that seemed out of place, Zak followed suit, but he couldn't have known what was out of place. All at once in that heat and humidity, he felt the chill.

Zak shuddered.

"What's wrong?" asked Hellestad of Ida Grove, Iowa.

"I don't know. I feel cold."

"You sick or something? Maybe one of these will help." Hellestad shook a pack of Pall Malls toward Zak. Zak reached out, grabbed a cigarette, but dropped it. Stopping and stooping, Zak heard Hellestad say, "Maybe you feel cold because—"

Ka-fump. And just like that, Hellestad had become a crumpled pile on the ground.

Somebody snatched Zak's arm—harshly. It was Braxton. "Didn't you hear me, goddammit? Get down."

Zak dropped.

Zak turned to what was left of Private Hellestad. He wished he wouldn't have. The bones he saw belonged to Hellestad's spinal column.

By this time, most men were shooting and cursing and shooting some more, most except for Braxton and Zak. "Cease fire," yelled Braxton, but the gunfire increased in sound and fury. "Goddammit, cease fire."

A few men stopped and echoed Braxton's order.

Doc, the name usually given to all navy corpsman, covered what was left of Hellestad's torso with an Ace bandage the size of a pillow.

Once Zak stopped vomiting, Braxton lit Zak's cigarette, the one Hellestad had earlier offered him.

"When he got hit with that fastball," Braxton told Zak, "he didn't hear nothing, didn't feel nothing, neither."

Zak thought a baseball term peculiar for a sniper's bullet. However, from that moment on, Zak fully relied on the chill as his personal warning system.

•••

Upstairs in the Metal Furniture factory, the sound of the machinery had stopped. "It's darker than a well digger's ass in here," Wing Nuts said aloud, "and I'm not stayin' in here another second." Pushing ahead by sliding numerous large boxes filled with metal furniture that would be shipped to state offices or universities, he made it to the exterior. *Pflip.*

What's that?

Pflip.

His eyes shot to the deep sink's spigot, where a drop of water dangled at its end and took its sweet-natured time to grow fat and heavy enough before it fell to the sink's bottom. *Pflip.*

Another took its place.

The zip gun's barrel, trigger mechanism, and hammer were made of steel. The rest was hard wood, painted flat black. Wing Nuts thought the weight was Goldilocks perfect—not too heavy, not too light, just right.

He fished for a .22-caliber long cartridge in his pocket, carefully pulled the hammer back, and dropped the bullet into the barrel's end nearest the hammer. Ever so cautiously, he aimed at a make-believe target. "Bang," he whispered his make-believe shot.

• • •

Zak figured the high number of Cobras sitting at or standing around the law library research table caused the chill.

Besides that, Jeremy Clark seemed to be checking his reaction. *Something's wrong.*

At Mortenson's desk, Zak rifled through the passes. "I don't see a pass here for Rico Rodriguez."

"That's because he's not—"

"Let me go." The scream definitely came from a female.

Mortenson's eyes were twice their normal size. "What was that?"

"Trouble," snapped back Zak. "That was Shirleen."

Johnny Sanchez slapped a shank to the side of her neck and warned Zak. "Take another step, dog, and I'll do this bitch real good."

When Cobra leader Rico Rodriguez grabbed Zak, Zak took a step back, fired the arm downward, freed himself, chopped Rico with an elbow, and body-slammed him against the wall.

At least fifteen Cobras, all wearing deadpan looks, formed an ever-tightening circle around Zak and their leader.

"Zak," Shirleen called out, "I'm all right. He's not hurting me."

Zak let go and held both hands high.

• • •

Rico Rodriguez had a dream the night before the riot. In it, he was like Pancho Villa sitting on a hand-tooled saddle, cinched to a high-stepping white stallion. Pulling slightly the reins, Rico steered the steed around throngs that applauded him. The place: Madison's Capitol Square.

Waving his sombrero to the Anglo university types dressed alike in khaki trousers, blue chambray workmen's shirts, and Hush Puppies, he threw kisses to their mostly small-breasted women in tie-dyed T-shirts and nearly white blue jeans. They were shod in combat boots, earth shoes, and flip-flops. The tiny titties swooned as Rico and his high-stepper passed by.

Governor Avery Todd awaited Rico's presence on the dais, holding on to a bronze medallion, intended to award the Cobra leader for exposing the prison guards who murdered Juan Medina.

However, looking at the mess and chaos that now occurred before his eyes, Rico knew his dream was like a Roman feast. Reality turned out to be a dog-shit sandwich.

•••

Johnny Sanchez held Shirleen while his latest lover, Esteban "Concha" Fernandez, who looked more like a teenage girl than an adult male, held out a roll of 3-M masking tape.

Her dominator snatched the roll with utter contempt in order to maintain respect from fellow Cobras. "Hold her, will ya," Sanchez ordered, pushing Shirleen to Esteban.

"Sit," Sanchez ordered Jack Murgatroyd, a library worker and now a Cobra hostage, since he stridently opposed the takeover.

Murgatroyd sat.

Sanchez taped his ankles, legs, trunk, and chest.

"Be careful so he can breathe," whispered Concha.

Finished, Sanchez rose and kicked Murgatroyd. "You're lucky, you snitch-ass punk, you ain't dead."

•••

Cobra guards opened the school's entrance door in order to let in additional groups of howling inmates claiming they wanted action, including Jughead Brewer and a number of Aryans. "Move them bookcases over to them windows so their sharpshooters can't see us," yelled Jughead.

Men grunted and cursed and pushed those heavy, loaded steel bookcases toward the outer wall while a number of books fell to the floor, the noise awful.

Rico felt he'd never get out of prison. *Why did I listen to Wing Nuts?*

•••

After Maj. Mark Ericson completed overseeing the movement of noninvolved inmates to their assigned cell halls, he stood below the school.

He had ordered Captain Bragg to check count in all cell halls, including Greenhouse. Bragg had reported back that all Greenhouse inmates were accounted for and that three-quarters of the inmates were in their assigned cells.

That means about three hundred are involved or are hostages or hiding. That puts me between a rock and a hard pla—

It was soft but nevertheless the noise was unexpected. It was close. And it was behind him. Ericson jerked. Startled, he was looking directly into the eyeballs of Gangs Captain Blake, no more than twelve inches away from Ericson's nose. "You could've warned me," said the major, figurative chunks of ice sliding down his spine.

Blake shrugged. "I didn't mean to scare you."

"You didn't scare me. You surprised me."

Blake shrugged and pushed an electronic bullhorn at Ericson. "Richardson says to use this when you talk to those assholes up there. ERU squads are suiting up. It's gonna be a helluva party. By the way, you're no longer Bar Four. You're field commander." Withdrawing a piece of paper from his shirt pocket with fanfare, he unfolded it. "I need notes, you know, with all this excite—"

"If the warden don't get up here in five minutes," yelled an inmate with a dark blue watch cap over his head, holes cut out for eyes, nose, and mouth, "we're gonna toss a dead teacher out of this window."

•••

Rico Rodriguez watched pathetically and helplessly as Aryans herded inmates wanting no part in the riot to the rear of the darkened library. Every last one directed hateful, angry looks at Rico as they marched by.

•••

Johnny Sanchez grabbed Shirleen's breasts and laughed.

Zak snatched Rico by the shoulders, spun him around, and lifted him off the floor. "If you want your leader to continue breathing, you'll let her go—now."

•••

The Cobra leader was uncertain of anything. One moment, he was lifted off the floor, and the next, he was slammed to the floor. At least that's what he thought. Something heavy was on top of him. He had trouble breathing.

Finally, the weight was gone.

Hector Soto pulled Rico to his feet, Rico staring at his open, bloodied hands.

Hector pointed to the mound on the floor, which turned out to be the big sergeant. "That's his blood," said Hector, "not yours."

Ben Dixon was so contrary that he did the opposite of the long ago admonition to "Go West, young man," because after Walla Walla, he traveled east and did stretches in Deer Lodge, Montana; Bismarck, North Dakota; Stillwater, Minnesota; and finally Waupun, Wisconsin, or as he called it, Wis-cow-shit. His longest stint on the bricks in twenty-two years was fourteen months.

Both parents had died, and the only relative who had anything to do with him was his sister, Beth, but even she had stopped doing anything with him. "You're always going to be in trouble, Ben, and that's unfortunate," she warned the last time she visited him in Stillwater.

"Oh, Joanne, honey. Oh, honey," moaned Antonio Cruz in J-20, trying to get Joanne Woodward hot.

With a profusely bleeding and suffering Christ on the cross wearing a crown of thorns tattooed to his back, Cruz ate at the same dining room table as Ben. This afternoon, Cruz showed Ben a picture of the actress Cruz had ripped out of a library magazine. He had inked-in breasts, nipples, and also added her lunch counter at the Y. "I'm gonna eat her out tonight," said Cruz.

"Damn it, Tonio, you come too quick."

Ben finished with another strip.

"Joanne, you felt sooooooooo good."

Ben grinned as he reached into the bottom of footlocker for his King James Bible. Although he knew nobody would be standing outside his cell, he still looked anyway before he opened the religious tome to page 353, the first page he began cutting a slot in order to hide a second pair of fingernail clippers he was not allowed to possess.

Deftly, almost lovingly, he touched them. He'd spent many nights sharpening the tool on the cell floor. He even questioned why Wisconsin cons were allowed to purchase even one pair. All the other joints he'd been in forbade them. If a con had a mind to, he could plunge one into somebody's eyeball and perform a swift lobotomy.

What the hell, he'd concluded a long time ago, even a ballpoint pen or regular pencil could become a lethal weapon, and there were plenty of both in Waupun.

CHAPTER FORTY-FIVE

Bedlam reigned. Inmate hostages, hands taped behind their backs, glared at inmate guards assigned to them as demented rioters flashed by, screaming, threatening everyone with some form of agonizing, end-of-life experience.

"Why'd you hit him so hard, dog?" demanded Rico.

"What you want me to do—kiss him?" Soto demanded in return as he pointed at the big sergeant. "Look, his chest. It's moving. He's alive."

Rico looked. "Good," he said. *That saves my ass—so far.*

A heartbeat later, Jughead Brewer and his followers surrounded the pair. Rico figured the group numbered at least twenty Aryans and maybe a dozen Chicago Black P-Stone Nation members.

"I got two questions," Jughead yelled at Rico. "Number one, when do we toss staff and snitches out those windows? And two, when do we get some pussy?"

"Pussy," the others yelled, "we want pussy."

Rico said something to Soto in a hushed voice after which Soto nodded.

"Talk to me, not him," insisted Jughead.

Hector stepped forward. Jughead backed off. "Rico says we ain't gonna toss nobody, and you ain't gonna get no pussy, either."

"Why?" demanded Jughead.

"'Cause that's what Rico says, and what he says is what we do." Hector's chest popped out as one man apparently warned him, lifting both fists, covered with modified file drawer handles that were now passable brass knuckles.

Hector glared.

The man tossed the handles to the floor.

"OK," screamed Jughead, "we agree. Rico's boss, but getting pussy never harmed nobody."

"Pussy," the others shouted, "we want pussy. Pussy, we want pussy. Pussy, we want—"

Jughead must have felt he had the upper hand. He strode to the door leading to Alice Broker's classroom and began shattering its windowpanes with bare fists. His blood splattered glass and walls.

Crazily, he turned to face Rico and Soto and supporters while grinning and licking at the blood. "That's real pussy behind that door." Jughead pointed to Mrs. Broker.

"Pussy, pussy, pussy."

Inside the classroom, Zombie rose from his desk and turned. Slowly, ever so leisurely, he made his way to the classroom door. He trumpeted loud enough for those in the hallway to hear. "Don't even think of coming in here."

Jughead turned to his followers. "Didja hear that?"

"Yeah," answered one follower, but the remainder of the group acted as if they were monks who had taken lifetime vows of silence.

Rico softly told Soto, "Take. Him. Out. Now."

Like a runaway cement truck, Soto stepped over and through some of Jughead's followers, seized the Aryan's windpipe with thumb and forefinger, and drove him into the wall and broken glass.

Jughead's eyeballs. They nearly burst from their sockets. It was obvious he couldn't breathe.

Hector turned to Rico.

Rico shook his head. "Not yet. We have to convince him we're serious, dog."

As Soto clamped harder, Jughead went to his knees as frog-like chirrups erupted from somewhere within him.

"OK," said Rico, "I think he's convinced."

When Soto let go of Jughead's trachea, he shoved the Aryan's face into a fractured glass panel, and when Soto yanked the head backward, shards stuck out of Jughead's chin and cheeks. One above the right eye caused blood to gush out. "What do you say now?" Soto demanded.

Jughead choked, "Rico, he's boss."

Soto let go. Jughead dropped to the floor like a rag doll.

Soto turned to Jughead's followers. "Nada," he said, pointing at Jughead. "He's about nada." With a flourish, he returned to Rico's side.

• • •

In the inky blackness where Zak dwelt, a spotlight suddenly lit up Major Than's face.

"I guess this is it. I must be dead," said Zak.

"Not yet."

"Then, why this—this nothingness?"

"You won't like my answer."

"Which is?"

"You and I are inside the brain that's in your head. That's why there's this nothingness."

"My head?"

"Yes," said the major, "the same one that Soto used a claw hammer on."

"And I'm not dead?"

"Not yet."

"Will I die soon?"

The major disappeared; the blackness returned.

• • •

Mark Ericson punched on the handheld. "Control, this is field commander."

"This is Control. Go ahead, Field."

"Riot spokesman says they're going to kill a teacher unless the warden meets with them in five minutes."

"That's a ten-fo—"

"We copy, Field," interrupted Ego. "Advise riot spokesman to use phone in principal's office. Sergeant Barnes is waiting to talk to him."

• • •

Alex Mortenson couldn't understand why he was being held hostage since he treated inmates as if they were his friends. He wasn't a hard-ass like a lot of officers he could name. "Rico, didn't I treat you and your Cobras right?"

Rico's huge bodyguard forced Mortenson to his knees. Mortenson made the sign of the cross.

"Are you Catholic?" asked Rico.

"Yes." Mortenson was obviously close to tears.

"You don't have to worry. We ain't going to hurt nobody as long as you and everybody else do what we say. Nobody's gonna get a scratch—nobody."

Rico couldn't tell Mortenson he wanted this thing to end, even more so than Mortenson. Rico could only hope that ninjas would soon charge their way up the steel stairs in a crescendo of boots, knock down the door, and stop this thing before anyone got hurt or worse, because it would be his ass plopped on the front burner of the criminal justice system's hot-burning stove.

• • •

With toilet paper applied to his wounds, Jughead surveyed his facial overhaul in the mirror outside the swamper locker. "You look like a clown," he told the face in the mirror.

"An extremely observant and cogent remark," observed someone nearby.

Jughead jerked. It was Troll Ostremski, appearing to delight in Jughead's discomfort. "It's also obvious Soto was trying to grind you into hamburger."

"That might be," said Jughead, "but at least I'm not uglier than a can of worms and as ruthless as a shithouse rat."

"And after the gendarmes take this place over once again—and they will—they'll assign a surgeon with Parkinson's disease to sew up that raggedy-assed face of yours."

"Enough of this love talk. Where were you when Soto was hammering my ass?"

Troll shrugged. "With the others, watching."

"Why didn't you help?"

"You didn't ask."

"I gotta ask?"

"That's all you had to do, and I would've taken care of matters—then and there—with this." Troll displayed a sharpened welding rod.

"Listen, bro, the next time you see an Aryan on the wrong end of an ass-whooping, assume he needs your help."

"And miss the show?"

Frustrated, Jughead said, "OK, you didn't help because I didn't ask. Now, I'm asking. Will you snuff Soto?"

Jughead winced as a gob of toilet paper fell to the floor. He unwound about five more feet from a roll, wadded it up, and held the clump to the wound until it bled enough for the paper to stick.

"Zombie disrespected you," said Troll. "Do you want me to take care of Zombie, as well?"

"No, I don't wanna piss off his men. They're out of this, and that's where I want them. Take care of Soto, and I'll finish off the big sergeant and his girlfriend."

"I'd like it better if you finish the sergeant and I get his woman."

"She's gotta be snuffed, not just corn-holed with a broom handle."

Troll flashed a crazed grin. "She's as good as wasted—that is, after I take care of my personal needs."

"It's a plan, then," finalized Jughead, *you ugly bastard.*

Ben Dixon was the inmate shipping clerk in Auto Tag, the vehicle license plate plant. Part of his job entailed cutting the twine that held cardboard that he folded into boxes that would hold fifty pairs of plates in them. He and a half dozen other inmates twice a week loaded the boxed plates into the trailer of a state-owned semitruck, its driver hauling them to Madison's Department of Motor Vehicles.

Ben began saving the cut twine, and when he was absolutely certain no one was looking, he concealed it under the bottom rollout drawer of his desk, adding bits of torn paper to the mix. He was quite certain second- or third-shift screws making a surprise search of the shop would likely assume they'd found a rodent's nest. Ben even added specks of dirt that could have been mistaken as mouse droppings.

Escape Day arrived. That's when Ben secreted the twine in his rectum when work was finished and he changed from work greens into khakis. On the march to the cell hall, the twine bit. His ass was raw.

He had been busy that day, having removed ink tubes from ballpoint pens he had boosted from the shop foreman, which is what he used to dye the twine and glue it to a piece of gauze for which he had to pay plenty to an inmate nurse. After that job was finished, Ben used nearly an entire bar of Fels-Naphtha for hand cleanup.

He then placed the wig on "Dummy," the head he had formed by tying a couple of prison towels into knots that formed a ball. Dummy was safely ensconced in his footlocker.

Inmates had most of the guards figured out. Charlie Tuna didn't use his light on the second and subsequent rounds. Ben accepted that as a fact of life.

Just then, he heard the cell hall's huge entrance door open and then shut, followed by Sergeant Jenkins's calling out, "Hi, Charlie. How they hanging?"

Two in a bunch," was the answer.

CHAPTER FORTY-SIX

Lee Summerfield carefully opened the warden's office door, shut it softly, approached Ego, and said, "We've four ERU squads suited up and ready. Do you want me to give them the go-ahead?"

"Not until state patrol arrives. Do you agree, boss?"

Palestine covered the receiver and said, "Do what is best, Marion," and then to the phone, he said, "No, Kyle, I was talking to my security di—"

• • •

Another desk flew out, followed by a third from yet another window, which is when Ericson asked Blake, "Where were we?"

Blake kept staring at the desks.

"Did you hear me? Captain, Captain Blake?"

Blake finally turned. "Did you see them? Those desks?"

"Yeah, I saw them. What about the state patrol's radios."

"Oh yeah, as soon as they get their antenna hooked up on the overpass roof, they're gonna hand out their walkie-talkies to us. That way, those assholes up there won't know what we're up to. Say, I gotta go."

"I could use somebody by my side, advising me."

"I can't. I gotta locate loose inmates. I found one guy in the Social Services Building, thought he was all alone. There he was in the hallway, jerking off. When I yelled at him, he zipped up so fast he got his foreskin caught. He was still moaning when blueshirts escorted him to the Greenhouse."

Ericson laughed for the first time since everything went nuts.

•••

Rico Rodriguez, certain the blueshirts were not going to rescue him, formulated plan B. "Hey, dog, go get Ms. Hammer."

Soto shrugged. "Sanchez—he got her."

"Sanchez don't count. Blindfold her and bring her here. Have her kneel next to Mortenson. Then, get the librarian and do the same thing, and then all the teachers, one by one, and have 'em kneel. After that, blindfold them."

"Sanchez won't like it."

Rico stared.

Soto shrugged. "You're the boss."

Rico watched as Soto said something to Sanchez. Lips curling in defiance, Sanchez pushed Shirleen at Soto who told Shirleen something before blindfolding her.

"Who wants her, anyways?" Sanchez screamed at Rico.

•••

As Shirleen was being led where she knew not where, she thought only of Zak. *Haven't seen him, haven't heard him, nobody's said anything about him. Please, God, let him be safe in your hands.*

Soto stopped her. "Kneel," he ordered, helping her to her knees. Then, he tied her hands behind her back.

•••

Reggie Walters pumped the Ithaca and pointed its barrel at a darkened library window. The school building's exterior was no more than twenty feet away.

"Officer Walters."

Reggie searched other windows.

"Down here," said the voice.

It was Ericson, standing by the school stairs.

"Yeah? I mean, yes, sir?"

"You are to comply with lethal force guidelines."

"I know them by heart, major. They're designed by judges and lawyers who don't have to deal with these jerks—but you don't have to worry, sir, I'll follow the guidelines." *I'll blow away the first son of a bitch who pops his head out of a window—and he won't hear any warning shot, either.*

•••

Sgt. Jimmy Helm blocked the entrance to the security office.

Dorothy looked up from her typewriter and glared. "Helm, can't you see I'm busier than a mother tryin' to breast-feed hungry triplets at the same time?"

"I see," said Helm, "but I want you—and everyone else up and down the chain of command—to be aware that I'm not gonna let anyone in or outta the overpass gates until a whiteshirt—or above—authorizes me to do so."

Dorothy sighed long and hard. "Look, as I said before, and I'm telling you once more, Mr. Richardson said all first-shift officers and civilian staff assigned to the Administration Building are to remain at their posts. That includes you, Helm." Dorothy rose and shouted at the other staff members. "And if you don't work in the Administration Building or this office, then you are report to the squad room."

That's when the group started shouting out questions.

"Now," said Dorothy, "not later."

"Who am I supposed to let in and who am I supposed to let out?" demanded Helm.

"Tell me, Sergeant, do I look like Mr. Richardson?"

"Can't you tell us how many hostages they have?" Helm asked.

Henry Wye, third shift, Tower Two, drove his bloated head through the doorway. "What's happening?" he asked.

"Report to the squad room," screamed Dorothy.

Wye turned to Helm. "Who rattled her cage?"

"That's it," screamed Dorothy. "Get out of here and leave me the hell alone."

That is the exact moment Officer Two Dan Weeks poked his head between Wye and Helm. "Where am I supposed to report?"

Dorothy pulled at her hair and screamed.

"Whoops," said Weeks, making a quick retreat.

"Don't sweat it," Helm cautioned Weeks, "I'm number one on her hit parade."

Sgt. Charles "Charlie Tuna" Crivitz's breath reeked like a rotting carp. Staff and inmates disagreed as to the source of halitosis. It was a toss-up between having gut cancer or Charlie's eating used cat litter.

While second-shift Sergeant Jenkins filled in Charlie, Ben Dixon's heart raced as fast as Big Daddy Garlits's Hemi-powered Swamp Rat rushed from the Christmas tree to the big end of the quarter mile in less than six seconds.

The sergeant's swivel chair's springs sighed from relief as Jenkins rose, moments before the coils gasped from Charlie's big ass settling down on them. A moment later, Jenkins called from just outside the big door, "Good night."

Charlie grunted his farewell before Jenkins keyed the lock shut from the outside. Charlie would be locked down with the inmates until five forty-five in the morning, when the first-shift sergeant keyed open the door.

Ben Dixon figured Jenkins would probably drive to Otto's Bar & Grill and quaff a few brewskis before heading home to his wife, Myrtle, who slept with her hair coiled around big-assed curlers. Inmates learn a lot by listening in on blueshirt conversations.

At ten o'clock exactly, Charlie groaned, Ben guessing he was just about to lift for the handle connected to the bell's clapper. A moment later, four loud gongs rang out, signaling lights-out.

Most cons were snail-slow in unscrewing the forty-watt ceiling bulbs because Charlie took at least a half hour before he made his round. If cell lights weren't off by then, he'd write tickets. Charlie didn't have to put up with any bullshit because he was vacation-holiday relief.

Cells' TV sets were allowed to remain on as long as the sound was turned low enough so men in adjoining cells couldn't hear. If anyone believed that bullshit, he was born yesterday. Simply, cons kept their sound low because nobody in his right mind desired to have his skull caved in on the rec field in an unfortunate "accident."

Many residents kicked their commodes' handles at about the same time, Ben thinking the entire cell hall was about to be sloshed down a monstrous shitter holding a lake's worth of urine and Waupun water.

CHAPTER FORTY-SEVEN

"You got three minutes, or we start killing hostages," the masked rioter yelled to the field commander.

Ericson paid him little heed as he listened to Laundry Officer Don Maxon, outfitted in ERU black. "No doubt whatsoever, sir, that's Pepe Cisneros. I know his voice anywhere. He's—uh, take that back—he *was* my runner, my right-hand man."

"Thanks," said Ericson, "Cisneros, he's—"

Thup-thup-thup-thup-thup-thup.

Maxon had to move in closer to Ericson, holding a hand to an ear.

Ericson yelled, "Gone."

Thup-thup-thup-thup-thup-thup.

The helicopter, hovering no more than a hundred feet above them, bore on its body a large red number four inside a yellow circle.

Rioters stuck their heads out windows, some not even bothering to disguise themselves. Ericson got out his notepad and started writing down names of inmates he could identify.

"Return to your squad," Ericson yelled to Maxon.

Thup-thup-thup-thup-thup-thup.

Maxon saluted and took off in a run toward the Southwest cell hall, the cameraman in the copter's open bay pursuing Maxon with his lens.

Ericson switched on the handheld. "Command, this is Field." He slapped the speaker to his ear and heard, "Go ahead, Field."

"We have a helicopter above us." By the time the speaker made it back to his ear, he heard, "Contact FAA."

Thup-thup-thup-thup-thup-thup.

A second helicopter appeared. Additional rioters pushed and shoved at one another in order to get front-row spots.

"Command," radioed Ericson, "we now have two copters."

The second copter's downdraft nearly drilled him to his knees. The pilot, chewing gum, wore a pencil mustache and mirrored sunglasses. As Ericson waved him off, the pilot nodded, gave a thumbs-up, and forced his craft to rise above the Food Services Building.

• • •

Shirleen was more worried about Zak's safety than her own. *Let me know you're alive, OK? Speak up. Let me know, some way. Yell, whisper, talk, be alive, be safe, and don't, please don't be a hero. This can't last forever. Why hasn't ERU come up here—what's holding them back? Don't they care? Zak, please, please let me know you're OK.*

One nearby rioter screamed, "There's two of 'em now, not just one."

"Let's get our pictures took," another yelled.

• • •

"Did Soto use the claw end of the hammer?" asked Zak.

Major Than Lanh was lit up once again in what a moment before was total darkness. The major laughed. "Might I use an American expression, 'Give the man a kewpie doll'?"

"Is Shirleen OK?"

"For now."

"When am I going to come to?"

"Whenever you're ready."

"I'm ready."

"Well, then—"

The major disappeared, but Zak remained in the black stillness.

• • •

"Command, this is the field commander."

"Go ahead, Field. This is Command."

"Both helicopters have left. They've flown in the direction of the Horicon Marsh. Weapon making in the welding class is continuing. We can see grinding sparks and weld flashes. I want electricity and water in the entire school building turned off. Jesus, they're—"

"Field, what's the matter? What are they—?"

"Rioters, they're hoisting Shirleen onto a window ledge. She's blindfolded. I think they're—no, they haven't pushed—they're yelling that they want to talk."

• • •

"Marion, did I hear correctly? Is Shirleen out on a window ledge?"

"Yes, boss, but they haven't pushed."

The warden lifted the red phone. "Kyle, rioters have placed our inmate advocate, Shirleen Hammer, on a window ledge. They haven't pushed yet. Our field commander, Major Ericson, is attempting to talk them out of it as we speak."

• • •

Hector Soto made his way for the bathroom but tumbled and then fell. Someone had tripped him. The big fellow was on the floor. That's when Troll Ostremski pierced Soto's ear canal with the nearly needle-size point of a sharpened welding rod.

Pulling it out, Troll blended into a mob of rudderless rioters.

• • •

Vietnam army medic Isidro Moreno wanted no part in the insurrection, but Rico Rodriguez told him, "Help Soto, or else."

"Or else, what?" asked Moreno.

"Or else you're gonna meet God this very day." Rico appeared as serious as cancer.

Moreno accompanied him to where Soto lay. He knelt, made a quick check of vital signs, and looked up to Rico. "There's nothing I can do. Somebody wanted him seriously dead. See those eyes?" Moreno pointed. "They're already fogging up."

"He's still moving," said Rico, pointing to Soto's legs.

"Yeah," said Moreno. "I saw that dance in the Nam many times. It's his last one. Is there anyone else you want me to look at?"

"Check out the big sergeant. See what you can do for him."

•••

Jughead kept telling the Cobra pair leading him down the hallway that he'd have met with Rico voluntarily. When they met up with Rico, he pointed at the dead Soto.

Jughead patted the toilet paper on his face. "I didn't have nothing to do with that."

"I had brought you here to ask you only one question."

"Yeah?"

"Where's your leader?"

Jughead shrugged. "Hell if I know."

Rico solemnly nodded. "I want you and all Aryans to know this has been a setup all along, and Cobras don't want no part of this—this fucking mess."

Jughead recalled Wing Nuts's warning. "But the Aryans do," he said.

"Then, you have it," Rico said with a wave of his hand. "We're finished."

•••

Sammy "Dime Bag" Mayfield, an Aryan lieutenant, tried not to stare at the toilet-papered face.

"We're taking over," said Jughead, "and I've got something I want you to do."

• • •

Rico announced to Johnny Sanchez and all other Cobras in shouting distance that Cobras were no longer involved.

Sanchez, with an arm draped around Concha's shoulder, asked Concha, "You know what time it is?"

Concha shook his head.

"It's time to lay back." Sanchez picked up what was surprisingly a yet complete chair. Before standing it upright, he kicked at the refuse that hid the floor. Moments later, many more Cobras circled around him and Concha.

They watched Dime Bag and a dozen Aryans haul student desks from classrooms to the library, where they placed them one behind the other, beginning at the entrance door. "What're you doing?" Sanchez yelled.

Dime Bag grinned. "We're the welcoming committee."

Dime Bag and his crew continued hauling desks until they had four abreast—from door to opposing wall. After that, they tossed books, magazines, and any and all flammable material, covering the desks nearest the door.

"If they try to come in," Dime Bag told Sanchez and the Cobras, "they'll be met with a wall of fire."

Ben Dixon would soon make his escape. Water pipes wheezed and banged throughout the entire cell hall. Then he listened to the sound of nothing, except for an occasional cough or throat clearing.

Although he heard Charlie Tuna asthmatically wheeze, Ben listened carefully for the groans of sergeant's chair springs.

Third-shift cell hall keepers had to personally witness the skin of each inmate as the sergeant made nightly rounds. Even if a man unwittingly rolled up in a blanket while asleep, the sergeant had to dutifully rouse the man and insist on seeing skin.

Ben saw the twitching light of Charlie's lead-weighted flashlight, which could be used as defensive weapon if the need arose. The jerking light flashed on wall, ceiling, and large exterior windows as Charlie made his way up the thirty-six steel steps and three landings to L-tier. Charlie walked the catwalk as softly as clouds pass overhead in the night sky.

Carefully, Ben Dixon placed the last cotton strip into the footlocker, shut the lid, lay on the bunk, and shut his eyes. His heart sounded like a clattering fan blade. Soon, he'd escape.

Charlie was the reason Ben chose this night. Cell hall keepers' post orders demanded two randomly timed rounds of the four tiers per hour. After each round, the sergeant had to telephone Control and make his report.

Charlie made only one round at night and another before he was relieved but phoned Control as if he had made the demanded rounds.

Finished with L and down on K. It didn't take long for the light to invade Cell Eleven. Ben's eyelids remained shut until the light left. He slightly opened them and watched the beam investigate the Sony Trinitron along with some books on a steel wall shelf. The beam swept down. Ben dared not follow it.

It rose, shone on the stainless steel mirror, where the light remained while Charlie must've tried to inspect his image.

Stop admiring yourself and get the hell outta here, will ya?

CHAPTER FORTY-EIGHT

A rioter at a window shrieked, "They're coming up."

All noise and confusion stopped, the placc almost as still as the dead Soto.

Having spent years in various lockups, Jughead knew it was only a matter of time. "How many?" he yelled.

"A hundred, maybe more."

"Maybe two hundred," broke in another lookout, standing at a different window.

"There aren't two hundred screws in the entire state," countered Jughead, making his way to the window of the man who made the initial warning. "And they're not coming up, either."

There they were, ninjas, a substantial number, grouped by the Southwest cell hall. Making a quick count, Jughead called out, "There's close to seventy, not two hundred."

Johnny Sanchez, ever the inmate no one wanted on his side, yelled, "They'll be coming soon, and then you guys can light your fire." He grinned.

"They remind me of a centipede," said the other lookout, "and guess who's on its menu?"

"You and me. We all are," yelled Sanchez.

"They're performing right now," yelled Jughead, "in order to make us nervous—so we'll make mistakes."

Ninjas herded themselves into a column of fours. The ones in front sliced glossy black batons before them. Jughead could hear the *foosh* sound from the batons' swift arcs. Next, all ninjas stomped left boots—*whomp*—following that with roars that reminded him of a nature TV show about red-mane lions on the Serengeti plain. "Mooove." Raising and slashing clubs in two rapid, opposing arcs—*foosh-foosh*—all Ninjas advanced a half step, clubs returning to port arms.

Foosh, whomp, "Mooove," *foosh-foosh. Foosh, whomp,* "Mooove," *foosh-foosh.* Behind the baton bearers were shotgun, rifle, and rocket launcher carriers, stomping in cadence. *No way can we outgun them, no way.*

•••

Troll's eyes flicked left, right, then straight ahead, appearing to be the reptile he was. With care and caution, he slipped into the principal's office. Many rioters, aware of his reputation, backed away.

Troll approached the window opening where Shirleen stood. "I'm going to help you down," he told her, and guided her from the ledge to the floor. "Are you all right?" he asked.

"No," said the still blindfolded hostage, "I'm not all right. What did you do to Sergeant Griffin?"

Nobody answered.

•••

Gangs Captain Kevin Blake entered the Metal Furniture shop where Ego's assigned dirty deed would soon be done. Blake entered the foreman's office. *He said lower right heat register behind the desk, and there it is.* Blake withdrew a security screwdriver from a trousers pocket, backed out the screws, pulled the plate, reached in, and found what he was looking for.

He brought out the baseball bat and, like a kid, traced the letters in the burned oval, *BIG LEAGUE.*

Exiting the office, he stood the bat on top the table of a huge shear, turned, reached back, fingers catching the taped grip, following the procedure a number of times, fingers finding their target. Satisfied,

Blake eyeballed the guardrail around the stairway that led to the basement. “It’s time,” he yelled.

He heard footsteps before he saw the big-eared Aryan. *Come and get it, asshole.*

• • •

Wing Nuts made his way slowly, counting each step, watching for Blake’s hand to move. *You think you’re gonna surprise me, but I’m the guy with the surprise.*

• • •

Shirleen called to the ERU below the window. “These men say I must tell you the warden and his associates must give these men what they want, or—” She held back the tears. “Or else he, they—will...kill...me.”

• • •

Officer Frank Kemp, disgusted with the lack of action, asked aloud, “Why wait? Let’s go up and knock down that door, get our asses inside, and save as many hostages as we can.”

“And the moment they see or hear us start up those stairs,” whispered Sgt. Nick Hayes, “what do you think’s gonna happen to her?” He pointed to Shirleen with his chin.

Kemp shrugged. “It might not be pretty for her, but this damned waiting is killing me.”

“It’s getting to us all,” said Hayes, so let’s keep calm. We’re the good guys. They’re the bad guys. We’re trained and disciplined. They’re not. Mark my word—we’re going to go up there and kick their asses.” The sergeant laid a hand on Kemp’s shoulders. Just have patience, OK?”

“OK, Pops.”

The unit broke out in grins. Even Sergeant Hayes couldn’t hide his.

•••

Zak's head ached, inside, outside, all around. Even his worst hangover could not match the pain he felt. He had trouble focusing but made out a hand.

"How many fingers do you see?" asked former army medic, Isidro Moreno.

Zak knew Moreno because of his military service. He also made out Zombie and Jeremy Clark along with a group of Brother-men, glaring at inmates passing by. Zak figured they were lookouts or guards, or both.

"Three," answered Zak.

"Looks like you're going to live," said Moreno. "I just want you to know I didn't want any part of this shit, but Rodriguez gave me an either/or. So, that's why I'm here."

"Rico sent you?" said Zak, not believing what he was hearing.

"Yeah, but close your eyes because Aryans are now running the show. You'll be OK if you keep your eyes closed because they'll think you're out cold, or dead. That way, you won't be seen as a threat, understand?"

"Understood." Zak closed his eyes.

Moreno put a hand on Zak's shoulder. "You're on your own now. I'm going back where I came from. I don't want any part of this."

•••

Sunlight shone through an opaque window, highlighting Blake's obvious attempt to make a subtle move, his right arm moving to the rear.

Wing Nuts extracted the gun, feinted left, then drove right, avoided the bat's trajectory, and seized Blake's arm, slamming the zip gun's barrel to the gang captain's forehead. *Pip.*

Blake's brain managed to signal the eyes to look surprised before all of him struck the floor, motionless. The bat, however, got a life of its own, turning here, there, rolling on the concrete floor. Finally, it stopped.

Turning to the mass that was Blake, Wing Nuts grinned and executed an over-the-top about-face before dramatically counting off, "One, two, and thuh-ree."

Bounding forward, he booted Blake's head. The returning sound was hollow. Wing Nuts stopped, raised hands above his head, and loudly proclaimed, "Extra point."

Then, he looked down and asked the heap, "Ain't life a bitch?"

The heap did not answer.

The soon-to-be escapee, Ben Dixon, listened as Charlie Tuna moved on to the next cell, certain he was making his usual review of each cell. Ben figured Charlie was six cells down. Slipping out of his bunk, he tiptoed to the bars, crouched, and jabbed the fingernail clippers forward. Clink.

Charlie's light beam propelled a ninety-degree turn, lighting up Ben's fingers before shutting off.

Under the blanket, breathing as heavily as a nervous rhinoceros, Ben knew his eyes were shut too tight.

Ease up, yeah, like that's possible. Slow down the breathing, or Charlie's gonna search your cage and find everything.

His heart sounded like a cluster of Yakudo drummers. He could feel Charlie, actually 100 percent feel him, although Charlie was on the other side of the bars. Why doesn't he say something, anything?

The beam struck Ben's eyelids.

Open 'em, dammit, or he's gonna know something's up.

On an elbow for support, Ben squinted, one hand shading the light's brightness.

Don't play too cool, or he'll have you in his sights. "What's up, Sarge?"

The beam inspected the cell. "What was that noise?" demanded Charlie.

Ben cleared his throat, giving him time. "It was me. Sorry about that, Sarge. We had chili for supper and my gut's on fire. I tried to put out the fire with maybe a gallon of water. Then, I got all this stuff slopping around in my gut. I try to lie down. What happens? It's burning again. I can't sleep. I get up. Not much to do in a cell, right? So, I have me a look-see down the catwalk for something to do—and they hit the bar."

"They?" asked Charlie. "What's they?"

"These," said Ben, exposing the pair allowed in his cell.

Charlie nodded. "Gut ache, huh? Want me to phone Health Services?"

"Nah, I'll be all right."

The beam turned off.

"If I'm not sleeping by the time you make your next round, you can make that call."

Ben awaited plan approval.

Charlie stood there, stood there, stood and breathed and reeked.

I'm gonna die if he doesn't get outta here.

CHAPTER FORTY-NINE

"I have nothing to lose," Troll Ostremski yelled at Major Ericson and the ERU forces. "Kneel," he ordered Shirleen. She knelt. "Bitch, it's time for your dessert."

•••

"Why can't we shoot that son of a bitch?" whispered Officer Two Terry Johnston.

Sgt. Maureen Kelly, unit supervisor, gave her sudden answer, "Because Ericson hasn't given the command."

•••

Vera Cabot of Milwaukee's TV 6 Action News stood in the alleyway that ran the length of the south wall of the prison from Madison Street to Drummond Street. Shaking, she punched the rewind button. Waiting only momentarily, she hit Stop, following with a quick punch of the play button. "Bitch, it's time for your dessert."

Oooooooooo-weeeeeee, do we have an ex-cloooooooooo-sive—or what? There's only one reporter in this whole, wide world that has that on tape.

Next stop, the Big Apple, maybe even Cronkite's chair.

•••

Aryans in the principal's office voiced opposition to killing Shirleen. "Doing her doesn't make sense," complained Don Feit, a former stockbroker, in prison for bilking hundreds of state retirees out of their life savings.

Fred Krueger, burglar, agreed. "I even see a problem with a blowjob because everyone up here gets twenty-five for that, me included."

"That don't go with me, not at all," said Jerry Gardner, in for manslaughter.

"Those screws down there can't stop me," declared Troll. "What makes you think you can?"

"We're not saying we're going to stop you. We're trying to make some sense out of this," said Feit. "Even if all my good time was taken away for being involved in this, I have five years, three months, and two days left before my mandatory release. What I'm saying is we're not looking to spend the rest of our lives in this place as you must."

"Who forced you to be up here?"

"Nobody," said Gardner, "but that's not the point."

"So, what is your point? Why didn't you return to your cage like most of the so-called men in this place? They're probably watching us on their TV sets this very moment."

"Partying was something to do," said Krueger as he looked around the room for support, "something to break up the, you know—"

"Monotony?" inquired Troll.

"Yeah," said Krueger, "that's it."

"I'll tell you what's monotonous, all this talk I'm hearing. Do you think those screws down there need a reason to kill us? Do you think desks or bonfires will stop them? Or will your weapons, or mine, for that matter"—he held the sharpened welding rod before him—"mean a tinker's damn to them? Look. Look for yourselves. They're armed to the teeth with real firepower, not pieces of furniture or homemade knives."

"Nobody said nothing about killing hostages," protested Ted Roth, rapist and loyal Aryan. "We're here because that Mexican kid was murdered by screws. That's what."

Troll laughed. "Tell me, do you think I believe in Santa Claus, as well? Where are the Cobras, the group that should be leading this takeover because one of theirs was supposedly murdered by screws, pray tell?" Troll then eyeballed each and every man in the room. "What's wrong? Cat got your tongues?"

He wasn't finished. "I'll tell you where the Cobras are. They're out there, with their thumbs up their asses. They don't care one whit about that man who killed himself—and neither do you. Those screws down there will be given their orders to come up here. First, they'll shoot enough tear gas up here so no one of us will be able to breathe, including hostages. Then, they'll blow that door down with a bazooka, shattering those desks as if they were furniture pieces in a dollhouse."

"Stop, you're scaring me," said Feit.

"You know what I said is the absolute truth," spouted Troll. "This is their time to get even. They're going to come up here, guns blazing. So what if they kill a few hostages? They don't like these teachers, anyway, because they make twice as much money as captains."

• • •

Zak would not be put off. "I asked if that was Ostremski who yelled at Shirleen, Ms. Hammer."

Zombie looked to a faraway spot. Finally, he nodded.

• • •

Wing Nuts headed for the stairway but stopped. Snapping his fingers as if he had forgotten something, he turned to what used to be Blake. "If you want to know where I'm goin', I'm off to see the wizard, the wonderful Wizard of Oz."

• • •

Vera Cabot heard shouts at the front of the institution and took off in a run down the alley until it intersected with Madison Street, and there they were, mostly male reporters, photographers, and TV cameramen, pushing one another—as two prison guards and an old man in a leisure suit exited the institution.

Soon, Vera pushed her way through the crowd until she could tap cameraman Scottie Riley's shoulder.

"Where've you been?" he asked.

Vera didn't answer because she zeroed in on the old duffer, dressed in that horrible, powder blue leisure suit with glossy white plastic trousers belt. *God, I hope he's not wearing white shiny shoes.* She looked. *Jesus, shiny fucking white.*

"Is that old guy in that awful leisure suit who I think he is?" she whispered.

Scottie didn't answer because he turned his camera to the guards, who were collecting what looked like a wooden podium from the back of a pickup truck. After they dropped the pulpit in front of the old man, they took their place at each side, both adopting mile-long stares.

Scottie answered. "Yeah, he's the warden."

And he's gonna be my ticket out of Wisco, she thought, rubbing Scottie's butt.

As the mass of reporters pelted questions, the warden raised both hands. "Please," he pleaded, "please."

"Looks like somebody shot at him and missed but shit at him and hit," whispered Scottie.

Vera snickered.

Nearby reporters and cameramen turned to the pair. "Shhhhhh."

"No questions, please," said the warden. "I'm not going to answer questions, but if you stop shouting, I have something important to read."

Screw your no questions, Pops. "Scottie."

"Sound's on and camera's rolling."

"Good, I'll be going for his family jewels."

Almost all male scribes put index fingers to their lips. "Shhhh," they warned.

"Shhhh your goddamn selves," shouted Vera. "Warden," she hollered, "do you realize—at this very moment—a female hostage—behind those walls—is likely being raped and possibly being mutilated by rioters?"

The old man started shaking so much it surprised even her.

Joe Stein, a Milwaukee print reporter from the old school, asked, "Is your question based on fact?"

"Firsthand," she shrieked. "I have it firsthand." *They don't have a clue.*

"Scottie," she whispered, "did you get that?"

Scottie grinned.

It'll be perfect for tonight's lead.

"I will now read my statement," said the visibly shaken warden.

Scottie fixed his lens.

"The Waupun Correctional Institution is presently facing an inmate takeover of part of this institution by a small band of inmates. For matters of security, safety, and the well-being of staff, inmates, and the general public, normal operations of this institution have ceased. Inmate visitors, attorneys, new inmates, and the news media will not be allowed into this facility until further notice. That ends my statement."

The guard to his left handed a sheaf of papers to Palestine. "These are copies of my state—"

"Jane Dilley, *Madison Cap Times*," screamed Vera's nemesis. "Warden, can you give us an estimate as to how long the siege will continue?"

Bitch, you don't know the first thing about news. Besides, the Clearasil you paint on your forehead with a four-inch brush isn't doing its job.

"I, uh—"

"Warden," screamed Vera, "as long as you're answering questions, I have one. I was standing in that alley over there—" She pointed the direction; Scottie pointed his lens there. *Scottie, you absolute genius.* "—moments ago, and I—I heard a rioter threaten—" She stopped, unfolded her notes, and read, "Major Ericson, E-r-i-c-s-o-n, or e-n, whichever—"

"O-n," obliged the warden.

His eyes. They're daggers. "—that if you, Warden Palestine—" *Now, Scottie.*

As if she had made the call out loud, the cameraman pointed the lens at the old man.

Scottie, you're a mind reader. "—permitted members of the media inside those walls to meet with rioting inmates, they would give up their takeover. They absolutely guaranteed that."

Every reporter present began barraging the old man with questions.

"What do you say to that, Warden?"

"Warden, is what she said true?"

"What's your answer, Warden?"

"Warden," Vera called out, "are you, uh, sir, are you experiencing physical problems? I repeat, sir, are you experiencing physical problems. Did you hear me? A female hostage is likely being cut into pieces at this very moment."

Although she had memorized Shirleen's name, Vera hesitated. She wanted drama as she made believe she was coursing through her notes. *Isn't life one big ball?* When she raised her eyes, she looked directly at Palestine. "Ms. or Mrs. Hammer, I believe the spelling to be, H-a-m-m-e-r."

The old man's forehead furrows quadrupled in number.

"I'm certain you don't want her harmed, do you, sir?" shouted Vera.

I can see it now, Walter handing his chair over to me before saying his final, 'That's the way it is.'"

Fellow reporters sounded like crazed hounds that had treed a coon.

The old man's lips trembled. "I have nothing further to add."

Scottie turned to Vera. "You're hot, Vera."

"You betcha, like a foundry," she rasped, waggling her tongue.

Ben Dixon envisioned his escape plans evaporating into thin air. If it wasn't for the fingernail clippers hitting the bar, Charlie wouldn't be here and I'd be on my way.

Charlie broke the dreadful silence. "I thought I saw some Rolaids in one of the desk drawers. I'll go down and get 'em."

"You don't hafta, Sarge." Why in hell don't you just be your normal, lazy-assed self?

"I know I don't hafta, but I'm gonna." Charlie took off.

Why? Why me? Ben sat on the bunk, and then his feet hit the floor. Time to urinate. Finally, when Charlie returned, he held out his right open palm. "These should put out that fire."

"Thanks," said Ben, biting hard, crunching, swallowing, smiling, and rubbing his belly. "They already have."

In his time, which was slower than a sloth's climb, Charlie moved on.

•••

Making count, first-shift Officer Gregory Reister, woozy from a night of partying, saw no fingers or knuckles grasping K-11's bars. Thus, he latched on to the bars, peered in, and roared, "Hey, you, time to get up."

Reister came to. Something's wrong. His head's up there, feet down there. Who's on the bunk? Jeezus, it's a fricking dummy.

Reister fell to all fours and saw what he thought he was going to see.

Standing and grabbing a guardrail, he roared, "Sergeant Foster, I need you. Now. Sergeant Foster."

Foster appeared below, looking a bit miffed. "Reister, was that you?"

"Yeah."

"What do you want?"

"The inmate in this cell—I think he's dead."

Foster raced back to his desk.

Reister turned back to the cell and looked in. He tried to detect breathing but could not. Neither could he have known that the inmate lying there, lifeless, had followed a plan to near-perfect execution. Ben Dixon had made good his prison escape.

CHAPTER FIFTY

With reporters baying like crazed coon dogs, Mitchell Palestine recalled Kyle Marston's warning: "Now remember, read the approved statement to the press. When finished, don't answer one question, no matter how benign it may seem. Those bastards will cut off your dick, stir-fry it, and hand it back to you. Am I making myself clear?"

"Very clear, Kyle, I understand."

Palestine's left eyelid jerked. Next, it noticeably twitched. The twitching became constant—and annoying.

Sticking a finger to the eyelid, the warden managed to halt the trembling. *Good.* However, when he removed the finger, the spasm's speed increased. Mitchell Francis Palestine was in unfamiliar territory. Members of the press used to treat him as if he were the president of the United States. Not now. Now, he was dead meat, and they acted like starved hounds that had not partaken in a meal in a very long time.

The baying intensified. Cameras lurched closer. Palestine was well aware of their intensity, their subjectivity. He knew they were recording his finality. The dogs tore at his flesh and masticated his bones while his heart yet beat. The pain of continuing had become unbearable.

•••

Blake should've finished searching all three floors of that building. Tower Officer Ben Holloway checked his watch. Eyeballing the handheld, he headed to it, lifted it out of its charger, inhaled deeply, and let out a long sigh before inhaling again. "Bar Six, this is Bar Twenty-Four, your twenty?"

"This is Command, Twenty-Four," squalled Ego, causing Holloway to nearly wet his skivvies.

"Go ahead, Command."

"10-33. Emergency traffic only. Stay off the radio."

He could've been easy on me and kicked me square in the nuts. With certain tenacity of the Irish, Holloway hit the button again. "Uh, Mr. Richardson, Blake, he, uh, Captain Blake, he went into Metal Furniture a good half hour ago and he hasn't come back out. I'm concerned."

Ego exploded. "Did you copy, Twenty-Four? Use your landline."

When Holloway's handheld crashed to the floor, he mumbled, "Ten-four and out, you bastard."

• • •

While the warden addressed the news media, Ego watched through the window of the command center, the warden's office. Administrative Captain Lee Summerfield, sitting at Ego's side, felt awkward when Ego ordered Holloway off the radio. "Uh, boss, should you have treated Ben that harshly?"

Ego grabbed the handheld. "Bar Six, this is Command. What's your twenty?"

After hearing Ego, Wing Nuts knew he'd better act fast. He cleared his throat and then cautiously pressed the switch. "This is Six. I'll be in the buildin' awhile longer."

"Ten-four, and out," confirmed Ego, waiting for anyone to question that voice. Seconds ticked. *Blake's done for. Griffin and Shirleen—they're gone, as well. And Theodore, I suppose right now you're feeling pretty good, but if you thought I'd let you escape my prison, you have another think coming.*

Astoundingly, the red phone rang at the same time as the warden's office doorknob turned. Rising to answer the phone, Ego twisted in order to see who was entering.

Palestine, skin ashen, he was having difficulty walking under his own power.

Summerfield rushed to help the old man to his desk as Ego got out of the way.

The old man literally flopped into the chair. Clawing for the red phone, he barely lifted it and managed to put it to his ear. "Yes, Kyle."

Ego watched a pasty white excretion form at the edges of the warden's eyes. "Yes, Kyle, I understand—I—"

The especially loud dial tone sounded like taps being played by a lone bugler.

"Marion?"

"Yeah, boss?"

"He wouldn't let me—"

A soft tap on the door.

Ego didn't even look but bellowed, "Who is it?"

"Mary."

"Come on in."

The door opened. Usually the figure of competence, Mary hid her lips with trembling fingers and spoke through them. "Warden, I can't believe what they're saying."

"Who, Mary, saying what?"

"The radio and TV. They're saying Shirleen—she, uh, she might be either raped or dead, and they're blaming you."

Leaving the door ajar, Mary returned to her desk where she whimpered and dabbed at her eyes with a soggy handkerchief.

After Summerfield closed the door, he eyed Ego.

"Yeah, what do you want?"

"From what Mary just said, I think we desperately need our investigating lieutenant and Detective Weems in the back so they can document everything."

Ego was beyond angry. "Judder? No, he's not coming in, no way."

"Marion."

The moment before Ego jerked to address the boss man, he fully expected to confront a pathetic, swayback nag, hardly standing before the glue factory's gate. Instead, he witnessed a slicked-down stallion with flaming eyes. "Yes, boss?"

"It's obvious to Captain Summerfield and me that it is imperative we have Lieutenant Brown and Detective Weems document everything, because the press will say or write anything that will tend to make me look like a fool—and Marion?"

"Yes, boss?"

"I am no fool."

Ego could not control his own shaking body.

"Right now," continued the warden, "the media—and thus the public—are rooting for the poor, downtrodden inmates instead of taking my, uh, the prison administration's point of view. So, I believe it is of utmost importance we document everything that takes place in the back in order for us to combat any false points of view. Am I clear on this matter, Marion?"

"Yes, boss." Ego turned to Summerfield. "You heard the warden. Make the calls." *And, Summerfield, when this is over, I'm assigning you to run Farm One. You'll be ankle deep in cow shit instead of being outside my office, sitting on your lard ass.*

Summerfield carried out the order. He lifted the black phone. "This is Captain Summerfield. I need an outside line. Yes," he added, "it's been approved by the warden and Mr. Richardson. Do you wish to speak to them? No?" Summerfield smiled before he added, "Well, then."

The male child's bulbous forehead almost concealed the mismatched, oddly angled eyes that mocked one another in their independent moves. Isolated, random tufts of pig's bristles dwelt on top of his head, where liver-colored birthmarks clashed with the too pink skin. His ears were a pair of morel mushrooms.

In kindergarten, fellow students nicknamed Norman Ostremski "Troll." Whenever he approached fellow students on the playground, the girls held their ears, squealed in mock horror, and ran as far away as they could. The boys simply avoided him. Few taunted Norman.

As an adult with a doctorate in political science, Troll gained political acclaim for helping first-time office seekers get elected. Even with his success, Norman curried the hateful memories of those long-ago taunts. Never could he forgive; never would he.

Purchasing auto salvage yards in states picked at random, he promptly shuttered each, and during political off-seasons, he sought "her" out. She had to exemplify "them." Her abduction could bear no witnesses. When time and fate coincided, he clutched a chloroform-soaked rag and stormed from behind. When she came to, she could not realize she was being held in the back of a semi, box, or delivery truck.

Each production began with Norman brutally sodomizing her. Next, he penetrated every orifice with a dentist's pick, delighting in her screams. Finally, he told her of her final but required act and said if she didn't bite him, he'd free her. Most victims believed him, and after he murdered them, he posed each with a wooden table leg thrust between her thighs.

A salvage yard south of Nekoosa, Wisconsin, was his downfall. An exhausted cross-country bicycle rider climbed into a sleeping bag alongside the fence line of an abandoned salvage yard. During the black of night, he was roused by horrible screams and feared for his own life and waited for dawn in order to get the hell out of there and report the incident.

Sheriff Al "Big Al" Westhuis, Jr., ordered deputies to check out the salvage yard. One deputy slowly made his way by the semitrailer. An ambulance rushed the poor dear to Riverview Hospital in Wisconsin Rapids.

Rounding up all his deputies from the three shifts, Big Al told them, "Tonight, some of us will wait in that ol' Monkey Ward truck trailer, and when that cocksucker comes in, we'll get 'im. That's for certain."

That night, when he heard the sounds only a rat would make, Big Al sparked the flashlight and caught the freak's startled expression. "Don't let 'im get away, boys."

Former Triple-A baseball player Vern Keller cracked the pick-holding hand with a pipe wrench as fellow law dogs plugged and kicked and bit whatever they could. Finally, the monster became still.

Big Al broke the silence. "Why'd you do it?"

"Those bitches—they called me Troll."

Big Al tapped a Copenhagen tin top, slipped it off, dug in, withdrew a gob of what looked like worm bedding, and mashed it betwixt lower lip and gum. "I ain't so pretty myself." A moment later, Big Al spat a gob of tobacco juice that landed slightly below Troll's contorted right eye, the tar-like secretion sticking like a leech.

CHAPTER FIFTY-ONE

After Shirleen screamed, Zak opened his eyes and said, "That's it. All deals are off."

Zombie nodded. "I understand," he said. "You have to do what you have to do, but you've been warned. You might cause her death and yours."

"That's the chance I have to take," said Zak, tossing away the bloodied towel that had been wrapped around Zak's head.

•••

The waiting on the ground while bedlam reigned in the school was frustrating the field commander, but Mark Ericson was certain the waiting could avoid horrible, unintended consequences.

"Major Ericson," some inmate from above called out. "Sir?"

Ericson looked up. It was David Adkins, an inmate library aide and certified public accountant on the streets. Adkins was sentenced to life imprisonment for murdering his wife and her boyfriend. "I represent a group of inmates who want no part of this," explained Adkins.

"How many are you?" inquired Ericson.

Adkins shrugged. "Fifty, maybe seventy, seventy-five. Maybe more. Sorry, I didn't make a head count."

"If you claim that you and they want no part of what's going on, why don't you open that door, come down those stairs, and give up?"

"No can do," said Adkins. "That door you want us to open is blocked. Once your troops break it down, they'll be met with fire, but I'll tell you no more. I live in this place twenty-four hours a day, seven days a week. You work here eight hours and go home. This *is* my home. Anyway—" Adkins turned and began talking to somebody inside the school. He then turned back to Ericson. "Sorry, I have to meet with my constituents."

"Adkins," yelled Ericson, "are you going to let me know what you and they have decided?"

"I don't know. We'll see."

Adkins disappeared into the darkness. A moment later, he was at the window. "Yeah," he said, "I'll be back."

Ericson felt he was between a rock and an extremely hard place. *I can keep on waiting, but waiting will give Ostremski time. Besides, I've not seen or heard from Griffin or Mortenson.*

• • •

Jack Koch, manning Tower Five, watched sharpshooter Jack Blaine's nose wriggle like a buck rabbit's sniffing at a doe's behind.

"Damn," hollered Blaine as he dove out of the tower and onto the catwalk. He held on to his gut with one hand and the top guardrail with the other. A streak of profanity streamed from his lips. Not once did he repeat the same foul word.

Koch laughed so hard his face turned the color of beets. "It was the beer and fried eggs."

"If I puke," yelled Blaine, "I'm coming in and puke inside your tower."

• • •

Eyelids twitched with every heartbeat as Wing Nuts Kopfmueller gnawed on a knuckle while scanning the scene below. The tower screw continued eyeballing the building's entrance door. *All bullshit aside,* Wing Nuts addressed the zip gun, *I got another job for you. Your target's that screw down there.*

Wing Nuts lowered the barrel and sighted in. *Not too high, not too low, itsy-bit-hiiiiiigher, nose, eyes, therrrrrre, eazzzzzzy, breathe innnnnnn, hollllld, don't breeeeeathe, stehhhhdeeeeeeeeeeee.*

Pip.

For two seconds at most, the target did its best to hold on to the guardrail. Knees buckling, it let go.

Lucky me, most of him fell back into the tower.

• • •

Edward "Nervous Ed" Seacrest in Tower Three shook his head, went to the sink, turned on the spigot, and sloshed cold water on his face. He had almost been lulled to sleep by staring at the old gray twine plant his tower faced.

• • •

"Hey, Blaine," Jack Koch in Tower Five yelled.

Blaine wouldn't even look. He had plunked his butt on an overturned steel mop bucket, which he'd snatched from the tower and slammed onto the catwalk's grating. *I was twelve when Grandpa gave me that old Stevens Model Fifteen single-shot .22. He got it from Great-Grandpa Blaine. I still have it, and some day my son and his son—if that ever happens—will get it. Twelve years old, I could shoot the eye out of squirrel thirty yards away with iron sights. If I had this scope, I could've easily shot out a gnat's ass.*

"Would it help if I said I'm sorry I shit in my pants?" yelled Koch.

Blaine rose from the bucket, a shoe's heel striking it. The pail tipped this way, then that. As Blaine grabbed for it, it fell and crashed to the cinder track below.

"Now, you did it," said Koch.

"I got a job to do up here," yelled Blaine. "So, why do you keep busting my chops?"

•••

Predictable as a gunnysack of weasels, Troll took note of Shirleen's bronze breasts under the snow white bra, abandoning her world and traipsing into his, where he could do her, where he had done all the others before he had actually done them, he still managed to hear the alarms of his supposed compatriots—such as they were. He ignored them.

"Look out. Here comes the big sergeant."

"I thought he was dead."

"Me, too."

"Why ain't nobody guarding him? He's coming in here as if he owns the goddamn place. Hell, this is our building now, not his."

Not one rioter was aware of Troll's reluctance to enter their insipid world. Reluctantly, he knew he must.

The sergeant was everything he was not. *He believes he has the nobility of cause.* "Sergeant Griffin, what brings you here?"

"Her," said the sergeant, pointing to Shirleen.

Troll's eye movements communicated no emotion as they made independent rounds of the room. Unbeknownst to the sergeant, Jughead was behind him, bent over and making quirky, jerky moves toward him.

"I thought," Troll addressed the rioters in the room, "that staff were our hostages. Why are we making the sergeant an exception?"

I have to give Jughead the necessary cover in order to save my day.

Troll almost laughed at the sight of the Aryan with toilet paper stuck to his facial wounds. Jughead clutched a chunk of steel in one hand, his free hand signaling Troll to continue talking.

"Sergeant, behind you," yelled Inmate Feit.

Zak jerked and zeroed in on the only threat-appearing figure, wielding a three-foot-long chunk of steel.

Jughead advanced until he must've figured he was close enough, holding the chunk like a bat and as if he were in the batter's box awaiting the pitch.

Zak turned, giving Jughead the narrowest view of his body and bent his knees at the same time both forearms shot up to ear level, one crossing the other horizontally just below the nose.

Zak knew what was coming. The arc was such that Zak had time to meet the steel chunk with the vertical forearm. When it and the piece met, Zak screamed. Although the pain was unbearable, he knew the forearm had done its job; it not only deflected the weapon's path; Jughead had involuntarily let go.

Yet screaming, Zak rose to full height and pumped his knees as he did in high school football practice, taking part in the tire drill. His feet pounded the floor, his body pretending to move left but a moment later moving right. He reached out with his good arm, grabbing Jughead's crotch area with his hand and squeezing as hard as he could, pulled back.

Jughead shrieked in pain and fell to the floor, knees to his chest while blood flowed all over parts of his face.

Next, Zak turned to face Troll as he pointed to Shirleen. "Let her go."

"Your sergeant wants me to hand you over to him," Troll addressed Shirleen. "What say you?"

"Need you ask?" she cried.

"Sergeant, if I willingly let her go, what will you do for me in return?"

"I'll let you live," said Zak, "nothing more."

Troll pushed Shirleen into Zak.

Zak turned to eye each man in the room before he winced and demanded, "Does anyone object?"

Zak and Shirleen made their way out of the room while rioters scrambled to get out of their way.

"Game's over," Troll announced as he sneered and looked down at the still-writhing Jughead.

• • •

Rigid and utterly tense, Judder stood at attention, his knees locked, muscles tensed. *Why did they call me in after what they did to me yesterday? After I called for a lockdown to avoid what is happening?*

Judder's disgust for their mendacity increased with each droning word. "We called you in, Lieutenant, because we want you and Detective Weems to be witnesses to...." Blah, blah, blah—

I warned you but you had better ideas, didn't you?

"Get a cassette recorder and the institution camera to document the...." Blah, blah, blah—

Judder began counting the number of times Summerfield's head bobbed. *You wouldn't be affirming them if you realized they want me dead because I know of their schemes. I am aware of their lies; I have personally witnessed their treachery.*

"Joe Weems and you will...." Blah, blah, blah—

Judder looked to the warden. *While you sit mightily on your throne, your toady jaws away. You must think I'm a buffoon.*

Palestine's eyes met Judder's. Judder purposely thrust a pinky into the right nostril, dug in, and snagged slime. Palestine was obviously disturbed as Judder dispatched the goo and one single nose hair to the desktop, performing a perfect landing after which he dragged the finger, leaving the sludge behind. The finger lifted.

The warden's forehead ridged as his jaw dropped, Judder counting gold crowns and silver fillings.

"Do you have any questions?"

Judder turned to face the toady. *Whatever you've said means nothing. I shall no longer abide by your counsel. You are the enemy, the state's enemy, my enemy.*

"Lieutenant."

Judder took too much time to say, "Sir?" *I warned you. I warned you two. A lockdown would've avoided this. I can see it in your eyes. You're afraid I'll talk. You've already conspired that I shall be KIA before the sun sets, but it is you who shall suffer the consequences of your lies, your deceit.*

Ego cleared his throat.

He wishes to be perceived as being in control.

"Goddammit, Judder, I just asked you a question."

I am aware of you. Are you aware of me? "Sir?"

"Were my orders clear?"

As clear as pig shit. "Yes, sir," answered Judder, "extremely clear."

"Then, get going, goddammit." Ego turned to Palestine. "Excuse the lingo, sir."

"I understand, Marion."

Judder came to full attention, right arm up cracked at the elbow. He made a full military salute. "Yes, sir."

Judder made an about-face, approached the door, opened it, stepped into Mary's office, turned the knob, and quietly shut the door.

Although most adults accept change as inevitable, Warden Mitchell Palestine did his best to discourage political allies from forcing him to hire women as correctional officers. Eventually, he accepted his fate. "We must obey the law of the land," he advised staff.

Jeffrey Cox, great-great-grandson of Waupun's founders, a Waupun native, and an ace reporter for the Madison Capital Times, wished to get the guards' point of view, and asked Palestine permission to interview Sgt. Jimmy Helm, union steward, and Cox's best buddy in elementary and high school. Cox received permission.

"With women becoming screws, cons are gonna be overcome by the dreaded disease, the Scottie Syndrome," Helm told Cox.

Cox scratched his head. "Scottie Syndrome? Never heard of it."

"Because I just made it up," said Helm, laughing. "Remember when we were kids and we got those little black-and-white plastic toy Scotties mounted on magnets at the five-and-dime?"

Cox chuckled. "Yeah, I remember you taking them to school, putting them on top of the desk, and playing with them. Old Lady Johnston confiscated them."

"When I placed those dogs facing each other real close and let one go, remember what happened?"

Cox chuckled. "The loose spun around, and when its behind was in the other dog's face, they latched together. Now, I get your drift. Scottie Syndrome? Yeah." Nodding thoughtfully, Cox added, "But aren't you forgetting that fraternization between staff and inmates has always been against the law, and isn't there a possibility some male officers are physically attracted to inmates?"

"Your calling my fellow screws fags is total bullshit, Jeff, and you know it."

As Cox searched Helm's eyes, Helm must've felt uncomfortable because he changed tack. "Jeff, do you agree women are physically weaker than men?"

"Generally, yes. However, I know some Madison Amazons who could pound you and me into the pavement without causing them to sweat."

"Yeah, but I bet you can't find one single screw here who'll tell you he'd like to have one of those dykes as his partner."

Cox's story was kind to Helm but nevertheless was picked up by the AP.

Betty Friedan of the National Organization of Women asked a New York Times reporter, "Where the hell is Wisconsin? You sure it's one of our states? Well, no matter, that guard's gotta have an IQ of a doorstop."

Phyllis Schlafly, Friedan's opponent, disagreed. "There are jobs for which women should never apply, one being guard in an all-male prison. That's just using a woman's good common sense," she clucked.

CHAPTER FIFTY-TWO

Lee Summerfield was surprised by both the warden and security director's behavior after Judder left the room.

"It's gotta be those pills," exclaimed Ego, laughing. "He ain't heading for the loony bin. He's already in it."

"Sir," said Summerfield, "tranquilizers have the opposite effect. They calm people down."

Ego sneered. "Oh, it's Dr. Summerfield, now, eh?"

"Captain Summerfield," said the warden. "Did you see the lieutenant pick his nose and leave *that* on my desk?" The warden pointed and eyeballed his security director. "Marion, could you—uh—?"

Ego snatched a Kleenex box from the credenza, pulled out a gob of wipes, bundled them into a wad, and swiped the desktop back and forth.

Summerfield had a devil of a time maintaining a sober look.

• • •

Jack Blaine's uneasy eyes moved like a typewriter carriage on steroids. *Something don't feel right.* As his sight line made it once again by Tower Four, eye movement halted. It was as if he had been zapped with electricity. Lifting the rifle, he peered through the scope. "Koch, look over there."

"Where?"

"At Tower Four."

Still, Koch sat back on his stool almost nonchalantly.

Blaine turned to him. "You didn't look, damn it."

Koch reached for the tower's binoculars, placed them before his eyes, and focused. A moment later, he snatched the handheld.

Blaine stormed into the tower and grabbed the radio. "Don't use the radio."

"What's wrong with you? You gone crazy?"

"No, I ain't crazy. Remember when Ego radioed Blake?"

Koch continued wrestling for the handheld, but Blaine kept backing away.

"Listen to me," said Blaine, "remember when Holloway radioed Blake?"

"Yeah," said Koch, "the boss got hold of him and that was that. Will you give me my radio?"

"No, at the time, I didn't think it sounded like Blake, but I kept my mouth shut. Now, I know for certain it wasn't Blake. It was somebody else, and that somebody else is most likely an inmate."

"Sounded like the captain to me," countered Koch.

"Listen to me, will ya? Are those Holloway's soles you see on that tower's floor, or are they a figment of my imagination?"

"But?"

"But what, for chrissake?"

"Bernie could've fainted or something, got sick, you know?"

Blaine dramatically pointed to the Industries Building. "See that white line running from Industries down to the tower's guardrail?"

"White line? What are you talking about?"

"Rope, I mean rope."

Koch let go of the radio and raised the field glasses.

"The way I figure it," continued Blaine, "one of those rioters answered the boss. I figure Blake's either dead or a hostage. But Ben over there, he's deader than a door nail—which means they gotta have a gun or a bow and arrow or something powerful enough."

"Which is why you don't want me to use the handheld. They'd hear me."

Blaine sighed. "Give the man a kewpie doll."

"Is it all right if I use the phone?"

"And while you do," said Blaine, "I'll keep watch on that line, I mean, rope."

•••

The warden's black phone made a half ring.

Ego picked up and shook his head. "No, Jack, you can't talk to the warden. He's busy. Yeah, I'll let him know. Uh-huh, uh-huh, uh-huh. You sure? Yeah, I heard you. OK, settle down, Jack. I know. Uh-huh, uh-huh, that's right, Blake was checking Industries. You guys could be right. I was—I wasn't even paying attention to the voice. Uh, we'll have to, uh, let me speak to Blaine. Yeah, let me. Yeah, I heard you. Let me talk to, now, to Blaine, yeah, on the phone."

Ego cupped the mouthpiece and addressed the warden, "Did he think I was gonna talk to Blaine with tin cans and some string?"

A voice on the other end cut in. "Yeah, boss?"

Ego brought the phone to his ear. "I heard, but listen to me, Jack. No, I said listen." The security director and warden shook their heads. "Jack, are you listening? Good. We don't know if Ben's—I know, I know—he could've had a heart attack or was"—two winks for the warden—"looking at one of those girlie magazines that we can never catch him with, and—damn it, Jack, how can you be—? Listen, are you listening? Good. Keep looking—that's what I said. Keep looking and if anyone moves—

"Yeah, that's the ticket: take care of everything on your end, and the warden and me will take care of everything on this end. That's the boy, ten-four and out."

Ego dropped the phone onto the cradle.

"What was that all about, Marion?"

"Officer Blaine, our sharpshooter, boss, is in Tower Five. He told me Tower Four's Ben Holloway is down and not moving. Blaine figured a rioter shot him, and that Holloway's either hurt bad, or dead."

"Why did he think Ben was shot?"

"There's a rope running from the third floor of Industries down to Ben's tower."

"Then, what you are saying is this riot is a disguise for inmates to escape?"

"Yes, boss, and that's why I told Blaine what I did."

•••

Judder made a hard right instead of the normal left upon exiting the warden's office. Entering the newly relocated armory, which was recently moved from Tower Eight to the rear of the warden's office, he signed for a .223 with iron sights. When he had to pass the warden's office, he kept the stock under his right armpit, the barrel moving in cadence with his right leg.

Once he reached the stairs, he exposed the weapon. "Thou shall not kill," he nearly screamed as he passed by ERU reinforcements, state patrol officers, and county deputies.

"What the hell was that about?" asked a deputy from Fond du Lac County.

"Beats me," said a state patrol lieutenant.

Most of the reinforcements shrugged as they busily prepared themselves for their eventual move to the back of the institution.

Sexual liaisons between female correctional officers and inmates occurred rarely. However, when discovered or uncovered, either chanced upon by other staff or hastened by inmate snitches, the affair became the institution's focus.

If caught "in the act," she was allowed to prepare herself properly before being escorted to the warden's office. In most cases, Ego led the way, the woman behind, two of the biggest male correctional officers at each side.

Warden Palestine addressed her failure to perform her job as a professional correctional officer. "You won't be charged with a felony if you resign."

Each woman signed her marching papers with quivering hand. After forking over her Department of Corrections ID card with a promise to return her uniforms at the front gate at a later time, the warden's office door burst open, the pair of gorillas in blue, making their exit. They eagerly waited to escort the offender out of the institution.

Some male officers raised fists and proclaimed, "We warned the administration this would happen."

After each affair, some inmates dared to toy with their scrotum whenever approaching a female officer. If she wrote a conduct report, the inmate had to appear in front of the institution's court.

"Did he scratch an itch?" asked the court's presiding official, who had never wanted women correctional officers, anyway. And what of the officer who wrote the conduct report? She was upset, of course, but carried on as best she could.

South Cell Hall Sergeant Barnes wondered why a male social worker stood so long before an inmate's cell. Barnes quietly climbed the stairs, inched his way down the catwalk, and surprised both inmate and staff member with his presence.

As the social worker backed away from the cell, he was unable to conceal his fully erect organ. The offending inmate was escorted to the hole.

Since the social worker fell under the auspices of the associate warden of treatment and not the security department, he requested sick leave, which was approved.

Hiring a local lawyer who knew judges in Dodge and Fond du Lac counties and their wives and girlfriends by first name, the shyster advised the social worker to attend Sunday church services, seek psychiatric help, and stay out of taverns and any other possible trouble spots.

After a long time, it was agreed the offending social worker be reassigned to the Department of Motor Vehicles, where he monitored written driver exams. He eventually underwent a sex change.

Female officers continued to bite the bullet while still having to outperform their male counterparts in order to be considered equal to the task.

CHAPTER FIFTY-THREE

Wing Nuts thrust the handheld inside his waistband before grabbing the side of the window frame. Jumping onto the ledge, he knelt, steadying himself. Then, he reached out and grabbed hold of the rope. "One, two, thuh-ree."

Dropping and hitting the building's harsh exterior, he skinned arm, legs, and side of his head. The blood didn't bother him; the rope did. It was like holding on to a jouncing, coiled spring.

•••

Nervous Ed in Three saw Wing Nuts. "Holy shit," he exclaimed, after which he stared at his shotgun and then at the rifle and then back to the shotgun before he turned back to the rifle. Nervous Ed couldn't move.

•••

Jack Blaine grinned nastily. "Will you look at that? A dope on a rope." He watched Wing Nuts dance his involuntary boogaloo. Blaine's trigger finger eased the squeeze. The resultant thunderclap caromed time and again against the inside walls.

Blaine followed the target to the concrete. Inhaling deeply, he then sighed and calmly placed the weapon crossways on his lap. Grabbing for his shirt pocket, he pulled out a pack of Pall Malls, stretched out a leg and found the Zippo in a trouser pocket, brought it out, examined it momentarily, shook his head, grinned, and flipped the cover and then the wheel. Firing up, he took a deep drag and exhaled slowly.

"You got 'im," yelled Koch inside Tower Five, looking through his field glasses.

"That I did," agreed Blaine, grinning. "That I did."

• • •

Rioters in the school heard the explosions ricocheting off the institution's walls. "They're shooting. Stay away from the windows," somebody warned before each man admonished the man next to him with the same cautionary message.

"They're shooting to kill," yelled Troll, enjoying their predicament.

• • •

The clutter was unbelievable where Alex Mortenson's desk had been, but it suddenly had become the only area where security prevailed.

Brother-men, arms against their chests, glared at anyone who paused in what was now their territorial imperative. "Move on," they warned trespassers.

"Yes," Zak confirmed to Shirleen, "that was a rifle shot."

"Maybe this is going to end soon," she said.

"Maybe," he said.

• • •

"Control," answered Bubble Sergeant Moen.

"This is Ed in Three. Is this Rita?"

"Do I sound like Rita? This is Moen. Ego says we can't let civilians operate the phone system, now, can we? No sir, I says. He doesn't think I got enough to do."

"I gotta talk to the warden."

"Sorry, Ed, no can do."

"But it's an emergency."

Moen sighed. "Everything's an emergency right now, Ed."

"Well, I don't know if I should be saying this, but that inmate they call Jug Ears or something like that, I saw him dressed in civvies. He's got blue jeans on. Somebody, I think Blaine, shot him right in front of me. I think the guy's dead. There's an extra-large pool of blood on the concrete."

"Jesus, Ed, are you certain?"

"It ain't cherry Kool-Aid I'm looking at. That's for sure."

Moen turned to Rita. "How do I get hold of the warden?"

She pointed. "Just like you did with the last call. Plug it into that hole and pull back on the ringer."

• • •

"Yeah?"

"Mr. Richardson, please."

"This is Richardson, Moen."

"Yes, sir. Nervous Ed in Three called and said an inmate, dressed in civvies, is below his tower, shot dead."

"Gotcha," said Ego.

• • •

Moen stared at Rita. "He hung up."

"Then, pull that out," she said, pointing at the plug.

• • •

Jack Koch was beside himself. "Damn it, why doesn't Moen answer?"

Jack Blaine was too busy scoping an ERU detail approaching his kill to answer. "ERU," he yelled. "It's Dunlop and his crew."

• • •

"That's Wing Nuts Kopfmueller," announced Morris Dunlop to his five-member team as they stared, Wing Nuts's head lying at a peculiar angle.

"Jesus, would you look at that," said twenty-two-year-old CO Two Alan Shockley, the squad's most junior member.

"I'll betcha a dime to a doughnut that chest wound is what killed 'im, not the broken neck," observed Dunlop.

"Yeah," said Ted Sweeney, "looks to me that after he hit the concrete, that's when his neck most likely broke. I wonder who shot him."

A moment later, Dunlop pointed to Tower Five. "There, it's Deadeye himself. See? It's Jack Blaine, looking through his scope."

"I hope he's got it on safety," said Shockley.

"He's looking all right," affirmed Dunlop, "but—"

"But what?" asked Ernie Williams, the first black correctional officer hired at the institution.

"I can understand Nervous Ed shitting his pants, but why didn't Bernie in Four nail his ass?" It didn't take Dunlop long to figure out the answer to that problem. "Look," he said, the team following his finger, pointing to Bernie Holloway's pointing mud stompers.

"Jesus," said Sweeney, "I wonder if Wing Nuts shot him with that zip gun."

"What zip gun?"

"The one lying over there."

"That was one heck of a shot," remarked Williams.

"Look, he had one of our radios, too," said Dunlop. "Check the bar number on it, will ya?"

Shockley advanced slowly and kicked the radio.

Dunlop was surprised. "Why'd you do that?"

"I wanted to make certain it wasn't jerry-rigged with explosives," said the Vietnam veteran. He bent over and picked it up. "Man," he said, looking up to the clouds, "that pisses me off."

"What pisses you off?" asked Williams.

"Man," said Shockley, scrunching up his nose, "I got his blood on me."

"That's not my problem," said Dunlop. "What's the bar number?"

"It's Blake's. Got his name on it."

"How'd he get Blake's radio?"

Officer Neil Jeffries, his eyes mere slits, spoke for the first time. "How do we know if it was Wing Nuts that shot Ben?"

Dunlop jerked.

"Yeah," continued Jeffries, "Ben could've been killed by a different inmate, or inmates. We really don't know nothing for sure, now do we?"

"Then," said Dunlop, "after they snuffed Ben, they crossed to his tower. You're right. Could be Wing Nuts was last one out. Listen up. Assume Jeffries is correct. There could be armed cons in that tower or in Industries. Ernie, keep a watch on Four and also those industry windows. Shoot anyone who shows his head."

"Gotcha," said Williams.

"Make sure it's not Blake, though."

"Gotcha."

"Shockley," said Dunlop, "I want you to report to Major Ericson and let him know what we found."

"Why can't you send someone else?"

Dunlop glared.

"OK," said Shockley, "I'm on my way."

"Tell 'im there could be a shitload of armed inmates hiding in that tower or in Industries. The rest of us, except Ernie, will be searching the Industries Building."

"OK," said Shockley, "I didn't mean no disrespect."

Dunlop grabbed the young man's shoulder. "Yeah, I know. Now, get going."

•••

In a semicrouch, Dunlop made it up the four steps and knelt before the door and tried the knob. It turned. Slowly, he pulled open the door and pointed inside. After he put a finger to his lips, his team members nodded and preceded him into the building.

•••

A light on the telephone system's board flashed. "Damn," said Bubble Sergeant Greg Moen, "it's like McDonald's at lunchtime." He plugged the hole below the light. "Yeah?" he demanded.

"Dunlop here. I'm in Industries, using their desk phone. I need to speak to the man."

"You and everybody else," said Moen as he prepared to pull the plug.

"Hey?"

"Yeah."

"Holloway in Four's been shot. I think he's dead. Also, I found Blake, Captain Blake, in Industries. He ain't breathing, either, shot in the head with a small-caliber bullet."

Moen connected Dunlop to the warden's office.

•••

"Command Post, security director speaking."

"Boss, this is Dunlop in the Industries Building. Ben Holloway in Four, and Captain Blake in here, have been shot and killed."

"Are you sure?"

"Pretty damn sure about Bernie, and it's a fact about Blake. He ain't breathing."

"OK, I'll pass that info to the warden. Retain radio silence. Got that?"

"Got it, boss."

Ego put the phone down. *Everything's going as planned.*

•••

Troll Ostremski was certain it was a bolt of lightning inside the building, so convinced that he went to his knees. For the first time, he was scared. Of what? Quickly, he concluded what he feared.

The blinding illumination had caused within him a spiritual transformation. Not everything had changed. He was still pissed off at good looking women and he looked down on most humans as being sheep minus a shepherd. Then, what changed? He knew at once. He preferred life over death, even if the rest of his life had to be lived in this Waupun shit hole.

Standing, he went forward on a mission.

Brother-men guards stopped him. "May I have a word with you?" he shouted to Zombie.

"What is it you want?"

"Whatever this is or was"—Troll looked around in disgust— "is finished. I'd surmise the screws are going to assault this building—and soon. When they do, there will be some—perhaps many—of us hurt and possibly killed, including you, me, the sergeant, and his lady. Why don't you go to the principal's office and tell the major that we'll give up if you and I—and twelve other men of your choosing—each accompany one hostage down the stairs, ensuring these so-called men up here that they'll live yet another day of their miserable lives locked up in this zoo."

"Let him through," Zombie ordered.

Gilbert "Gib" Melborp planned how he was going to receive a master's degree in English. He volunteered to be handyman for his thesis director, Dr. Jules Keenan. As far as Gib was concerned, it was the only way he'd receive the sheepskin.

His thesis sucked. So, he biked to Dr. Keenan's house, oiled squeaks, painted walls, varnished woodwork, fixed leaks, tore up old carpets, removed shingles from a leaky roof and did his best to align new ones. Professor Keenan's neighbors thought the shingles were nailed down purposely in undulating waves, you know, in artsy fartsy style.

At night, Melborp drank Jack Daniels while plodding through his thesis on a god-awful Royal typewriter, comparing the poetry of Gerard Manley Hopkins to that of Robert Bridges. Gib couldn't stand the works of either poet.

Hopkins and Bridges were friends during the mid-1800s and remained so, even after Hopkins converted to Catholicism, became a Jesuit priest, and was sent off to the British realm's biggest pain in the ass, Ireland. He died there in 1889.

In 1913, King George V appointed Bridges, an MD, as England's poet laureate. Bridges edited Hopkins's book of poetry, published in 1918.

Professor Keenan, also a former Jesuit priest, was a close friend of the department head, who approved Melborp's thesis, sight unseen. Keenan advised his one and only tattooed graduate student to teach the "hard to teach."

After receiving his master's degree from Ohio's Kent State University in 1967, Melborp hired on as the English teacher at the Wisconsin State Prison and introduced the Hooked on Books program, bringing in paperback books by Fitzgerald, Salinger, Faulkner, and Hemingway, among many other recognized American authors.

The front gate officer directed the teacher to Ego's office. Upon entering the room, Gib saw Ego holding up a copy of The Catcher in the Rye. "Who gave you permission to bring in this fuck book?" demanded Ego.

"That's not a fuck book, sir. It's a contemporary classic."

"It's a fuck book to me. You're fired. Get the hell outta my institution."

Two blueshirts promptly entered the office and escorted Gib to the front gate and out of the prison. Melborp didn't know what to do. He didn't like Ego. Looking under the heading of "Attorney" in the phone book, he chose the name of Hooker. Interesting. Melborp thought all lawyers were hookers. The teacher explained to the lawyer why he was fired.

Hooker phoned the prison. "Hello, Marion, this is Ed Hooker. Yes, we met at the golf course some time ago. Say, I have Mr. Gib Melborp in my office. Yes, he's my client. Marion, the long and the short of it is no court of law will allow you to fire this young man for bringing in classic books, and because he has a master's degree in English, that makes him an authority on literature, don't you agree? Well, good. I'll send him back. Have a nice day, Marion."

Addressing Gib, Ed Hooker warned, "If you want the job, you have it, but stay out of that man's way."

For the most part, Melborp followed Hooker's advice for the next twenty-seven and a half years.

CHAPTER FIFTY-FOUR

Even the most stone-hearted individual in Channel Twelve's Milwaukee studio gazed intently at the monitor as Vera Cabal, live from Waupun, had forgotten to insert her earpiece.

Jane Flaxmore, news desk co-anchor, attended to by Mary Lou, the makeup girl, shook her head and said, "What a dumb bitch."

Mary Lou was aware that Vera had lured Jane's boyfriend, Tom Hayden, to her boudoir not that long ago. Jane tossed everything that belonged to Tom in a Goodwill bin and changed the lock to her apartment. He was persona non grata.

"Jane, we're on," said Tom, who used more makeup than a supermodel preparing for a photo shoot. He gently tapped the crystal of his Rolex Daytona, which Jane had purchased for him with money she had inherited from her mother's estate.

Don't get your undies in a bundle, you two-timing bastar—

"Done," announced Mary Lou, backing away, rechecking her work.

Jane rose, approached her chair, and sat. "How ya doin', big boy?" She pointed to the monitor. "Better than she is, I hope."

"You don't have to worry about Vera," retorted Tom. "She's a professional."

"Yes, I'm told she gives fantastic blowjobs." Jane then tossed her raven tresses and inhaled deeply, lifting her mortar shell-sized breasts in a very sexual way. She was certain Tom looked at them lovingly. "You used to call these your teddy bears, remember?" Turning to Camera One, she softly hummed the melody from "Tie a Yellow Ribbon Round the Ole Oak Tree" as her fingers did the walking to Tom's genitalia. *What have we here?*

Camera One's red light flashed.

Jane led. "Good afternoon, everyone. Welcome to Milwaukee's TV Twelve's action-packed news. Jane Wheatley, here."

"And Tom Hayden," said the creep.

"We seem," said Jane, looking to Tom, "to be having some technical difficulties at the Waupun Correctional Institution." *Vera is so clueless, but Tom's more interested in other, more pressing matters, aren't you, big boy? It's as hard as a cast-iron pipe.*

An unidentified flying object bounced off Vera's forehead. *She looks like a rabbit that just spotted a coyote with hasenpfeffer on its menu.*

Studio folks snickered.

Jane halted the petting.

"Don't stop," snarled Tom.

Oh-oh, your bitch finally put in the earpiece. Now, she's hoisting the mike.

Vera began with, "Hello, Jane and Tom. This is Vera Cabat, reporting live from Waupun Correctional Institution. This gothic-like fortress you see behind me was commandeered this morning by armed inmates, holding seventeen staff hostages, mostly teachers in the prison school. The rioters are threatening to kill their hostages if the mutineers don't get what they want, and that's to meet with us, members of the news media. But their demand was turned down by the prison administration. Meanwhile—"

"Vera," said Tom, "have you been told if any hostage up to this point has been harmed, or worse yet, killed?"

Good going, Tom, old boy. Vera looks both clueless and pissed off.

"No," responded Vera, "but I personally heard a rioter claim he was going to murder a female hostage—that is after—and I must warn parents that what they're going to hear next, they may want to ask their children to leave the room or shut off the sound."

Shit. "OK, Vera," said Jane, who looked straight into the camera. "Did you hear that, parents? What you are about to hear might not be advisable for children to listen to. Please continue, Vera." Vera lifted the cassette recorder.

"Thank you, Jane. The rioter said he was going to murder her after he forced her to perform oral sexual acts on his person."

As I assume what you do with numb nuts sitting next to me every night, thought Jane.

"You can now turn on the tape recorder, Vera. Our TV audience has been warned," said Tom.

Vera punched a button on the recorder and placed her mike near it. "Bitch, get your dessert."

The studio director howled, "Four and Six have nothing like this. Vera's got the Murrow Award cinched."

"Jane," whispered Tom, "don't stop."

"Do it to yourself."

"It's not the same."

"No shit, Dick Tracy. You'll have to wait for her return."

"The hostage," continued Vera, "was—excuse me—*is*—a Milwaukee native. She has been identified as Shirleen Hammer, a former Milwaukee police officer and Wisconsin Department of Justice employee. She is presently the prison's inmate advocate. Interestingly, Ms. Hammer's brother with another last name, Davis, an Earl Davis, was sentenced to this institution by Judge Christ Seraphim for drug-related matters. Davis was murdered inside those walls, apparently in a gang fight."

"Ba-whoom," announced the director.

Jane had never seen the director like this.

Vera and other reporters ducked as if someone were shooting at them.

"What the hell was that?" shouted the director.

Jane covered her mike. "That was a rifle shot."

"This is what *it's* all about," shouted the director. "This is what we're all about."

Give me a break, thought Jane. *We're all about making money.*

Vera and a number of other reporters were excitedly talking to one another before she stopped jabbering. Facing the camera, she announced, "Only moments ago, that noise you heard apparently came from a high-powered rifle, fired from one of the guard towers here, we're being advised. We're receiving unconfirmed reports that a prison staff member has been murdered. Remember, it's unconfirmed, but this is what we're being told."

"If she doesn't get the Murrow," screamed the studio director, "I'll eat an entire plate of fried Amish horse turds on award night."

"Jesus, Jane, you started it," Tom gnashed betwixt clenched teeth. "So, now finish it."

"Tom, you're just going to have to wait for the Edward R. Murrow recipient's return. I'm certain she'll accommodate you—that is, if she ever comes back to this two-bit outfit."

"If you think working out on that iron pile is going to change Wilson's mind, think again, babe. Two years ago, this Hollywood-blond muscle-beach jackoff wouldn't give Wilson no bootie, neither. So, what does Wilson do? He pitches Hollywood over the fucking tier. Wilson gets a year in the hole, and get this, after he does his time, he dicks Hollywood in the ass while Hollywood kneels on the wheelchair in which he's gonna spend the rest of his miserable life. Go figure.

"And then there's Sommers. You know Sommers, don't you? He's the hunchback with one eye. With that eye, he's looking at you, babe. I swear he copped with Frankenstein on the bricks. With this claw he was born with, he rips this dude's tonsils out because the dude won't give him no sugar.

"A box of Salems, Pall Malls, or Camels in a pinch—each week keeps 'em at bay.

"I know, I know. Some dudes say they'll cover you for free? Yeah, and I'm the fairy godfather. The fact is, babe, they'll bore your bunghole to the size of a manhole cover. After that, they'll pay some chump to kick your teeth out and sell you on the rec field as an all-day sucker.

"Besides, I'll get you anything you want, even pussy.

"What'd you say? Say, babe, pussy's all around you, staff bitches is what I'm talking about. They give the right dudes their poontang because we're not like their chumps on the bricks who slave their eights, come home smelling like dog shit, pop a brew, turn on the tube, flop on the couch, and don't pay the bitches no never mind.

"If you get caught, nothing to it: you do ninety in the Greenhouse.

"The bitches? They get marched out of here like they're being led to a firing squad. Turns out to be no big deal, babe. All they lose is their jobs.

"Let me lay it out for you. I know at least a dozen cons that want to kick off a cluster fuck on your virgin ass. Screws ain't gonna protect you. Your social worker will demand sloppy seconds, and the chaplains? They'll pray. So, what do you say?

"You said—one box? I do nah-theen for one box. I don't even get up in the morning for a box. That's all you can afford? You gotta have wax buildup in those ears, babe. Put in a kite to see the nurse. Her aide, a buck nigger, is an animal. He'll force you to go down on him, or else he'll break your arms and legs. You haven't been listening, babe. Waupun's a jungle is what I've been saying all along.

"OK, I'll say it again. I said Salems, five boxes each Friday, personally delivered to my house.

"Or what? Or fucking else, babe, that's what."

CHAPTER FIFTY-FIVE

Rioters screamed, "Amnesty. We demand amnesty."

"Amnesty's not going to happen," Major Ericson warned Zombie, who was leaning out of a school window, attempting to end the takeover.

"What'll work?" asked the Brother-men leader.

"No deals, period."

"I didn't ask you for any deals. I asked, what'll work?"

Ericson stopped, seemingly in deep thought. Slowly, he nodded. "First, staff hostages must be released. Second, rioters must throw down their weapons. Third, inmates, one at a time, must exit the building, hands in the air. They must submit to all lawful orders and they shall be strip-searched."

As the screaming continued, Zombie turned to the rioters. "How can I get anything done when I can't even hear what the man's saying?"

When the noise died down, Zombie told Ericson, "I don't know if they're going to agree."

"Then, there's no need for us to continue," warned Ericson, checking his watch. "I'll give you five minutes. No more."

"Five minutes," said Zombie before he disappeared into the school's darkness.

•••

"Command, this is Field."

"Go ahead, Field."

"Rioters say they want to give up. I've given their spokesman five minutes to surrender unconditionally. I don't know for certain if they'll accept my terms."

"Ten-four, Field. Good work. So far. Keep us posted."

"I'll do that." Ericson turned his attention back to the window. Nobody was there.

•••

Mary, with pomp and circumstance, threw open the door, marched up to Palestine's desk, and declared, "Warden, it's on the radio. They said Major Ericson is negotiating an end to the riot."

"Boss," said Ego, "may I go out back?"

Mary was certain her boss looked as if he had just stepped in a pile of fresh dog doo-doo. Turning from Ego back to her, the warden forced a quivering smile. "That is good news, Mary. Would you please close the door?"

Like a Japanese Geisha who blew an earsplitting fart while engaged in a tea ceremony, Mary shrank away and closed the door so softly it barely clicked shut.

•••

Zombie was back at the window in little more than three minutes. "What have you decided?"

"Me?" screamed a visibly upset Zombie. "This isn't about just me; it's about *us*."

"OK, I apologize," said Ericson.

"Accepted," said Zombie. "Major, here's the deal. These men won't give up until you agree to one proposition."

"And that is?"

"We want inmates up here—former rioters—on the ground to be witnesses to any funny stuff your guys might try—we're not saying they will—but if we have our guys on the ground, there'll likely be no funny stuff happening. Here's how we think it could work—that is, if you'll agree."

"Continue, I'm listening."

"OK, an inmate of our choosing, not yours—one at a time—with hands held high, will follow one staff hostage at a time down those stairs. That'll mean, when all our hostages are down there on the ground, there'll be fourteen of our guys down there, as well. And you have our guarantee that if any of our witnesses try any tricks whatsoever, your guys can shoot to wound, no questions asked."

They could hide weapons behind them or on the hostages, and then when they'd get down here, they could—"Look," said Ericson, "I'll agree as long as each hostage also holds up her or his hands and inmates and hostages will keep their hands up until we give an order to put them down. Is that clear?"

"Clear." Zombie left but returned shortly thereafter, Ericson figured, in order to check with other rioters. "We accept," Zombie said.

"Now," warned Ericson, "you have to give me five minutes so I can check in with my superiors and get their approval."

"Done," said Zombie.

•••

Warden Palestine smoothed his mustache delicately. "Marion, let me answer the major."

"No problem, boss," said Ego, "I just thought that—" *Since I been answering all this time.* Ego handed the radio to the warden.

"Major Ericson, this is Warden Palestine."

"Go ahead, sir."

"It is obvious to me that you have handled your task with courage and good sense. I approve of your proposal that will end this, uh, inmate takeover. One rioter is allowed to accompany one staff hostage at a time down the school stairs so the fourteen rioters can be witnesses to our treatment of their fellow lawbreakers. I wish to make it clear to all staff who can hear me that I sincerely appreciate their professionalism in handling their tasks through this trying time, as well. That is all."

"Thank you, sir," answered Ericson. "Ten-four and out."

Aware he had crossed an invisible line, Ego said, "Sir, I, uh—"

"Marion, I have to assume the governor's office has heard the news." As if Palestine had planned it, the red phone began to ring. Smiling, he said, "There you are. No sooner said than done. After I finish briefing Kyle, we, Marion—you and I—we shall have the media to contend with."

The warden lifted the phone. "Hello. Oh, it's you, Governor. I thought it was Kyle—no, I was just about to call you. Major Ericson only moments ago briefed me with a proposal to end the takeover. I have accepted the major's and inmates' terms. Yes, that is good news, Governor."

•••

While law officers and ERU members waited, most had heard the radio transmission between Palestine and Ericson.

With unexpected suddenness, the school door opened with a *ker-flam*.

Nearly all eyes on the ground focused on that door. A moment later emerged Shirleen, eyes blinking, likely from being in the darkened school and entering the sudden brightness. She held one hand above her head while the other tried to hold her blouse together.

Behind her exited Zombie, his eyes also blinking, both hands in the air. After he said something to Shirleen, which Ericson could not hear, she stopped.

All weapons were aimed at them.

"Come on down," urged Ericson, letting out a long sigh.

The pair came down the stairs as Zak and serial killer Norman "Troll" Ostremski emerged.

"Thank God you're safe," Ericson said to Shirleen, pointing to Joe Weems. "Would you stand over there by Detective Weems? He's—"

"I know who Joe is," Shirleen angrily fired back.

Ericson wondered if he had said something wrong, and if he did, what he was about to say might cause Shirleen to go ballistic. "We need to pat-search hostages," he told the troops, looking at no officer in particular. Would some female officer please do so?"

"Aye, aye," answered Sgt. Maureen Kelly, smiling and approaching Shirleen, giving her a quick pat-down. "She's clean, major."

"Thank you, Sergeant."

"Major?" It was Zombie.

Ericson was fast losing patience. "Yeah, what do you want?"

"Where do you want me to stand?"

Ericson pointed to a spot by Food Service's exterior wall. "Over there," he said. "All inmates from the school will stand over there."

Zombie approached the spot.

Ninjas backed off, their weapons trained on him.

"That's far enough," said one.

Zombie stopped.

"Search him," ordered Ericson.

"Pat or strip?"

"Pat now, strip later."

"Yes, sir." A ninja pair quickly worked Zombie over.

"No weapons," they advised.

Troll was next.

"Once you finish with the pat search," the major advised them, "they can put their hands down, but only then."

"OK," a ninja told Zombie, "you can put your hands—"

"Hey, Major. Yo, Major Ericson."

That calling out of Ericson came from the staircase.

Ericson turned to it. "Yeah, who said that?"

"Me, Gib Melborp." Melborp, the English teacher, seemed as perturbed as Shirleen.

"Yeah, what can I do for you?" asked Ericson.

"I don't like those guns pointing at us. What are you planning to do, shoot us? For chrissake, we're the good guys."

"I realize that, Mr. Melborp, but Department of Corrections' SOP is to treat all hostages as possibly having Stockholm syndrome."

"Wasn't it bad enough," countered the teacher, "that you guys permitted this riot to happen?"

We permitted what? Ericson took a few moments to pray for patience. Then, he spoke not only to Melborp but to all the hostages. "I know you're not going to like this, but we have to consider the possibility that one or more of you could be holding weapons for the rioters."

"That's preposterous," screamed the irate Melborp.

"Look," said Ericson, "at this moment, as far as I know, everyone who was in the school's alive. When I return to my home tonight, I shall be certain it was due to my officers taking all the necessary precautions to maintain your safekeeping. Now, does that answer your question?"

"It does for me," shouted Alice Broker, who stood behind Melborp. "I want to thank all of you down there, including inmate Randy Smith, who personally protected me from being hurt, or worse. Thanks to you and him, I'm going to be at home tonight, safe with my family, with my husband and my sons. So, I, for one, don't care how many guns are pointing at me. You and your officers and all those lawmen are just doing their job."

The other hostages standing on the stairs with their inmate escorts, except for Melborp, agreed, some more enthusiastically than others.

Ericson waited. "Thank you, Mrs. Broker. Now, let's get that stair—"

"Major."

Griffin. What does he want? "Look, Sergeant, I need to establish some order here. Can you wait?"

"No, I want you to know that Zombie and the Brother-men had nothing to do with what was going on up there. He and his men protected me and Shirleen. They saved our lives."

"Sergeant, as you well know, I wasn't up there. We'll get everything all straightened out—when I and my officers have time, and right now, we don't have that time."

"I just wanted you and everyone else to know what happened up there."

Shouting and cheering started up. It came from the direction of where inmate witnesses stood. Ericson saw some Brothermen high-fiving one another. “Listen up,” he warned the inmates, “there’ll be no talking, no cheering, no whispering, no signaling, and no passing anything.” Ericson took in a deep breath. “Do I make myself clear?”

Few inmates looked straight into his eyes, but their silence signaled understanding and assent.

Satisfied that he had made his point, Ericson turned to the staff hostages. “You guys,” he said, breaking into a grin, “you can talk and laugh all you want, but please refrain from passing anything to anyone, understood?”

School Officer Mortenson shouted, “The only thing I’m gonna pass is ga—”

“Didn’t you hear the major?” It was Judder Brown. “He said no passing.” Judder aimed his rifle at the inmate group.

More startling to everyone there was the explosion that followed.

• • •

Zak identified the fallen inmate, Zombie.

“That was his high school diploma, you idiot,” screamed Jeremy Clark.

• • •

Shirleen felt Zak’s muscles tighten. She grabbed hold of his arm. “Don’t,” she pleaded, “please don’t.”

Zak gently but forcefully removed her hand. “I have to.”

A moment later, Zak broke through armed ninjas, and an instant later Zak grabbed the rifle barrel and placed it against his chest. “Go ahead,” Zak yelled, “shoot me.”

“Why?” pleaded Judder. “Once upon a time, we were the good guys.”

Zak pulled the weapon from Judder's grasp. Losing his balance, Judder fell to the concrete and whimpered like a puppy removed from his mother that very day.

Zak tossed the rifle to a county deputy. "Hold on to that, will you?"

"Sure enough," replied the startled deputy.

Zak then made his way to Zombie and discovered it was a shoulder wound. "You're going to be OK." Zak removed his shirt and stuffed it inside Zombie's shirt. Then, Zak turned to Ericson. "He's going to need an ambulance."

Next, he asked Jeremy for the diploma, studied it momentarily, and returned to Judder, shoving the document to within inches of Judder's face. "You see this?"

Judder kept whimpering.

"I asked, do you see this?"

"Yes."

"It's a high school diploma," said Zak. "That man wasn't passing anything. He was proud that he received this. He was showing this to his friend."

"He failed to obey a direct order," countered Judder. "He didn't obey the major's direct order."

The subject in St. Peter and Paul's Catholic eighth-grade religion class was the soul.

"Sister," said Catherine Moriearty, her father a circuit court judge, "my father said when he was in the army and one of his buddies was killed, he saw his buddy's soul leaving his body. Father said it looked like a tiny star."

Sister Mary Elizabeth, school sister of Notre Dame, brought hands together above a bleached white cloth that covered black that covered white that covered undetected breasts.

"And, "said the nun, "a judge would never lie. That man's soul was going to heaven in order to join God, Jesus, the Holy Ghost, and our mother, Mary."

The nun's thumbs latched together. Opposing fingers fluttered like wings of a dove. As they flapped above her head, fingers and palms reformed themselves into a sphere.

The boy who would become Smooth rose from his desk without raising his hand.

"Yes?" queried the nun, her eyebrows inverted V's.

"What the judge claimed to have seen cannot be, Sister."

The nun's fingers tapped nervously on her trembling lips.

Nevertheless, the boy continued. "Dr. Henry Gray, the world's authority on human anatomy, performed many postmortems and concluded he could find no such thing as a soul."

The nun's right hand clawed for the brass Jesus on the black crucifix that rode at the end of the large, beaded rosary hanging at her right side.

"There shall be no classroom schism." Sweat drops beaded above her upper lip. "Did you hear him, children?"

"Yes, Sister," some students answered.

Performing a military about-face, the nun strode to the chalkboard, picked up the wooden yardstick, turned, and directed her eyes to the heretic. "Come here," she ordered.

The boy dutifully approached. He could smell her distinctive halitosis, what smelled like a mixture of soured mayonnaise and Sen-Sen, tiny licorice pieces, the size, color, and shape of mouse turds, sold in tiny paper packets.

"Your hands," she shrieked.

Most students gasped; Rocky, the classroom bully, giggled and said, "He's gonna get it now."

"And I mean now," ordered the nun.

"Please, Sister, if you break a finger, I won't be able to become a surg—"

Kawack.

Fourteen years later, Smooth visited Sister Mary Elizabeth at a Milwaukee hospital. Put down by a stroke, she was unable to speak. That night, she died in her sleep. "Massive stroke," concluded the coroner in his report.

CHAPTER FIFTY-SIX

Jane Wheatley faced the camera with the red light. "Yes, we heard, Vera, as I'm certain did our viewers."

Jane wore her most solemn look and turned to face an equally severe Tom.

"Yes, I agree, Jane," he said, "it did sound like a rifle shot. Have you any confirmation, Vera?"

"I have no confirmation," said Vera, thinking of New York and the desk she would inherit from Cronkite, "but thank God, we in the media remain out of harm's way—at least for the moment."

"Thank God," echoed Tom, an avowed atheist.

Jane turned off her mike and whispered to her co-host, "Your mama." She stood and ripped off her earpiece.

"Where you going?" thundered the studio director.

"To hell," said Jane, "if I don't change my ways."

•••

The Truck Gate sergeant and his crew of four blueshirts thoroughly searched the ambulance. Then, using his key, a large, steel, club-like object with the proper male fitment, he inserted it into the female opening of the huge, steel-covered gate on steel tracks, its mammoth jaws slowly parting.

Two emergency medical technicians checked Zombie's vital signs, gave him initial first aid, and only then lifted him onto a gurney.

Moments later, the ambulance reentered the Truck Gate's sally port. With its siren blaring, the driver headed the vehicle to Waupun's Memorial Hospital.

•••

Ninjas erected a makeshift booth in order to isolate one inmate at a time for a strip search. Behind the booth, each man stripped. Officers bagged the clothes, tagged the bag with the man's name and serial number, and tossed the bag into a waiting laundry basket for a thorough search when time permitted.

After a full-body cavity search was completed, four officers escorted each naked inmate to his assigned cell, where he was placed in TLU status, pending investigation.

•••

At ten p.m., Channel Six's Tom Hayden figured he'd better look as if he'd just been told he had a week to live, or else he was heading to the Fargo, North Dakota, affiliate. "Good evening, everyone," he said soberly. "Jane Wheatley is not with us tonight. She is ill." *Yeah, probably drunk on her ass right now.* "It has been confirmed that two correctional officers and two inmates at the Wisconsin State Prison have been confirmed dead in addition to one inmate being wounded in the aftermath of the Waupun prison riot. Here is Channel Six's reporter on the scene, Vera Cabot, to give us an update." *She's already got a ton of job offers flowing in—and not one in our shit-kicking market, either. What the hell? I can always return to Jane.* "Vera, can you tell us what happened?"

Vera somberly nodded as she snuck a look at the notes she held in her free hand. Slowly, the mike rose, as did her eyes. "I'll do my best, Tom. In today's riot, two correctional officers and two inmates were murdered and one inmate was shot and wounded—after the riot had been terminated. This day turned out to be the deadliest in this institution's long history. Added to that, we have been advised by people in the know that the riot itself was a well-orchestrated con job, and I mean con job, perpetrated by the Aryan Nation gang, a white hate group."

"A con job, you say? That's remarkable," observed Tom.

"Yes, Tom," Vera continued after checking her notes again. "Institution authorities here tell us that Theodore Kopfmueller, convicted murderer of two Milwaukee police officers in 1965 and the local Aryan Nation's gang leader, shot and killed two correctional officers today with a prison-manufactured zip gun, most likely fabricated in the institution's machine shop. The riot, itself, ended shortly after a guard sharpshooter shot and killed the armed Kopfmueller, who was attempting to escape over the back wall of this institution. Yet another inmate, a Hector Soto, also of Milwaukee was found in the school. He, too, was murdered, according to prison authorities."

"So the riot was a ruse for Kopfmueller's escape. Is that what you're saying, Vera?"

No shit, Dick Tracy. "Yes, Tom. While teachers, a librarian, and a civilian school clerk were being held hostage in the prison school by numerous rioters, Kopfmueller hid in an industrial shop where he murdered Capt. Kevin Blake of Waupun." She stopped, again checking her notes. "Blake had entered the shop, looking for inmates who might have been left behind in the initial commotion. The captain leaves behind a widow and two young daughters. Then Kopfmueller must've aimed his weapon at—"

Vera eyeballed more notes— "Tower Officer Benedict "Ben" Holloway, who leaves behind a widow and four adult children."

"But what of the inmate who was shot after the riot was over?"

Would you give me time to get to that? "I was getting to that, Tom. Although we have not been given the particulars of the situation, we know this much. After the riot ended and rioters were being herded outside the school building in order to be searched for weapons, inmate Randy Smith, also of Milwaukee, was shot and wounded by a correctional officer supervisor, whose name is being withheld. We don't know why the supervisor shot Smith. I'll let you know as soon as I find out.

"Wow, Vera," said Hayden, "this has just been an incredible day for you."

"Yes," agreed Vera. "According to Warden Mitchell Palestine, the riot started early this morning when inmates took over the academic school and library on the second floor of a one-hundred-year-old limestone block building within those drab, gray walls you see behind me."

Vera turned suddenly. "Warden, Warden Palestine," she called out.

"Yes?" Palestine was now on camera alongside Vera.

"What is your take on today's events in your institution?"

"Well," said Warden Suave, "the riot was, in reality, a diversion contrived by Aryan Nation gang members who wrongly assumed our staff would not recognize the takeover as a ploy to deceive us.

"They ransacked the inmate academic school and manufactured knives, spears, and machetes in the prison welding shop located directly below. They blindfolded and tied up hostages and threatened to kill them." That's when Palestine placed a bandanna before his eyes as an improvised blindfold.

Cut to Vera alone. "As our viewers can understand, it has been quite a day in Waupun. Thankfully, inmates are now locked down in their cells. Investigations continue and we will remain on the scene in order to update our viewers regarding this terrible tragedy."

Cut to Tom. "Thank you, Vera. What a day. What a night," he told his viewers. "In other news around the state and nation...."

• • •

Shirleen, Zak, and the other twelve hostages left the institution that night after Ego told them not to speak to the press, that they'd be expected to report to work the next morning, and they'd be spending the next few days writing conduct reports regarding the actions of individual rioters.

When they passed through a gauntlet of reporters, not one hostage uttered a word.

Vera Cabat chased after Shirleen and shoved a microphone at her—time and again.

Shirleen stopped.

"Are you Shirleen Hammer, and if you are, would you care to share your experiences with our viewers?"

Shirleen pushed at the TV reporter with all her might. Vera Cabat went down. Scottie zeroed in on the disheveled and obviously frustrated reporter.

•••

"I'd rather be alone tonight," Shirleen told Zak.

"I understand," he said. "I feel the same way. I guess I had my moment of clarity up there."

"Huh?"

Zak smiled. "That's what we say in AA. There's a lot of stuff going on in my head, none of it bad, but I need to wrestle with some stuff."

"I love you, Zak."

"And I love you, Shir."

When Zak got to their apartment, Reggie was not there. Zak chose a George Jones album. After Lonesome George began singing his tales of woe, Zak plopped on the bed, closed his eyes, and promptly fell asleep.

•••

The next day, a media horde descended on Waupun. Some outstate news folks had to check into motels fifty miles away. In the morning, they congregated either at Betty's Corner Café or at Otto's Bar and Grill.

Waupun citizens told one another that media members gagged down meals like half-starved wolves and drank like sailors on twenty-four-hour shore liberty.

A few locals received their fifteen seconds of fame. With cameras focused, a grandmotherly type said, "The murdered staff members were good people, family members, hard workers, and churchgoing folk. The city of Waupun was their chosen home, not that prison, where those inmates are sentenced for committing heinous crimes."

"Inmates preying on one another seems to be the norm in that place," said a Protestant minister.

"It doesn't matter that most inmates were not involved in the riot. All are being punished in an institution-wide lockdown," sniffed Joanne Feathers, spokesperson for WAIT, Wives Are Inmates, Too, her husband a convicted child molester.

"Never," one Waupun senior citizen said, "has staff been killed, and only once has staff killed an armed inmate. Now, all that's changed."

"That guy who wounded that inmate, his name is Judder," said a man who identified himself as a retired correctional officer. "Ever hear of a name like that? Neither have I. Although I don't blame him for shooting the man, I heard he was on drugs, which seems to explain things."

Meanwhile, both the Dutch Reformed minister and St. Joseph's Catholic Church's Franciscan pastor researched spiritual tomes for appropriate quotations for approaching funerals.

Werner-Harmsen and Kohl's funeral homes kept their doors open extra hours, greeting processions of common citizens and dignitaries, alike. Governor and Mrs. Avery Todd avoided Mitchell Palestine and his wife as if they were carriers of the bubonic plague. State legislators were on hand as church bells knelled solemnly.

Hundreds of law officers from Wisconsin and adjoining states drove their squads to Waupun. With lights flashing and sirens wailing, they led the two corteges, shiny, silent, and black funeral cars behind them, and stopped in front of the churches.

Correctional officer pallbearers stepped to the vehicles' rears.

"Atten-hut," Sgt. Morris Dunlop boomed in basso profundo.

A blueshirt firing squad in white dickeys and leggings came to attention as coffins were eased out of hearses onto carts, their wheels silenced with well-oiled bearings. The pallbearers lugged the boxes to the churches' entryways, TV cameramen waiting like vultures eyeballing a dying coyote.

•••

Hostages rode roller coasters of emotions. Governor Todd announced they'd be given two weeks off with pay. With a grinning Reggie Walters by his side, Todd also told reporters he'd go along with forming a prison guards' union.

"Blueshirts applaud your move," said Reggie.

Because Personnel Director Jon Powers followed Delmar Winston's questionable memo, Powers charged the days off hostages took against their earned vacation time.

After Gib Melborp, English instructor, examined his paycheck stub, he telephoned Powers. "This is Gib Melborp. What the hell's going on with deducting my vacation time for those two weeks off the governor gave us?"

"I can't help it. Those were orders from headquarters," explained Powers.

Melborp telephoned the *Milwaukee Sentinel* editor and explained the situation. The next morning's issue carried a front-page story with a three-inch headline regarding the snafu. An accompanying editorial on page eighteen denounced Gov. Avery Todd's mendacity.

That afternoon, the explosive governor told reporters, "I, nor any other politician, had anything to do with the mix-up. Those two weeks off were special. This morning I advised former professor at UW-Madison's law school, and now corrections chief, Delmar Winston, to right this wrong. At once."

Winston telephoned Powers. "I am ordering you to not charge hostage time off against their vacation allotments. I further advise you to not talk to the press about this matter." That said, Winston hung up.

Powers pulled Winston's memo that ordered Powers to debit days off against the hostage-employees' allotted vacation time. "Thank you, Jesus," he said aloud. After telephoning the *Milwaukee Sentinel* editor, Powers left the institution and drove straight to Milwaukee, where he met with the editor and two reporters. A copy of Winston's memo with a heavy black frame appeared on the *Sentinel's* front page the next morning.

"I'll betcha," Powers told his wife at breakfast, "right now Winston's bladder is malfunctioning."

Powers's wife smiled. "Would you like more coffee, honey?"

•••

Two weeks after the riot, Mitchell Palestine stood by Governor Todd's side and announced, "I have been the Waupun institution's warden long enough and am announcing my retirement from state service with full retirement pay. I intend to read, fish, hunt, and hopefully take part in my grandchildren's upbringing."

"Thank you, Mitch, for your long-term loyalty."

Palestine's resignation was duly noted by state print media on inside pages. A student sit-down at the University of Wisconsin-Madison's administrative offices was front-page news that day.

A week later, the governor invited Delmar Winston to the governor's mansion for breakfast, large bowls of Captain Crunch cereal, topped off with cream, sugar, and fresh strawberries, each as large as a plumber's thumb. Todd lifted a berry. "You can thank Governor Moon Beam for the strawberries."

"You mean California's Governor Jerry Brown?"

What a dipshit. "Also got a case of Napa Valley choice wine. Me and Moon Beam had this bet on the Rose Bowl. If I lost, I had to send him a shitload of blue ribbon Swiss, Colby, and cheddar plus a case of Sheboygan brats—the sausage, you know—and, of course, good old Milwaukee beer."

"You're kidding."

Todd belched. Lifting the Irish linen napkin from his lap, he dabbed at his lips and chin. Truth be told, the sight of Winston was enough to make him vomit. Todd turned to Moses, the governor's black civil-servant servant, dressed in white coat, white shirt, black bow tie, black trousers, a shiny, black, two-inch silk piece running down the sides, and lastly, black spit-shined shoes.

Moses, having anticipated the moment, had already reached with white-gloved fingers for the box of premium Havanas, opened the lid, and let the governor grab one. "Yassuh," said Moses, grinning.

"Wanna Havana?" Todd asked Winston.

"Uh, no sir, I don't smoke."

Too bad. You should. Todd eyeballed Winston like dirty old men eyeballing women with big hooters. He then blew a cloud of smoke at the corrections chief. "Delmar, you do enjoy pissing with the big dogs, don't you?"

"Sir?"

"You got ears, don't you?" Todd's demeanor changed to that of a pit bull on speed. He took an extra-long drag on the stogie and exhaled a heavy fog bank.

Aware that Winston hoped to catapult from his corrections chief post to a national-level Democratic Party assignment, Todd continued his act, screaming. "I'm waiting."

He rose and headed to a large casement window that overlooked Lake Verona and pushed aside a gossamer curtain, looking sideways so Winston could see his scowl.

"Waiting for what?" pleaded Winston.

"Goddammit, Winston, I made you chief of corrections, doubled your law school salary, and all you had to do was to keep the lid on my prisons."

"Sir, I didn't—"

The governor flew from the window, his nose crushing against Winston's. "Listen, you little shit bag, you accepted my appointment, you sit with me in my mansion, you eat my food, and now you don't—don't what? You want to piss with the big dogs? Well, then piss like a big dog, Delmar. You don't squat like a little Chihuahua bitch."

• • •

Standing at the doorway, Kyle Marston made mental note to award Todd—naturally, in a private ceremony—the Oscar for best performance by a governor.

• • •

Todd was on a roll. "Delmar, I'm reading your mind. You're now wishing you would've stayed in that law school, am I right?"

"Sir, I object, I—"

"I won't let you object. Don't you understand, you little pipsqueak, you're finished. Never in hell would I let you return to that law school, you—" The saliva accompanying Todd's righteous indignation hit Winston.

The governor faced Marston. "Kyle, do we still have that Amish outdoor shithouse inspector's job open?"

(Neither the governor nor his aide, they later agreed, could believe what happened next).

Winston dropped to the floor and knelt, hands pressed together as in prayer, tears streaming down his cheeks and chin, his snot faucet turned on to full, body heaving in spasms. "What can I do?" he slobbered. "What can I do?"

"The first thing you can do," screamed Todd, "is to pick yourself up, blow your goddamn nose, and wipe that shit off your face. I'm just about ready to puke."

• • •

Kyle helped Winston up, reached for his handkerchief, and offered it to Winston.

Winston shook his head. "No, I'll get it dirty," he blubbered.

"That's OK, sir."

"Call me Delmar, please."

"Delmar," agreed Kyle, certain his former pain-in-the-ass professor was actually a Chihuahua bitch and would eventually realize who the big dogs really were. "Delmar, the governor's office, as you well know, keeps its fingers on the public pulse. Recently, we've been losing favor with minorities and females."

"Waupun," questioned Winston, still sobbing, "has caused those problems?"

"I'll tell you what Waupun has to do with them," interrupted Todd, "every goddamn thing."

"Delmar," continued Kyle, "we want you to call a press conference."

"To announce my resignation?"

"No," said Kyle, "you're not going to announce your resignation—not yet."

Todd applauded Kyle by tapping together his index fingers.

"If you play your cards right, you're going to announce that Waupun will have its first African American female warden, Ms. Shirleen Hammer, presently the inmate advocate and, by the way, a former Waupun prison hostage."

On cue, Moses entered the room and exclaimed in his best Stepin Fetchit, "Praise the Lawd, we done reached the Promised Land."

"With God's help, you'll lead a good life and go to heaven," Marcella Richardson told her son, Marion.

"Ah you going to heaven, Mummy?" asked the boy.

"Someday, yes, Mummy hopes to be with God and all the saints and angels."

"Then I want to go to heaven, too."

The woman drew the boy to her, kissing his forehead. "That's a good boy, but it's time for some seriousness."

"What's seiousness, Mummy?"

"Seriousness," she said softly, "means there's always the opposite side to every coin. The opposite of heaven is hell. If you choose the devil as your partner, instead of spending eternity with God and me, you'll spend eternity with the devil and all the horrible sinners."

The boy shuddered. He'd seen pictures of Beelzebub. "What's eternity, Mummy?"

"Eternity, son, is very difficult for even Mummies to explain."

"But, what is it?"

"You'll have to give Mummy time to think."

Marion rested his head against his mother's warmth while she pondered the vexing question.

At long last, she smiled. "I believe I can now explain eternity.

"Oh, goody."

"Close your eyes, Marion, and picture a tiny bird, the tiniest bird on earth."

Dutifully, the boy scrunched his eyelids and announced, "I can see the bird."

"Good. Now, this teensy-weensy bird once every one hundred years flies toward a huge, steel ball as large as earth and brushes its little feathery breast against it."

"A ball as big as earth, Mummy? That's a big, big, big ball."

Smiling, she turned a thatch of Marion's hair into a curl. "Yes, and just think what kind of effect that tiny little bird's breast would have on that big steel ball."

"Not much, Mummy."

"What a bright boy I have. Now, since that bird's tiny breast touches that big steel ball only once every hundred years, how long do you think it would take for that little bird's breast feathers to wear away that huge steel ball into nothing?"

"A hundred-billion-zillion years?"

"My, what an intelligent lad, and that hundred-billion-zillion years would only be the beginning of eternity."

"The beginning?"

"That's correct. Now, Marion, think hard. Where would you rather spend all that time, in heaven or in hell?"

"In heaven, Mummy."

CHAPTER FIFTY-SEVEN

If by happenstance, someone miraculously discovered the narrow passageway that led to the ordnance room, that person would step on a wired rubber pad. If that pad was disturbed by no more than four ounces of pressure, a relay would emit an electrical pulse that would cause the entire house to disappear in a mushroom cloud seconds later.

The only thing that could've saved that house from total destruction was the knowledge of the hidden mercury switch on the passageway wall.

After Smooth's fingers found the switch, eyes expectantly and momentarily aggrieved by the lights' brilliance, he advanced to the first gun cabinet, opened a door, and touched a button, and a hidden drawer swished open. He reached inside the drawer and held before him a velvet-covered case that held the tiny Baby Browning with gold-inlaid floral pattern.

Val Browning, only son of John, designed in 1926 a special presentation vest-pocket .25-caliber pistol, serial No. 778226. It, too, had a gold inlaid floral pattern. Although 77826's existence was well-known by firearms aficionados and highly desired by the wealthiest of them, they knew that only one existed.

Unknown to everyone except Val and Smooth, Val produced 77826's twin in all respects except for its serial number, which Val kept for his personal protection.

After removing 778226A, he touched a button. The drawer disappeared. Next, he turned slightly and slid aside a concealed pocket door. Just like that, he was in the attached garage, where he checked the right saddlebag of the full-dress Harley. The cassette player was still there, as he knew it would be.

The bike glimmered, its wine-berry-painted tank, frame, and fenders buffed to diamond brilliance, the chrome pieces surpassing radiance.

Straddling the pan head, he pressed a button that opened the garage door. He lifted and came down on the starter. The engine coughed and soon its *potato-potato* resonance soothed his very core. Testing the saddle, he peered in the rearview mirrors one at a time, patted head hair into place, and felt for 778226A, assuring himself it was yet on his person.

Squeezing the clutch handle and kicking the peg, he gave the throttle a slight twist, let the clutch out, and headed the scoot north, his destination Waupun via a most circuitous route north to Green Bay, south to Lamartine, and west to County Highway M.

•••

With the office door closed, Dodge Country District Attorney Glen Matthews placed both feet on his desktop as he told the sitting Sheriff Nehls and Joe Weems, "As I see it, there's really not a damn thing I can do to that lieutenant—legally that is."

"I understand," said Weems, "but as far as I'm concerned, he shot that inmate without cause."

"And you're most likely correct, Joe, but I could never face a jury that was told the field commander had just finished ordering the heretofore rioting inmates not to pass anything to anyone. Although he was showing his high school diploma to a friend, he was violating the order. Anyway, it was a time of high tension. You agree to that, don't you?"

"I agree," said the sheriff, "but Joe—he's closer to this thing than me."

Matthews grinned. "I'll say this for him—his first name's Judder, isn't it?—kind of weird when you think of it—he comes across as a nut bag, but I can't prosecute him for being a head case, now, can I?"

"No, I guess you'd have plenty of problems with that," replied Joe.

"Anyway," added Matthews, "his attorney tells me the lieutenant's seeking psychiatric help."

"I hope so, for his sake," said Weems. "It's still a shame. The inmate he shot was responsible for helping to end the takeover."

"Sometimes, we just have to shrug and go on with our lives," advised Nehls.

"You're one hundred percent correct," said Joe. "By the way, do you know what the definition of a gentleman is?"

• • •

Shirleen and Zak had attended Tower Officer Ben Holloway and Gangs Captain Kevin Blake's funerals. They requested DOC approval to visit inmate Randy "Zombie" Smith at Madison's University Hospitals. Approval was granted.

They were keyed into the maximum-security secure ward by Turnkey Sgt. Tom Scott, who pointed to a bed. Sitting on a chair next to Zombie's bed was a bespectacled and regal black woman with salt-and-pepper hair. Dressed in a navy blue suit, white blouse, and black sturdy shoes with laces, she wore well the navy blue and white straw hat sitting straight on top of her head.

Shirleen was flabbergasted. "Why, that's the choir director in Auntie's church, the Tabernacle Community Baptist Church."

The woman was built large but was not at all fat. Zak thought she was stunningly beautiful.

As the pair approached her, the older woman said, "My, my, if it isn't Shirleen Hammer. I heard you were working at Waupun. How are you, girl?"

"I'm doing fine, Mrs. Flippin." Shirleen smiled as she leaned down and hugged the older woman. When finished, Shirleen stood and told

Zak, "Zak Griffin, this is Mrs. Dorothea Flippin. She was the choir director of Auntie Louise's church in Milwaukee. Mrs. Flippin, this is Zak Griffin, my very good friend."

"My goodness, child, I still am the choir director. I'm pleased to meet you, Zak." She offered her hand, which Zak shook.

Mrs. Flippin then addressed Shirleen. "Of course, you couldn't have known I was Randy's mother because we were never formally introduced, and I suspect your Auntie Louise wouldn't say much about anyone's past, including mine. Auntie Louise is a saint."

"Amen to that," said Shirleen. "I only knew you as our choir director and also loved your singing voice, which is heavenly."

"Why, thank you, child, it is he, the one above, who gives me the voice to praise him and shout my hallelujahs as long as he gives me strength. And he's blessed me with a son who is finding his way to the righteous path—finally." With that said, she turned to Zombie.

He lay in bed, grimacing. "That's Sergeant Griffin, Moms. He's the one I was telling you about."

"Did Zombie," Zak asked Zombie's mother, "—I mean Randy—tell you he saved my life? It's because of his actions that we're both alive today."

Mrs. Flippin trembled as she reached to touch her son before she signaled Zak and Shirleen to come to her bosom. As the three hugged, the older woman's body shook from her crying. "You don't know how good it is to hear what you just said, Sergeant. After all the trouble Randy brought onto himself, he has finally found it in his heart to follow the righteous path, praise be to Jesus, Amen. I am so grateful to God, above, that my son was finally able to write a note to me in his own hand. As a boy, he hated school, and how do you think he treated his mother, a teacher? Well, you have to know there were many troubling times for both of us. After Randy's father and I divorced, I took back my maiden name, which gave my son another reason to loathe his mother."

She glanced at her watch. "My second husband said he was going to have one cigarette, but I'll wager he's on his third. No matter, he'll be so pleased to hear what you two have to say about Randy. Could you stay awhile longer?"

Shirleen turned to Zak and squeezed his hand. "Yes," she said, "we can and we shall."

• • •

"Amber," yelled Delmar Winston DOC chief. He seldom ventured from his office, because there was always a distinct possibility he'd have to talk to an underling. "Did you make that phone call?"

"Sir, I'm calling right now," yelled Amber while making faces at Beatrice Rosenblum, probation and parole consultant, who had plopped her behind atop Amber's desk.

The person on the other end answered.

"Hello, this is Delmar Winston's secretary. Is this Shirleen Hammer? Good. Please hold, Miss Hammer. Mr. Winston wishes to speak to you."

Amber covered the receiver and shouted, "Mr. Winston? It's Miss Hammer."

She then whispered to Beatrice, "I'll betcha he's playing with his little thingy again."

Beatrice nodded, covered her mouth, and sniggered.

• • •

When Joanie Richardson put the Sears vacuum cleaner in the hall closet, she heard the front doorbell. Not expecting anyone, she snapped the closet door shut. Hopefully, whoever was there wouldn't be Jehovah's Witnesses or, worse, an encyclopedia salesman.

She approached the screen door. Whoever he was, he was young, a sharp dresser, and movie-star good-looking with a pleasant, white-tooth smile. He was not carrying encyclopedia or *Awake* but held something that looked like a portable radio. He wore dark trousers, a white shirt, a dark blue tie, and a beige windbreaker. She made certain the hook was in the eye—meaning the door was locked—before she spoke. "Yes, may I help you?"

"Hi," he said pleasantly, "I'm Tom Zimmerman, reporter for the *Milwaukee Sentinel.*" He then lifted before him a *Sentinel* picture ID card at Joanie's eye level.

Because her husband had trained her well in personal security matters, Joanie took time to carefully check out the card. "Sure enough," she said, "it says you are who you say you are."

"And might you be Mrs. Marion Richardson?"

Joanie smiled. "I am."

"Is your husband home?"

"No, he isn't, but it doesn't matter because he won't talk to members of the press. I can assure you of that."

"Which is typical of most heroes."

Joanie was thrilled this young man, this good-looking young man, who reminded her of Clark Gable, used her pet name for her husband. "What's typical of most heroes?" she asked.

"For certain, Mrs. Richardson, heroes don't like talking about themselves." The good-looker turned around to leave but halted and turned again. "Well, if he won't let me interview him, do you think it's possible I could interview you and get his wife's point of view?"

"Me?" said Joanie, shaking her head. "You wouldn't be interested in anything I have to say. I'm just a housewife, although it might be time people saw my husband as I do. He undoubtedly is both a dedicated state employee and a hero." She unlocked and opened the door. "Come in, Mr....Geez, I already forgot your name."

"Zimmerman. Call me Tom. Everybody does."

"Well, Tom, sit down on that couch over there while I go to the kitchen and get us some lemonade. You will have some lemonade, won't you?"

"Why, thank you, ma'am. I am a tad thirsty, and lemonade sounds marvelous." He retrieved a pen from his shirt pocket and a pad of paper from his jacket. He also put down the radio. "This is a tape recorder," he explained. "While I usually rely on my written notes, having this along helps me quote my interviewees word for word. You don't mind if I use it?"

"Heavens to Betsy, no," said Joanie as she left the room.

•••

George, Zak's AA sponsor, selected a booth at Beaver Dam's Walker's restaurant. "Two high-tests, Annette," George called to the smiling waitress behind the counter.

"Hi, Georgie. Two high-tests coming up," returned Annette.

George leaned over, attempting to keep his spoken words private. "When I first sobered up, I didn't understand the concept of living in the moment, either."

"You're saying I should forget the past?"

"No, that's—"

Annette was already at the booth. She gently set two cups of steaming-hot coffee before each man and an insulated plastic, copper-colored and black carafe between them.

"Thanks," the two men said together.

"Enjoy," said Annette before she was off and running.

"No, I didn't mean that at all," said George. "Our past is the sculptor that hammers and chisels us into the people we are this day. Each subsequent day becomes the past, continuing to hammer and chisel, taking out unneeded stone, and smoothing out the rough spots, trying to make our forms perfect, which will never be achieved."

"I've never thought of it that way," said Zak.

"And I'm certain someday—I'm not saying when—but someday you're going to know what you need to do concerning that photograph. All you need is time for the sculptor to continue his work. Trust me, you'll eventually know."

"I'd like to believe that," said Zak.

"Well, then, you're ninety-five percent there, and whether or not Jane Fonda and her fans see it my way, it doesn't matter one hoot. I believe each and every one of us owes you and the all of our fighting men a debt of gratitude for what you guys did by putting your very lives on the line for our freedom."

•••

"I assure you Mr. Richardson shall find his future in state service a not-so-pleasant task," Delmar Winston told Shirleen.

"What you really mean, Mr. Winston, is you're not going to do anything. From what inmate Clark told me, I believe Richardson is responsible for causing my brother's death."

"But, as you know, he was not a witness, was he? Winston's eyes looked her way but for a nanosecond. "Shirleen, my specialty is the law, and no judge would ever let that case into his courtroom. Too much of what you've been told is hearsay, not factual evidence, but—"

"But what?" Shirleen demanded.

"You still haven't told me if you'll accept the warden's position."

•••

The lemonade pitcher had tipped on its side, its contents growing into an ever-enlarging spot on the carpet. Next to it sprawled Joanie Richardson, looking like a department store mannequin that lay at an awkward angle. Although her eyes remained open, they were deprived of animation. Blood trickled out of her right temple, caused by a small-caliber projectile entry wound.

With gloved hand and utmost respect, Smooth slipped the tiny pistol into his jacket pocket, checked, double-checked, and even triple-checked everything in the room before he pressed the play button of the microcassette player.

After exiting the house through the rear sliding glass door, he took off his gloves and stuffed them in a jacket pocket.

Nonchalantly, he walked across Ego's back forty, entered the woods, and was soon swallowed by thick brush. After the brush, he made his way among red oak, sugar maple, and balsam pines.

All of a sudden, he stopped. There, only thirty feet in front of him, were a browsing whitetail doe and her fawn. The doe must've sensed his presence because she lifted her head, twitched her ears, looked here and then there, back to here again, and then returned to her browsing while all that time, the fawn stared at him.

Eventually they and he moved on.

After removing branches and brush that he had used to camouflage the Harley motorcycle, he removed his tie and exchanged jacket for a shirt that had been stored in the saddlebag. Aryan Nation members would be pleased, although he nearly broke their bank with his fee.

He intended to head the scoot to Fond du Lac and then east to Sheboygan, taking the indirect way home. It would be nice to have Lake Michigan at his side for a while. Besides, it was such a glorious day for a ride since he had made yet another score.

•••

Zak turned up the car's radio. Jim Croce was singing "Bad, Bad Leroy Brown." He couldn't have known that twenty miles in back of him, Shirleen sat in the backseat of a state car. Neither she nor the driver had said one word to each other.

•••

Ego approached the front door and heard a woman's voice. It didn't belong to Joanie's. He wondered who it could be. "My name is Ann Secamore," said the woman.

Then, a man spoke up. "Could you speak a little louder, please, and spell your last name?"

Ego heard her cough and clear her throat. "Excuse me, I thought I was speaking loud enough. It's Secamore, S-e-c-a-m-o-r-e."

"And Miss Secamore, where do you reside?"

"I live at three-oh-nine West Main Street in Waupun."

"You said three-oh-nine West Main Street in Waupun."

"I did."

Oh, no, Joanie must've found the tape. With foreboding, Ego opened the door and entered.

•••

Sergeant Biggs got out the Approved Visitors' book. "Clark, under the Cs. You haven't been here before, have you, ma'am?"

"No, this is my first time."

Biggs nodded. "I thought so. I have a pretty good memory, you know. Clark, you say? How do you spell your first name, ma'am?"

"It's spelled just like Alice with an A at the end, A-l-i-c-e-a."

"And by golly, here it is, Mrs. Clark. See?" Biggs's index finger drew her eyes to the name.

The woman's eyes lit up. "Yes, that's me."

"Could you remove all the metal you have on your person, including pocket change, Mrs. Clark? We'll have to send you through the metal scanner."

She lifted her left hand and pointed to her wristwatch. "Including this?"

"Yes, ma'am, including that—and your belt buckle, too. That'll set off the buzzer. Even something as small as a twenty-two bullet will set it off."

•••

A blue Chevy with a state official license plates stopped behind Zak's car.

Shirleen popped out the rear door and ran full tilt. As she slammed into the big guy, he lifted her off the roadway. "Oh, Zak," she cried, "I wouldn't. I couldn't."

Zak held her hard to him. He'd find out later what she would not or could not do.

•••

Alicea Clark thought she'd be escorted to a room, sit on a steel chair, and talk to her son via telephone. Instead, the Visiting Room was large and open and brightly painted, set up like a huge living room with many couches and chairs and even toys for kids.

Inmates were already sitting with other visitors. They wore khakis and a few of them held children. Others had their arms around wives, sweethearts, and mothers. Most everyone was smiling except for one young lady, who was crying. The others talked and laughed as if they were home—not in a maximum-security prison.

The tall, good-looking sergeant rose from his desk. His name badge stated, Sgt. Robert Kell. "Ma'am," said Kell, "I see this is your first visit. Thus, I need to advise you that you can only hug and kiss your visitor twice, once before the visit, and once afterward. You will be doing your visitor a disservice if you hug and kiss him more than that. You'll have four hours in which to visit. If you want to leave earlier, that is up to you, but once the four hours are up, I'll call out your son's name, and he will have to leave. At that point, you can give him your second hug and kiss, but please don't let it linger."

"Where is my son?"

"Officers are shaking him down as we speak, ma'am. We want to make sure he's not bringing any contraband into the Visiting Room, and after your visit, he will be shook down again so we can be assured he didn't receive any contraband here."

"Oh," she said.

"You can sit in that green chair over there." Kell pointed. "When your son comes in, I'll send him over to you."

"Thank you, Sergeant," said Mrs. Clark, "for explaining things so well."

"Just doing my job, ma'am."

• • •

As the tape droned on, Ego no longer listened to the words. No one or nothing mattered anymore, not the job, not Blake, Holloway,

Kopfmueller, Davis, Zak, Shirleen, not even the Cobra pair. Smith did not matter nor did Secamore, Brown, Winston, or Vergenz.

Ego gazed at what really did matter, what used to be his living, breathing, devoted wife, Joanie.

After retrieving his .44 magnum revolver from the gun safe in the hall closet, he collapsed on the couch. He watched a tiny bird brush its breast feathers against a massive steel sphere as large as the earth. At the same moment, he heard Wing Nuts Kopfmueller say, "Everyone's got a price to pay, includin' you."

Ego pulled back the hammer. It clicked in place.

His lips encircled the barrel's tip. He began the steady compression of thumb against trigger. He heard nothing. He felt nothing. He was no longer in the scheme of things. Ego had become past tense.

THE END

AFTERWORD

When Zak Griffin retired from state service as Waupun Correctional Institution's major of the guard, Warden Maureen Kelly thanked him for his years of exemplary service and fair treatment of subordinates and inmates alike.

When Zak received his twenty-five-year AA sobriety medallion, he was the featured speaker at an open AA meeting. "In addition to Shirleen, I'm most grateful for our kids, Irmadine, our eldest, a second-grade schoolteacher at Jefferson Grade School, her husband, Jeb, a Waupun correctional lieutenant, our other two daughters, Louise and Jeanne Marie, who are in college and high school, and our son, Zak Jr. They have never seen their old dad take a drink."

Shirleen and Zak's kids applauded the loudest.

Zak and Shirleen joined Jerry Dixey in a Street Rodder magazine road tour with fellow gear heads in Shoo-fly Ply, their '35 Plymouth coupe hot rod. Although the nation's capital wasn't one of Dixey's stops, Zak and Shirleen made a special side trip there.

At the base of the Vietnam Wall, Zak leaned against it a sepia-tone picture. After Shirleen wiped away Zak's tears, she took a picture of him with the wall as background.

As the same time Shirleen clicked the shutter, neurosurgeon, Dr. Thu Ngoc Thanh of Cho Ray Hospital in Ho Chi Minh City, drank tea at her desk while gazing at a sepia-tone picture of her and her father, Major Lanh Ngoc Thanh, who'd lost his life in battle at Dong Ha. He had died a hero.

The Reverend Jeremy Clark, Waupun Correctional Institution's Protestant chaplain, reveals to inmates his past, including his murdering a fellow inmate. Clark's wife and children attend Sunday services inside the walls.

"He's not just a chaplain," said Reggie Walters, former correctional officer and now head of the state employees union. "The Reverend Clark is a prime example of what prison rehabilitation is all about. Inmates have personally told me he challenges them to make needed changes in their personal lives."

Randy "Zombie" Smith is an English teacher at Milwaukee's Martin Luther King Jr. High School.

Jack "Rude Boy" Worthington hired on as a youth counselor at the Milwaukee Boys Club, teaching boxing to at-risk kids, helping many lads to give up their lives of petty crime and follow the path of spirituality and righteousness.

Theodore "Wing Nuts" Kopfmueller's remains are buried in the inmate cemetery next to Farm No One's piggery. He did not mark any religious preference on his face sheet, but the Catholic chaplain nevertheless prayed for the repose of the Aryan's soul.

After Governor Todd fired Delmar Winston as chief of corrections, Winston headed east and landed a low-level position with high-level Democrats, including a short stint as Hillary Clinton's chauffeur. When he couldn't get it up, she fired him.

Judder Brown quit state service and attended UW-Madison and the UW law school. A successful criminal lawyer, he is retired and living in Fort Myers, Florida, in the winter and in Elk Rapids, Michigan, during the summer.

Smooth, the professional hit man, resides in Portugal. Or is it Ireland? Nobody really seems to know.

The Waupun Correctional Institution, in existence for more than 150 years, is still in full operation, its cells filled to capacity, its walls bearing pastel-tinted mortar from the 1980s, now fading into grayness.

Sodium lights, attached to prerusted, 150-foot-high steel poles, hover above the institution and light up the evening sky. Their flashing red lights prompt some out-of-town folks to claim they saw UFOs.

A new Administration Building has elevators and ramps so that people with physical disabilities can enter and exit the institution with relative ease. Disabled parking is available not far from the main gate.

The Greenhouse is no longer the set-aside for the state's most miscreant offenders. A super-max institution was built in southeastern Wisconsin—a concept altered by a federal judge who ruled the institution could no longer be called super-max nor could its inmates be termed as the "worst of the worst" although the institution is a super-max and its inmates are Wisconsin's worst of the worst.

Laws are yet broken. Some people who break laws are apprehended. Of those apprehended, some are charged. Those who are charged usually accept a reduced plea bargain. Some receive probation. A few are sentenced to serve time. Some do their time at Waupun. If they refuse to do their time in Waupun, they can sit back in their cells, and the state will do their time for them.

There's always a price to pay.